TALES OF THE
SHADOWMEN
Volume 19: Demi-Monde

also from Black Coat Press

TALES OF THE
SHADOWMEN

Volume 19: Demi-Monde

edited by
Jean-Marc & Randy Lofficier

stories by
**Tim Newton Anderson, Matthew Baugh,
Atom Mudman Bezecny, Matthew Dennion,
Brian Gallagher, Martin Gately, Travis Hiltz,
Rick Lai, Jean-Marc Lofficier, Randy Lofficier,
Rod McFadyen, Nigel Malcolm, Christofer Nigro,
John Peel, Anthony Perconti, Jean-Paul Raymond,
Frank Schildiner** and **David L. Vineyard.**

cover by
Aurélien Maccarelli

A Black Coat Press Book

ISBN 978-1-64932-177-0 First Printing. December 2022. Published by Black Coat Press, an imprint of Hollywood Comics.com, LLC, P.O. Box 17270, Encino, CA 91416. All rights reserved. Except for review purposes, no part of this book may be reproduced or transmitted in any form or by any means, electronic or mechanical, including photocopying, recording or by any information storage and retrieval system, without permission in writing from the publisher. The stories and characters depicted in this anthology are entirely fictional. Printed in the United States of America.

Table of Contents

MAURICE LEBLANC

ARSÈNE LUPIN

contre Herlock Sholmès

FRANETTE GUÉRIN

LE LIVRE DE POCHE POLICIER

Texte intégral

Introduction
The Lupin Quest

It was in the summer of 1975 that I embarked on a search that would change my life. I was following the trail of the most brazen character in the world: Arsène Lupin.

I had discovered the existence of this daring criminal in a 1971 anthology edited by Hugh Greene, *Cosmopolitan Crimes—Foreign Rivals of Sherlock Holmes*. Created by Maurice Leblanc, Lupin was a fascinating arch-felon whom I loved as a fictional character, but detested as a person. He was pompous, arrogant and even cruel. A selfish womanizer, he was guilty of driving one woman into a nunnery.

While reading the early tales, my sympathies were totally with Inspector Ganimard, the policeman constantly humiliated by him. Despite my qualms, I made a solemn vow: I would perform the daunting task of reading all the Lupin tales.

Remember this quest was undertaken in 1975. The Internet did not exist. The English-language translations of the Lupin novels had been published primarily during 1900-30s, and one had to spent a lot of time in libraries and used book stores to find them Also, one needed to get on the mailing lists of used book mail order catalogs. So it wasn't until the 1980s that I largely completed my quest by buying a three-volume Lupin omnibus of the original French texts.

In many of Leblanc's stories, Lupin battled an English detective quite familiar to me. The British editions called him "Holmlock Shears," while the French and American editions used "Herlock Sholmes," but the character was clearly meant to be Sir Arthur Conan Doyle's Sherlock Holmes. In fact, the earliest French edition had called him "Holmes" until Doyle had threatened legal action. (Currently, the latest English translations by Black Coat Press do use the Holmes name.)

I was both delighted and dismayed by Leblanc's depiction of the duel between Lupin and Holmes. My delight came from the mere fact that these two fictional giants could coexisting together. My dismay cane from the transformation of Holmes into an embittered adversary who inadvertently killed Lupin's wife. My discomfort with Leblanc's unflattering portrayal of Holmes prompted me to theorize claims that Lupin had circulated misleading accounts of his conflicts with Holmes. It wasn't until many years later that I published my theory as "The Holmes-Lupin Rivalry" in Rick Lai's *Secret Histories: Daring Adventurers* (Altus Press, 2008).

Shortly after discovering the Holmes/Lupin crossover, I read Philip José Farmer's *Tarzan Alive* (1972) and *Doc Savage: His Apocalyptic Life* (Revised Second Edition, 1975). Both postulated a shared universe populated by fictional characters whose ranks included Holmes and Lupin. Farmer's crossover universe, now known as the Wold Newton Universe, fascinated me, and I started to write speculative articles expanding on his concept. While Farmer created an entertaining genealogy, it mainly linked heroes and only included a few villains. Therefore, I added more villains to the family tree. I also started to link the villains by creating vast global criminal networks for them to populate. Discovering that my speculations worked best with strongly constructed timelines, I also focused on creating chronologies for various fictional series.

Thus, I had evolved from a fan of popular fiction to a published theorist of escapist literature. I owe this transformation to Philip José Farmer. However, a second wondrous transformation awaited me. I would transition from theorist to storyteller. One person is primarily responsible for that metamorphosis, Jean-Marc Lofficier.

My quest for the Lupin series had led me to other great French fictional characters, such as Monsieur Lecoq, Rouletabille, Fantômas and the Phantom of the Opera. I loved these characters so much that I wanted to write pastiches of them, but I couldn't conceive of any publisher wishing to continue the exploits of these iconic characters.

Then the Internet came into existence and through the auspices of Win Scott Eckert, I met Jean-Marc. Thanks to his *Cool French Comics* website (http:www.coolfrenchcomics.com), I was introduced to other fantastic French characters whose existence I barely suspected. These included Judex, Irma Vep, Dr. Cornelius and, most importantly, Paul Féval's Black Coats series of novels.

It was the launching of the *Tales of the Shadowmen* anthologies by Jean-Marc and his wife Randy that finally gave me the opportunity to become a writer of escapist fiction. I joined the ranks of Shadowmen scribes with the first volume with a story entitled "The Last Vendetta", starring Arthur Gordon of Texas and Josephine Balsamo, Countess Cagliostro, who coincidentally are also featured in my contribution to this ninetieth volume, almost twenty years later.

Unfortunately, health issues have caused me to virtually cease writing. Thankfully, I was able to make the anthology's deadline both this year and last. I was only able to do so because of Jean-Marc's incredible patience and support.

Thank you, Jean-Marc, you are a true friend!

Rick Lai,
October 2022

Alphabetically, Tim Newton Anderson again opens this year's collection with a good old fashioned English public-school tale featuring a collection of very diverse boys brought together by fate under the same roof. Murder, intrigue and cricket are the elements that propel the suspenseful "rippin' yarn" that is...

Tim Newton Anderson: *The Brasher Bat*

Dulwich, 1900

The dead man was pinned to the floor like a butterfly in a collector's case. A cricket stump had been nailed through his chest and his hands grasped it tightly as if trying to remove it.

"Crikey, it's Quelch," said Plum. "What a bally horrible way to die."

I looked at the prefect standing next to me in the cellar below Dulwich School's kitchen. Even though he was six years older than me, he was only a couple of inches taller. I had just had a growth spurt and was pretty tall for 12. I was certainly a few inches taller than young Dickson who had come with us to the cellar.

I admired the way Plum was handling things so matter-of-factly. I had seen a few dead bodies back in Chicago. There were parts of the city where polite folk didn't go, but I had been there a few times to try and find my father in one low dive or another. That was before my mother had finally had enough of his alcoholism and brought me back to England to stay with her family. I was more surprised at Dickson's reaction to the corpse. At his age, I would have expected him to be horrified, but he seemed more curious, as if he came across this every day.

I looked at the body again. With his teacher's cloak spread on the floor like giant black wings, he looked more bat than butterfly.

"Do you notice anything strange?" Dickson asked.

"Apart from a man run through with a stump?" Plum said. I admired his dry sense of humor as well.

"There's no blood on the floor," Harry said. "That stump looks to have gone straight through his heart so there should be a pool round him where he bled out."

"Crikey, Dickson, you're right," he said.

He walked up to have a closer look. Even without the gloom in the cellar and with his spectacles on, he was as blind as a bat. Getting a stronger prescription was the first thing on his agenda when he left school after the cricket competition.

"There's something else which is even more noticeable," I said. "Look at those teeth. He's got two incisors that would do a sabertooth tiger proud. I've seen hustler's shivs less sharp."

We could hear noises above us as the domestic staff started to cook breakfast. We had sneaked down in the hope of finding some treats that were being hidden from the boys for the masters. Plum was convinced we would win the competition against Eton and Greyfriars and wanted to lay down some provisions for a feast at the end of the week. The trophy—the Brasher Bat—was always hotly contested and it had been a couple of years since Dulwich had won.

"I suppose we better call someone to help," he said. "Don't want any coves thinking we did this."

We had only met the dead man the day before, and English public schools are not known for training up homicidal maniacs, but I saw his point. Besides, the Bull would want to snoop round to see who they could pin it on. I wanted to have closer look round the whole room before we called anyone in, though.

"I'm going to have a look round, to see if I can spot any clues," Dickson said. He obviously had the same idea as me.

"Like that Holmes chappy?" Plum said. "Does that make me Sherlock or Watson? Actually, as you are my fag, you should be Watson. You can write everything down and sell the story for a fortune."

Plum was a lot cleverer than he appeared—his upper class accent hid a pretty decent mind. I still felt he was a bit out of his depth with investigating, though. I'd been here a week—my grandmother thought it would be good to settle in before term started—and I'd got to know him quite well since I had been assigned to his dorm. Good man and good cricketer, but probably poor detective.

"We can decide that later," Dickson said. "The priority now is to see if we can find anything that might reveal the identity of the murderer. Don't touch anything in case we get accused of tampering with evidence, but look round carefully and jot anything you see down in that notebook of yours."

Plum had ambitions to be a journalist so was forever scribbling things—observations, ideas, a few sketches. I had some ambitions as a writer myself and was slightly put out that the youngster had chosen Plum over a fellow American. I was also not sure why he thought he should be in charge of the investigation. He was the same age as me, but seemed to have even more of the typical Yankee self-confidence.

"Actually, it would be good if you could draw the scene as well. Where the body is, where any clues are," I said.

"Right ho," Wodehouse replied brightly.

The cellar floor was made of stone slabs and must have been cleaned recently. There was no dust to show footmarks. The only easy entrance was via the door we had come in through. There was a barred window at the far side of room, which was giving enough light for our survey, but nothing bigger than a cat could get in that way. In any case, the window was shut and bolted. It was at ground level and the staff didn't want to risk rainwater coming in and spoiling the food.

That stump sticking out of Quelch's chest could have come from anywhere. However, there were three bands painted round the top in Dulwich's colors, so it must have belonged to our school. I made a note to check the kit room later and see if any were missing. Whoever put it there must have been pretty strong, or used a mallet. If the latter, there was no sign of it. I gently lifted the body from the floor, and as Dickson said, there was no sign of blood underneath. In fact, there was no blood anywhere in the room, so even if the body had been brought here from somewhere else, it must have been completely exsanguinated first.

Sherlock Holmes was always finding cigarette stubs or other things dropped by the killer, but we had no such luck. It was almost as if the body had been dropped there from the heavens, or flapped in on that bat wing gown and landed in the center of the floor. However, the door had been locked from the outside so anyone could have come in, done the deed, and locked it up on the way out. There was no sign of theft and I couldn't think of a reason for brutally killing a schoolmaster outside of him setting particularly punishing Latin verb conjugations. We would need to talk to the other pupils and teachers, especially the lads from Greyfriars, because as far as we knew, they were the only ones who knew Quelch.

"Any sign of anything?" I asked Plum.

"Nary a sausage," he said. "I've finished the sketch."

He showed me. It was pretty accurate. Dickson seemed less impressed, but kept quiet for once.

"We had better leave, then," I said. "We tell people we opened the door, saw the body, and came straight out to raise the alarm."

"Won't the cooks know we've been here a while?" he asked.

"It was dark, we didn't see the body at first. It took us a couple of minutes until our eyes adjusted."

He nodded.

We went back out of the door, locked it behind us, and walked back up the stairs to the kitchen.

It was half an hour before the Police arrived. In that time, we had accepted the sweet tea the head cook had offered us, and the caretaker had gone downstairs to verify our story. When the police Inspector returned from the cellar, though, his face was red with anger.

"What sort of game are you schoolboys playing?" he said. "It's not a joke, wasting Police time."

Plum, Harry and I looked at each other in bafflement.

"There's no body there," he said. "I'm not in the mood for schoolboy pranks."

The caretaker jumped to our defense and said he had seen the body as well.

"It's probably one of the other pupils," Inspector Lestrade said. He was a weasel-faced man in his late fifties dressed in tweeds with a bowler hat that was rattling on his shaking head like the lid on a boiling pan. "Some clown has staged this and then sneaked off as soon as your back was turned."

"I swear we saw a body," said Plum. "It was Quelch, the master who's here with the Greyfriars boys."

I nodded. "If it was a prank, would we be so stupid as to get the staff to call in the cops?"

Dickson kept his silence, but looked thoughtful.

The policeman also looked thoughtful. I suspected he'd reached his rank more by stepping into dead men's shoes than natural ability, but even he saw the logic.

"Are you a Yank?" he asked.

"I've lived there most of my life," I said. "I just arrived a couple of weeks ago. My grandmother lives nearby and she wanted me to have the best education."

"Be careful you don't learn the wrong things from these public schoolboys," he said. "Some of them grow up to be very rum coves. Just because they're educated, they think they're above the law. I've arrested quite a few of them in my time, and there's a few more I would like to get behind bars. The worst criminal I ever knew taught at a public school. Brain the size of a planet, but Holmes and I ran him to ground. In fact, his nephew is at school here, so you had best watch out for young Moriarty."

I knew who he was talking about, but Moriarty seemed as nice as Plum. Apart from my friend, he and the other Irish boy, O'Hara, were our best cricket players.

One of the other Dulwich boys came in as Lestrade was talking. I'd met Tootles—as he was called—before, and instantly noticed his quite thick London accent and a dark skin that was obviously colored by an outdoor life. Many of the boys—like Plum—had parents living overseas, but spent most of their time locked behind the school gates and had pale flesh which hours on the playing fields hadn't darkened.

"The Head wants to see Chandler and Wodehouse," he said.

"So this is where the old man sent you, is it?" asked Lestrade. "One of his charity cases. Still, I hope for both your sakes it pays off."

Tootles blushed slightly.

"I'm doing very well, sir," he said. "Everyone's been very good to me and helped me catch up with the education I missed before I came here."

The Inspector nodded.

"I'll talk to you two boys later," he said. "My men will see if they can find this Mr. Quelch and if they do, I want to find out more about what happened here. I don't appreciate my time being wasted when there are villains to catch."

Plum and I were only too keen to go and see the Headmaster. I knew some Heads have a reputation for caring more about the cane than for textbooks, but ours seemed very decent. We took our school caps out of our pockets and put them back on our heads.

As it transpired, the Head didn't want to see us for anything serious. He just wanted to go over the batting order for this afternoon's match against Eton. Plum had stayed on specially to captain the match, and the Head wanted me to learn as much about cricket as I could before I took to the field. I'd only played baseball before so using the strange flat bat was a challenge, but I was skilled at fielding. Catching a baseball or cricket ball was much the same.

The competition trophy—The Brasher Bat –was in the center of the Head's desk. Six inches long, it was a solid gold bat mounted on a wooden plinth which had a silver plate engraved with the names of the winning schools. Last year, it had gone to Eton who had brought it back ready for this year's contest.

Plum had told me its history. It had been presented by a former pupil—the eponymous Brasher—who had had it made in China where he had been stationed in the army. The gold came from a village in the interior where he had been given it by a Buddhist monk. It had been a large medal taken from someone the monk had described as "a devil" and he gave it to Brasher because he felt it polluted the holiness of his temple. Brasher had no such superstition and had it made into the bat, which he had then sent back to his *alma mater* as a prize. It may be it wasn't that lucky, as Dulwich had only won once in the last five years, and Brasher himself had recently died in the Boxer Rebellion.

It was quite attractive, but with the brassy beauty of a high-class harlot.

When Plum and I had finished going through the lists with the Head, we went back to the kitchen to find the Inspector and his men had left. We were astonished to find Quelch had turned up alive and well and persuaded the police to write off the incident as a foolish prank. He undertook to find the culprits and mete out his own form of justice with the switch he held permanently at his side.

"Misdirection," said Dickson. "Like the stage magic I have studied. The question is, what it was meant to distract us from."

I wanted to investigate more. I was sure that had been Quelch and was equally sure he had been as dead as a weekend in Woking. However, Plum persuaded me to do some batting practice before lunch.

On the way we met some of the boys from Eton—Wimsey, Drummond and Petrie. Drummond was every inch the typical sportsman, hard bodied with the expression of a bulldog on guard. Wimsey was deceptively slight with sandy hair, and Petrie was of that unexceptional type that could have come off Ford's assembly line, if he made schoolboys rather than cars.

13

The trio were watching a sign writer add the names of former pupils who had died in battle. As well as Brasher, there were some who had perished in the Boer War and others who had died in the silent wars of the Great Game with Russia in the East. Russia was still keen to extend its influence in Afghanistan, but seemed to have reached an understanding over China as both they and Britain were more wary of Japan than each other. Apparently, they were even helping each other defend their embassies in the current Boxer Rebellion.

"Hopefully no-one will die on the field of battle this afternoon," said Drummond.

He always presented a pleasant front, but I suspected he could be a bit of a bully

"If it is it will be one of you coves," said Plum.

I wondered if, like me, he was speculating if Drummond and his friends had been involved in the prank.

"Feeling confident, aren't we?" Drummond sneered. "You know our new coach, Mr. Raffles, was a top-flight cricketer?"

"If he was actually playing, we might be worried," said Plum. "But the bunch of useless drones you and Greyfriars have assembled are no match for our top squad. Plus, Chandler here is our secret weapon."

"An American. He can probably only play that ridiculous rounders game the Yanks like."

I may have been six years younger than Drummond, but he didn't scare me. I stepped up until I was only a couple of inches from his face.

"Do you want to put your money where your mouth is, Limey?" I snarled. "How about a bet?"

"As long as you don't expect to pay in dollars, certainly. I think I can risk a fiver. How about you boys?" Drummond said, turning to Petrie and Wimsey. They both shook their heads. Although Drummond was still sneering, he did take a step back. Like a typical bully, he only wanted to take on someone who was scared of him.

Plum held me by the elbow and tried to guide me away.

"We'll see you on the field tomorrow," he said.

As we walked out of the school towards the cricket nets, he leaned in to talk to me quietly.

"Are you mad?" he said. "I thought you didn't have any money? Didn't you say your mother was on her uppers? And I can't imagine your grandmother being pleased to stump up five pounds to cover your gambling debts within a week of you arriving here."

"I'll think of something," I said. "You can't let bullies win. A person has to have standards."

As we approached the nets, I saw the some of the Greyfriars boys were already there—Wharton, Nugent, Cherry, Bull and Singh were present, but Bunter was probably off searching for some food—there was a rumor he'd even been seen eating flies and mice. Singh was to one side of the others, talking to my schoolmate O'Hara. I knew O'Hara made regular trips to India, so perhaps they were reminiscing. Singh was supposed to be some kind of Hindu Prince, but his English had less of an accent than mine, apart from occasional deliberate jokes like saying "clickee ba" for cricket bat.

Dickson was there as well, and was talking to the other boys and jotting down notes in an exercise book.

I was more curious to see Quelch standing there. It definitely looked like the same man we had seen dead in the cellar, although he didn't have those oversize teeth anymore.

"Ah-ha," he said. "The two boys who thought I was a corpse. I can tell you the rumors of my death have been greatly exaggerated. I'm as alive as I have ever been."

"It must have been some other boys playing a prank," said Plum. "It was jolly convincing, though. I could swear they'd made one of them up to be the spitting image of you."

"Rest assured," said Quelch, "If I find the boys responsible, they will be thrashed within an inch of their lives."

I was studying Quelch closely. If it hadn't been his body we found, it was certainly a very good impersonation. Then I noticed his waistcoat. Just over his heart was an area that had been sewn up. Right where the stump would have entered.

"Are any of the stumps missing?" I asked. "It might give a clue as to who was responsible."

He gave me a withering stare, as if I was something he had just scraped off his shoe.

"I'm surprised you can recognize a stump, being from the Colonies," he said. "I am perfectly capable of making my own inquiries without any suggestions from you."

He swung his cape free of his arms and strode off.

"Don't mind old Quelch," said Nugent. "His bark's worse than his bite."

"Yes, but his cane is worse than his bark," said Cherry, laughing. "Rest assured it wasn't any of us played the prank, although if we had thought of it, we may have done. We were all in our dorm having a feast until the early hours. I'm afraid we're night owls."

I wandered closer to Singh and O'Hara. Their conversation seemed to be intense and I was curious to know what was so important. These were the two Dickson had been talking to a few seconds ago.

"I've had a telegram from my Uncle Hurree," Singh was saying. The redhead and the Hindu prince were pretending to watch the action in the nets and standing side by side rather than face to face. "Both the Russians and us are looking for an artefact stolen from China a few years ago. It's causing a bit of stir amongst elements in the Chinese Court. One of the sparks that lit off this

Boxer Rebellion apparently. Whichever nation manages to get it back will increase their influence in China significantly."

"What is its nature?" asked O'Hara.

"Some kind of badge taken from a Buddhist temple. Strange story, it's supposed to belong to one of Seven Golden Vampires, of all things. Obviously rubbish, and I would have expected better of the Buddhists. They're not normally that superstitious. Still, it seems whoever it did belong to wants it back and has considerable influence with the Chinese government, There's some talk of a powerful Mandarin being involved who wants to banish foreigners from China. He was a key player in the Chinese opium market, but was pushed out when we got involved."

It was obvious what they were talking about, and O'Hara must have put the pieces together too. I quickly turned on my heel and strode back to the main school building, taking Plum and Dickson with me. I wanted to warn the Headmaster before someone tried to steal the Brasher Bat.

The door to the office was wide open and I could see the Head slumped across his desk. What I couldn't see was the Bat.

The new school librarian, Mr. Giles, was also standing behind the desk, checking the Head for a pulse and clucking over a bloody scalp wound.

"Go and get nurse, quickly, and ask the caretaker to call the police," he said. "It looks as if he's been hit by a heavy object. I've touched it gently and his skull doesn't seem to be broken, though. He's still breathing, just out for the count."

There were no bloody statuettes or red spattered paperweights, but Giles may have some information.

"What happened, sir?" asked Dickson, who had the same thought.

Giles kept looking round the room, especially at the partly open window. Was that where the burglar had fled?

"I was popping in to see the Head to check on a consignment of books from a former pupil's library we are expecting," he said. "I knocked but there was no answer, so I opened the door and found the Head like this."

"And they must have stolen the Brasher Bat," said Dickson.

Giles looked intently at the desk and shook his head.

"My god," he said, "I hadn't noticed. Someone must have broken in to steal it."

Plum came back with the Nurse, who bustled us out of the room.

"Did you notice he pushed his glasses back on his nose," said Dickson. "It must be a nervous tick he only uses them for reading. Why did he have them on? If he was going to show the Head some paperwork, he would have put it on the desk as soon as he saw his employer's condition. And the desk was completely clear. There are a couple of things that don't add up. First, whoever has taken the Bat has left a lot of other expensive silverware on open display in the study. The Bat may be the most valuable single item, but a quick rifle in the trophy cupboards would have at least tripled the value of the haul. Second, how did Giles know that the Bat was on the desk—and in the very spot he looked?"

I remembered the letters and books Plum and I had seen on it when we had been discussing the team selection.

"Giles kept looking at the window," Dickson said. "Shall we have a look from the other side?"

"Right ho," Plum said. "As that cove Holmes would say, the game is afoot. Except he spent a lot of time in cabs, from what I remember."

I gave a wry smile. Lots of times Plum was very witty, but this wasn't one of them.

The Head's study was on the second floor—or first floor as the English would count them. However, as the school had high ceilings, it would have been a bit of a drop for anyone leaping from the window.

"There are no foot marks in the flower bed or lawn fringe as you would expect if someone had landed there from that height," said Dickson. "They have been well watered, leaving the ground quite soft. There were no recent scuff marks from a ladder in the lintel of the window. Besides, the window is in plain view from the nets and one of us would have seen something. The culprit must have exited through the school, and if no one saw a stranger, they must be a pupil or staff member at one of the three schools."

Unless they flew away, of course.

We were at the front door as the Head was helped out to an ambulance and the Inspector returned with a couple of uniformed constables.

"I need to speak to that man," he barked.

"I'm sorry sir, he's suffering from concussion and needs to be checked out urgently at hospital in case he has a blood clot or other brain damage," said the doctor.

The Head pulled himself together a bit.

"Sorry, Inspector, there's nothing much I can tell you anyway. I was attacked from behind and it all went black as soon as I was struck."

Lestrade huffed but waved the doctor to continue.

"Are you three involved in this again?" he said.

"We weren't the first on the scene this time," said Plum. "That would be the Librarian, Mr. Giles. He was already there when we arrived."

"And where can I find him?" the Inspector asked.

Giles walked forward through the crowd of staff and boys standing on the steps.

"That would be me, Inspector. If you would like, I can take you to my study and tell you what I know."

The two men strode through the double doors into the school, with the two constables scurrying along in their wake.

Eton's cricket coach, Mr. Raffles, had appeared, together with Mr. Quelch. I realized I hadn't seen either of them since well before the attack on the Head.

Raffles hadn't been present at all this morning and Quelch had walked off from the nets as I was listening to O'Hara and Singh. I had also not seen the fat boy from Greyfriars, Bunter, all day. I should talk to the cooks as his favorite place seemed to be the kitchen.

"All right, boys," said Quelch. "We can't allow this barbarism to get in the way of the competition. We've lost an hour of this afternoon's play, so we shall just have to add an hour onto the end. My school and Dulwich need to get into their whites as quickly as possible and we can make a start."

It was a perfect day for the match. Sunny but with a slight cooling breeze. The groundsman had watered the grass that morning so it had some softness, but the sunshine had dried the creases enough to make it a bowler's wicket. Both Plum and O'Hara were excellent fast bowlers

We won the toss and opted to bat first. To give everyone an equal chance the competition was played over 20 overs a side rather than the interminable test match option. The winner would be whoever did best over all three matches.

Harry Wharton proved to be an excellent fast bowler, although his best friend, Bob Cherry, was not in the same class. Bunter had now arrived and I was surprised to find he was quite a decent wicket keeper. Our two openers—Tootles and Darling—were both caught for only a dozen runs each.

I hadn't talked to Darling much since arriving at Dulwich—largely by choice. Although he was leaving after the match like Plum, and despite his enthusiasm for his upcoming military career, he seemed even younger than me. Forever chattering about pirates and Red Indians.

The double act of O'Hara and Moriarty piled on 50 runs each before being bowled and then run out, and the next pair—Plum and Ruthven—also added good scores with Plum nearing his century from several splendid sixes when Ruthven was caught in the slips and it was my turn to bat.

Ruthven was what Plum would have called an odd cove. He kept himself to himself and I gathered from my friend he was prone to enlisting the younger pupils in secret societies rather than mixing with boys of his own age. He seemed keener on the Greyfriars' boys' company than that of his schoolmates. They were always in a huddle somewhere - perhaps he was trying to set up yet another secret cabal.

I was nervous. I was a reasonable batter at baseball, but this was different. You had to keep a close eye on the ball as its bounce could send it anywhere, especially on a fast wicket. Wharton was bowling and I had seen his spin ball.

The first ball hit the ground and angled right. I managed to get it a good whack and sent it to the boundary for a four. I could see Wharton analyzing my stroke and rubbing the ball against his trousers to get the right level of friction so he could send it where he wanted. I was also reading him, though, and as I guessed the next ball spun to the left to test me. I surprised him by stepping forward into the ball and this time hit it for a six.

Behind me, I could hear Bunter mumbling and hissing. Not really cricket, as Plum would say. I could sense him waggling his head to tell Wharton where to place the ball. I stepped and sent the ball straight back over Wharton's head for another six. And that was the end of our 20 overs for a score of 262. In the end, we won by a comfortable margin of 43 runs.

"The Head should be back tomorrow. Fortunately, he has no broken bones or concussion, just a nasty scalp wound that needed stitches," Giles said when we got back to the school. "They are keeping him in overnight just in case, so I will be looking after you tonight."

Supper wasn't quite as bland as some of the food I had experienced during the last week. Chicago had quite a lot of its food based on its Irish American heritage, but in the past few years, immigrants from Germany, Poland and Scandinavia had literally spiced things up. This meal started with Kedgeree—a sort of curried rice dish—and ended with an apple crumble spiced with cinnamon and some kind of aniseed flavor. I went to bed with a full stomach and the tiredness that comes from hard physical effort and the feeling of a job well done.

I was sound asleep enjoying pleasant dreams when Dickson shook me awake.

"What's happening?" I said groggily. "Is the place on fire?"

He smiled. "No, but my brain is," he said. "All of this robbery and violence stuff doesn't make sense. My money was initially on Raffles, but why go to all that bother only steal the trophy? If you ask me, the whole thing is bats."

"Sound thinking," said Plum who was also sitting up in his bed. "I think we need to do some investigating of our own. Starting with a sneaky look at the Greyfriars dorm. Those fellows are rummer than a drunken sailor in a distillery."

"Agreed," I said. "If the dead Quelch was a prank aimed at diverting attention, it's only really Greyfriars who would choose him as a false murder victim. Dressing up the body in that elaborate way has to be Wharton and Co.'s work."

Dickson said he wanted to do his own investigation.

Plum and I dressed carefully in long black running gear to blend in with the shadows. It would look a bit more suspicious than pajamas if we were caught, but we could bluff that we were off for a midnight run. In term time, the risk of being caught would be higher, but with so few staff and boys around, we managed to get to Greyfriars' dorm in the Orchard without the alarm being raised. There was a drainpipe Plum and I could climb.

As it was a warm and close night, Greyfriars had left the window open, but closed the thick drapes. We moved to either side of their concealment and listened to the conversation inside.

It was muffled but seemed to be some kind of chanting in Latin. I hadn't had any Latin lessons yet, but Plum was—as he described it—a bit of a whiz.

"They seem to be doing some kind of ceremony," he whispered. "Something about honoring their master with a sacrifice. Their pronunciation is deplorable."

Before we could hear any more, the curtains were pulled aside and we were confronted by Quelch, but a Quelch with the big teeth—big teeth that had blood dribbling down from them.

We could jump down 20 ft and risk breaking a limb, or try and push past Quelch and make it to the dorm door, but before we could choose, Wharton and Nugent grabbed our arms and pulled us into the room.

The dorm was lit by long candles. Two of the beds had been placed on top of each other, with sheets draped over them as a makeshift altar. Tied to the bed head with pajama cords was Bunter, struggling to escape and whining and complaining through the pillowcase gag in his mouth.

All of the Greyfriars crew were there, except Singh. To my surprise, Ruthven was there too. Like Quelch, they all had elongated canines, and blood around their mouths. Judging from the blood on his neck, it was Bunter's. Despite the warmth of the night, I started shivering.

Bunter had his shirt torn open. The white buttons flashed on the floor in the candlelight like a scattering of pearls. There were cuts on his chest as well as neck. I had seen a man with similar wounds in Chicago when a window had exploded, but these but these were slices from those teeth. His eyes were rolling in terror and pain.

"We were not expecting visitors," said Quelch. "You can get into a lot of trouble sneaking into other dorms at night."

"I had guessed we were in trouble," said Plum with a steadier voice than I think I could have managed. "Is this one of your midnight feasts?"

"You're in no position to joke," said Bull. "You shouldn't have pushed your noses into our business."

"What are you doing to Bunter?" I asked. "This is not some harmless prank. He's terrified. Why aren't you stopping this, Mr. Quelch?"

"Because he's a bally vampire," said Plum. "I've been wracking my brains to remember where I had heard Ruthven's name before. He was that vampire chappie in the story by Byron."

"Polidori," said Quelch.

"Whatever," said Plum. "But Ruthven was hundreds of years-old, not sixteen. And how does he go out in daylight and eat garlic?"

"You are confusing my bloodline with Dracula's," said Quelch. "Your Ruthven is my son by blood, as are all of these boys."

"Except Bunter," I guessed.

"An interloper," said Quelch. "One of Dracula's get sent to spy on us, just as we sent my son to spy on you and pave the way to steal the bat."

"So that was you?" I said.

"No, someone else got there before us," said Quelch. "I thought pretending to be killed would draw out the opposition, but you two fools found me instead"

"How do you know we aren't the opposition?" said Plum. "We could be here with lots of our accomplices standing just outside that door."

"I can smell you," said Quelch. "I would have found Bunter if he had been converted by Dracula instead of simply succumbing to his mind control. You are just foolish schoolboys. For now..."

Wharton and Nugent held us tighter while Bull and Cherry moved over in case we tried to escape. Not that we could move in the iron grip of the two boy vampires. Quelch's fangs seemed to grow even longer as he strode towards us.

Then there was a knock on the door.

"I hope you boys are all decent," said Mr. Giles. "I'm coming in for a dorm inspection."

Wharton and Nugent let go of our arms and the vampires seemed to shrink as they resumed their normal appearance. The only thing unusual was poor Bunter still tied to the improvised altar. Wharton quickly removed his gag as the door opened and the librarian entered.

"What's been happening here Mr. Quelch?" he asked.

There were bulges in both his pockets that looked suspiciously like revolvers.

"Some ridiculous prank," the vampire elder said. "I heard the noise from my room down the corridor and was just ordering the boys to let poor Bunter go."

"He's in a bad way," said Giles. "I'll take him to the nurse. I'll leave you to deal with your boys. We can talk about what happened here in the morning."

Quelch was rightly worried about what we would say, but didn't have much choice unless he was going to kill Giles as well. With a thinly masked curl of his lip, he allowed Giles to untie Bunter and Plum and I lifted him up and supported him out of the door. It wasn't easy. He was a dead weight in our arms.

"Shall I wake up the nurse?" asked Plum.

"Not yet. We need to go to the library," Giles said.

My arms were shaking with strain by the time we got to Giles' book-lined kingdom. Harry Dickson was already there and sitting in an armchair. There were no settees in the room, so we sat Bunter down in another armchair.

Giles unstoppered a bottle of water and I thought he was going to pour some for Bunter. He did, in a way, as he poured it over his head to rouse him.

"Stop it, you rotter," Bunter shrieked in his high-pitched voice. "I'll tell mater and pater what a beast you've been."

Bunter seemed pathetic, but I could see the cowardly cunning behind the eyes. He seemed destined to end up running a squalid bar somewhere in North Africa or running round the world pursuing something that would make his fortune with a fall guy in tow to absorb the heat.

"Drop the act, Bunter," said Giles. "It won't wash with me. I know who your master is."

"What is all this vampire stuff?" said Plum.

"I don't think I can stay skeptical after seeing the fangs on the Greyfriars gang," I said. "They hadn't bought those in a theatrical costumier's. What I don't get is why the Brasher Bat is so important—wrong type of bat, surely."

"Everyone wants it," said Dickson. "Including this man and his masters. You're a member of the Watchers' Council aren't you? Or is it the Diogenes Club?"

"At the moment, both," said Giles. "I'm a Watcher, but we're working with Mycroft Holmes's organization on this. I'm looking after the vampire side of things and O'Hara is handling the political side."

"That would be why he was talking to Singh about China," I said. "Some political game between us and Russia."

"The Great Game," said Giles. "O'Hara was active in India and Afghanistan and Singh's Uncle was his handler. Mycroft is worried the truce between Russia and us in China is just a smokescreen to hide their ambitions."

"I still don't see how the Bat fits into this," said Plum.

"I suspect it's not the Bat but the gold it's made of," Dickson said.

"Well done," said Giles. "It was a medallion worn by one of the Seven Golden Vampires. Or six, as they are now. Their cult is incredibly powerful, behind the scenes. We think Dracula wants to take over, following his failure in England. If he can get the gold back and remake the medallion, he can use it as a tool to become their leader and rule China. Neither Russia nor we can countenance that, but if they get it first, they may use it to control the sect themselves."

"And Ruthven presumably has the same ambitions," the youngster continued.

"So we believe," said Giles, smiling. "I'm impressed."

"Elementary," Dickson said. Plum smiled at the reference.

"I think that settles which of us is Holmes," he said. "I'm surprised the great man himself isn't here himself in disguise. The cook, perhaps."

"He's busy," said Giles. "But he did ask one of his ex-Irregulars, Tootles, to keep an eye on things."

"Not Raffles then as you suspected, Dickson," I said.

"Don't be so quick to dismiss him," said Dickson. "I searched his rooms and there was no sign of the Bat, but there were some interesting papers. It seems he, too, is after the Bat, on behalf of an international criminal organization known as the Black Coats. I will talk to him tomorrow."

"It's clearly not Ruthven's crew, or they wouldn't have bothered torturing Bunter," I said, turning to the fat owl.

"Don't look at me, chaps," he whined. "I may have pinched the odd postal order or bit of tuck, but not the bally Bat. I certainly wouldn't have bashed a chap."

"I believe him," said Giles. "Apart from anything else, he's too big a coward to withstand any interrogation from half a dozen hungry vampires"

"Speaking of which," I said. "What's going to happen to them?"

Giles adjusted his glasses and rubbed his hand through his hair.

"We send them back to Greyfriars, but keep a close watch on them," he said. "They can spend eternity as a bunch of schoolboys endlessly recycling slight variations on the same year and never getting any older. Ruthven is safer there than out in society."

"Does that mean the cricket tournament is off?" asked Plum. He sounded more dejected than he had facing down a roomful of vampires.

"Greyfriars will forfeit their match and Dulwich can play Eton for the trophy," Giles said.

Plum smiled again. He had only stayed on at school for the competition and I knew what it would mean to him to lead a winning team.

"If you are going to play tomorrow, though, you need some sleep," Giles said. "I will deal with Bunter and the rest of the Greyfriars crew."

Plum, Dickson and I went back to our room. Although we were all tired, it was hard to sleep and we talked for an hour until we eventually dropped off.

"I can contact Holmes to see if he or his brother know anything about this. I'm sure Tootles will take a message," said Dickson. "This Bat seems to be important, and we need to know why. Giles has explained the vampire's interest, but why are the Black Coats involved?"

Next day's game was a lot closer than the one against Greyfriars. Although Eton were a few years from the unbeatable team they would build with the next generation of players, their existing squad were no slouches at batting or bowling.

Batting first, Wimsey, Drummond and Petrie laid down impressive scores before being bowled by Plum and O'Hara. Their final tally of 302 was an impressive target, but Plum changed the order of batting, putting O'Hara and myself in first. We did well. By the time Plum came on to join Moriarty, we were only 50 away from Eton's score with two overs to play.

The first added two sixes, two fours and a single. Six balls and 30 runs left. Plum's first two balls added another 12 and he then hit one for three runs, leaving Moriarty at the crease. He hit another three, leaving two balls and 12 to score. Brave strikes on two of Drummond's dangerous fast balls gave another two sixes.

A win. The match, and the trophy. We all threw our caps in the air in a storm of navy and blue and the rest of the team charged onto the field to hoist Plum on high.

I saw Dickson slip off after a lone lemonade, with the excuse of having left something in his locker. I followed him. Moriarty and Raffles were there and inside Moriarty's locker was a glint of gold.

"I was pretty sure it was you, Moriarty," Dickson said. "There was the hint from the Inspector about your family, but what clinched it was a scrap from your other trousers on the lintel around the roof where you climbed down a rope ladder to get into the Head's study."

Raffles drew some strange kind of gun from his pocket.

"I will not be thwarted by a group of meddling kids," he said. "You English public school boys are full of privilege. This dart gun should puncture your pomposity."

"Actually, we're American," said Dickson. "My friend Mr. Sherlock Holmes knows all about you and your masters, Mr. Raffles—if that is who you are. His colleague, Dr. Watson, was the person who attended the Headmaster and his observations and my investigation gave him all he needed. He is outside now with the Police."

There was indeed a noise outside and Raffles, or whoever he was, turned towards the door.

It gave me the chance I needed. My bat was still in my hand and I swung it, knocking the gun from his hand. I could see a moment of indecision before he ran to the far end of the locker room and climbed through a window.

Moriarty looked as if he would follow, but remembered the bat in my hand.

"I wouldn't bother trying to run," Dickson said. "I've already told Mr. Giles, who is rounding up the rest of his agents at the school to take you in."

"My family have friends in the Police force," he said. "I'll say it was just a prank and they will get me off."

"I'm sure they would, if anyone was going to call in the Police," said Harry. "My mention of Holmes was a bluff. Giles has everything in hand. I know both your father and the Black Coats are after the real thing because of the gold's potential to power devices that will further their schemes."

Moriarty looked worried. He may come from a family of career criminals, but he was still only a 16 year-old boy.

"What are you going to do with me?"

"Nothing," said Giles as he walked in. "You will have to leave, of course. I'll tell the Head we found the trophy and you confessed, so we asked your parents to take you out of school. Not much of a lie. I'm sure your father will think of some appropriate punishment for failing to get the Bat for him and his clients, be they the Russians or the Black Coats. We will substitute it and keep the real thing in our Black Museum for safekeeping. We can't afford the Golden Vampires or other criminal organizations to get hold of it, and it's too risky to try and smuggle it back into China."

A black chauffeur-driven car pulled up half an hour later and Moriarty was thrust into the back seat with his trunk thrown into the car's boot.

"Holmes may have done for his uncle, but Colonel Moriarty is every bit as bad as the Professor. He just hasn't been caught yet," Giles told us.

"I suppose you'll be recruiting young Dickson here?" Plum said.

"You would be welcome," Giles said.

"I already have my career planned," Dickson said. "I would welcome some training from your organization, though."

I had a slight moment of jealousy, but realized I would rather read or write about crime than try and solve it. In the U.S., murder is simple—it is committed in the heat of the moment with whatever is at hand, or by career killers and hoodlums. It is done for the normal motives of greed, revenge, or passion and not as part of some bizarre dance with rules even more complex than cricket.

Plum left the next day as the competition was over, after being presented with the copied trophy on behalf of the school. Dickson had finished his trial week and was bound for some other public school as part of his training.

I hung around for another day or so before going back to my grandmother's house. My own trial week had been successful, according to the Head's report, and of course there was no mention of the mystery—just cricket. I looked forward to a simpler term at the end of the summer. With no vampires.

A change of pace for Matthew Baugh who draws on his vast knowledge of Mexican wrestlers & horror films to pen this amusing little tale, starring his Russian Vampire Yvgeni, last seen in our tenth volume....

Matthew Baugh: *Hercules and Samson vs the Russian Vampire and the Zombies of Frankenstein*

Veracruz, 1974

Mexico had been a bad idea.

These were my thoughts as one massive hand gripped my chin and the other the back of my head. Powerful arms wrenched, and I heard a horrible crack as my head rotated 180 degrees out of position. A quick downward glance revealed that my body had not moved at all. My face now looked out over the back of my suit and the heels of my expensive shoes. My head was on backward, something that would have proved instantly fatal had I not already been one of the undead.

A vampire can survive such *outré* wounds. We can even heal them, though it does take several moments of concentration. Alas, my focus was entirely taken up by the soles of a pair of boots as they rushed at my face in a most athletic kick. The blow didn't hurt me much, but it did send me pitching forward to crash on the front of my body.

As the back of my head struck the cement floor, I realized that having one's head on backward makes maintaining one's balance difficult. This was most undignified, especially for a *wurdulac* of the line of Vseslav. I tried to rise, but my confused physiognomy misunderstood my brain's signals and humped forward like an inchworm. Before I could figure out how to correct my error, two of my brawny assailants caught hold of my arms and twisted them behind my back until my fingers touched my chin. My strength is that of twenty mortals, but my situation was uncomfortable and rather confusing from an anatomical perspective. I struggled but could not break the grip.

"*¡Rápidamente, clavad la estaca en su corazón!*" One of them said to the third man, who remained standing.

"*¡Sí Sí! Sólo déjame encontrar...*" came the reply. "*Ah, esto funcionará muy bien.*"

I heard wood snapping, and my third assailant stepped into view. He carried the thick end of a broken pool cue, which he raised like a spear, preparing to impale me with it.

This misadventure had started at a ruined chateau in the Pyrenees several months before. Word had spread through the undead community that an elder vampire needed an envoy. They say, "the dead travel fast," and that is twice as true of gossip among the dead. The problem was that it grows as quickly as it travels. By the time it reached me, the elder was Dracula himself, and the reward power and riches beyond imagining.

I was skeptical, of course. My last 400 years have held many such opportunities. Sadly, they had usually been the inflated posturing of minor vampires and had never ended in riches and power. Still, I had been reduced to a homeless fugitive, sleeping under piles of tumbled rocks and preying on animals and the occasional village idiot. As little as I wanted anything to do with vampire society, I had no good options. As the rumor directed, I went to the chateau at midnight the night of the next new moon. I stood near the main door and howled like a wolf.

Vampires, I should mention, love this sort of melodrama.

After a moment, the door creaked open, and a sepulchral voice called out, "Enter freely and of your own will."

I let out a sigh and walked through the door. The invitation was a formality, for our kind cannot enter a dwelling without being asked. Still, it seemed that the voice's owner cared at least as much about theatrics as security.

The place was as full of dust and cobwebs as I had expected. A small, red ghost light that floated at head level broke the darkness. That was a nice trick. I followed, and the light led me to a grand hall with an absurdly long dining table. At the far end sat two men whose faces shared a familial resemblance.

"Greetings, brother," the taller said.

"Please join us," the shorter added. "I fear we have no plate for you, for we didn't know you were coming."

I took the seat at the foot of the table where the ghost light had paused to hover. The shorter stabbed a piece of pale flesh on his plate and gobbled it down with relish. The taller raised a glass goblet of thick crimson fluid, and I smelled blood. I had to restrain myself from leaping on the table and running its length to snatch the glass, but I reasoned that might upset my potential employers.

"We have been searching for someone to fill our position for months, and you are the first to reply," the taller said.

I thought about pointing out that their recruitment methods were rather impractical. However, the drama had screened out any competitors, so I let it go.

"What is your name?" The shorter asked.

"Yvgeni."

"Ah!" His face lit up. "A Russian! No doubt you were a great boyar before you turned?"

"No, I was only a Cossack, poor but loyal."

"I see. But no doubt you know who we are."

"I have no idea unless the rumors I heard are true and you are Dracula."

The shorter man barked out a laugh while the taller merely raised an eyebrow.

"Which of us do you think is Dracula?" He asked.

"Whichever you like, my lord," I said. "If you are willing to pay for my services, you can both be Dracula for all I care."

The shorter laughed again, and the taller let a smile creep onto his face.

"We are the brothers Ténèbre," he said. "I am Jean, and this is my brother, Ange. As you may have observed, he is an *upyre* while I am a vampire. He feeds off the bodies of mortals while I drain their blood."

Jean raised his goblet for emphasis. It seemed arrogant that he would explain such things to me when they were common knowledge, but elder vampires must have their posturing.

I glanced at the meat on Ange's plate. Flesh meant nothing to me except an upset stomach. On the other hand, Jean's glass was driving me mad with desire. Not trusting my voice to hide my appetite, I remained silent. I've found this a helpful strategy among my kind, for vampires love the sound of their voices better than any others.

"We have some questions about your qualifications," Ange said, looking up. "For example, can you walk in the daylight?"

"I can, though it weakens me and causes pain," I said.

"What about garlic?" Jean asked.

"I don't like the smell, but it doesn't hurt me."

"What about the cross or the consecrated host?" Ange said.

"They frighten me. I haven't ever touched either holy symbol, but they sap my strength when I am near them."

"Interesting." Ange's voice was thoughtful. "Were you religious in life?"

"Of course!" I said.

"I've often wondered if the power of holy symbols has to do with the faith of the vampire, the faith of the human wielding them, or something else. I should like to convert you to atheism and see if that allows you to overcome your weakness."

"Please, sir," I said. "I may be a thrice-damned creature of the night, but I am a Christian creature of the night. I have never shirked in my duty to kill Tatars, Poles, and other enemies of the Christ."

"I meant no offense," he said. "But I wonder, have you ever been affected by the holy symbols of other religions?"

I thought about that for a moment. I have traveled a great deal in my existence and have an unfortunate tendency to run across exorcists and vampire hunters wherever I go. I remembered a Japanese shrine maiden who made me helpless by throwing a scrap of paper with some writing at me. In the Middle East, I had been driven away by the chanting of Hindu mantras and Muslim sutras. In America, a Navajo wise man had nearly destroyed me by sprinkling corn pollen on my body. Then there was a particularly bothersome rabbi who wore a little box strapped to his forehead. This object held me at bay while he gave me a thorough tongue-lashing, after which he drove me away with a blast on a ram's horn. It seems I am allergic to holy objects of any sort, though it might not be wise to admit that to the brothers.

"No," I said. "I have never had that happen."

There were a few more questions, mainly concerning my weaknesses and strengths. The brothers were disappointed when they learned I could only shape-shift into a wolf and delighted that I could survive with my head severed from my body. Ange had wanted to test that, but Jean had dismissed the idea with a wave of his hand.

"We have no reason to doubt the good Yvgeni. He suits our purposes admirably."

Ange made an ugly face but nodded his assent.

"Europe has become too crowded," Jean said. "We wish to relocate to a country where there are currently no elders so that we can establish our dominion. We have concluded that Mexico is the best place to do this."

"Mexico?" I said.

"Our investigations have shown no significant vampiric presence in that nation," Ange said, "that is, except for a woman called Pandemonium. However, she operates near the American border. We plan to establish ourselves in Central Mexico, so there should be no problem."

"Are you certain," I asked. "I had heard a rumor that Dracula—"

"No!" Ange said. "There was a minor vampire named Baron Brakola whose domain was in Mexico, but he perished several years ago. Dracula has never been there!"

"But—"

"There is no one, I tell you!"

"You must forgive my brother," Juan said. "He is sensitive on the subject of Dracula. There is a history."

"Of course," I said.

"We believe Mexico is safe for us," he continued. "Nonetheless, we want you to go ahead and check it out. We also need you to procure a dwelling for us and some undead servitors. We will provide you with sufficient funds, of course."

"Of course," I repeated, though I had no idea where I could purchase undead servitors.

Two days later, I arrived at the *Museo de Antropología de Xalapa* in Veracruz and knocked at the service entrance. A small mustached man in a security guard's uniform opened the door.

"Casimiro?" I asked.

"*Sí,*" he replied. "*¿Estás aquí por los zombis?*"

"I do not speak Spanish."

"English?"

"Yes, some."

"Good! Please follow me, but quietly. I'm not the only night watchman on duty; my new partner wouldn't understand."

I followed him to the basement, wondering what we would find. He chattered on the whole time about his adventures. He hadn't met a vampire before, though he said he had met a werewolf. It had attacked his girlfriend, and he had beaten it to death with a torch. That seemed unlikely, as did his claims that he was a descendant of D'Artagnan, the musketeer, the Count of Monte Cristo, and the masked hero, El Zorilla."

"Do you mean El Zorro?" I asked.

Casimiro shook his head with an apologetic smile and opened the door to a large storage room. Behind a curtain at the rear, I saw what I took to be a dozen or so manikins. It was only on touching one that I could tell they were cold flesh, not plastic.

"Why are they standing like this?" I asked.

Casimiro smiled and pointed to the belts they all wore.

"These are not the zombies of legend, señor. These are controlled electronically by the belts they wear, using this." He swept a sheet off a table, revealing a black box covered with knobs, dials, and lights. He threw a switch, and the machine buzzed to life as the lights began to flash, and an electrical arc climbed the space between two antennae.

"Who made this?" I said, with a sense of awe.

"It is Dr. Frankenstein's machine. The zombies are his creations also."

"Victor Frankenstein made these?"

"Oh, no, señor," Casimiro replied. "It was a lesser known relative of his, Dr. Irving Frankenstein."

I decided that too much conversation with Casimiro would give me a headache, so I changed the conversation to more practical matters.

"How does it work?"

"Very simply, señor." He produced a handheld microphone which he plugged into the side of the device, then spoke into it.

"Zombies, face me."

They obeyed, without the precision of soldiers, but each shambled and stumbled until all faced a position the little man, who beamed with pride. I looked over the squad of walking dead. They were all men and appeared to be farmers or laborers. Hardly the stuff of a fearsome undead army, but they would do for a start."

"Casemiro?" The deep voice came from the doorway. Turning, I saw a man about six feet-tall and powerfully muscled with a face I knew all too well.

"Maciste?"

His heavy brow knotted in thought. "You… You're that vampire. The one who led us to the city of Selene…"

It had been several hundred years since I had seen him, but there could be no doubt this was the same man. If my heart had still functioned, it would have skipped several beats. Maciste was inhumanly strong, and I knew from experience he could break me like a twig.

Snatching the machine from Casemiro, I raised the microphone to my lips. "Zombies, attack the big man. Tear him to pieces!"

My unliving soldiers surged forward, and Maciste met them with a grim smile. I caught Casemiro's arm and moved to the door. Pausing for a moment, I spoke into the microphone.

"Four of you, kill him. The rest, come with me."

The zombies complied, a third of their number swarming Maciste, who stumbled under the sudden rush.

"My poor friend," Casimiro said as I hurried him through the museum halls. "Those monsters will kill him!"

I didn't reply, but I knew he was wrong. The whole dozen would have been no match for Maciste; four would only slow him. We would be lucky to reach my rented truck before he caught up, and I didn't want to think about what would happen then. My kind can recover from almost any injury, but being crushed and mangled still hurts.

I ordered the zombies into the back of the truck, but as I forced Casimiro into the cab, a whistle sounded behind us. I spun to see a police officer, his revolver drawn. I hissed and bared my fangs to frighten him away.

"¡Madre de Dios! ¿Qué clase de hombre eres?"

"¡Corre, hombre!" Casimiro shouted. "¡Es un vampiro y su legión de muertos vivientes!"

To his credit, the officer was brave enough to level his weapon at my chest and fire off all six rounds. The bullets passed through me harmlessly, and I let out my most sinister laugh. (I have practiced this for three hundred years.) The man dropped the pistol and backed away with a horrified expression as I hauled Casimiro into the truck's cab.

"No se preocupe, señor. ¡Pediré refuerzos!" The officer shouted.

"¡No! ¡La policía estará indefensa!" Casimiro screamed back.

At that moment, Maciste came running from the museum. His shirt was in tatters, but otherwise, he looked unharmed. I shuttered to think how my poor zombies must look. I jumped into the passenger seat and turned my most potent hypnotic gaze on Casimiro.

"Drive, you fool!" I shouted.

The little man's expression went blank, and he turned the key to an already running ignition, causing a horrible sound. A moment later, he shifted into gear, causing a grinding sound from beneath the truck. I regretted the circumstances that had led me to abduct an incompetent driver. But then the gears caught, and the truck started with a lurch. As we pulled into the street, I saw that Maciste was losing ground. Had I still lived, I would have breathed a sigh of relief.

We passed through the dark streets at high speed. Veracruz is known for its nightlife, but the traffic was light enough not to cause problems.

31

"Casimiro," I said.

"Yes, master?"

"What did the policeman say to you?"

"He told me not to worry and that he was calling for reinforcements."

"What did you say to him?"

"I told him not to. The police are no match for one such as you."

"Good!"

I settled into my seat, trying to relax. However, after only a few moments, I heard a siren behind us. Checking the mirror, I saw that the noise came from a 1930s style roadster with the top down. As it drew closer, I could tell that the driver was a burly, shirtless man in a silver mask that concealed all of his face. The passenger was dressed similarly, except his mask was blue. A third masked man rode on the running boards. His mask was more elaborate and sported a red letter "M" on the forehead.

"What is the name of all that is unholy…" I said.

"The policeman must have called them," Casimiro said.

"Who are they?"

"They are three of our greatest wrestlers. The driver is Santo; the others are Blue Demon and Mil Mascaras."

"Wrestlers? Why would he call for wrestlers?"

"They are also great scientists and adventurers, señor," Casimiro said. "They protect our land from all manner of monsters and evil scientists. Even from Martians!"

"That was alarming, if bizarre, news. Had the brothers known there was this kind of resistance in this country? And what could three men, no matter how strong and skilled, hope to do against the undead? I have had a long history of underestimating enemies, but three unarmed men? Surely, I had a better chance fighting them with the zombie horde than trying to outrun them in the ancient trunk.

"Pull over," I said, indicating the parking lot of a building with a sign that said, *Cantina a mi Gusta*.

The truck had scarcely stopped moving when I sprang out with the control box under one arm. I threw open the back and raised the microphone.

"Out, my minions. Kill the three masked men!"

The zombies moved into action, albeit slowly and awkwardly. They were almost all out of the truck when the roadster pulled into the parking lot. The masked men barreled out and plowed into the mob without any hesitation. Despite the numbers, it looked like a mismatch as the wrestlers easily suplexed, body slammed, and power bombed the zombies. After several moments it became clear that the undead creatures recovered instantly, to return unhurt to the fight. I felt a surge of exultation as I realized that the masked men would eventually tire, but the zombies never would.

"Hermanos, estas criaturas no mueren," the blue mask said.

"Tengo algo para esto," The red M said. He headed to the back of their car, breaking away from the zombies.

"He luchado contra los zombis de Frankenstein antes," silver mask said. *"Su debilidad son sus cinturones electrónicos."*

He grabbed the belt of one of the zombies, ripped it loose, then stomped on it. The electronics shattered, and the creature collapsed into a heap. Blue mask laughed when he saw it and tore off the belt of another.

The fight had shifted to the wrestlers' favor when red M reappeared with an odd pistol that looked like something from a science fiction movie. He pointed it at a cluster of three zombies and pulled the trigger. A gout of flame erupted from the weapon, setting the three ablaze. My Gand had gone from eight members to three in a matter of seconds.

I heard a siren from down the road and saw a lone police car approaching. Somehow I knew it was the officer from the museum. He pulled into the lot as the last zombie fell. The three wrestlers turned to face Maciste, his shirt now entirely gone as he leaped out of the car. I used the momentary confusion to throw away the useless control box and run into the cantina. The interior was dim, and there were only half a dozen customers. I bared my fangs, and several people screamed.

I grabbed hold of a barmaid as the door burst open to admit Maciste and the masked wrestlers. I placed a hand to her throat and caused my fingernails to lengthen into talons.

"Leave me alone!" I growled. "If you try to stop me, I will kill the woman."

The four brutes stopped, the chivalry of their kind betraying them. I allowed myself a triumphant smile. Then I noticed that my enemies were looking at something behind me. I suspected a trick, but then a black object like a boomerang shot around my wrist, wrapping it in a strong, thin line.

Maciste sprang forward, plucking the woman from my grasp. I turned and had a brief impression of a tall figure in a long cape, a black cowl that resembled a bat with pointed ears. I had heard of such a crime fighter in the United States who had fought and beaten vampires. I cursed my luck that I should encounter him.

Then the wrestlers piled on me, and I fought for my life.

Mexico had been a bad idea.

Blue Demon and Mil Mascaras pinned my arms while Santo raised the broken pool cue like a spear. He was about to impale me when Maciste placed a big hand on his shoulder.

"Wait, friend. I have a better use for this creature."

The man in the silver mask slowly lowered his weapon.

"Tengo la sensación de que debería confiar en ti." he said. *"¿Eres tú al que llaman Hércules?"*

"People sometimes make that mistake. I am not Hercules; my name is Maciste."

"Ya veo. La gente a veces también me llama erróneamente Sansón. Soy Santo y mis compañeros son Blue Demon y Mil Mascaras."

I'm glad to know you," Maciste said. "And also your other friend."

I saw then that the bat-like figure was different than I had thought. The cape, cowl, gloves, and boots framed a voluptuous woman's body whose only other clothing was a dark blue bikini.

"Hola, me llaman la Mujer Murciélago."

The five questioned me for several hours, and I confess I gave up on the Ténèbre brothers after only a short time. I would have held out much longer, but after Mil Mascaras discovered that the money they had given me was counterfeit, my feelings of loyalty vanished. I told them where to find the brothers and everything I knew about their strengths and weaknesses. I didn't know much, so I mostly made up details.

The five pledged to go to France and end the Ténèbre brothers. I heard later that they found the chateau abandoned and no trace of Jean and Ange. Those two seemed to have led a slippery existence and had often vanished for long periods when things got tough. As for me, Blue Demon and Mil Mascaras wanted to stake me quickly and be done with it. Maciste said that I wasn't a bad sort, as undead predators went, and Santo argued that mercy was a good thing, even for a vampire. The bat-woman broke the tie with the suggestion that they return me to my homeland, sealed in a coffin, and that if any of them come across me again, they destroy me.

And so, I find myself sealed in a coffin, deep in the bowels of a Cuban cargo ship, headed for the Soviet Union. I'm sure the customs officials will be surprised to find me on board, and I am not looking forward to that. Still, it will be far better to be back in Mother Russia than anywhere the cursed Ténèbre brothers may be. And it will be a million times better than the Americas.

Mexico had been a bad idea!

In this tale, Atom Bezecny revisits Orpheus, *a 1950 French film directed by Jean Cocteau and starring Jean Marais. It is the central part of a trilogy, which consists of* The Blood of a Poet *(1930),* Orpheus *(1950), and* The Testament of Orpheus *(1960), all inspired by the ancient myth of Orpheus, and already adapted by Cocteau in an eponymous play in 1926. The film embroiders on the theme of the hero's relationship with Death and takes place at an undetermined time, in neutral contemporary settings with fantastic sequences. Death here is a pale-faced woman played by Maria Casarès, who is accompanied in her works by two motorcyclists, who intervene where she must operate. Her mission orders are transmitted to her by "personal messages" of the style of those used on Radio London during the World War II. If she keeps her aura and her mystery in the world of the living, in the Beyond, she is considered as a mere agent working for a mysterious celestial bureaucracy...*

Atom Mudman Bezecny: *Orpheus Omega*

Orpheus cursed. "That machine of yours has really done it this time, Doctor."

Doctor Omega ran a hand through his slicked-back silvery hair. "I can't understand it," he whispered. "I just can't understand it."

"I know I'm not the first to tell you that you can't control that thing. And when it has the ability to go anywhere, anywhen, that's nothing short of a recipe for disaster."

Omega withheld his usual retort, that he could, in fact, steer the *Cosmos*, but it was just too finicky at times.

His vessel had taken them to a strange place indeed, a place so strange he was at a loss for words. He couldn't recognize the burning ruined city that surrounded him—not from any era in Earth's history, and not from any of the alien worlds he had visited in his travels. This wasn't unusual by itself—what was truly bizarre was the odd feeling in the air. It was a feeling which he knew it would be foolish to ignore, even though he didn't know what it was.

The man known as Orpheus, as a French poet, was able to find the words that Omega could not.

"This place doesn't seem *real*," he said, in that bitter tone of his. "It feels like how I feel when I'm lost in the rush of writing a poem. It's like this is a place of *ideas*—a domain of the human mind."

The Doctor took a while to answer. "As advanced as my ship may be, I don't believe it possesses the power to enter realms that lack physical substance," he said finally.

"Are you sure about that? When I first started traveling with you, you called your ship a possibility machine. And you've always said it could go *any-*

where. Forgive me, but is it not possible that even metaphorical realms are within its reach?"

The Doctor did not answer. In part, this was because these ruins reminded him of the cities he'd seen destroyed by the multitude of evils that he seemed destined to battle again and again. But beyond that, he had an odd certainty that Orpheus was right. Somehow, the ship *had* taken them in a place which didn't really exist.

That was a contradiction in terms—at least, at first glance. Nonexistent places, the Doctor realized, had to exist in some form, being defined by their nonexistence. The only true nonexistent places were ones that had not yet been defined, not yet thought of, or imagined...

He pulled at his lapels and sniffed. That line of thinking was more in Orpheus' department than his own. He was a scientist, and he knew there had be a scientific explanation for this mysterious realm, beyond the subjective terms of the mind.

"I suppose if these are questions we want to answer... There's nothing we can do but try to learn what we can of our surroundings," he said.

"Let's be careful," Orpheus replied, gesturing toward the falling flames and burning rubble.

Without a further word, the two travelers set out into the dreary landscape.

The air hung quiet as they walked. Their feet carried them for miles, over the course of what felt like hours. There was no variance in their surroundings. Wherever they went, there found only smashed buildings burning in the night. The ground was blasted and seared, as if with struck with an atomic bomb. The ship's scanner had detected no hazardous radiations, but the Doctor knew he could never be too careful.

"This place reminds me of a strange dream I once had," Orpheus said at last. "I don't know why, because it doesn't resemble the dream at all. I was in a far-off place which I didn't recognize. I watched as lamp-light glittered off the casing and lens of a great telescope. It must have been some sort of observatory. In that place, I was visited by a strange figure, who came to me dressed in the clothes of an 18th century aristocrat—his coat was two hundred years out of style, and he had a powdered wig and tricorn hat. He spoke to me about the nature of imagination, and imagination's relationship with death, and time. He had traveled through time to meet me, past the historical point of his own death. He told me such amazing things about art and poetry, which I'm realizing I can only just now remember..."

"Yes, my memory is tickled too... it must be something in the air. I remember when I wore a tricorn hat, when I looked a little different. Perhaps I was the one in your dream..." The Doctor shook his head. "No, that's ridiculous. That never happened. Least of all because I have never changed. Not since I was..."

"Born?" Orpheus suggested.

"Yes, something like that," the Doctor grumbled back. "There must be answer to what happened to this place. Perhaps somewhere, beyond this city, we can find someone living..."

Orpheus, who was looking behind the Doctor, let out a small gasp. He pointed off in the distance, and Omega whirled around to look at what he'd seen. From the basement of one of the ruined buildings, a figure was emerging. A woman with a pale face, dressed in black, with the bearing of a princess.

Once she came into full view, she stared at the two men. "Back again, Orpheus?" she mused. "And you, Doctor... I did not think it was yet your time."

"My time?" asked Doctor Omega. "Do you know me, young lady?"

"I do... though, like Orpheus here, you probably don't remember me." The dark-dressed woman grinned wickedly. "The mind is a fragile thing. It blocks out everything it fears—and there is nothing it fears more than its own nonexistence. It is therefore difficult to remember one's brushes with Death."

Orpheus at once seemed to understand.

"You claim to be Death, young lady?" Omega scoffed. "Death is not a person. It is a natural phenomenon, without persona or soul."

"Did I say I had a soul? Did I say I was a person? You are curious as ever, Doctor—both in that you desire answers, and in that you're a curiosity yourself. I sense in you the questions which only dead men have the wisdom to ask. But like I said, it is not your time, and you are still living..."

"I know this woman, Doctor," Orpheus said then. "I knew her as the Princess, but she *is* Death. At least, she is Death in a shape you and I can comprehend." He paused a moment, before saying: "Don't you remember, Doctor? I have been dead all this time."

The Doctor shuddered.

"You can't be dead, Orpheus. If you are, how did you come to travel aboard my ship?" the Doctor asked. "What about our journey to Tormance, or our battle with the mad poet Glenarvon—?"

"You intercepted me, on my way to... this place. To the Underworld," Orpheus interrupted. "I died before, but I was allowed to come back. I was returning to Death because the life I went back to was only an illusion. I couldn't look upon my own wife, Eurydice, even though I was reunited with her. And so I have decided now to face my eternal end."

He looked firmly then at the Princess who was Death. "Do you still love me?" he asked.

"In this iteration, perhaps I do," she replied.

"I can accept that," the poet said then, gaining the first hint of hope Omega had seen in him. "Come with us, Doctor. I'm sure a being of your stature won't need to *remain* in the Underworld. You could just visit and leave again, under your own power."

"The Doctor is always welcome in my domain," said the Princess, continuing to smile. Once more, a chill ran down Omega's spine.

37

And yet, his eternal curiosity—the source of all his glories and failures—tugged at him. The Underworld? That was something he had to see.

Nodding his head slowly, like he was dreaming, the Doctor agreed to the offer.

The Princess led the two travelers back towards the dark from whence she came. At first, it seemed only to be a little enclosure, but soon the darkness within it yawned up and swallowed them. The Doctor realized that they had passed into the ice-cold night of the afterlife. He reached out, seeking something familiar—matter, form, shape, time—but none of them greeted his senses. In moments, he was completely unaware of how far he had traveled into the void, whether it was yards or miles.

But his will was strong. He clutched his fists tight, feeling the cold metal of his signet ring press against the palm and fingers of his left hand. So long as he resisted giving in to this place—whatever that meant in the moment—he could endure and survive.

He realized he was slipping away into Death—dying. But as the Princess herself had said, it was not yet his time. Though he was standing close to Death, he was not yet dead. Now he knew that he had stood many times before next to her, without knowing it. Sometimes, out of the corner of his eye, he had glimpsed her—but only for a moment.

"What purpose can there be in this place?" he inquired. "What could one possibly learn here?"

"There is no purpose in Death," the Princess said, "save to be dead. There is nothing to learn, save for the meaning of nothingness."

This idea horrified Doctor Omega, who had always delighted in the *fullness* of existence. To face emptiness was a terror that he had never before fathomed.

But he would not give in to that terror without challenging it, interrogating it. He sensed *something* within this place, beyond the darkness, and that something called to him. All he had to do was answer the call. His thoughts strained against the void, as if he was locking it in a mind-bending contest. After much struggle, his mental grip triumphed, and he was able to speak his piece.

"I have always believed, at heart, that time is cyclical in nature," the Doctor pronounced. "I believe that Omega is Alpha, that the end is the beginning. Many fixtures within time are as circular as is the timestream that cradles them. Extremes are not opposite each other—they are adjacent. The point of ending and beginning occupy one simultaneous point. This is clearly a world where conventional reality does not exist. And without reality, we are close to these cosmic extremes. Within this nothingness there is... everythingness. And vice versa."

Though he could not see her, Death once more grinned at him.

"Yes, Doctor, we are bodiless here, without substance or matter, and that opens us up to all kinds of infinities. You truly are a wise man, for you know how to walk to Heaven from Hell."

"Doctor...?" Orpheus whispered, from the darkness.

"I will not deny you your final rest, my boy," Omega assured him. "But I wish to see the realm of Life before I leave your company." He gazed at where he thought he'd heard Death's voice. "That is what that place could be called, correct? If this is the realm of Death?"

"Life, creation, imagination—death, entropy, oppression. These are two sides of the same coin. And yet, I cannot accompany you to the realm of Imagination," the Princess said. "I am bound here. Instead, you must seek another guide."

The Doctor was at the point where he didn't feel like questioning the idea of a "spirit guide," though the urge tugged at him.

Suddenly, he could see in the dark, and became aware that there were now two Orpheuses. But as he gazed upon the second "Orpheus," the Doctor realized that he wasn't Orpheus at all. In fact, he wasn't even human. Instead, he looked to be like some sort of alien—a bestial humanoid, a man sporting features of a bear and a wolf. This Beast seemed embittered by Omega staring at him.

"Are you the one guiding me into Imagination?" the Doctor asked.

"Yes," the Beast growled. "I am a native of that realm—I am something of a spirit of magic."

"Magic?" Omega chuckled. "My dear boy, I am afraid that even with all this, I am still not a believer in magic. What we are experiencing right now may be a different form of reality than that in which I normally reside, but to dismiss the qualities of this world as magic seems overly simplistic."

"You deceive yourself, Monsieur le Docteur. Inside, you are still the child who dreamed of magic and wonder. We all are, no matter how many years or centuries may pass."

The Beast began to walk away, leading Omega and Orpheus away from Death's company.

"When I was a child, I was uneducated. My sense of the universe was vague," the Doctor said.

"And yet, you dreamed of exploring it. Were those dreams not magical?"

The Doctor couldn't say they weren't. While he prided himself on what he had learned as a grownup, everything that he was today was because of the childish giddiness that had thrived in his soul. No matter how hard he tried, that side of him was always stronger than the old man on the outside, who often denied things out of hand from pure stubbornness.

Now, the world around him was lightening, its dark burden releasing from his shoulders. Only then did he realize how afraid he had been, sensing the closeness of Death. In an instant, she was gone, and reality changed again.

They stood in the corridor of a building, which resembled to Omega's eyes a hotel from early 20th century Earth. Doors lined the hallway, and the Beast strode confidently past them, speaking to his guests as he moved.

"This is where magic is alive and well. It's like a studio—artists of the Beyond live within these rooms and create their scenes and situations. But unlike in the real world, here, there are no limits on what they can create."

He opened one of the doors and bid the Doctor and Orpheus to look inside.

Inside was a young man working on a painting of a human figure, whose face he was now detailing. Slowly and meticulously, he shaped the image's mouth. He glanced away for a moment, and to the Doctor and Orpheus' befuddlement and horror, the mouth began to move, as if straining to speak. The artist looked back up at his work and observed this miraculous change. He moved his hand up to the canvas and tried to wipe the mouth away, but instead the pigments transferred to his hand, and the orifice continued to try to speak, as part of his body.

"Here, there is no division between reality and imagination," the Beast said, "just as in Death, there is no division between reality and oppression. Here, creation is reality, and in Death, there is not even the concept of freedom. Creation is the antithesis of Death because Death is Entropy. The Creation of new matter, new energy, with *ideas*, is the antithesis of Entropy's gnawing cancer. Creation is Life within Entropy."

"And yet, these realms are only accessible to the dead," Orpheus said. "To those who have forsaken matter."

Doctor Omega looked at his companion with a sharp look. "What do you mean by that?"

Neither figure answered—instead, the Beast led them further down the hall.

"There is more," he said, opening more doors.

The two travelers observed a man slicing open a woman's eye with a straight razor, and a figure resembling Christ leading a young woman back inside a blood-soaked castle. Other images included strange, impossible deserts, oozing clocks, and spinning wheels of yin-yang light.

"Here, freedom thrives, almost to the point of exhaustion. If you were to gaze downward into this world, you would see more minute fairy-scenes playing out, losing their imaginal qualities as they spiral down into material reality."

"I feel it, Doctor," Orpheus said. "Here, one can do *anything*. That Zone, the one which preceded the Underworld, nearly had the same properties, but *this...*"

He raised his hand, and from the floor of the corridor rose a sphere, pulled from the raw matter of the tile. He moved his fingers, and the sphere became a pyramid, and then an octahedron. This shape then turned into a bundle of roses, which tumbled gently to the floor. Orpheus laughed, delighted by the power in his hands.

"And there are places on Earth where rabbit-holes open into this world," the Beast said. "How they were opened, I know not. But if you wish, Doctor, that is your explanation for magic, on Earth at least. The 'wizards' of the world ventured into places where they could work their will without limits."

"I have heard of such a place in Russia," Orpheus said, "though I have no idea who I heard about it from. They say that a meteor crashed there, or maybe aliens, and created a Zone. And at the center of that Zone is a Room, where one's innermost wishes come true."

"I have never heard of such mysteries in all my travels on Earth," the Doctor confessed.

As he spoke, he felt a strange nausea well up in him—for a moment, it felt like his body was wearing thin. He frowned, but only for a split second. But the Beast had seen the lapse of strength in his eyes.

"You should not be here, Doctor," he said. "Admittedly, in describing these realms, I have been bound to the limits of human language. It is easy to think of this bright place as the realm of Life and that dark void at the home of Death. But both of these places are immaterial. They are outside of that which sustains your form."

"Of course," Omega mused. "How could magic and imagination be bound to physical substance? I suppose then I have been wandering here bodiless, like you, or else, some fluke of nature has allowed my form to endure here. But I cannot stay permanently, I presume?"

"No. If you remain here, you will become a fictional character. In fact, that is one of the less horrible fates that awaits a living man here." The Beast sighed. "There are some apotheoses that mortals, even ones who are nigh-immortal, cannot face in life. There are some stories that don't shine until after their author is dead."

"Hmm, yes... I believe that the only way to live forever is to leave something that people will remember. We become immortal by the good we do, and the lives we change. Even if we reach a point where we cannot recognize ourselves—some fragment of who we once were remains in those who remember us, promising buried hope." The Doctor giggled. "I realize that this atmosphere is toxic to me, sir, but I must confess it has been quite some time since I've enjoyed such enlightening discourse."

"You may not remember this conversation when you leave," the Beast warned.

"Oh, but that doesn't mean it didn't happen." Once more the Doctor tugged at his lapels. He turned to face Orpheus. "My dear boy," he said, "I believe this is where we part ways. This is where you belong. Here, you can capture all human experience in your poetry."

Orpheus laughed. "Even in eternity, my friend, there is not enough time for that."

The Doctor shook his hand and bid him goodbye. This was, for Orpheus, a fine ending. By the time the Doctor turned his back, his shade would have faded away, looking for a room in which to get to work.

Omega turned back to the Beast.

"Will you do me the service of escorting me back to my ship?"

"Through here," the Beast growled, opening one of the hallway doors.

The Doctor peered into the room, and to his surprise, he saw the familiar shape of the *Cosmos* within. He did not question how it came here from the Zone outside the Underworld.

He started to say goodbye to the Beast, but before he could speak the Beast interrupted him. "There is no need to show me good sentiment, Monsieur le Docteur—I am a simple Beast. It is my lot to suffer, until a young maiden sets me free. Over and over again, all throughout history, I am reborn, fated to no kindness but that of my *belle*."

"I will thank you all the same, sir, for what you have done for me. I do not believe in any fate that denies one kindness."

The Beast, for the first time, seemed taken aback. The Doctor was not a young maiden—though maybe once he had been, a very long time ago. Regardless, he had acted outside of the cyclical loop which the Beast considered the primal definition of his life—the entirety of his power.

"Perhaps you do belong here after all, Doctor—you are a creature of magic."

The Doctor did not believe that to be so, but now as he surveyed his ship, he wondered if maybe, somehow, the *Cosmos* had been pulled from this realm. It was, as he once told Orpheus, a possibility machine.

In many ways, the ship was like a poem, or a painting—a window into the infinite.

As he stepped aboard, he realized he wouldn't be leaving this place at all, so long as he had his vessel. And in a sense, that meant he'd always carry with him a part of Orpheus, whom he already missed.

Not a crime thriller this time, but a swashbuckling mini-epic from Matt Dennion who, in the following tale, brings back two of the best swordsmen from popular fiction...

Matthew Dennion: *The Worthiness of the Wielder*

Vézère Valley, 1625

A cool wind blew across the valley as the cloaked figure made his way toward the small inn on the outskirts of town. The man was dressed entirely in black. He was tall and well-built with a somber countenance. His face was gaunt with cold eyes that were partially hidden by a slouched hat. Around his waist were a rapier, a dirk, and a pair of flintlock pistols.

In his right hand, the enigmatic figure held an ornate walking stick that had a feline shaped head atop of it. When he reached the door to the inn, he opened it and walked in without greeting anyone. The figure simply walked to a table in the corner and sat. The people who worked at the inn, or went there for occasional food and drink, were used to seeing strangers and nomads entering the establishment, but there was something about this man that chilled them to the bone.

Most of the people in the room took one look at the man and then turned away so as not to incur his attention. There was only one set of eyes that were fixed on the stranger. These captivating feminine eyes watched the newcomer from the shadows, but without looking directly at him.

The innkeeper did not wish to bother the stranger. Instead of addressing the black-clad man directly, he sent over a tavern boy to see what the intimidating nomad wanted to drink. As the young man went over to the stranger, the cloaked woman who had been watching him casually made her way over to the counter.

The tavern boy quickly got the newcomer's order and then returned. The shadowy woman listened as the young man passed on the stranger's order.

"He only wants water, bread, and beef stew," said the boy.

The innkeeper was surprised. "That man only wants water?"

"That's what he said."

The innkeeper quickly set to filling the man's order. As he was doing that, the cloaked woman shifted her cloak so that it rested on her back and revealed her shapely body. She then shifted her clothing to push her ample breasts forward. Lastly, she pushed back her hair, to better accentuate her full lips and stunning face.

When the innkeeper turned around with the stranger's order, both he and the tavern boy were awe-struck by the beautiful woman who suddenly stood before them.

43

She smiled at the two men. "Excuse, would you mind if I were to take that man's food and drink over to him?" She shook her head. "I feel I may be in danger and I think he is the type of man who might protect me."

The innkeeper nodded while taking a long admiring look at the woman's cleavage.

"Of course, by all means," he replied. "A bit of warning though: that man looks like he could be dangerous in his own right."

The woman smiled. "Oh, he *is* dangerous, but that's why I need him."

She then took the food and drink over to the stranger. As she approached the black-clad man, she was surprised that he did not stare at her. In all of her years of using her charms to distract men, she had never met one yet who seemed as indifferent to her as the stranger did.

Realizing that the man she had sent for might be one of the few that had control over his lustful feelings, she quickly altered her approach. A simple change of posture and gait toned down her overt sexuality. A slight alteration of the way she was breathing changed how her chest rose and fell. In a matter of a seconds, she had switched from seductress to damsel in distress.

She sat down at the table and placed the food and water in front of the stranger.

"Begging your pardon, but when I saw you enter the tavern, I knew you must be the man I sent for," she said. "You are the Puritan known as Solomon Kane, are you not?"

Kane nodded. "Indeed, I am. I received word that a young woman here might have information regarding a great evil that needs to be destroyed?"

Her eyes portrayed a mixture of hope and dread as she looked into the cold eyes of the nomadic warrior. She whispered in a frantic voice as she grabbed the tall man's gloved hand:

"My name is Milady de Winter. I'm the widow of Baron Sheffield. Currently, I live in Paris in the service of Queen Anne. In my duties, I have had the misfortune of overhearing numerous secrets, but none so dark as one that I have recently heard. I was entering her room to gather her linens when I heard her speak with her confidant, Constance Bonacieux, about a weapon of incredible power."

With a nervous look on her face, Milady scanned the tavern to see if anyone was eavesdropping.

"Milord Kane," she continued, "I fear people may overhear what I'm about to say." She squeezed his hand. "Perhaps, if we were to retire to a room upstairs, we could speak in private?"

Kane shook his head. "Please call me Solomon. There is only one who should be referred to as Lord, and it is his will that I not be alone indoors with a woman. As we speak, I am watching the entire tavern. I would notice if anyone was paying undo attention to us. Just as I noticed you paying attention to me when I first walked in, despite your attempts to conceal your actions." He gestured to the door. "We can speak outside if you wish. A great field surrounds this tavern. We would see if anyone was within earshot..."

Milady considered the offer and shook her head. "No, Solomon, I can see that you are a man of honor. If you feel you can protect me, I will believe you." She moved closer to the puritan and continued in a whisper. "The Queen spoke of a war she believes is coming with England. She feels that, in order to win that war, France will need a weapon of great power—one that possesses the power of a heathen god and that, if wielded by the right person, could lay waste to an entire country. I heard her say to Madame Bonacieux that this weapon was once used by Joan of Arc herself. She said it was it that led her to victory at Orleans. Prior to her capture, she hid it in an ancient cave located in this area..."

Milady began to tear up. "Solomon, please believe me. During my time in service of the Queen, I have always been loyal to her, and I have grown to love France. When I was with my dear departed husband, I grew to love England, as well as her people. I couldn't bear to see so many countless lives ended and their souls sent to Hell by the power of a pagan weapon."

The door to the tavern opened and Milady immediately wrapped her cloak around her body and face. She held her breath as she quickly looked at the two persons who had just entered. In that brief moment, Kane saw terror in her eyes.

"Are you concerned that someone has come looking for you?" he asked.

"Not for me, but they may yet find me. Madame Bonacieux is here, looking for this weapon and she is not alone. She is here with her lover, a young musketeer known as D'Artagnan. His skill with a blade is only surpassed by his cunning." She looked away from Kane. "I'm ashamed to confess that he once lured me to his bed with promises of marriage, only to send me away after a lust-filled night."

Milady remained silent for a moment before continuing. "He is infatuated with Madame Bonacieux and, as a musketeer, he is fearlessly loyal to the French Crown. They have been searching the area for the weapon. Thankfully, they have not found it yet, or they would already be on their way back to Paris. No doubt, they plan to continue their unholy quest tomorrow."

Milady turned her fear-filled eyes toward Kane. "I'm sure that, whether by the lack of my duties being carried out, or the Queen's dalliance with black magic, my absence has already been noticed. Were either of them to see me here, I fear they would accuse me of treason, and execute me without a second thought."

Kane nodded. "I understand." He slid his hand to the hilt of his sword. "This D'Artagnan may be a skilled swordsman, but he has yet to face a man with the power of God himself in his blade. Once more, I assure you that while you are in my presence, you have nothing to fear."

"This is why I reached out to you, Solomon. When I heard of the Queen's intentions, I first went to Cardinal Richelieu for help. He told me however that the Church would not oppose the Queen. It was then that I remembered a friend of my husband, an English Puritan named John Felton. I recalled him speaking to us of a warrior of his religion who hunted down and destroyed evil, a man who knew no fear, and was unequaled in the art of battle. With nothing but prayer on the wind itself, I sent a letter to several Puritan establishments looking for a man named Solomon Kane in hopes that this noble warrior would lend his strength and skill to helping prevent a great evil from being unleashed."

Kane shook his head. "The sin of pride often comes before the fall. All of my accomplishments come from God working through me. They are not of my volition. It is his will that your letter found me as quickly as it did."

Milady nodded. "Of course, through God all things are possible."

Kane used his peripheral vision to keep an eye on Constance Bonacieux and D'Artagnan without directly looking at them. The young man wore his musketeer uniform and his pistol and rapier were on full display. The newcomers ordered wine and food before sitting at a table on the other side of the tavern and soon engaged in a heated discussion.

Milady kept her head down as she addressed Kane. "Solomon, they cannot be allowed to locate this weapon and use it against England." Her voice softened even more. "Nor do I believe that this heathen weapon should be wielded by anyone. I beg you, please help me. When they find it, we can take it from them and destroy it before it can be used on the people of England—or anyone else."

Kane briefly looked in the direction of D'Artagnan and Constance. He took the measure of the musketeer and then he slowly looked away.

"God has brought both of us here for a reason. I can see that you are skilled at hiding your presence, as am I. I will join you in following these two emissaries of evil, and together, we shall put an end to the apocalyptic weapon they seek."

For over a week, Solomon Kane and Milady followed D'Artagnan and Constance as they searched the caves in the area. Kane and Milady were always careful to stay far enough behind the musketeer and the Queen's confidant so as not to be seen. As they moved through the numerous caves in the area, Milady continued to work Kane into a fervor. Her ability to read people and manipulate them was unmatched. She understood that Kane's obsession was to rid the world of evil and fed into this fervor by giving him a mix of half-truths and well-crafted lies.

After a week of filling the Puritan's mind with misconceptions about D'Artagnan and Constance, the holy warrior was prepared to slay them at a moment's notice if they tried to wield the weapon they sought.

On the eighth day of their quest, Kane and Milady entered a cave they had never seen before.

The Puritan and the spy had waited until the Queen's emissaries were deep within it. It only took a few steps before Milady gasped at something she saw on the wall. Kane looked at it and he immediately made the sign of the cross. He then walked closer and commented upon these depictions of all manner of animals and demons.

"I've seen elephants like the ones pictured here and lions in Africa," he said, "but I have never seen fur-covered elephants or lions with long fangs like these. These paintings are obviously the idolatry of witches. This must be the right cave. We must make haste."

Kane could see the light of D'Artagnan's and Constance's torch ahead of them. With no more need to conceal themselves, he quickly lit a torch and he and Milady moved after their prey.

The Puritan suddenly saw the light ahead stop moving; then he heard D'Artagnan voice say:

"Look at them, Constance! I can feel the power coming off them! Those must be what we are looking for!"

Upon hearing these words, Kane and Milady broke into a sprint. They turned a corner and found the two French agents looking at a hammer, a set of metal gauntlets, and a belt placed upon a carved-out shelf on the cave wall. The hammer was clearly a weapon of war and, as Kane and Milady stared at it, they saw what looked like lightning arcing off of it.

Milady's eyes went wide as she stared at the mystical artifact and spoke its name. "Járngreipr, Mjölnir, and Megingjörð! The weapons of Thor!"

D'Artagnan and Constance turned around and looked at the duo that had been following them. The musketeer sneered as he set his eyes upon the seductress.

"Milady, we do happen upon each other in the most unlikely of places."

The spy turned her eyes on Constance and replied:

"Indeed, we do, and it always seems to be the same places as Madame Bonacieux. I hope for her sake that her encounters with you do not leave her as unsatisfied as they did me."

Constance ignored the spy's remark and turned her attention to Kane.

"Good sir, I must inform you that we are here on the official business of the Queen. I would also inform you that the woman whose company you currently keep is a spy, a liar, and a criminal. I would ask that you please depart and leave this fugitive in our custody."

Kane shook his head. "I cannot do that. I am no subject of your queen. My name is Solomon Kane and I answer to a higher power. The lady tells me you are looking for a heathen weapon to give to your Queen—a weapon she will use against England to kill countless people."

"No, Monsieur Kane, that is not the truth. Milady works for the Cardinal who desires war with England and the downfall of our Queen. She only sent us here to retrieve those artifacts and use them to defend herself against the Cardinal, who bears her much ill will. She has no desire to use them in an offensive manner."

Kane shook his head and held up his staff. When he held it up, the eyes of the cat carved into its handle began to glow. "The Lord has seen fit to provide me with this staff. It is a mystical artifact capable of detecting evil..."

He shifted the staff toward the gathered artifacts and the cat's eyes began to glow even brighter. "Those things—the weapons of Thor, as you call them—they come from pagan gods. Their power is steeped in darkness. I cannot allow them to exist. I must destroy them. Be warned, I shall show no quarter to any who stand in my way."

The young and brash D'Artagnan drew his sword.

"Solomon Kane, I have heard your name spoken of in whispers. Your skills are legendary. I would consider it an honor to be the first among my brothers-in-arms to best you in single combat. Be warned though, Monsieur Kane, you have yet to encounter a man with real skills in the use of a blade."

The Puritan unsheathed his rapier. "You've been warned, boy. This is your last chance to stand aside!"

D'Artagnan shook his head. "I shall not stand down. *En garde!*"

The musketeer flew at the older man with the speed of a falcon. Kane barely had time to raise his sword in defense of D'Artagnan's initial blow. The younger combatant was a blur of stabs and slashes as he drove the Puritan back with the sheer speed and quickness of his attacks.

Kane had almost been backed up to the cave wall without making a single offensive attack. It was clear to the Puritan that the Frenchman was superior to him in pure swordsmanship, but Kane was more than just a fencer. He was skilled with all manner of weapons. He blocked an overhead strike from D'Artagnan with his rapier and then brought the thick end of his staff crashing into the musketeer's face.

The blow knocked back D'Artagnan and sent blood flying out of his mouth. The youngster brushed the blood off his chin and smiled at the older man.

"First blood goes to you, Monsieur Kane. Well done! However, rest assured that you shall not catch me with the same attack twice."

The agile musketeer then renewed his strikes.

As the two legends crossed swords, Milady and Constance were staring each other down in front of the Norse artifacts. The Queen's agent knew that she was no match for Milady in personal combat. Still, despite being overmatched in physical prowess, the young woman refused to let the seductress have the weapons her Lady had ordered her to retrieve.

"Flee now, Milady. D'Artagnan will defeat the Puritan. You know this to be true. And once your puppet has fallen, my lover will either arrest you or run you through."

The spy laughed. "Your lover has already run me through and yet here, I stand. He's welcome to try again when I possess the powers of the Norse gods. I am confident that even he will be defeated at my merest whim!"

48

Sparks and loud clangs from the clashing swords of the dueling warriors echoed through the cave, as Constance shook her head.

"Will you ever grow weary of using your body to control men? Your actions and lies only serve to lessen yourself and all other women."

"The first time I used my body to seduce a man to get what I wanted, I grew weary of it," said Milady. "Every time I tell a half-truth to make a man perform the task I need him to do in order to reach my goal, I grow weary of it." She looked over at the ancient weapons. "With the power of a god, I shall no longer have to use my body or my lies to bend men to my will. Járngreipr, Mjölnir, and Megingjörð will give me the power to force anyone to do my bidding. The Crown, the Church, the Musketeers, no one will be able to stand against me!"

She smiled at Constance. "You, Madame Bonacieux, are the only obstacle that stands between myself and ultimate power. I assure you, that is not a position you wish to be in."

With the fury of screaming harpy, Milady charged Constance.

Meanwhile, Kane and D'Artagnan continued their battle. The speed and agility of the younger man had allowed him to land a few cuts on the Puritan. But while Kane was bleeding in several places, the old warrior knew these cuts were nothing more than a few flesh wounds.

D'Artagnan had the advantage in speed, but Kane was far stronger than the musketeer. Each blow that D'Artagnan blocked felt as though he was stopping a barbarian's axe. He was also unaccustomed to fighting a man with a rapier and a staff. Kane had managed to land several blows with his stick that D'Artagnan was certain had cracked, if not outright broken, bones.

While Kane's staff was proving to be a dangerous weapon, the musketeer was timing his foe's attack pattern with the cudgel. When he was sure that a strike was coming, the young man ducked, and then stuck the tip of his sword into Kane's left shoulder. The stab was not deep, but D'Artagnan knew that the wound would hamper Kane's ability to strike again.

The musketeer pulled his sword from Kane's shoulder and he was about to deliver a killing blow when he heard Constance scream his name from behind. Thinking only of his lover, D'Artagnan turned around to see Constance lying on the floor with a beaten and bloody face. Behind her, he saw Milady reaching up to claim Thor's weapons.

The infatuated youngster took two steps toward Constance, but then Kane's staff struck him in the back of the head and sent him falling to the ground.

The Puritan stood above the musketeer with his sword drawn and he was about to end the young man's life when he saw Milady trying to put her hand into one of the magical gauntlets.

Kane screamed, "Milady, no! That thing is filled with dark magic! It mustn't be wielded by any human!"

49

The spy ignored the Puritan's warning as she jammed the gauntlet on her arm. She then reached for the hammer. But the instant that she tried to wield it, lightning ran across her body. The electrical discharge burned not only her skin but her very soul.

Milady screamed in pain as she tore off the gauntlet and threw it and the hammer to the ground. She then sprinted past the two warriors and ran out of the cave.

D'Artagnan used the momentary distraction to re-engage Kane. The young man was still flat on his back when he attempted to drag his sword across the Puritan's chest, but Kane avoided the attack by shifting his torso back, causing the musketeer's sword to only tear his shirt.

The Puritan responded by bringing his sword down, which D'Artagnan easily blocked. The musketeer was expecting a blow from the staff, but when it never came, he became puzzled. His confusion ended when Kane's boot came crashing into his chin and caused the back of his head to snap back and hit the cave floor.

Seeing D'Artagnan laying on the ground and about to be slain gave Constance the strength she needed to crawl over to the artifacts. The young woman had seen what they had done to Milady, but with the life of her lover at stake, she dared to wield them.

As Constance slid the gauntlets onto her hands, she felt her fingers tingling with power. Prior to grabbing the hammer, she wrapped the belt around her waist. The instant she clasped the belt, Constance felt a surge or strength throughout her body. The young woman then grabbed the hammer and, as she held it over her head, lighting wrapped her body and tore the majority of her clothes to shreds. As the electricity swirled around her, it also healed all of the injuries she had suffered at the hands of Milady.

When she was fully bonded with the weapons, Constance felt as if she had the power of a god. She looked at Solomon Kane standing over her lover with fury in her eyes.

"Back away from him if you want to leave this cave alive!" she shouted.

Kane stepped away from D'Artagnan and moved toward Constance.

"I shall do so—not because of your threat, but because my business is now with you and the unholy weapons you possess."

The Puritan held out his staff, as the cat eyes on the top of it gave off a dark blue glow. "I, too, have a weapon from the world beyond. Mine has the power of the One True God, while yours relies on that of a False God. Shall we see who possesses the more potent weapon?"

As Kane spoke, D'Artagnan rose and walked over next to Constance. The young man's eyes were transfixed by his lover's beauty and the aura of power coming off her.

Constance glared at Kane. "I have heard of you, Solomon Kane. It is said that you are a righteous man. Please know that I am a just woman. I only wish to use these items for the protection of my Queen and benevolent purposes."

Kane sneered. "That's what everyone who picks up a sword or musket says, but in the end, they all use their power to get what they want. I've seen ordinary weapons corrupt even the most pious souls." He gestured to the now tattered clothes covering Constance. "I can't imagine that a weapon that would leave you with less clothing than a harlot would push you to use it for the betterment of others, and I don't intend to let it corrupt you!"

The Puritan lifted his sword over his head and charged at Constance. In response, the young woman simply held out the hammer and lightning streaked out of it, struck Kane in the chest and then slammed him into the wall. The beams of energy continued to flow from the hammer and kept him trapped against the side of the cave.

As the hammer pinned Kane to the wall, she could feel the energy coming off the Puritan's staff. Constance moved closer to her trapped opponent and she looked into his eyes.

"You claim that these magical artifacts will possess me, yet what about the weapon that you wield?" she asked. "I can feel its power as well. Has it corrupted you?"

Kane shook his head. "My faith in the Lord protects me from letting the weapon pull me from the path of righteousness!"

Constance glared at Kane. "And my faith in my Queen will allow me to do the same!" Her voice softened. "Perhaps, we can use our respective faiths to find an acceptable compromise..."

She stopped the flow of energy emanating from her hammer. She then placed the weapon against Kane's staff. "I do not know if you can feel this as well, but our two weapons are communicating. As you said, they are both from realms beyond. I have no wish to slay you, as I know you to be a righteous man; however, I cannot have you trying to kill D'Artagnan or myself."

Constance placed her free hand over her heart. "As such, I offer you this truce and my word. I swear that I shall only ever use the power of these weapons to protect my Queen and one other time of your own choosing. Should you ever meet an evil threat beyond your ability to defeat, you may use your staff to call on my power one time to aid you. Conversely, should I use my powers for any other purpose other than those stated, your staff will know that I have been corrupted, and then you may come and end any evils I may have caused."

She looked at D'Artagnan. "Dearest, I beg of you as well, should this power corrupt me, you must aid Solomon in defeating me. Even his skills are no match for the power I now possess."

D'Artagnan shook his head. "I could never hurt you, no matter what you did."

She gazed upon her lover with pleading eyes. "If you truly love me, you will make this vow."

The musketeer sighed. "Very well, I swear upon our love that should you turn evil, I shall find this man and aid him in bringing your life to an end."

Constance directed her eyes back to Kane. "This will be a two-way deal, Monsieur Kane. The power of Mjölnir connects me to your staff. Should you ever lose control, I will know about it, then with it and D'Artagnan at my side, we shall come to end you. Are these terms agreeable to you?"

Solomon Kane gritted his teeth and took a long breath. "I suppose we shall both have to prove ourselves worthy of the weapons we have been chosen to wield. I accept your terms."

Constance released Kane. The Puritan bid the two French agents farewell and then left.

After the Puritan had gone, Constance found D'Artagnan staring at her with her ripped clothing leaving little to his imagination. The musketeer shook his head. "You had him at your mercy."

A small stream of energy circled around Constance as she held the hammer. "Yes, and I used that to my advantage to have him accept that I shall only use Mjölnir for the two purposes to which we agreed."

D'Artagnan smiled. "You could not have requested one more use for Mjölnir?"

Brian Gallagher has written a new chapter in his WWI saga featuring Gustave Le Rouge's criminal mastermind & mad surgeon, Doctor Cornelius Kramm, originally penned in 1912-13, translated by Brian Stableford and released as a trilogy by Black Coat Press. A note here about Professor Marcus and the Saturnians. Saturn against the Earth was a remarkably inventive Italian comic book series written by Cesare Zavattini & Federico Pedrocchi and drawn by Giovanni Scolari, published between 1936 and 1946. It was also one of the first foreign comic to be translated into English and published in America in Future Comic, in 1940.

Brian Gallagher: *The Projector of Death*

The Isonzo Front (The War between Italy and the Austro-Hungarian Empire), August 1916

The Slovenian soldiers were terrified. Before them, hovering over the trench, was Death itself. The horror of it was heightened by blazing sunshine of the day—one expects this sort of thing in the night, surely? Things were bad enough—the Italian invaders had almost taken the town of Gorizia—but now this?

Instinctively, they opened fire on the being. The bullets had no effect. They seemed to disappear through the specter, making it shimmer slightly. The soldiers stood their ground, fighting their fear. Death, garbed in cloak and hood, had his traditional scythe in his right hand. He raised the scythe and a bolt of black lightning flew from the tip of it.

Lance Corporal Frančišek Zupančič was from Radvanje. He was not only terrified, but regretful. He was never very keen on going to church. *I must apologize to Father Krajnc,* he thought. He was then hit by the lightning. He seemed to glow black and collapsed.

His fellow soldiers fled the trench. None wanted to be next to be claimed by Death. The Specter faded away. The Lance Corporal lay dead, his body unattended, his pike grey uniform blackened. Fear was etched on his burn face. Later, his parents would be told that he had died from a fire caused by shelling. The Habsburg Empire did not want the truth of things to get out, lest it cause panic.

Days later, a Captain Marić of the 25th Zagreb Home Guard Regiment was riding slowly through woods under Austro-Hungarian control. He cursed. It was early dusk, and he had an important briefing to get to. *Damn these Italians,* he thought. They had invaded in May of last year—taking advantage of the war—in order to annex his homeland.

The Italians had finally scored their first victory in taking Gorizia, although they had paid dearly for this advance. And now, there was a story that the Italians had enlisted Death to their cause—a story his superiors had told him to suppress. But was there something in it?

His mind went back to his journey. *There should be enough light to get to the regional HQ in time,* he thought. There was a path of sorts, with trees on either side. He stopped his and looked forward. *Was that a man I saw?* He rode very slowly forward, taking his side-arm out of its holster. He was well within his own lines, but this did not feel right. He could see something moving behind a tree. It looked like a man, with his hand on a tree. The thing revealed itself. The Captain shuddered. What stood just before him was a specter. A man with a skull rather than a head, garbed in some kind of foul-looking garment.

The Captain looked at the creature, fearful. He had heard of what had happened to Lance Corporal Zupančič. And yet—could it be merely a man in a mask?

Then, the thing started to levitate. *Not a man in a mask*, he thought. Captain Marić had no intention of ending up like the unfortunate Lance Corporal. "Back to Hell, you go!" he shouted, and fired at the specter. His horse started momentarily but remained calm. The Captain was pleased at how well he had trained the beast, but less so as his bullets went through the specter, causing the shimmering he had heard about in the previous incident.

Fear gripped the Captain, as it would anyone in such a situation. He then noticed his horse was still calm. Surely, if this was Death in front of him, the horse would be reacting?

The specter started to raise its hand to point at the Captain. Although this thing had no scythe, the soldier reckoned that perhaps this thing did not need one to fire its black lightning. He dismounted fast—the woods here were a little dense around the path for the horse—and moved into the woods.

Black lightning flew from the finger of the specter, but missed the Captain completely. *Death appears to be a bad shot*, thought Marić. He then noticed a small thin line of light—barely perceptible—coming from the other side of the woods to the specter.

He fired at the source of the light beam. The specter suddenly turned sideways in mid-air and then fizzled out. There were shouts, but not in the Italian of the invaders, but in French. "Retreat!" he heard.

The Captain was an educated man. French was a language he had long mastered. He felt he had the advantage. He fired again and started moving towards the shouts.

He could see some figures moving off at speed. And then he saw an Italian soldier on the ground, struggling to get up. "Do not leave me!" the man shouted, in French, at his retreating fellows.

Marić did not give chase, lest these obvious Frenchmen decided to stand their ground. No one would know about this if he got killed. And he had a prisoner. He looked at the fake Italian soldier, trying to crawl away. He was bleeding from the shoulder. One of his bullets had hit home.

The soldier stopped crawling and turned around. "I surrender," he said in French.

"What is a Frenchman doing here in Italian uniform?" Marić asked.

An obscene gesture was the response he got. Marić groaned inwardly. *It was going to be quite something to get this man to HQ.*

Italian military facility, near the front.

Simon Hart considered the base given to his team to be ramshackle. Did these Italians not realize how important their French allies were? It was little more than a large hut with a smaller one nearby to act as his team's sleeping quarters. Still, his men were happy about it; it meant they would be slightly more inconspicuous.

He had come here directly from Paris. Things here were not going as well as they should be. *Where is that damned Professor Marcus?*

He went outside and spoke to a nearby soldier. A few minutes later, the door opened and the Professor was shoved in by a soldier.

Ah, thought Hart, *Warrant Officer Duval had found him. Excellent man, that Duval.*

"How dare you treat me like this?" spluttered the Professor.

The two men made something of a contrast. Simon Hart was clean-shaven and well-dressed as befits a French intelligence officer; the Professor, who was balding with a goatee beard, wore a lab coat.

"I have been waiting long enough for you. Please be seated," said Hart brusquely.

The Professor muttered some obscure Italian oath and sat down.

Hart started with the reason why he was here. "I have heard the report from Warrant Officer Duval about what occurred. He says that, quite against his advice, you ventured with the projector too deeply into enemy lines. Consequently, one of my men is now in the hands of the enemy."

The Professor responded. "Your men failed to realize that the charred body of an enemy officer, killed by Death itself, would create tremendous fear in the enemy, especially so far behind their lines. This war must be prosecuted more fully. Italy must take the territory promised by the allies to her."

Hart knew that Professor Marcus an Italian irredentist, a follower of the crank Gabrielle D'Annunzio, was mostly concerned with laying claim to territories beyond their borders—specially the Slovene and Croat parts of the Habsburg Empire. The Professor did keep going on about it. Expansion was the reason why Italy had joined the war.

"And as I say, one of my men is now in the hands of the enemy. Who knows what he has been subjected to in order to make him talk. We are fortunate that you did not come across a whole group of Croat troops. Suppose the projector had fallen into their hands?"

"I would use the projector to its fullest ability to deal with them," said the Professor. "I would die before being captured. Furthermore, only I know how to work the projector."

"I am sure the *Evidenzbureau*[1] would at some point be able to work it out. After all, you only know how to work the projector because of our expertise and resources. You came to us, remember?"

Indeed, he did remember. Marcus well recalled that. Through his sources, he knew that the French had advanced research into esoteric technology. He also knew the Austro-Hungarians did as well, but he had considered them an enemy even before the war. The French, it had to be, as his homeland did not have the same level of facilities Paris had.

"And might I add," continued Hart, "that you manipulated the research so that only you could work the projector."

The Professor almost snorted, but didn't. That was certainly true. However, the French scientists he worked with would not take too long now to understand how to operate the projector fully. It concerned him that the French would use it for their own ends, rather than it being used to further the ambitions of Italy.

On thinking of that, the Professor snorted anyway. "It is not my fault that your scientists, useful though they were, were not able to master the projector completely."

"Regardless, you and the projector are to be moved to the Western front, where we shall use it to defend France and create fear amongst the German army. The military will direct its use, rather than you."

The Professor scoffed. "You will find, *mon ami*, that my government will not agree to that."

"They already have. Italy is keen not to upset us, given that the Allies have promised them Adriatic territories."

The Professor was furious, but he was no fool. He decided to be calm.

"I see any protest by me would be of no consequence—although you can be sure that I will protest. Then, I will do as you ask. I will not disobey my government," the Professor said.

"I respect that. Make your protest swiftly. We leave tomorrow. In the meantime, can I see the projector?"

The Professor nodded and rose. He went over to a table with some maps on it and moved it aside, along with a mat underneath. There was a small hatch on the floor, padlocked. He unlocked it and there was what looked like a small grey box, about the size of a brick. He took it out and put it on the table. He put his

---

[1] The Habsburg Empire's military intelligence service. Formed in 1850, it was the world's first such organization.

hand on the top of it. The box started to glow in many different colors. And then an image of Death appeared before them.

If the Professor had intended to startle Hart, he failed. He was unmoved. "It works well," the Frenchman said.

"Yes, I have become more attuned to it. The controls seem to intuit what I want. It records paper images I show it and then projects them at my command. I now believe this has a dual purpose. First, communication over long distances by its beam, perhaps projecting the image of the user to another person. I also suspect it is a form of entertainment, projected to an audience in a similar fashion to our Kino, but in three dimensions. Further, it must have been used as a weapon, one that uses some form of light to destructive effect."

Hart had heard much of this before, he knew the Professor enjoyed talking about his theories. It was a useful way of finding out more from the Professor, as the scientist could not resist discussing his new theories.

"You said the craft from another world crashed near Genoa in 1911, near your observatory. Surely, it can't be that much of a threat if these pilots crash so easily?"

"I suspect there was something in our atmosphere that caused a problem," the Professor replied. "I had spotted it from my observatory, stationary high up in the atmosphere, directly above me. And then, something went wrong, and I saw it crash. I went to the crash site, much of the craft seemed to dissolve into the soil, except for the projector, which at that point seemed misshapen.

"My idiot superiors thought it to be a meteorite and suggested it be put on display in a geological museum. It is fortunate that, after further examination, I saw it change into the rectangular box shape we see here, and brought it to your department. When Italy is under firm leadership, I will command the observatory. Strength will be needed to deal with these Saturnians."

That last bit was new to Hart. "Deal with these Saturnians? What do you mean?"

The Professor looked at the box. "The projector... it connects with the mind. Your organization is aware of the potential of telepathy, and here we have a weapon that our minds can command. And yet, it seems to contain information. I have been able to sense--I would put it no more than that—that this was an unmanned reconnaissance mission, from the sixth planet, sending back information about our world. It seems to have wanted to know our level of scientific development, which explains their position above my observatory. I have a particular interest in Saturn. I believe the Saturnians seek empire. We must prepare for the future."

Hart looked unconvinced. "These Saturnians, why are they delaying? Surely, they would have invaded by now?"

"Who knows what their strategy is? However, a strong Italy will defend Europe and the world!"

Hart was dubious about that, but said nothing. However, the Professor's words simply meant that the projector had to remain under French supervision.

"Indeed," he said, humoring the Professor. "Very well, I have other matters to attend to. We start back to France tomorrow in the morning."

Both men bid each other a good day and Hart left.

"Keep an eye on him, Duval." Hart said to the Warrant Officer who was standing guard outside. "He seems cooperative, but you never know. I shall return in a few hours, I have to see an old friend."

The Sergeant nodded and smiled. It was well known that Hart had a number of mistresses—he would always claim to be seeing an 'old friend.' It was one of the reasons he was so popular with the soldiers attached to this branch of the *Deuxième Bureau*[2]. Duval was also glad to be leaving. He was none too keen on having to wear an Italian uniform to conceal the French presence here from the enemy.

Inside the hut, Professor Marcus activated the box by simply placing his hand on it. In front of him an image of Hart appeared, exactly as he looked a few moments ago. Hart had no idea that the projector could perfect such a likeness, thinking it could only produce crude replicas from magazines of images of Death. Indeed, previous use could only project images of humans that were not that detailed and transparent. However, his work with the projector had gone a little further. It was able to study Hart for a few minutes, seeing him in three dimensions—there was only a slight transparency, which could be seen only from a couple of centimeters. He switched the image off and projected it outside—a small beam of light going through the wall door and outside. *It's still daylight, the Sergeant won't see it*, thought the Professor.

Outside, the Sergeant noticed Hart coming back. "I almost forgot," said Hart, "Could you inform our liaison Captain Esposito of our intended departure times tomorrow? Best to do it now, to prevent any offence. I think the Professor can't get up to much mischief for a few minutes."

The Warrant Officer agreed, and moved off, happy to help Hart get to his rendezvous on time.

Professor Marcus swiftly left the hut, with the projector in his hand.

Later, Hart was furious. At first, he did not believe Duval's story. Then reports came of the Professor leaving the military area in the company of an Italian officer, who claimed he was elsewhere at time.

Hart let his fury abate. After all, the Sergeant could not have known that the Professor had improved the use of the projector. Further, he was incommunicado for a couple of hours due to his own assignation, which he didn't want too many people to know about.

---

[2] The French military intelligence service

A couple of days passed and then came a report of a Death sighting, in relation to a robbery. The report was in Slovenian newspaper. *What was the Professor doing in enemy territory?* wondered Hart. Marcus was too much of an Italian irredentist to become a traitor. No, he was up to something. Whatever it was, there a huge risk that the Habsburgs may capture him and the projector. And his assets in the Habsburg Empire were somewhat limited. However, he knew a man who could bring back the Professor from there—for a price.

Inverlair Lodge, Scotland.

A scarred wreck of a man was speaking to his wife. It was not going well. She was pleading with him.

"Astor, you must believe me! I am going to stand by you. You must believe me! I am not going to leave you. Have I not stood by you for the last two years? Have I not moved here from London to be with you?"

The wreck of a man responded, "You will betray me, Ellenor, like the weaklings in the government have. They have imprisoned me here," he said, waving his hand round the room, which was little more than a bedroom with a table and washing facilities.

"Astor, you are here for your own good, to be treated for your injuries."

"No! My injuries have been treated as much as they can. What can anyone do about this?" he waved his hand across his scarred face. "They cannot make me a proper man again."

She looked at his burnt face. Gone were the handsome features of the man she had married, replaced with a burnt face. Gone was the confidence of the adventurer Lord Astor Burydan, the man who, with his friends, had taken on the master criminal Dr. Cornelius Kramm. The Doctor had once imprisoned her, testing some foul drug on her, and was responsible for the death of her sister. Lord Burydan and his allies had crushed Dr. Cornelius, his brother Fritz, and their Red Hand criminal empire. She had married this man—her hero. Now he was just this paranoid, wounded man. However, she was his wife, and she took her vows very seriously.

"You are as great a man as any," she replied. "Few have had the adventures you have. We will return to London soon, and you can plan the future. As soon as the doctors here say you are better, we can go."

"Doctors! This is a prison for the inconvenient, the building lent to the government for the war. They will never let me go."

"You are a free man, Astor, if you want to leave now, you could."

"They would stop me, have you not seen the guards here?"

"I can see we are going nowhere again today. I shall return tomorrow, when perhaps you are in a better mood." With that she strode out of the room.

As soon as she left the corridor, she turned around and saw an orderly leave the adjoining room and knock on her husband's room. She thought nothing of it—the orderlies sometimes went to check on him after her visits, to make sure he was not distressed.

The 'orderly' received no reply to his first knock. He tried again. "Go to hell!" came the reply. The orderly simply walked in.

Lord Burydan took in the thin, bespectacled bald man in front of him.

"Dr. Cornelius!" he hissed. He tried to leap at him, but he only got up from his chair and stumbled forward, his injures preventing him from doing anything else. Cornelius took Lord Burydan's shoulder and firmly pushed him back into his chair.

"Criminal scum! I should kill you!"

"Why would you wish to harm me, Lord Burydan?" the master criminal asked. "We were, at least technically, on the same side the last time we met.[3] Do you not want to know why I am here?"

"To kill me, no doubt." He then laughed strangely. "Look at me. I have no objection."

"Why would I wish to kill you? No, I am here to make you an offer."

Lord Burydan stared into the Doctor's eyes. "What kind of offer?" Burydan knew his tone gave himself away. He tried to suppress it, but hope was suddenly within him.

The Doctor knew immediately that he would be able to convince the man. "To restore you. Am I not, after all, the sculptor of human flesh? I can change men's faces," he gestured to Lord Burydan's body, "and their bodies."

"For a price," said Lord Burydan.

"Of course. The price is simple. You will accompany me to help capture a man and a special weapon in hostile territory, and perform a special task. And then you will be free, with your face and body restored."

"I am no criminal."

"Indeed not. This mission is for your ally, the French. You remember Simon Hart, from our last encounter? He is the one employing me. For you, this is a war mission."

"Does my government know of this?"

"I have no idea, Lord Burydan. Your involvement is my concern only. You are committing no crime, as far as I am aware. Furthermore, I understand you a legally a free man. If you disappear from this residence, again you will have committed no crime."

"How do you know that I won't walk away after you've restored me?"

Cornelius smiled. "The initial treatment will be temporary. Should you escape me, you will revert to your present form within 48 hours."

Lord Burydan responded angrily. "You could have a hold on me forever!"

---

[3] See *The Doctor of Sarajevo* in *Tales of the Shadowmen* 16.

"It would be bad for business if it got out that I reneged on my agreements. You may even kill me in a fit of rage. And anyway, if I did do that, would it still not be better working for me than living out your days like this?"

Lord Burydan looked at the floor. Then he looked up again. "What is this special task?" he asked.

"Our mission is likely to be interfered with by the adventuress Countess Petrovski. Your job will be to kill her."

"Kill a woman!"

"Spare me your mock horror. Let us recall that, in the past, you cold-bloodedly killed two of my employees by throwing them to alligators."

Lord Burydan laughed, but this time it was more the laugh of his old self. "Yes, I recall," he said, with a certain relish. "The world was better off without them, but a woman?"

"A woman who is an enemy of your country..." *And now*, thought the Doctor, *the killer blow*. "...and also the woman who pushed you into the fire, creating your current predicament."

Lord Burydan froze. He recalled the events of two years previous, where he had possession of a super-weapon that could destroy whole cities. Who cared if the Hun were killed in their millions? The war would have been won. And then, on the ship carrying the weapon, the Habsburg agent, Countess Irina Petrovski, had intervened, destroying his plans. He suspected he had been pushed into the fire, but he could not quite remember. One moment, he was on deck, the next in the flames. And yet, he had heard her cry "Farewell, Lord Burydan." Yes, yes, it made sense now. It was the Countess!

Cornelius could sense he was near. Now to finish it. "You could be a whole again, be a man again for your wife. Do you wish to see her go off with another man?" Lord Burydan flashed a look of hate at him. Cornelius went on, "Everything can be yours again. Come with me now, and within hours, you will be restored. My equipment is not far. In the morning, you will enjoy the Sun on your unscarred face. This could be your last night spent like this."

"Let us go. I wish to settle with the Countess."

"Excellent," said Dr. Cornelius.

He was delighted. His former enemy now worked for him. And what's more, Lord Burydan thought the Countess responsible for his disfigurement. That was amusing to him, because it was he who had pushed Burydan into the fire, not the Countess.

The island of Brač, Dalmatia, Austro-Hungarian Empire

Countess Irina Petrovski looked out onto the Adriatic. She could see the city of Split in the distance, a few kilometers across the water, with the Dinaric mountains behind. She was in the village of Sutivan, seated at café on the small Riva, near to the main village church. She looked to her right, and saw her friend

Josip walking past the small castle *Marjanović* and towards her. She waved at him. He was pleased to see her. She looked striking, an auburn-haired beauty wearing the most fashionable Viennese clothes.

Josip sat down. "My dear Countess, you look as beautiful as ever."

"Ever the charmer," she replied.

He sat down. "Why are you here, Irina? I am aware you are kept busy with nursing duties and your journalism work. I hear that Vienna holds your work in high regard, including certain military circles."

The Countess knew that Josip was involved in politics—he was a member of the Croatian People's Peasant Party. Clearly, he had heard something about her exploits beyond nursing and the occasional piece in the fashionable Vienna Press.

"I do my duty to my people and the Empire, Josip."

Josip smiled. He knew that she was a Polish nationalist, deeply concerned with the fate of her people and politically wanting a united Poland, currently split between three powers within the Habsburg Empire.

"I know, Irina. And your interest in fair representation of the peoples of the Empire is well-known and appreciated by people like me. I do hope you can put in a good work with the Emperor, and his heir Karl regarding our cause. We believe some form of Croatian unit, within the Empire at least combining the lands of Dalmatia, Slavonia, Croatia..."

The Countess interrupted him. She was sympathetic, and loved discussing politics, but right now she needed information.

"Josip, forgive me. I do have some important questions for you. First, I would just like to thank you for looking after my property here for me..." *Which is why the* Evidenzbureau *assigned me this mission, my links here provide excellent cover,* she thought. "...But I also need your help, your knowledge of the area, here and on the mainland," she pointed towards Split.

"How can I be of service?" he replied, sensing immediately something important was going on. He had also noticed a couple of upright-looking gentlemen on another table who he noticed kept glancing at them.

They changed subject when the waiter approached, speaking about her holiday home in the village, how her seafaring friends, the Lukšić family, were and so on.

After the waiter left, Josip leaned over to her across their table. He glanced with his eyes over to the table with the two gentlemen.

"Ah," said the Countess, "Captain Marić and Lieutenant Vuljanić" she said quietly. They are with me, part of my entourage, shall we say, along with my butler and maid."

Josip realized there was much truth in the rumors about the Countess.

"Josip," she said, "have you heard anything about these tales of a man dressed up as Death robbing people? And the incident in Supetar two days ago?"

Supetar was the island's administrative center, not far away from Sutivan, where Josip lived.

"I have. In fact, I have spoken to the man who was robbed. The press reported a man dressed up, but he insisted that it was real. That Death appeared before him and demanded money. He admitted to me that he was drunk and on his way home. He's a sensible enough fellow once sober, but when drunk, he is rather less so. I would not be surprised if he simply lost the money and invented this story to placate his wife, who would not be amused at the loss of his wages." Josip nodded towards the two officers. "Also, when he went to the police, he was then questioned by two mysterious men." He glanced again at the officers.

"I am sure they had their reasons," said the Countess, smiling. "After all, we are at war, and these robberies have taken place all the way from the Isonzo front down to Split, where there have been a cluster of such robberies. I am interested in writing about them for a Vienna newspaper. Have there been any unusual happenings of late? Any strangers?"

"We are at war, everything is strange. However, there is something. There is an Austrian visitor in Supetar, a Gerhard Huber. He has been flashing money about and has been staying at the *Praha* hotel for the last week or so. He speaks German, but with a strange accent. He keeps saying that the Dalmatia will become part of his country, which is odd as we already come under Vienna, as the barmen keep telling him."

This interested the Countess. "Has he been spoken to?"

"Yes, his papers are in order. He claims to be here to look at the stars. He's been here a for a week or so, with a couple of trips to the mainland."

"The gendarmes have not informed me of this individual," the Countess said, thoughtful.

"I am sure he is harmless. I met him myself. He's an accountant with an interest in astronomy. He rambled to me about Dalmatia being his and then bored me rigid with talking about the stars."

At the other table, the two officers were speaking to each other, whilst carefully looking around the area. They spoke of the war, both agreeing the recent Italian advance would be repelled; despite their numerical superiority, their enemy had not made much progress since entering the war.

For the Captain, this was all new. He had been swiftly seconded to the *Evidenzbureau* to work with the Countess on finding the fugitive. The soldier he had wounded had died from infection, but he was clearly French and could barely speak Italian. They also knew that the Italians were hunting a man with certain unspecified equipment, and that this person had disappeared. The *Evidenzbureau* had put things together. It was likely that a French soldier had, for whatever reason, stolen the mysterious device and was now on the run, using it to get cash in robberies.

The *Evidenzbureau* further believed that a certain unit of French intelligence was behind the device, and now, they had to get it, before the French agents did.

At that moment, a rough-looking man dashed over to the café, collapsing in a chair.

"Rakija! Now!" he shouted at the waiter, banging his fist on his table.

The Countess looked disgusted at this uncouth person. "I've seen him around for the past few months," said Josip. "He moves around the island, looking for the odd job to pay for booze."

The waiter simply looked at him—they occasionally had to deal with his sort. "That ghost in the newspapers! He's in Ložišća, he was robbing people by the church! It's not a man in a mask, he's real! It's Death! Death!"

The Countess went over to him. "Describe what you saw," she ordered. Her tone brooked no dissent. The Captain and the Lieutenant stood by her, reinforcing her authority. She knew the village he mentioned –about six kilometers away.

"People were going to evening prayer, then Death appeared, demanding money for their sins! They refused to give it, holding their crosses against him. He pointed his scythe at one of them—and lightning of some kind hit the mayor, burning him to death."

The two officers exchanged a brief glance. That fitted with the first attack in the trenches, the details of which had not been publicly released.

"I ran all the way here, without looking back," the man said.

The Countess looked at him suspiciously. "Did no one come with you?"

"Every man for himself. The others no doubt ran to their homes. I wouldn't stay there. I'm off to Split on the first boat out."

"The Countess turned to the two officers. "If this man is telling the truth, we have to move fast." She then spoke to Josip, "Keep an eye on him. Send for my butler to assist you." She promptly left with the officers in tow.

Nearby was her vehicle, which she named *Elizabeth*, specially armored for the war, parked next to the castle Marjanović.

She and the officers got in. "I'll drive. I know the way."

The two officers piled onto the back seats.

"Hang on to your hat, sir" said the Lieutenant to the Captain.

The car headed off, picking up speed and running along a rough road out of the village.

"How is this possible," asked the Captain. "We must be going at 60 km an hour across this road."

"It was a present from my British friends from before the war. And its secrets defy our expert's knowledge—as it did my friends."

There were a number of mysteries regarding the vehicle. Professor Saxton and Professor Wells had given it to her as the only appropriate reward for helping saving London in 1912. They had not been in contact since the war began.

Within minutes, they were approaching a small bridge over a ravine.

"The *Franz Joseph* bridge is up ahead soon," said the Countess. "The original bridge was destroyed in a flood, the locals petitioned our Emperor for help and he paid for this new one, hence its name."

On the far side of the bridge, a square-jawed man leaned on one side of the stone bridge. He was on the external side, standing on a piece of ground just before the ravine. He held a rifle, an Enfield P14.

Dr Cornelius certainly knows how to get the best weapons, I'll certainly say that for him, he thought. He saw the car he was waiting for in the distance. He let it come closer, to get his shot right. *Perhaps it might fly off the bridge and into the ravine—that would be a fine spectacle!* he thought.

The man moved away from his position. *Why not let that Hun see have a glimpse of who did this, and thus why she is going to die.*

Lord Burydan moved to the middle of the bridge and raised his P14.

The Countess saw a man on the other side of the bridge and started to brake.

The British Lord took his shot.

A bullet hit the windscreen, but bounced off. The Countess halted the *Elizabeth* on the bridge.

Lord Burydan remained standing. He fired more shots at the Countess. The bullets bounced off the windscreen. The Countess stared at the man.

"Lord Burydan!" she exclaimed.

She picked up her Doppelpistole M1912 by the side of her seat. On the bottom of her windscreen, she moved a small slat, put the barrel off of the gun through the revealed slot, and opened fire.

Lord Burydan dived aside, having seen what she was doing. He rolled back to lying behind the bridge wall, with the ravine just a few centimeters away, and out of the line of the Countess's fire. The occupants of the car then heard a noise.

"Is that… laughing?" the Lieutenant asked.

"Yes," said the Countess. She remembered the British Lord from their last encounter. He was quite unhinged then. What was he like now?

The British peer was exhilarated. What fun this was! *The Countess is keen to provide some sport!* He started to move down.

"We have to get out—take the fight to him," Captain Marić said. "If you cover me, I will go back and around the side—try and flush him out with a few shots. He must be pinned down right there."

Before the Countess could say anything, he leaped out of car and ran back. He had his Rast & Gasser M1898 service revolver with him. Within seconds, he was back at the beginning of the bridge. He looked around the side and saw nothing. Where did the man go? It was certainly getting darker, but he should certainly be visible.

Someone shouted. The Captain whirled around—and took a shot in the arm.

Lord Burydan had somehow appeared on the other side of the bridge, right next to the car, rifle now slung on his back. The sides of the car had armored plating, but he saw an observation slot.

Lord Burydan had a pistol, a Webley, which he stuck into it, twisted the barrel to where he thought the Countess was, but it was forced up from the inside by the Lieutenant. Then the car moved backwards. The Briton was dragged along and was forced to let go of his pistol. He fell to the ground, his rifle coming off his shoulder.

Now he was almost in point blank range of the Countess's gun. He jumped over the wall of the bridge before she could fire again.

"I'm all right, it's a flesh wound, stay inside—he must still be here," the Captain said. He moved as fast as he could toward the car door and got it in swiftly.

At that moment, a number of men approached the bridge, from the direction of Ložišća. The Countess recognized one of them—Ložišća's priest. He approached the car, his hand shielding his eyes from the glare of the headlights.

He came nearer and recognized the driver. "Countess? Are you well? We heard shots"

"Until next time, Countess—which will be very soon" came a voice in English, preventing the Countess from replying.

She saw Lord Burydan in the nearby field, waving at her. He then ran off into the dark.

"See to the Captain," she ordered the Lieutenant and got out of the car. The priest and the other men were rather startled to see the Countess wielding a machine gun. She also had what seemed to be a pair of opera glasses. She looked across the field in the near dark with the glasses. The image she saw was largely green, but she could see no figures. Lord Burydan was out of the range of her optical instrument. Pursuit might be difficult, given it was unclear which direction he had headed off in. More importantly, there was another place to get to at once.

"I am sorry to have disturbed you all, Father. Has there been a major incident in Ložišća tonight?"

The mystified priest shook his head. "Nothing at all happened," he said.

"Thank you, I thought as much. I am sure someone will come to explain it to you shortly—and I shall return at some point to explain in person also," she added.

She looked at something on the bridge. She saw a rope attached the side, hanging down. She spotted a couple more. She rolled her eyes and got back into *Elizabeth*, and reversed off the bridge, turned and went back the way she came. She knew she had to drive more slowly due to night having fallen, which could cost her the mission.

"He's gotten away. We must head to Supetar. How is Captain Marić?," she asked the Lieutenant.

"I'm perfectly fine," the Captain said, keen to show he was not incapacitated. "A flesh wound."

She glanced at the Lieutenant who was bandaging him, who nodded.

"You mentioned something about a Lord Burydan... Is that the English adventurer?" asked the Captain.

"The English lunatic more like," the Countess replied. "Did you notice those ropes? He was swinging underneath the bridge, jumping from rope to rope. That's how he was confusing us."

"Is he an acrobat?" asked the Captain.

"An exhibitionist, certainly."

Lieutenant Vuljanić looked puzzled. "I've read the report on the Pula affair. How can be here? He was severely burned."

"Quite so," said the Countess. "They were burns no man could recover from. Surely, Lieutenant, you must know who we really face? It is Dr. Cornelius Kramm."

"The master criminal? The Lord of the Red Hand?" asked Marić. "I read in the papers that he was killed in America. That would have been before the war. And wasn't Lord Burydan one of his arch-enemies?"

"He certainly is not dead," the Countess said. "He now operates in Europe. He sells his criminal services to the highest bidder. Perhaps the French have hired him. His surgical abilities are far beyond anything known to medical science. Only he could have restored Lord Burydan. And no doubt, he was now working for Dr. Cornelius in return. Given Burydan was unhinged in the first place, I daresay whatever enmity Lord Burydan felt for him has been very easily set aside in return for restoring him."

"What has this got to do with our mission?" asked Vuljanić.

"This was plainly a trap, no doubt to eliminate us. Dr. Cornelius is after the same man and weapon we are. He may have been hired by the French or tghe Italians, or even possibly operating on his own to get this weapon. It is likely that he is in Supetar right now, going after the man Josip told me about."

"Thanks for the warning shout, by the way, but I could not make it out," said the Captain to the Lieutenant.

"That was Lord Burydan," the Countess said. "I think he has some kind of warped sense of honor. I suspect he just did not want to shoot you in the back, although he was quite happy to try and destroy whole cities last time I met him."

Elizabeth returned to Sutivan, by the Café where her butler and Josip were standing by the man whose information had led them to Lord Burydan's trap. She called the 'butler' over.

"Sergeant, that man led us into a trap. Find out what he knew about it. We have to get to Supetar." With that, she drove off.

The Sergeant, who was another of the Countess's group of operatives, went over to Josip. "Sir, do you have somewhere private where I could speak to our friend here in private?"

Josip nodded. The man jumped up, but the Sergeant shoved him by the shoulder back down. "Now, my friend, you don't want me to use this, do you?" The sergeant moved his jacket, revealing a pistol.

The Sergeant spoke in German, which the man could not speak, but he understood perfectly, promptly deciding that full cooperation was best.

In the dark, Lord Burydan was walking in the direction of the sea, where his boat was. He, too, had a pair of glasses that enabled him to see in the dark—another piece of the Doctor's equipment. He was exhilarated. He had never thought that he would do such things again. Dr. Cornelius would not be pleased with his failing to kill the Countess. However, the good news was that he would likely get another chance. And the other good news was that the Countess would be too late in getting to Supetar. He laughed out loud in the dark. *What entertainment this all was!*

In Supetar, Dr. Cornelius was waiting outside the *Praha* hotel.

"You are sure that's him?" he asked the rough-looking man next to him, showing him a photograph of Professor Marcus.

"That's him. First saw him in Split, now he's in there."

"He had best be, Darko, given how much I am paying you for this information."

"No more Red Hand to work for, Doctor. Got to pay my bills. And you can afford it."

The man was insolent. He was a former member of the once-feared Red Hand organization, which Dr. Cornelius and his late brother had run. In the old days, he would simply have had the man killed for his tone—or perhaps be subjected to his surgical experiments. Things were different now. To eliminate him would be to ensure others would not work for the sculptor of human flesh.

A few people left the hotel, heading for the nearby port area, where a boat to the mainland waited.

"That's him," Darko said, pointing a balding man in the group. "Name of Gerhard Huber. I'm told he has a ticket to the mainland tonight."

Dr. Cornelius was satisfied. This was Professor Marcus. What a fool the man was. No attempt at disguise and committing robberies within a small geographical space. He stood out here on the island of Brač in the last few days. The Doctor was surprised the police had not already picked him up.

"There are too many people around," the Doctor said. "Let's follow him."

Professor Marcus got on board the boat. His pursuers bought two tickets and got on board, keeping a discreet distance from their target. Shortly, the boat set off.

It was some minutes later that *Elizabeth* roared into the town. The Countess and the officers ran over to the hotel, with Captain Marić firmly banging on the door. He was determined to show that his wound was minor. The startled owner came out.

"I understand a Gerhard Huber is staying here. Is he present?" demanded the Countess. Her imperious tone brooked no dissent.

"No, he's left on the last boat to Split," replied the owner.

"My men must check. Check the hotel register and his room."

"This is my property…" started the owner.

"I am the Countess Irina Petrovski. I trust you have heard of me?"

The hotel owner indeed had and became more respectful. "Yes, of course. I have read some of your articles and I know you have property on our island, but why are you so interested in my guest and who are these men?"

"We are on important business for the Empire. Help us, keep quiet, and I shall give your establishment a mention in an article I am preparing." The owner was delighted and quickly showed the officers the man's room which was on the first floor—he indeed was not there.

They came back down to report to the Countess.

The hotel owner volunteered some information. "If it is of any help, the fellow did say he was going the *Hotel Bellevue* in Split."

"Likes to live well, this one," said the Countess. The Lieutenant suppressed a smile. Much the same could be said about the Countess.

She looked over to the harbor. There was a boat there that had brought over *Elizabeth*. Its captain was an intelligence agent, prepared to move at a moment's notice. She turned to Vuljanić.

"Get our boat ready, captain, we leave for Split at once. Then take *Elizabeth* and pick up the Sergeant. I'd like to know what he has found out from that man in the café. Make sure he is restrained until he can be taken into custody, his actions nearly got us killed." She looked around. "Just where is Dr. Cornelius? The sooner we get to Split, the better."

It took around 45 minutes to set off. The Countess wondered if that gap of time would see the man they were after snared by Dr. Cornelius.

Dr. Cornelius himself was not amused. First, he and his minion were not able to get to the Professor coming off the boat. There were far too many people about, despite it being night. There were also the odd gendarme. And people were suspicious—there was a war on, after all. They followed the Professor along the Riva from the harbor towards the *Hotel Bellevue*. They stayed outside, whilst he went in.

"What now?" asked Darko.

"We enter after him," said the Doctor. "Some improvisation may be required to get into his room and to persuade him to come with us. I have a spray to render him unconscious if need be. We will use it on staff if we have to—

69

better someone finds a sleeping body than a corpse." The Doctor cared nothing for human life, but he did know that a corpse would create a much bigger commotion just when he did not need it.

Lord Burydan suddenly bounded up to them.

"Splendid boat, you've got there, Cornelius. It got me here quickly." he said in English.

"Silence, you idiot," replied the Doctor. "The English language is not one the locals will ignore if heard. How did you find us? You were supposed to return to our hideout."

Lord Burydan beamed at the Doctor, and then switched to German, and said in a lowered voice, "Well, old man, I got back here and parked the boat right there…" He pointed to a mooring area by the Riva. "…I wanted to have a quick look round this place you know, in case of trouble. Spotted you very easily, you stand out with that bald head of yours."

Dr. Cornelius was about to explode, when Lord Burydan continued. "Didn't manage to kill the Countess—that car and bloody villagers appearing on the scene." He thought best not to mention the loss of his weapons and considered himself fortunate he had left a spare Webley on the boat he used.

"You failed!" the sculptor of flesh hissed.

"No, no, old boy," replied the Briton. "A temporary delay. You must admit she's not caught up with you, so the ruse worked to that extent. Er, she didn't capture the target?"

"We have not seen her, and the target is in there," the Doctor said, pointing to the hotel. He suppressed his rage. "We now have to get in and get him out. We must deceive the hotel receptionist, or perhaps bribe him, into giving us his room number."

"Leave it to me, I can act Kraut," said Lord Burydan.

With that, he strode into the hotel lobby and straight up to the reception desk. As it was night, there was only one person on duty, a young man, sitting in a chair. He stood bolt upright when he saw the Briton marching towards him. Lord Burydan slammed his hand on the desk. "Gerhard Huber. Get him down here at once, Pig-Dog! [4]"

Dr. Cornelius and Darko rushed in behind him.

"Mein Herr," said the young receptionist, "we do not simply call down the guests". He turned to ring a bell behind him, which would summon other staff. The man was clearly a drunk.

"Don't you 'Mein Herr' me!" shouted Lord Burydan.

He leaned over the desk, turning the young man round and lifted him up by his lapels. "What number room is he in?" the Briton menacingly asked.

"204!" the terrified young man said.

---

[4] German: *Schweinhund.*

Dr. Cornelius sprayed something on the man, and he immediately lost consciousness.

"Put him down into the chair—gently" the Doctor said.

Lord Burydan did so.

"No one appears to have heard you," Cornelius said. "We are fortunate."

"That's due to not dilly-dallying and taking action instead."

Cornelius stared at him. He had had enough. "Your luck ran out once. And it's thanks to me that you stand here so arrogantly. Do not make me reconsider our arrangements. Enough of your rash actions."

Lord Burydan suddenly looked concerned. Then he gave a theatrical bow. "My apologies. Let us get the man we are here for."

The three men swiftly went upstairs.

In room 204, Professor Marcus lay down on his bed. Things were going well. His room even overlooked the Prokurative square next door, its Venetian style stirring his irredentist feelings. He thought of how he had gotten to this position where greatness was within his grasp.

The war had not gone so well, despite Italian numerical superiority and the recent victory. This had enraged the Professor. How dare these Slovenes, Croats and the rest defy the Italian invasion of their lands? Further, how was it that the Italian military leadership bowed to the French on the use of the projector? *If only Gabriele d'Annunzio was in charge!*

Shortly after his escape from Hart's group, he had made contact with irredentist sympathizers. After demonstrating what he could do, he informed them that he wanted to do something to smash the Austro-Hungarians. He proposed he go to Vienna and assassinate their Emperor, which, he thought, would hasten Italian victory and deliver annexation of lands promised through the Treaty of London.

Time was of the essence—not only the French, but officially the Italians were seeking to recapture him. The irredentists were none too keen on assassinating Franz Joseph—it was too risky, they felt. However, they suggested another target that would soon arrive in Spalato—the Italian name for Split—on the Dalmatian coast. They had good information leaked to them by intelligence sources. And this target may be more politically useful.

The Professor was not so sure, but he was persuaded by one of the irredentists, who pointed out the target's potential threat. The Professor was both convinced and impressed by this man, who already had a reputation and was now an NCO in the Italian army. *Along with d'Annunzio, this Benito Mussolini was one of the men needed to lead Italy!* the Professor thought.

His train of thought was interrupted by a knock on the door. "There is a fire, we must evacuate" came a voice from outside.

Fire? The Professor was suspicious. He kept quiet.

Another knock. "Mr. Huber, please! You must come out immediately!"

The Professor could hear nothing. Surely, there would be commotion throughout the building? He looked out of the window onto the square. A few people were idling about. No sense of alarm there. He quickly took the projector out of the bed and activated it.

Outside, Dr. Cornelius had hoped the Professor would simply open the door. He nodded at Darko. The man took a sharp tool from his pocket and stuck it into the lock. After a few seconds, he stood back and gestured at the lock to indicate it was now unlocked. Lord Burydan prepared for action.

"Open it," commanded Dr. Cornelius.

Darko opened the door and was struck by the visage of Death within the room. This version floated towards the men. Darko looked terrified.

"It's just an image, idiot!" said Lord Burydan.

The Briton grabbed Darko and shoved him in, following. Darko unwillingly flew at the specter—and went through it. The creature flickered and the unfortunate Darko seemed to burn, twisting in the room, making a gasping sound. He collapsed, a blackened corpse.

"Slight miscalculation!" said Lord Burydan.

The Professor pushed his hand deeper on the projector, and another Death image appeared.

"Off," said Dr. Cornelius to the Professor. He had used the moment of Darko's burning to get to the Italian and hold a pistol directly to his head.

The image disappeared. Dr. Cornelius took the projector from the Professor. He noticed it tingled his hand slightly.

"Who are you?" asked the unnerved Italian.

"I am Dr, Malbrough. and this is…"

"Lord Astor Burydan," exclaimed the Professor. "And you are in fact Dr. Cornelius Kramm, the so-called sculptor of human flesh. I recognize both of you from the newspapers. I followed the whole Red Hand affair very closely. You are supposed to be dead, but clearly you are not. However, I thought the both of you were mortal enemies?"

"The war makes unlikely allies, Professor."

"It certainly does," said Lord Burydan, beaming. The Professor thought that there was something not quite right about that man.

"Let us leave," said the Doctor. "I will have my gun on you at all times, Professor. My instructions are to bring you in alive, but the retrieval of the projector is paramount. I will kill you if need be."

"Nonsense. Only I know how to operate it."

"I have my instructions, and it's not open to debate. Move."

"One moment," said Lord Burydan, who was looking out of the window. "Looks like a gendarme or some such out in the square. Looks bored. My sense is that he's not on alert. Let's wait a few minutes until he clears off."

72

Dr. Cornelius nodded. He spoke to the Professor. "I am curious, Professor. What is the origin of this projector?" he asked, holding it up in his other hand.

"Hart has not told you?" asked the Professor.

"He told me what it does, not its origins. I don't think you invented it, it seems a little advanced, plus your field is astronomy. My pardon if I am wrong."

The Professor looked a little ruffled. "Well, I do have an interested in other sciences. However, you are correct. Hart did not tell you—very well, I will. Just to spite him."

He told him about the alien craft and the crash.

Still keeping an eye the gendarme, Lord Burydan laughed. "From space? What tosh!"

"I suspect he's telling the truth, Lord Burydan," said the Doctor. "Censorship, bribes and disbelief keeps such matters out of the newspapers. Your government have specialists to deal with these things, including old friends of the Countess, incidentally. In Sarajevo, the Austro-Hungarians have a repository of mysterious technologies and strange relics, including some of otherworldly origin.

"By Jove!" exclaimed Lord Burydan.

The Professor became animated. "When Italy wins, you can be assured that I will be given full access to what is held in Sarajevo. I will find out all their secrets."

"The gendarme has gone—seemed to leave the square heading away from us," said Lord Burydan.

"Wait!" said the Professor. "Do you not want to know why I am here?"

"No doubt some scheme to attack the Dalmatian locals. It matters not. We have caught you and it's time to go," replied the Doctor.

The Professor remained where he was. "Hear me out," he said. "I am here to use this projector to assassinate Archduke Karl, the heir to the throne. He is due here for a meeting. I will use the projector to kill him in front of many witnesses. Death itself will be seen to have intervened in the war. It will be a terrible omen for the Austro-Hungarians, and will demoralize them. Let me do this, and then I will leave with you quite willingly. We will be heroes to Hart!"

"Could we get a bonus for this?" asked Lord Burydan of the Doctor.

Dr. Cornelius considered this, whilst noting the Briton's unheroic interest in money. "What meeting is he here for?" he asked.

"It will be secret, held in the cellars right under Diocletian's Palace tomorrow evening. It's just a few minutes from here. Archduke Karl will be meeting with the Croatian politician Stjepan Radić, to discuss reform in the Empire including a unified, autonomous Croatian unit. There is talk it would encompass even Bosnia-Hercegovina. Your allies the Serbs would not like that, and of course, we Italians would be concerned."

73

Lord Burydan scoffed. "Concerned? No doubt, given the limited gains of your army. Have to give it these Habsburg Hun types—they certainly have your measure!"

"How dare you! Our gains have been glorious!" said the Professor, despite knowing the truth of the Briton's words.

Lord Burydan continued laughing.

Dr. Cornelius cut in. "I have no idea how Hart, or his government might react to such an assassination. No, we will do only what we are contracted to do."

The Professor spat. "Money—is that all that motivates you?"

"Very much so," replied the Doctor.

Lord Burydan simply grinned and said, "Let's be off then!"

"What about him?" the Professor asked, pointing at Darko on the floor. He was still twitching.

"He will be dead soon enough," said Cornelius. He was happy to let the man die slowly for his insolence. He would pay the man's family his fee with a bonus—which would leave his reputation intact.

The three men left the room and went down the stairs. The Professor doubted he could escape these two men, at least not at the moment, with their guard up. They exited the hotel.

At this point, Fate decided to give the Professor a chance. They were surrounded by a group—three men and a woman, all pointing guns at them. Dr. Cornelius groaned inwardly. The Countess and her friends. That idiot Burydan's failure to kill her meant they were about to fail in their mission. *Where was the Englishman, anyway? He was with us only a moment ago*, he thought.

Cornelius swiftly aimed his own weapon at the Professor's head, grabbing hold of him and twisting him so that the gun was clearly aimed at the man's head. "Countess, I will kill this man if you do not move out of the way," he shouted.

"Don't be ridiculous," the Countess replied. "Hand him over, and you will be fairly treated."

Meanwhile, Lord Burydan had bounded upstairs to the first floor, revolver in hand. He had spotted the group an instant before leaving the hotel. *The Doctor lacks my experience in combat. I saw them a mile off*, he thought.

He stuck his head of the window on the first floor and looked down. His line of fire to the Countess was obscured by one of the men –so he aimed at him.

"Good night, servant of the Boche!" he shouted, and fired.

All of the Countess's group had turned upon hearing him. The shot hit the Captain, knocking him into the Countess. The Lieutenant and the Sergeant fired back, but Lord Burydan was already gone.

The Professor took the chance that was offered by the chaos. Lord Burydan's surprise attack had momentarily distracted the Doctor, and his gun had moved away from his head.

The Professor grabbed the Doctor's arm and twisted it. The gun fell out of Cornelius's hand. With presence of mind, the astronomer shoved him away, grabbed the gun from the ground and aimed it at Cornelius.

Without a word, the Doctor gave him the bag containing the projector. He was not going to die for it. The Professor grabbed the bag, took out the projector, and then disappeared.

All present were non-plussed, not helped by people coming from all over, to see what the commotion was. The Countess aimed her weapon at Cornelius. Vuljanić went over to the Captain, who lay on the floor.

"He's dead," said the Lieutenant.

"Cover that window," said Vuljanić to the Sergeant. "I am going in to get that Englishman."

"I think not," said a voice.

They turned around. Lord Burydan had come from behind them, and had his Webley aimed at the gendarme he had seen earlier, now taken hostage by the Briton.

"Drop the weapon, Countess," ordered the Englishman. "Doctor, come to me."

The Countess did not comply. "He can go, but we are not dropping our weapons," she said.

"Very well. I will kill you some other time, Countess."

The sculptor of human flesh went over to him. "We are going back into the hotel, now," said the Briton.

The three of them backed into the hotel with their hostage, and slowly up the stairs. The Countess and the Lieutenant followed.

"Stay back, Countess," Lord Burydan warned.

They turned the corner of the stairway and were out of sight.

The Countess and Vuljanić slowly moved up the stairs when the gendarme ran down and said: "They jumped out of a window!"

The two men ran away from the hotel, with Dr. Cornelius limping as he ran. His landing onto the Prokurative had not been a very controlled one. They ran down the Split Riva and, within moments, had boarded the boat Lord Burydan had moored nearby.

Burydan activated the motor and the boat moved off at speed. "You know Doctor," Lord Burydan said, "jumping out of windows is a specialty of mine, very useful in the adventurer business. I must teach you how to do it!"

Dr. Cornelius cursed.

A passer-by informed the Countess of men who had jumped into a boat. She and the Lieutenant looked out to sea. It was dark; all that could be seen were one or two lights on the islands opposite.

They headed back to the hotel. The Countess was angry and upset, but maintained her composure. The lunatic Englishman had killed a good man.

The Professor was streets away. He was pleased. The projector had intuited that he wanted an image in front of him of what was behind him. It was lucky it was getting so dark; otherwise all present would have seen some movement in the air, the drawback with that tactic.

He felt now that the projector was understanding him more, linking more with his mind. *This projector must have had some kind of symbiotic relationship with its Saturnian creators, and now its relationship with me is growing stronger* he thought. Tomorrow, he would unleash its full potential.

Dr. Cornelius and Lord Burydan traveled not far along the coast and docked the boat just outside of Split. They left the boat and headed into a dilapidated house by the sea. They took the engine of the boat. Both men had night goggles on, enabling them to see where they were going. Lord Burydan had asked Cornelius where he had obtained such equipment, but the sculptor of human flesh merely said he had a good supplier of advanced items in Berlin.

They entered and walked over to a wall, against which, there was a cabinet. They moved the cabinet revealing a trapdoor. "Go down and wait for me," said Cornelius. "I have to make contact with Hart. It is not a straightforward process. It will have to be a few hours. Get some sleep. Use the escape tunnel if you need to."

The Briton nodded and Cornelius left.

The Countess entered room 204. The crowd been swiftly cleared by the gendarmes, and the lieutenant stood guard over the Captain.

"Have you found anything?" she asked Sergeant Mayr, who had been searching the room.

"No," he replied.

The Countess looked over to the blackened body of the minion. "A lesson there for those who consort with the likes of Dr. Cornelius. Let us hope we can help provide a similar fate for Lord Burydan."

The Sergeant nodded his approval.

The body suddenly groaned. "Help me," he croaked.

The Doctor returned to the house in the early hours of the morning. Lord Burydan was already awake, and in the house, rather than the cellar.

"Good morning, Doctor!" said the Briton. "What have our employers told us?"

The Doctor replied "We have a new task. We must capture the Professor, but prior to his attempting at assassinating Karl, even if that means killing him. Hart is concerned that such an assassination could eventually implicate France, blackening their name, but would also see French leaders become targets in the future."

"Are we going to get a bonus for this?"

"No," lied the sculptor of human flesh. "Hart thinks we should have captured the man and his projector by now. He expects results today. And we shall deliver."

"Indeed!" cried the Briton.

Cornelius looked at him. He was intrigued by this interest in money, not that he was paying the man anything bar his treatment. The Doctor could exploit that.

"Have you looked at yourself today?" he asked Lord Burydan.

Concerned, the Briton took out a small mirror from his pocket. He looked at his face. He could see some greyness on the skin. "I need my treatment," he said.

"Yes," said Cornelius. "However, this is an excellent time to again mention that I am less than amused by some of your behavior. You failed to kill the Countess, letting her interfere later on. Further, your blundering into the hotel could have raised the alarm."

"Hang on, I did manage to get out us out of there. We were outnumbered and outgunned."

"Yes, but from now, you must control yourself more. If we fail, I will not be paid. And if you have contributed to any failure through your behavior, then I will discontinue your treatment."

Lord Burydan could feel his mind suddenly under strain. He had been given a new life. He could not let that go.

"I apologize, Doctor," said the Briton, in a tone of voice less exuberant than usual. "You must understand, the way I operate is much different to yours. However, I will adjust."

"Excellent," said the Doctor. "I have been considering what happened earlier. It is my guess that the Professor's disappearance was not due to his actually becoming invisible, but rather his usage of the projector. I suspect he did something that projected the street behind him, in front of him."

"Damned clever, these spacemen," said Lord Burydan. "Pity that Italian has the projector. We could make a lot of money from it."

"We could. However, it would not be long before the French found us. It is best to take the money. However, there is no harm in taking a look at the projector when we have it. But that is for later. Tonight, we will head to Diocletian's Palace. Unlike the Countess, we know where the Professor will turn up. We must be cautious until then. I shall provide a new face for myself, but not for you. The underlying damage to your face and body could complicate the permanent setting of your face. You may dye your hair… No, shave it all off. It may cause a momentary failure in recognition at some point—a moment you can exploit."

Lord Burydan looked appalled, then laughed, "Yes, I think I can manage that."

"Good. Let me give you your treatment for your face, and then we shall prepare in earnest."

Later in the day, in Split's Civic Hospital, Darko was on the verge of death. A priest entered the room where he had received treatment.

"I understand I am needed?" he asked the Countess, who was standing by the bed, along with the Lieutenant.

"Thank you for coming, Father," said the Countess. "This man is a criminal. His way of life has led to this." she pointed at the man, his face and arms visible above the sheets, but blackened with burns. "His only words were to ask for the last rites. There can be no question of denying him."

The Priest nodded and performed the rites. Darko turned his blackened head to the Countess and in a rasping voice said, "The doctor abandoned me… To hell with him. The Italian who was with him, he spoke of killing Archduke Karl and the politician Radić…"

He then fell silent. The Countess went over to him. "He is dead." She turned to the priest. "Thank you, Father. We must take our leave of you. Please do not repeat what you have heard—we will deal with this."

The priest nodded his assent. The two Habsburg agents left the room and exited the building.

Outside the hospital, the Countess turned to the lieutenant. "It seems we were wrong. We are not looking for a Frenchman using a weapon to rob members of the public, but an Italian wishing to assassinate the heir to the throne and the Croatian politician, Stjepan Radić."

"I saw Radić earlier on, he's here in Split," said Vuljanić. "He spotted me and called me over; he knows my father. He is here in Split for a meeting. He mentioned he's staying at friend's residence. It was just a few meters away."

"We must go there, at once; you must lead the way," said the Countess.

They got into *Elizabeth*, where the Sergeant was at the wheel. Vuljanić gave him the directions, and the vehicle moved off. The briefed the Sergeant on what they had find out.

"Who is this Radić, and what has he got to do with the Archduke?" asked the Sergeant.

"He's head of the Croatian People's Peasant Party. He wants more rights for Croatia within the Empire. I can see why an Italian would want him dead, but the main target must be Archduke Karl, who of course may have the power to help Radić," responded the Countess. "I can only assume he must be meeting the heir here somewhere—information it seems that was not given to us, neither

78

by our superiors or the authorities." She would have words with people about that, she thought.

Vuljanić spoke. He knew a lot about the Croat politician. "Radić has popular support, not like the Yugoslav committee in London, the capital of one of our enemies, a group which wants union with Serbia, a country that will accommodate Italian demands to our land along with their own territorial ambitions," he said angrily. "At least, the Empire fights the invader."

The Countess nodded. She sympathized with politicians such as Radić, whom she felt had had similar goals as herself—autonomy for a united Poland within the Empire. There was talk of some kind of Slavic unit within the Empire, under the Emperor, but no longer split under between the separate rule of Hungary and Austria as now; it would invariably be run in Zagreb. Such talk had displeased not only Belgrade, resulting in the assassination of Archduke Ferdinand, but no doubt Italy too.

The Countess was concerned. Emperor Franz Joseph was elderly, his time would be soon. She had expectations that the heir to the throne would be sympathetic to Polish autonomy. Whatever this Italian had planned, it must be stopped. She wondered what Dr. Cornelius was up to at that moment.

It was early evening. The Doctor and Lord Burydan were near on the seafront by the south entrance to the Diocletian's Palace. It had been built by the Roman Emperor as retirement home for himself in the last years of the third century with him moving into it in 305 AD. Since then, the city of Split had grown in and around it. However, some parts of the original remained.

Not that either Dr. Cornelius or Lord Burydan knew or cared about any of this history. Their concern was the gate to the lower level of the palace at the South wall. It had been closed off, and a couple of gendarmes stood nearby. Both Cornelius and Burydan had been observing it during the day, at a distance. Currently, they were talking as if they were locals merely stopping for a chat. They had passed the entrance a number of times that day.

"These gendarmes are not very good, are they? They've not spotted us lurking about all day," said Lord Burydan.

"Indeed not," replied the Doctor, now sporting a full head of hair, beard and mustache. He disliked changing his face—he was concerned that frequent use may do damage—but if Professor Marcus had recognized him, so could others. "Be alert, it's almost 8 p.m. The meeting begins in half an hour. The Archduke and Radić will soon be here."

The Countess and her party arrived at the place where Radić was staying. He was just leaving the house, when he was startled by *Elizabeth*.

"Of course, I know of you, Countess. And yes, I know that you are a wartime agent of the Empire."

"Mr. Radić," said the Countess, "you must believe me. Your life is in danger, and so is that of the heir to throne."

"It's very secret. Only tomorrow will it be announced he is in Spilt, but only in regard to his duties as a Field Marshal. We are meeting to discuss the position of Croats in the Empire."

"Where?"

"Below Diocletian's palace. I am due to be picked up..."

"Get in," the Countess ordered, and the Sergeant bundled the protesting politician into the back of *Elizabeth*.

By the entrance to the Palace, Dr. Cornelius momentarily turned to the sea. Before him, a specter of Death appeared, different to the one in the hotel. Dressed in a dark cloak, its skeletal hand beckoned at him—the skull seemed to be grinning.

"He's here!" Cornelius hissed at the Briton.

Lord Burydan turned around. "Where?" he asked.

The Doctor looked back to sea. The specter had gone.

"I saw one of those projections. Look around, he cannot be far. He must have somehow recognized us."

They walked around but could saw only a few passers-by.

"He will need to have sight of the Archduke. You walk a few meters that way, I shall go in the opposite direction."

Lord Burydan took a few steps. He could see a man approaching.

Behind him, Dr. Cornelius headed the other way, and spotted a car approaching. *This can only be the Archduke*, he thought, as a gendarme told him to move away.

Lord Burydan turned around, hearing the car in the distance and turned back the way he was headed—and suddenly realized the man in front of him was Professor Marcus.

He did not dare take out his gun—there suddenly seemed to be a number of gendarmes milling about and, given what had happened in Sarajevo two years back, they would shoot at him if they saw him with a gun.

He intended to get near to the Professor and see if he could surreptitiously point a gun at him. That was the plan agreed to with the Doctor, but liable to go wrong. He quickened his pace, and nearing the Professor, he moved across the road towards him.

"Excuse me..." he said in his best German, moving his hand to his hidden revolver.

But Professor Marcus had seen him and reached into his bag.

Suddenly, there were shouts and screams. Specters of death had started appearing all around, including right in-between the Briton and the Professor. Lord Burydan backed away. A specter aimed its scythe at him and a bolt of black lightning fired from it, missing him by inches as he ducked out of the way.

"Too slow, old man!" said the Briton pulling out his Webley and firing at the specter. The thing shimmered as the bullets flew through it.

Dr. Cornelius had heard the shouts and saw the Archduke's car still approaching. He noticed some of the specters moving his way. And he felt fear, but was not sure why. It must be from the projector. He ran into the way of the vehicle.

"Stop! Go back! There is an assassination attempt!" he shouted, making sure he was not too close to the vehicle, lest he be mistaken for the assassin.

The driver looked in horror at the creatures behind the Doctor and reversed.

The specters were firing at the car, but the bolts fizzled out after a few yards, and then they seemed to slow to a stop.

Limited power. Yet, clearly there are more of the creatures than on previous occasions, the Doctor noted.

The Professor could see the Emperor's vehicle reversing, and was furious. More specters were appearing around him, producing a kind of wall and firing at Lord Burydan, who was able to duck and dive from the bolts of the slowly-aimed scythes and fingers, laughing whilst doing so.

The Countess arrived in *Elizabeth*. She jumped out, followed by the Lieutenant, Sergeant Mayr and Radić. The heir to the throne, appeared to be arguing with a bearded man. The driver stood by the heir, warily pointing his revolver at the Doctor.

"Never mind, what those creatures, are! Go!" shouted the bearded man.

The Countess recognized the voice—Dr. Cornelius!

She ran to the Archduke. He recognized her immediately.

"Countess?" he said.

She pointed at the Doctor. "This man is an enemy of the Empire, and those creatures are here to kill you."

"But he saved my life", the Archduke protested.

"Yes, but for his own ends, no doubt." She turned to the driver. "Get in the car! You are to take His Majesty out of the city and far away to safety."

"No! I am not going anywhere, Countess! I am not leaving any of my subjects to the mercy of these demons."

Lord Burydan dashed up to them. He was going to shoot the Countess, but noting her weapon, and those of her colleagues, he thought better of it. The Countess looked at her operatives and shook her head slightly, effectively telling them to stay their hand against the killer of their colleague.

"What news?" the Doctor asked nonchalantly.

"The projector has melded itself to Marcus's chest. It's like they have joined together."

The Doctor was irritated at Lord Burydan's blurting out of the Italian's name. However, at this point, he was more concerned over his fee. Whatever else happened, if he had saved the Archduke, he might get a least the bonus from Hart.

"I must go now, Archduke. My work here is done. And may I remind you that I am not subject to your authority."

"Such impertinence!" shouted the heir to the throne at the Doctor. "But yes, you may go. I am not ungrateful. Countess, let them go."

The Countess aimed her gun at the Doctor. "The Emperor says he will stay and you can go—and as his subject, I must obey his orders. So you and this British madman can leave, but first, what do you know of this Professor Marcus?"

The Doctor could see he had little choice, it was best to give her the information she needed. "Professor Marcus is an Italian astronomer and irredentist. His machine is an off-world projector of some kind. Its powers grow stronger by the minute. It now seems to have taken to emitting waves of terror. Destroy the projector, or the man, or both, and you will stop this. Can I leave this to you now?"

Further conversation was curtailed by the appearance of a Death specter above the Palace, some three hundred feet-tall, scythe in hand. In the dark, it seemed like a floating skull, with the metal of the scythe next to it, creating if anything an even more terrifying image.

Across the channel, in Sutivan, Josip stared at the specter on the mainland.

"By Jingo!" exclaimed Lord Burydan.

And then waves of terror assaulted them, and the whole city.

A voice came from the creature. It spoke in Italian. "Come to the Peristyle, Karl. Come and face execution. This war shall be over, and Italy will reign in these lands. Fail to comply, and I will start killing the citizens of this city. Follow my minion!"

Professor Marcus stood exultant. The Peristyle was an open-air square within Diocletian's Palace, with columns on three sides. He was on the south side, where four columns held a triangular gable above a semi-circular arch. On his left, there was an ancient sphinx; to his right, he could see the Church of St. Dominus, with its tower and belfry. The historical setting pleased him enormously, but the location was also strategic. He stood on a stone platform under which was the exit from the cellars to the square. It amused him that his foes would not spot him immediately.

Symbiosis with the projector was not a surprise to him, but its increasing power was. Indeed, there were no more beams of lights projecting the images. Perhaps the energy was always there, untapped due to not being properly integrated with the operator? The Professor laughed. There would be much time later to contemplate the projector's mysteries.

The heir to the throne walked towards the entrance of the palace, beckoned by a death specter.

"No!" cried the Countess.

The Archduke turned to her. "I must... I will not see my subjects killed. Whatever, happens Countess, I order you sure to ensure this man fails in his ambition."

With that, he strode off.

The Countess could barely move out of fright, and had dropped her weapon without realizing it. What did Doctor Cornelius had said? The terror came from the projector? That meant it was not real, merely an addition to actual fear. She drew from deep within herself, from her faith, her belief in God to resist this fear. She slowly started walking after the Archduke. Behind her, Dr. Cornelius and Lord Burydan had also started moving, drawing on different reserves.

Dr. Cornelius could fight back the fear with his rationality. He saw the Countess' discarded weapon. He picked it up and slowly walked forward. He saw Lord Burydan alongside him—smiling!

"You provide such entertainment, Doctor!" said the Briton.

Clearly, his madness was helping him deal with the terror. Behind them, came the Lieutenant, the Sergeant and Radić, all drawing on some reserves to fight the terror, but they were knocked back by fleeing people seemingly coming out of all directions, some in their night clothes.

The Archduke walked up the stairs from the lower level to the Peristyle. A number of people were there, paralyzed with fear. The heir to the throne turned around. The Italian Professor stood there, a little above him, with the projector attached to his chest.

"What you are doing," shouted the Archduke at the Professor, "is against all norms of war! Stop terrorizing these civilians! The civilized world will not accept what is happening here!"

The Professor scoffed. "A new way of thinking is coming, Karl. The future will be decided by the strong, and the weak will be washed away. Men of vision—Italian men!—will lead the way. Sooner than you think, with the help of this device," he pointed to the projector, now melded to his chest.

"Now, Karl. In front of all your subjects, renounce your claims to Dalmatia and the other lands we covet! Accept they must be given to Italy."

Professor Marcus noticed the Countess emerging on the square from the stairs.

"And you must be Countess Irina Petrovski. Yes, Hart told me all about you. An aristocrat? Look at you crawl."

He turned his attention back to the heir to the throne. The Countess did not know what to do—she had no weapon. She cursed herself for not picking it up, but the fear was making it difficult to think. She could barely get up off the ground.

"Countess!" came a hissed whisper from behind her.

She looked around. Dr. Cornelius was on the stairs, just outside of the Professor's sight—with her projector gun. The fear was paralyzing him. He did not have the Countess's strength. But he had her Doppelpistol. He managed to shove it across to the floor to her.

She grabbed it and pulled herself up to her knees. *God must have a sense of humor to send me such a helper*, she thought.

She aimed at the Professor, who was just a couple of meters in front of her, and fired.

A volley of bullets smashed into the projector on the Professor's chest. It seemed to explode into light, blinding everyone there.

The Professor fell to his knees, screaming, cuts all over him. Remnants of the projector were melting off him, flailing onto the floor, with parts of his burnt flesh. He felt a hand over his mouth, and then a whisper in his ear.

"Do keep the noise down, old man."

After a couple of minutes, the Countess's vision started to recover. She looked around to see Dr. Cornelius. He raised a hand to her in farewell and disappeared back down the stairs. There was no time to pursue him; she had to see to the heir to the throne.

Dr. Cornelius dashed out of the entrance, easily eluding the Sergeant and the Lieutenant amongst the dazed crowd. Where was Lord Burydan? *To hell with him*, he thought. *Let him revert to his scarred state.* He went over to *Elizabeth*. The vehicle was locked. The Emperor's vehicle had gone. No doubt the driver had used it to flee. Unless Lord Burydan had taken it?

No projector, no professor. At least, he would get the bonus for his role in saving the Emperor. Such an irony—French money paying for saving one of their enemies.

The Doctor started his journey back to the hideout.

In the palace, the Countess went to the Archduke.

"Where is our foe?" he asked.

"Probably dead," she said. "That sludge and blood over there," she pointed to the remains of the projector on the stone platform, dripping onto the stairs, along with some blood. "That appears to be what remains of him. Given his screams, I doubt he escaped."

The Archduke looked at her. "Countess, once again the Empire is in your debt, and more so myself. Ah, Mr. Radić…"

The Croatian politician had appeared, with Vuljanić and Sergeant Mayr as well.

"I am pleased that Your Majesty is well," said Radić.

"Thanks to the Countess. Our meeting must proceed tomorrow, in the morning. We will not let tonight's events prevent that."

"Your Majesty, what are the public to be told?" asked Radić.

"Traditionally, information on such science, whether from Earth or the Heavens, has been kept from the public in order to prevent panic. Is that not so, Countess?"

The Countess nodded. "It is a wise policy, especially in this time of war. No one knows how people may react."

"From the Heavens?" asked Radić. "I have heard stories about what is kept in Sarajevo, but is this true?"

The heir to the throne looked a bit sheepish. The Countess swiftly rescued him. "A turn of phrase used in incidents such as this. The *Evidenzbureau* will prepare some form of story. Indeed, I will likely contribute. You need say nothing on the matter. Specialists will be summoned to deal with all this. It is best His Majesty takes his leave now."

Dr. Cornelius entered the hideout and opened the trapdoor. He could see that no one had been here in his absence, due to the precautions he took.

As he climbed down, a voice took him by surprise.

"There you are, old chap! Beginning to think you would never arrive."

A lamp came on. Sitting on a chair was Lord Burydan.

"Present for you," the Briton said, pointing to his side. On the floor, bound and gagged was the Professor.

"He's in a bit of state. Seems to have passed out. Lots of burns to his chest. Grabbed him whilst you all seem blinded, went round the back with him, appropriated the bloody Hun's car and here we are. Thought it best not to grab you as well—just got him out damn fast before anyone could see. I knew you would find your way out."

"You did well," said Dr. Cornelius. He went over to the Professor. "I will be able to treat him." He looked over at the Briton. "What did you do with the car?"

"In the sea, old man. Along with that complaining driver. Didn't seem to appreciate my gun to his head."

Dr. Cornelius nodded, looking impressed by the Briton's actions—and his spotting the various clues that would have alerted him to intruders. "I will deal with the Professor's wounds, but first..." he went over to his equipment and flipped a switch.

"A bomb, set to detonate and destroy my equipment if I failed to return," he explained. "It would have gone off in about 30 minutes time."

Now, it was Lord Burydan's turn to look impressed.

A few days later, the Countess was back in her property in Sutivan, sitting by her window, looking out to sea. She looked at one of the Vienna newspapers she had ordered. A story by her had appeared, relating her witnessing a propaganda action by Italian agents. They had used cinema projectors stolen from Germany to project an image of Death over Split. They had been foiled by local people, but had escaped.

There was, of course, no mention of the Archduke or Radić, let alone her role and that of Dr. Cornelius. There were rumors of sightings of the Archduke Karl and Radić, but the *Evidenzbureau* had ensured these had not seen print.

Despite foiling the plans of Professor Marcus, she felt uneasy. The war grew ever more terrible. She still hoped for the Empire to prevail, and for Poland to be united and autonomous within it, but she was now concerned over the designs of their ally, Germany.

Her maid, Kata—another *Evidenzbureau* agent—came in. "We are ready to leave, Countess."

The Countess got up. She was going to return to her nursing duties, but first, she would journey to Zagreb to visit the wife and family of Captain Marić, to tell them what a brave man he was, who had died defending his homeland.

At the same time, Dr. Cornelius and Lord Burydan were on a motorboat approaching the French Riviera. Their escape from Split had been circuitous. Smugglers of the Doctor's acquaintance were piloting the vessel.

The Doctor and Lord Burydan were discussing recent events. Cornelius had reverted to his own face. The Professor was sitting sullenly nearby. His chest wounds had been bandaged up.

"You know, we've done rather well," said Lord Burydan. He drew closer to Cornelius. "Now, I think we have worked well together, yes?"

The Doctor agreed. Despite some of his behavior, Lord Burydan's retrieval of the Professor had ensured the fee and the bonus from Hart would be paid. The Doctor intended to restore the man's face permanently. Lord Burydan was a more resourceful man than he had given him credit for. Best to simply conclude their business and let him go.

"Now, old chap, back home, I had certain... financial difficulties shall we say—adventuring did cost money, you know, and I was unable to earn whilst being stuck in Inverlair. I'd be interested in further collaboration."

"You wish to work for me?" asked the startled Doctor.

"Not for you, old boy, with you. Just so long as we do nothing against my government. They retired me and virtually imprisoned me, so I owe them nothing, but I'd rather they did not come after me for any reason."

"And your wife? She will guess who restored your face, and she will not forget who was responsible of her imprisonment and the death of her sister."

Lord Burydan recalled these incidents from before the war. It now seemed so long ago. The war had changed everything.

"My wife was looking to leave me. We will remain married of course, but I will certainly be going my own way. What do you say?"

"I accept your proposition, Lord Burydan." The sculptor of human flesh took great pleasure in this. The great adventurer Lord Burydan now reduced to working for a criminal mastermind. Not that the man seemed to mind too much, it seemed. The Doctor also was none too keen on the physical aspects of his work these days. This Briton could come in useful there.

"One thing," said the Doctor. "I have been instructed by Hart that the Countess is to be left alone. Again, he seems to fear that any harm that might come to her may trigger retaliatory assassinations on the likes of him. However, should she interfere with any future operations, that would be a different matter."

This was a lie, but he did not want the Briton to go after her and somehow find out who really pushed him into the fire.

Lord Burydan shrugged. "It will keep."

The men fell silent for a while. Then Lord Burydan looked over at the Professor. "What a miserable git you are, just sitting there."

The Professor said nothing.

Lord Burydan laughed. "You should have seen the look on your face when you spotted me at the gate. You weren't expecting us, were you?"

The sculptor of human flesh wearily joined in. "He had spotted us, Lord Burydan. He projected one of his Death images on me, just prior to your approaching him."

The Professor perked up. "I certainly did not. How would I have recognized you?"

"Not only was he surprised," Lord Burydan said, "but the projector was in the bag, not already in his hand, He brought it out, and let me tell you, he must have wet himself when he recognized me!"

"I certainly did not!" protested the Professor, with Lord Burydan laughing loudly at the Italian.

A dark chill went up the sculptor of human flesh's spine, a sensation he was not familiar with. What they said made sense. And that specter was different from the other ones. What had he seen *really*? And why was it beckoning to him?

Surely, it was all the projector, somehow? Surely?

Martin Gately has just written a new chapter in the saga featuring Jules Verne's Robur—more precisely, Young Robur, since this is about the early days of the future would-be Conqueror and Master of the World

Martin Gately: *Young Robur and The Thirst of Shiloh*

Morganton, North Carolina, 1867

> *"What's past is prologue... and sometimes,*
> *what is yet to come is also prologue"*

Frycollin was a courageous and intelligent man, but right now he was frightened out of his wits. Most especially he was terrified of losing Seraphina and that the life she carried inside in her womb would be snuffed out. He turned his back on the ghostly Ku Klux riders, and walked to the well, as instructed. He unlocked the winding handle and let the roped bucket fall to the water far below. After a moment he began to winch the sloshing bucket back up, and as he did so his mind drifted back over the last few hours, meditating on how he had got into this damnable mess.

1. The Picnic

The airship *Venger* was now nestled incongruously in the volcanic bowl of the Great Eyrie, near Morganton, its existence undreamed of by the local population. The dirigible's First Mate, Tom Turner, had—with his usual efficiency—overseen the setting up of the military camp; canvas tents had been broken out and swiftly put up in regimented order. Robur was surprised that the airship's hold also contained prefabricated structures—cabins and huts—for use as command posts and ammunition storage.

After the camp had been set up, Robur broke the news as gently as he could that they had been displaced backwards in time by the passage through the green aurora which had appeared over Africa (which had only been accomplished via the detonation of their radium bomb). The crew's reaction was a combination of skeptical and sanguine, yet they were pleased to be far away from the global war in which they had previously been combatants. Frycollin reported that Morganton—seen only at extreme distance and high altitude—had looked much as he remembered it. He believed they had returned to their own "present" of 1867, but he was very keen to confirm it.

"What we need is today's copy of the *Morganton Gazette* so we can know the exact date," said Frycollin.

Robur agreed that Frycollin and Seraphina would be the most inconspicuous of the crew to undertake this recce of the local terrain and town. During this decision making, Frycollin was again forced to point out—and this time with rather diminishing authority and enthusiasm—that Robur did not hold the rank of "captain" in anyone's army, navy or air corps, even though the British crew of the *Venger*, particularly Turner, had taken to calling him by that appellation. Challenged on the point, Turner argued that Robur had saved the ship twice now and should therefore be regarded as its acting captain. Particularly since it was now suspected to be fifty years removed from its legitimate chain of command.

It would be a long hike from the rim of the Eyrie to town, and so Frycollin raided the galley for the makings of a picnic—cheese, bread, wine and some cured meats—and loaded up a pair of backpacks with the food and a blanket. He and Seraphina could pause at a pleasant spot to refresh themselves. Robur and Turner were drinking tea outside the command post when Frycollin and Seraphina waved them a casual goodbye and started the awkward climb to the rim of the Eyrie crater.

"Where to next?" wondered Turner. "We cannot be holed up in this crater forever. But decades before flight is a matter of routine, we will call undue attention to ourselves by flying during the day—the newspapers will be full of reports of phantom airships!"

"Perhaps the only places I would wish to visit are my old homes in Arizona—the hidden religious community of the Woodlanders' Haven—and the Hopi Indian caves of the Anu Sinom," said Robur.

"I doubt if we'd have enough fuel to make it to the western desert territories of America," considered Turner. "And even if we did, our detailed charts are of Africa and Western Europe—I don't know how we would navigate effectively."

Robur nodded.

"Yes, you've mentioned before that the motors run on something called 'diesel'—but that is unknown in this time. Here, internal combustion engines are powered by something called coal gas."

"I don't know if we could make a conversion to gas, but the operations manual has emergency instructions for converting engines to consume wood alcohol. The necessary parts should be in the stores. It would take a little time though—though I don't suppose we have anything better to do."

"I still say we should've brought a weapon with us; a revolver or a carbine," insisted Seraphina.

"You don't know the south of this era like I do, girl," said Frycollin. "It might be enough to get us shot on sight. I doubt if law enforcement would even query our deaths. And the best-case scenario is that we'd be arrested for stealing the guns."

"Then we should've brought some of the British with us, their whiteness might've afforded us some cover," said the Amazon.

"Oh, those guys stick out like a sore thumb and would be impossible to account for. The locals would probably think the War of 1812 had started up again," joked Frycollin.

They had now picked their way down the rough, boulder-strewn side of the eyrie and had entered a series of pine meadows down which ran small silver streams in gentle cascades. The pair followed the largest of the streams in the belief that it would be the most direct route down the mountain. It meandered a little but eventually led them down to what looked like the beginning of a well-used trail. As they stepped onto the trail a couple of white-tailed deer exploded out of the high meadow growth and hared down the trail kicking up a surprising amount of dust as they went.

"We could've had venison for dinner," commiserated Seraphina. "If we had brought a carbine."

"Yes, I reckon Robur would've enjoyed that," agreed Frycollin.

In the high bows of the pines, blackbirds with red markings on their wings rebuked them noisily as they continued to hike down the incline. Frycollin never normally paid much mind to birds and didn't even know what these crow-like creatures were called, nevertheless, they struck him as a bad omen.

They walked for another hour or so and the terrain gradually flattened out. They were both starting to get hungry and it was well past lunchtime. They arrived in the grounds of what must have been an abandoned or demolished farmhouse. There was really little of it left but the remains of the stone hearth, and over to one side, the yard well. Someone had renewed the well's rope and bucket quite recently—so the property was not quite so abandoned as Frycollin had first thought. They laid out the blanket on a patch of rough grass beside the well and commenced to eat with gusto. Frycollin gnawed greedily at the delicious cheese, while Seraphina took time to delicately assemble sandwiches, as if she wanted to be at some Dahomey palace buffet.

Leading Airman Ellenshaw—on duty as a lookout on the eastern edge of the Eyrie Crater—gave a low whistle, the signal that he had spotted something of interest, in the direction of Robur and Turner who were drawing up plans and inventories on a map table outside the command post. Surefooted Robur ascended the steep slope like a mountain goat while Turner trailed slightly behind.

Ellenshaw handed his binoculars to Robur.

"Y'know, sir, I smelt it on the wind before I saw it. A kind of strange sweetness..."

Robur looked down the mountain in the direction of the airman's pointing arm. Perhaps two and a half or three miles away was a curling plume of feathery smoke—almost like steam—rising above the pine canopy. And, yes, there was a very faint but pleasant aroma wafted on the air. It was difficult to characterize, cereal being cooked perhaps but, with a tang of sugar overwriting it.

"What have we got here?" queried Turner.

"Someone down there is being very industrious," replied Robur. "I grew up in a religious community with a preoccupation with plants and trees, and I was taught about how syrup is made from maple sap in far off New England. But this must be something different. We're in a pine forest without a maple tree in sight."

"Well, I can take a wild guess," suggested Turner. "Bearing in mind our current location—the illicit production of alcohol—a moonshine still."

"Oh, I very much hope that you are right, for that would furnish us with some real possibilities. Particularly if it is a large operation. For it seems to me that if our engines can be converted to run on wood alcohol, they could probably be finetuned to run on grain alcohol. There must be very little chemical difference," mused Robur.

"Even better, we wouldn't have to trade or buy it. They are criminals... so if we relieve them of it, who will they complain to?"

"I think you'd better outfit six men with carbines and sidearms so we can scout this place out," suggested Robur.

Frycollin wasn't even sure why they had opened and quaffed so much of the second bottle of wine. But the afternoon had taken on a warm and indolent feeling, one of a quiet rural idyll to be recaptured rather than an errand to be run. It felt like they were playing hooky, far away from Robur and the men of the *Venger*. The mission to establish the exact date had started to feel slightly pointless, and Frycollin and Seraphina had both gotten sleepy. They had then cuddled together, barely fitting on the picnic blanket, and falling asleep. An atypical dereliction, but somehow, he was cherishing this time alone with Seraphina. Robur always seemed to find her an annoyance, and resented the intrusion on his previously close friendship with Frycollin, so it was almost a relief to be away from him.

The clatter of horses' hooves awoke Frycollin with a start and he cursed himself. How long had they slept? It was almost dark. They'd slept away the entire afternoon and long into the evening. Frycollin looked in the direction of the approaching horses and felt all the blood drain from his face. He also felt Seraphina stir at his side.

"Make no move. Say nothing," he rasped.

There was an intense duality to his perception of the white-clad riders. On the one hand, he knew them to be just men. On the other, he had been trained—indoctrinated—since childhood by both his own family and the white overseers to believe in superstition and the supernatural, no matter how foolish the belief might be—from the good luck brought by carrying a rabbit's foot to placating the spirit of the log pile when bringing in wood to burn; let alone the reality of the spooks of the vengeful dead, as these so obviously were. Bleached skull faces, bleached grey-white uniforms. These were the Confederate dead returned from their battlefield graves to hunt for disloyal blacks, carpetbaggers and renegades.

"What have we here?" asked the muffled sepulchral voice from behind the painted canvas of the skull mask. "Looks like a couple of sleeping lovebirds, just minding their own business. But I have a job for that strong-looking boy."

Frycollin stood up. His posture deferential. His head slightly bowed. This sickened him. What he wouldn't give now for a six-shooter in his hand or a landing party of carbine carrying British airmen at his side. He knew one thing for sure, at the least sign of disobedience or even sullenness he would be killed, and probably Seraphina too. The Ku Klux riders hated the "uppity negro" above all things, and reserved the most disgusting and ignominious deaths for any they found.

"Get me a bucket of water from the well, boy" said the lead Ku Klux rider.

"Yessir," said Frycollin quietly.

He dared to glance up for a split second at the face and even in a roundabout way at the ghostly steed, which was draped in an outfit reminiscent of what a horse might wear for a medieval jousting match. The lead rider's sheet-like mask came down far below the chin. It was crudely, but effectively painted with a greyish white paint—phosphorescent perhaps? He perceived that the rider wore some kind of helmet, a spike topped metal European army type thing, over which the sheet mask was fitted. Glittering pale blue eyes stared from out of the skull mask's ragged eye holes. The eyes roved over Frycollin, but could perceive nothing other than the debased humbleness that they wanted to see. Frycollin turned his back on the lead rider, and walked to the well, as instructed. He unlocked the winding handle and let the roped bucket fall to the water far below. After a moment he began to winch the sloshing bucket back up. Then he untethered the bucket and passed it to the eager hands of the Ku Klux rider.

The rider partially lifted up the mask sheet and poured the cold well water into where his mouth should be below the mask. It was like some odd conjuring trick. Not a drop of water seemed to be spilt. It all just disappeared... glugging away into the ghost's unquenchable gullet. After a few more seconds the bucket was empty.

"Lordy, that was good," said the Ku Klux rider, as he passed back the bucket. "That was the first drink of water I've had since I was killed at the Battle of Shiloh."

There was a strange chittering laughter from beneath the masks of the other riders.

"You two look like good negroes," continued the Ku Klux rider. "Now git back to your cabin, and don't be caught out again when spooks are around."

The riders reined their horses into a trot and headed off across the pine meadows, kicking up a sweet-scented needle dust cloud as they went. Frycollin was sickened. At least they had survived unscathed.

"Those men were your old enemies," puzzled out Seraphina. "Even unarmed, you and I could've killed a few of them... driven off the rest of them... escaped..."

"No, they are more than men. More than even ghosts. They are an idea. A concept of supremacy and repression which poisons everything. One day I will destroy them all, but today is not that day."

If Robur and Turner had expected an army of guards protecting the moonshine still, they had been disappointed. There had been only four men present, two guards—partially inebriated, armed with ancient ill-maintained shotguns. Besides that, there were just two older men in filthy and stained denims taking care of the fire and general operations.

Robur felt bad because he had advanced with Ellenshaw and struck one of the guards across the face with the butt of his carbine before he had realized the man was drunk. Robur's slight discomfort at the easy victory in this non-skirmish had amused Turner, who had previously thought of the man he had begun to address as 'captain' as a leader by virtue of his scientific, engineering and logistical solutions rather than martial skill. But at this early stage in his life, Robur was still subject to his own bull-headed impetuosity and a desire not to let his own side down. Running alongside that was something that would never change, his conviction not to eschew the threat of force or the use violence to achieve long term pacifist aims. Although, it was not just war which featured at the core of his thinking. His glimpse of the future war of 1916 had shown him that Man must ever be directed away from conflict, the possibility of the return of the institution of slavery to the United States had shocked him into the realization that the most extreme measures would be justified in preventing such a tragedy. And, finally, though Robur was deeply religious—he despised most of all that unfortunate tendency for religious devotion to become a tool of repression rather than a route to spiritual salvation. Since his return to the United States, the seed of an idea... a plan... had begun to form in his mind to free the inhabitants of the Woodlanders Haven from the yoke of Grand Pater Platanus.

"We need to get the ship's clerks down here to record the precise procedures for the operation of the still," said Robur to Turner. "These men need very gently interrogating."

"And there's two dozen barrels of moonshine stored in and around this shack. Not a bad little haul," observed Turner.

"There's going to be a lot to figure out here and now," judged Robur. "The copper still will need transporting to the Great Eyrie crater for our immediate use. Could it, or a version of it, be installed on the *Venger* for our use? Personally, I doubt it, but I just don't know. I don't even know what our fuel consumption or range will be. Will we need to set up fuel dumps and supplies across a range of projected routes? Or manufacture a set of stills of our own as refueling stations?"

Robur's musings only ceased once an airship medical orderly began to treat the bleeding of the guard Robur had injured—a process he observed with some interest. Turner, on the other hand, was concerned about who was in charge of this criminal enterprise. They had declared war on the local moonshiners, and they would doubtless want their property back. He was impatient to get back to the more easily defensible position of the Great Eyrie crater, especially now the sun had set.

After all these years since his last visit, the outskirts of Morganton were unfamiliar to Frycollin in the spreading darkness. He couldn't see the little church spire or the roof of the central hall. New farm buildings had been constructed recently—a smart new farmhouse with a large barn which had previously been a just a vacant lot had been put up. The buildings were well illuminated. Someone was still working in the barn. But some kind of instinct gave Frycollin the idea that this was going to be the place to hide out. After all, they could not return to their "cabin" as instructed by the Ku Klux riders who had not suspected for one moment that they did not belong to this area. He particularly did not want to enlist the assistance of freed slaves in assisting them and thereby adding to their troubles. Yes, he and Seraphina were on their own, and sensing that, they'd progressed from a mock casual stroll along the road to something stealthier in the direction of a patch of undergrowth; she was sticking to him like glue—moving like the elite bodyguard she was—with all her honed hair-trigger reflexes, but still regretting her lack of a single proper weapon.

Crouching in the darkened bushes by the edge of the road with Seraphina, Frycollin observed that the barn had a high pigeon loft with exterior windows and doors; what might be expected for racing or messenger pigeons. And now they were closer he could hear from within the contented billing and cooing of the birds themselves, accompanied by the melodic voice of the pigeons' keeper, a young woman who could be glimpsed in partial silhouette through those same upper windows—a young farmer's wife, or perhaps a farmer's daughter. A woman who enjoyed her work and kept everything on a tight and well-structured schedule. Possibly she was collecting pigeon eggs for tomorrow's breakfast?

At this point, a minor inspiration occurred to Frycollin, which was simply that a highly organized farmer's wife would probably have tacked to her kitchen wall a calendar with appointments and reminders marked on it. A brief sight of the calendar, even if only through the window, would obviate the need for hanging around until morning to procure a newspaper, as per their original stated mission. It was only a few minutes later that the young blonde woman—she did not look older than about twenty-four—exited the barn with her oil lantern and headed back to the house.

"I'm back in now, father," said the girl.

"Good. You spend too much time fussing over those darn pets anyway," said a gruff voice. "There's more important work to be done... fix my supper."

So, the young woman's life had not been as pleasant in this fine new farmhouse as Frycollin had perhaps first supposed. But there were worse things than an overbearing father. The older man's meal looked as if it would be prepared and served in the kitchen. The plan to look through the window for a calendar would therefore have to be abandoned, for now. It was just an unfortunate truth that the sight of an unknown black face at a window would be taken to be a presage to crime and mayhem—enough to trigger local alarm and a possible manhunt. Frycollin had noted that the barn had only been bolted shut rather than padlocked. He beckoned Seraphina to follow. They slipped into the barn intending to spend the night out of the way as comfortably as they could. A pile of fairly fresh straw and some sacking sufficed. Frycollin remembered the picnic blanket in the backpack, removed and draped it over Seraphina.

"I'm not cold," she protested. "I'm not even tired. I don't think I can go to sleep this early. You sleep, if you like, and I'll keep guard over you."

She was right. The initial lethargy from over consumption of wine—hours ago now—had rather worn off. But Frycollin had long since learned the benefits of seizing the opportunity for slumber while it could be had. He rolled over and willed himself towards the arms of Morpheus. But the birds in the pigeon loft had still not ceased their billing and cooing—they missed the attentions of their mistress—and Frycollin was kept awake for quite a while.

Countess Elsa von Merck had decided to rid herself of the appalling Erich von Rugen at the earliest opportunity. And it was not just the nauseating sexual overtures which had come to the fore of late. It was the association with the stench of failure which hung around him like a breath from a charnel house. The events in Oro Grande and the conspiracy to foment an uprising by the normally peaceful Modoc Indians had been all-encompassing in its unmitigated disastrousness. They had been lucky to escape by faking their deaths as per their pre-arranged plan—she in a most spectacular stagecoach crash, he by means of his prototype bulletproof vest. The Secret Service agents—thinking von Rugen shot through the heart—had left his body unguarded, and that was the only opportunity he had needed. The quality of a man cannot necessarily be judged by his ability to save his own skin.

So, they had made their weary way by train back to the East. So markedly different for them both to the indefatigable and arrogant mood in which they had first encountered their deadly adversary, Secret Service Agent Captain Steve Clarke, on an almost identical train—their inability to kill him by trapping him in the baggage car and uncoupling it was a portent of how he and his allies would frustrate the 1752 Conspiracy at every turn more accurate than supernatural prophecy ever delivered to *shamen* or witch doctors poring over split gizzards.

The countess and von Rugen had abandoned their aliases as Trina Dressard and Alex Morel and improvised less showy ones. The first humiliation. It was not long before von Rugen claimed to have made contact with higher authority back in Prussia, and that there would be a new mission for them. To this end, they traveled to Morganton. The countess had not been impressed with either Morganton or the nature of the mission. Doubts had already begun to form in her mind. Von Rugen had been cagey about the communication with Prussia and how it had been achieved—devoid of protocol, not associated with the proper diplomatic channels via the consulate in Washington, DC. Without accessing the messages to decipher them, she was suspicious that von Rugen had made the whole thing up—some sort of ruse to keep her near him while he sought to make romantic overtures. But then, as messages did start to arrive, and she was allowed to decode some of the more basic ones—as they built a network across the area of low-level contacts—she realized that it was just her ego swollen by a touch of narcissism that had made her think of deceptive romance. No, this novel element of a renewed version of the 1752 Conspiracy, in which she found herself embroiled, was all too real—as real as von Rugen's carnal desire for her. The problem was, it seemed overambitious and woefully under-resourced—a plan to disrupt society in the Post-Bellum South which might take decades to lay the foundations of and decades more to bring to its turbulent fruition. A generational plan to pass onto her daughter and granddaughter to fulfill. No, thank you.

The countess had always found it easy to kill, whether as a caprice or as part of a mission requirement. The difficulty for her had always been to hold her murderous temper in check. It had not taken long for her to begin to hate von Rugen. To hate his stupid face. To hate being trapped with him in this false domicile. The constant pawing and artlessly crass attempts at seduction—which, Heaven help her, she had almost been tempted to give in to due to sheer ennui. Yes, his face would have to go. It would have to be ruined beyond recognition. The stupid bulbous nose—painted red by Schnapps—then, as so often, disguise make-up reapplied to conceal it. But this would not just be a mindlessly cathartic exercise. There would be method to it in that this would not appear to be a crime committed by a woman. The countess had honed her art of disguise in this town, vastly improved it since her persona as barroom entertainer Trina Dressard. She looked, acted and dressed like a slip of a girl in her early twenties when the reality was that she was well over ten years older. With the right misdirection, she would be above suspicion. Why, there weren't even any competent law enforcement officers in this sorry town anyway.

Von Rugen, sodden with schnapps, had adjourned to the parlor couch and was snoring deeply. The countess moved swiftly and quietly. The scene had to be set and dressed, and nothing could be left to chance. She removed his ashtray from the side table—which was full of cigar ash and stubs—and replaced it with his long-stemmed clay pipe and tobacco pouch. Likewise, the lead crystal schnapps glass and empty bottle were replaced with a chipped shot glass and a half-full bottle of rotgut whiskey, which was strategically laid on its side on the rug. Yes, there were no detectives likely to arrive at this crime scene, but even a bumbling yokel neighbor might ask what von Rugen was doing consuming foreign luxury goods.

There was only really one logical choice of weapon. She didn't want to go out to the woodpile to retrieve the timber axe, and it was an inconveniently large thing to be attempting to heft in the fairly cramped space of the parlor. It had to be the small hatchet used for chopping wood for the boiler in the cellar. The countess wrestled momentarily with how to avoid the spray of blood getting all over herself and her clothing. Stripping nude was not as practical as it might first have seemed, especially if anything went wrong and she had to account for herself to others who had entered the house. She instead opted to strike the blows from her kitchen step-ladder—reaching over von Rugen from behind—with the effectively inverted hatchet. The blood spurts would then, in theory, just arc out over empty space spattering the floor and furniture.

She did the deed, obliterating every trace of the hated man's face. The sound of the blows was surprisingly similar to the hatchet's routine chopping of wood—just a little more muffled. The clearing up was the work of moments. The step ladder was replaced in its kitchen nook and there was no blood on it. The countess took the bloody hatchet out to the pigeon barn for what had become the most serendipitous part of her plan. She had seen the black man and the black girl sneak into the barn earlier and she had been unable to believe her good fortune. The imaginary scapegoat of her original plan was forgotten, replaced by the full reality of this unfortunate pair. Whatever they said would simply not be believed.

Entering with extreme stealth, the countess judged that the pair were really sleeping rather than feigning sleep in their position partially obscured by straw, sacks and a blanket. It was an almost Shakespearean moment as she stained the handsome negro's clothing with the sticky coagulated blood from the hatchet blade and then left the weapon only a couple of inches from his hand. A risk worth taking. She stalked out, looking back only once.

The sound was like a toll of doom echoing from the edge of the world to the center of Frycollin's consciousness. It was the sound of the barn door being kicked open with as much force as someone could muster. Light from flaming torches and oil lamps spilt across the intervening space and played across the surface of the straw. As Frycollin's eyes adjusted, the first thing he saw was the hatchet and suspecting that the men entering now were armed, he grabbed it, purely by instinct. Seraphina had snapped to instant alertness, her posture already cat-like, a killing energy barely held in check.

Kitty McKenzie—flanked by the knot of men entering the barn—raised her slim arm and pointed a delicate index finger accusingly.

"That is the man who just killed my father."

No one doubted it. No sane man would have done.

"Now, wait a minute…"

The words and the desire to say them died in his mouth. No explanation was going to suffice.

The shotgun barrel was already being levelled at Frycollin. The fact that it would be fired was as inevitable as gravity. Frycollin tried to dive clear of the blast, but he did not succeed, pellets caught him in the thighs and both knees. While still in the air, he hurled the bloody hatchet, sending it spinning into the midst of the men—though, horrifyingly, only narrowly past the shoulder of the beautiful young farmer's daughter, Kitty McKenzie.

Seraphina had made a rather acrobatic diving roll to behind the limited cover of a couple of hay bales, her status as an expectant mother pushed from her mind in the general interest of survival.

"I'm hit… get out of here. Get back to Robur."

That was all Frycollin managed to say to Seraphina. She weighed the options in that moment and could see no better course of action, though it tore her apart heart and soul. In her egress from the barn, she considerably restrained herself and only maimed two of the men. Once outside, they stood no chance of catching her. They never saw her again.

The downed Frycollin was hit across the temple with the butt of the same shotgun that had blasted him. It wasn't enough to render him unconscious, but it made a vertical split in his skin which ran up high into his scalp.

"To the nearest tree, or to the Sheriff's Office," asked one of the anonymous men, his words only just audible over the sobs of Kitty McKenzie.

"We'll take him to Sheriff Ashermann, there will be no lynching tonight," said the apparent leader. "And hurry to Doc Fielder—Benny and Jake look pretty badly hurt—that gal dislocated their jaws like a prize fighter and wrenched out their shoulders like some lunatic wrassler."

Nevertheless, Frycollin's wrists were tightly bound and a hemp rope was placed around his neck before he was led from the barn. Due process would only be slightly slower than a lynching. The nearest judge would be called upon to preside over a perfunctory hearing with the death sentence doubtless pronounced by mid-morning and carried out at noon. In his mind's eye he foresaw his only hope, and he knew it was a forlorn one, a daring aerial rescue busting him from his cell… the British airmen with their carbines blazing… all of them ultimately hoisted up to the waiting *Venger* and an unstoppable getaway. Just too many variable factors; the largest one of all—would Robur really be prepared to reveal the existence of the airship to the general population at such an early stage?

Frycollin feared that Robur would take a stealthier approach, and one that would be too late to be of any use. His thoughts now turned to Seraphina. He hoped she was running up the pine meadow trails towards the Great Eyrie as fast as her legs and her condition would allow.

Upon arrival at the Sheriff's Office, Frycollin was immediately untied and placed in one of the office cells where he could be closely observed. He did not ask for nor expect to receive any medical attention. Slow blood oozed from the pellet strikes in ever expanding stains on his pants. But it looked like nothing vital had been hit. With his scalp wound spattering the floor he took the opportunity to tear a strip from his sleeve to improvise a bandage.

All this time, Sheriff Ashermann listened with kindness to Kitty McKenzie's tale of finding her father murdered—struck with multiple axe blows—and then seeing a figure with a hatchet run from her home to the barn. The girl was obviously telling the truth. For Frycollin it was the most ridiculous misfortune. He would be the perfect scapegoat for some deadly local dispute someone had with the girl's father, or else some wandering maniac was getting away scot free. And there was nothing he could say that would not worsen the situation.

To identify himself as an Arizona Territory deputy sheriff here in a place which barely even accepted black men as free men… sounded like a fantasy, or worse, a calculated lie… something slow and difficult to check, something to buy time. Plus, he had been missing from Arizona since the day he first encountered Robur, and he did not now know if that was weeks or even months in the past. Even worse, his name might trigger a recollection in someone. He did not know this sheriff but had encountered a previous incumbent while escaping from slavery with the Underground Railroad. In this town he had intervened to stop a white man whipping a black woman slave and a girl-child in the street. That had nearly resulted in a lynching and it had been a miracle that the Underground Railroad Captain posing as Frycollin's owner had talked and bribed their way out of it. It would take a handful of miracles this time.

Eventually, a widow neighbor of Kitty McKenzie arrived to care for her and nurse her through her state of shock. The men who had cornered Frycollin in the barn gradually drifted away, certain now that the sorry and injured figure sitting on the edge of his cell cot was no longer a threat. But they still gave backward glances and exhortations to the sheriff and his deputy to watch him with care. It was almost dawn when Frycollin awoke from a sort of semi-concussed half sleep still sitting upright on the edge of his cot. Loss of blood was probably the main factor in him sleeping at all. Something vaguely familiar was happening, or repeating itself. A sing-song teasing voice was calling out insistently from the street. It was a voice Frycollin had heard before.

"Lordy, Sheriff Ashermann, why are you sheltering some black bastard killer of a white man in your jail?" said the voice. "Why don't you bring him out to the Thirsty Ghosts of Shiloh? We can alleviate you from a tedious chore and put a fine decoration on the nearest tree. A decoration and a warning."

Sheriff Ashermann took a Remington shotgun down from the cherrywood rack by the door and loaded it. At the same time, his deputy eased his six-shooter out of his own holster.

"I recognize your voices... I know who you are," bluffed the lawman, for in truth, he had no idea. "Go back to your farms and take off those painted sheets. There'll be no lynching here today nor any day."

"Lordy, Sheriff," continued the wheedling tones of the leader of the riders, "of course, we know where you live too. Your wife and daughter are in our hands... in our very power. The last thing we want is a conflagration at your home. Send the killer out to us and that can be avoided."

Frycollin was cynical of all this. Was it a drama being played out purely for his benefit? There was certainly something false or hollow about it. Ashermann addressed Frycollin for the first time.

"Did you hear what the riders said, boy?" barked the sheriff. "They may have my wife and child. Do you understand me?"

Frycollin rose slowly from his cot.

"Yeah, I understand you. This won't be something you can easily believe—but it happens to be true—far away from this place, I am a deputy sheriff—and I would not give up a prisoner to a mob. No true lawman would."

"You put a different complexion to it. So, you are a black deputy sheriff from some far-off state"

"Something like that."

"Which means you are innocent of the murder of Farmer McKenzie?"

"Of course."

"You just happened to pick the wrong barn to sleep off your liquor while snuggling the murder weapon and a violent accomplice."

"I can see how it looks, but however damning the evidence against me, I am still entitled to presumption of innocence and a fair trial," stated Frycollin, as forcefully as he could.

"You talk more like a shyster than a deputy sheriff," observed Ashermann's own deputy somewhat coldly.

"What is the hold up?" demanded the leader of the Ku Klux riders. "Give us the killer! You have only minutes now until your wife and daughter burn."

Now Ashermann looked as pale as the robes of the Thirsty Ghosts of Shiloh.

"If you are a lawman," said the sheriff, "you have a duty to uphold the law and save lives too. Would you go out to them willingly to save my family's lives?"

"Go out like some meek Black Messiah to save the white folk from their doom, when you could've cooked this drama up between you? Nossir. Why the hell should I? I have my own life to live and I should not be called upon to sacrifice it. You'll have to drag me out. In my injured condition you're hardly likely to find it much of a problem. But I'll struggle and fight you every inch of the

100

way. And be careful you don't knock me out or kill me while doing so, for then you'll have cheated the Ku Klux—and then you will have invoked their wrath even further. For they won't want to lynch an unconscious man, or worse yet, a corpse, they'll want to murder a freshly broken black man with an absence of hope in his eyes. And that is something they will never see in me. I won't give up hope on my friends and allies until after my final heartbeat. Even though it would be a miracle just for them to know the trouble I'm in."

"Your time is up, Sheriff," screeched the leader of the riders in a wavering falsetto filled with rage. "I have sent two ghosts to torch your domicile."

"Wait! Wait!" bellowed Ashermann. "Call them back... I'm bringing him out."

"Well, that is more like it," and this response was accompanied by a succession of raucous and impatient whoops and hollers.

True to his word, Frycollin violently resisted being handcuffed. But he was concussed and had already lost a lot of blood due to the shotgun injury. His movements felt like they were being made underwater, and the lawmen continued to rain blows on him. They targeted his kidneys with elbows and fists—blows that did killing-damage in their own right—until the fight was drained out of him. The best Frycollin could do then was to lock his joints in place. He did not move a single step, they had to move him out like a recalcitrant blood-stained statue.

What surprised Frycollin the most was that the entire town seemed to be out there waiting for the lynching, quiet, patient and complicit in what was now the early light of a greyish dawn. Pain and fatigue were causing him to disassociate. He was becoming an observer at a distance of his own death. A dismounted Ku Klux rider placed a hemp noose around his neck in an almost business-like way, and then dragged him towards the oak tree at the crossroads at the edge of town. The hollers of the riders became muted and then turned to practical conversation about the mechanics of the lynching and the best way to haul Frycollin high up into the tree and secure him there. To be a real executioner, a proper hangman, was a skill and, in some countries, actually a profession. Frycollin noted wryly that his death would be at the hands of amateurs, and probably all the more painful for it.

In the end, the dismounted rider hurled the coil of hemp up high over an oak branch and watched it unspool to the ground. The leader of the riders then tied off the rope on his saddle pommel and rode forward at a sudden gallop. Somehow, Frycollin had expected... well, didn't know quite what... more ceremony, more mocking, more scourging... the Ku Klux equivalent of a civic function. But no, the only thing these people wanted now was his swift death.

There was an extraordinary feeling of explosive pressure around his neck as he was lifted up off his feet into the boughs of the tree. A wet crunching and sliding of his vertebrae as his neck broke was accompanied by the snapped twig sound of his trachea rupturing. His vision turned to scarlet, but he could still think. He could still think.

Great clouds of blackness were swarming towards him. His lungs had collapsed. He anticipated that he would see his life play out again before him, as drowning men are supposed to. But this was not happening. Naturally, he felt cheated. But he could still think. He could still think. So, he thought about Robur. He had been lucky to run into that boy. He thought about Seraphina. And he had been lucky to love her, even if for so short a time. Now it was too tiring to think. The blackness of the clouds enveloped him.

2. The Postcard

Of course, Seraphina had not been able to leave Frycollin to trek back up the mountain to the *Venger,* she had rationalized it in various different ways. It reeked of unnecessary abandonment, and when she had seen him handed over to the Thirsty Ghosts from her position of concealment, she had known that she was right. There would have been no time for her to reach Robur and launch a rescue, but at least she had seen the manner of his death. There had been fragments of moments where she had entertained futile fantasies of rescuing him, of sacrificing herself... of joining him on that hanging tree. The long walk back through the pine meadows had been a kind of nightmare. Her grief was a slow poison moving through her system. Her mind was shutting down without her realizing it. Her steps were those of an automaton. She wandered in circles, scratched by briar. Eventually spotted by lookouts, a patrol was sent to recover her.

Robur looked into Seraphina's glassy eyes. She was sitting in a sickbay cot propped up by pillows, gripping the sheets with clenched fists.

"What is the matter with her? Why can't she speak?" Robur asked Turner with some frustration.

"I've seen something like it during the early part of the war in Europe. We used to call it 'shellshock'—an over-exposure to battlefield trauma... the sight of too much death. It can cause muteness and this almost somnambulistic state."

"She is a warrior. What battle can she have seen here in this place?"

"She returned without Frycollin—something which seems unthinkable. We must prepare ourselves for the worst. It seems to me likely that Frycollin is dead," said Turner, flatly.

Robur visibly blanched, and the ironclad innards of his ostrich-like digestive system ached with a sudden and convulsive nausea.

"We—you and I, only—will go down to the town. Incognito with concealed weapons. We will try to establish what happened. In doing so, we run the risk that we, too, will not return. Therefore, with your consent, I will give orders to the crew that the *Venger* be piloted to the most remote possible location—a South American jungle or some unknown island in the South Seas—where they can live out their lives quietly and dismantle the anachronism that is this airship," said Robur.

The man on the horse was a wide-shouldered giant, and normally his features had a cheerful and buoyant set, even in the most-deadly of circumstances, but not with the sight that his eyes were now having to drink in. He wore a white wide-brimmed hat so ostentatiously wide that on anyone less physically imposing it might have seemed comedic, on him the color alone seemed to be a signal as plain and unambiguous as the sound from a rattlesnake's tail: *Warning—I'm on the side of right.*

The photographer angled his box camera upwards on its tripod, taking aim at the corpse hanging in the tree. The photographer's head was invisible under the dark shroud of the black sheet which protected the photographic plate from premature exposure. The wide-shouldered man reined his steed to a halt next to the photographer right in the shadow of the oak.

"Why the need for a photograph, friend?" asked the big man.

"When there's been a lynching—there's always demand hereabouts for a lynching postcard," said the photographer in a rather wheedling, sing-song tone. "They'll be available in the general store and the post office come early afternoon. Send 'em to your relatives so they know how we deal with negro criminals in this State."

The big man narrowed his eyes and looked up at the face of the hanging dead man. Swollen though the face was, there was no mistaking it.

"I cannot account for why he is so far from home—but I know that man and he was no criminal—in fact, he was an Arizona Territory Deputy Sheriff called Thaddeus Frycollin."

The photographer packed up his equipment and started to scuttle away.

"If you wait here, I'll go to the sheriff's office and send him to you," offered the photographer. "Say, stranger, what is your name?"

"I appreciate that. My name is Idaho Jones and I am a Wells Fargo detective seconded to the United States Secret Service."

The scuttling was at maximum speed.

Sheriff Ashermann rode towards Idaho Jones sheepishly. Jones held out his identification in plain sight for the sheriff to see. His eyes took in the measure of this sheriff with a quick glance and found him wanting. Idaho Jones' first impressions were normally pretty accurate.

"I know you say you recognize this dead man," said Ashermann. "But what brings the US Secret Service to my town?"

"I have an arrest warrant for a woman called Trina Dressard, who I believe may be living under an assumed identity here. I found indications, clues really, pointing to this in her room in the Commercial Hotel in a town called Morgue, in California."

"So which matter do you want to deal with first?" asked Ashermann.

Idaho Jones was a man of steely self-control, but a close friend or associate would have seen a flickering change in his expression as he quelled his momentarily rising temper.

"First of all, you and I are going to carefully cut the deputy sheriff's body down from this tree and start to make the arrangements for a Christian burial."

Robur and Turner blended in as best they could with the small crowd of people who had paused in their normal business to observe the taking down of Frycollin's body from the tree.

Robur did not know how much longer he could hold in check his desolate grief. So far, he had kept himself from openly weeping, but the urge to howl and scream his rage to the high firmament was building within him and it originated in some primal section of his brain over which his intellect had only the most rudimentary control. Worse yet, it felt like an anvil had been thrown through his chest. He knew little of medicine, but it seemed that the cardiac muscles of his heart ached abominably. He had read once that it was possible to die of a broken heart, and this he could now believe. His heart had been beating in an irregular pattern since he first saw Frycollin's corpse. The finest man he had ever known had suffered an ignominious death. And there would now be a reckoning. A very terrible one…

He did not wonder now that Seraphina had been struck mute by witnessing this murder. He only wondered at the level of complicity amongst the townsfolk. Was there anyone amongst them who could be judged not guilty? Yes, perhaps one. For Robur had been surprised by the reverence with which the man the sheriff had called Idaho Jones had taken down the body and wrapped it in a white shroud.

Edging closer, Robur had picked up some conversation between the sheriff and Jones. That Jones knew Frycollin seemed almost too fantastic to be true, but it marked him out as a potential ally—as well as someone Robur was concerned the town might turn on and seek to eliminate, if he sought to deliver them to justice.

Robur and Turner spent the rest of the day moving around Morganton as inconspicuously as they could—mainly listening, but daring occasionally to ask questions—as indeed many others were doing—about the horrible murder of Mr. McKenzie, and how his beautiful young daughter was coping.

The man with the long lugubrious face and fancy waistcoat listened with rapt attention to the conversation taking place between Sheriff Ashermann and Idaho Jones. The man was sitting in the same cell in which Frycollin had been prisoner last night. Indeed, Frycollin's blood still spattered the floor of the cell and stained the bed sheet upon which he made himself comfortable. Not that anyone around here really seemed to care, but the man's name was Gideon Spilitt, former Union Army war correspondent and now a senior reporter for the *Poto-*

mac Clarion. No one cared because the local populace, in the general heightened state of hysteria following the murder of Lionel McKenzie had incorrectly, though enthusiastically, identified Spilitt to be a Northern carpetbagger come down to stir up disaffection amongst ex-slaves, make them want to claim their voting rights in forthcoming elections, and perhaps even urge them to commit the random and shocking murders of pillars of the community. As far as the people of Morganton were concerned, there was enough similarity between the elaborate embroidery of his waistcoat and what they imagined a yankee carpet-bag to look like for it to be damning proof positive of his guilt. After being frog marched to the sheriff's office, Ashermann had taken the opportunity to place the reporter in protective custody. Spilitt could not have been happier. This was going to be one hell of a story.

"Sheriff, I am just one man. I cannot take on your entire town to solve the mystery of who your white robed lynch mob of fake ghosts are. In a Southern town like this, brim-full of hate and prejudice, with an upside-down view as to what constitutes both patriotism and treason, every man would be one of my prime suspects. You should know better than I who the most hardened fanatics are—those with the greatest longing to return to the days of the Bonnie Blue Flag," said Idaho Jones, who was normally a man of very few words indeed, and disliked speechifying.

"Then what is your plan from this point forward, Mr. Secret Service Agent?" demanded Ashermann.

"The warrant I carry is for Trina Dressard, and my every instinct is that she is at the root of any problems you have had in this town. The woman is a living poison," said the detective without exaggeration. "I don't know how yet... but it's possible that Frycollin was on her trail and she somehow implicated him in the murder of Lionel McKenzie to get him out of the way."

"I don't see how," said Ashermann, "It was Kitty McKenzie herself who identified Frycollin as the killer, and he was hiding in her barn at the time."

Idaho Jones' eyes narrowed.

"Where is Kitty McKenzie right now?"

"Last I heard she was still recovering at Widow Foy's house, over on Pine Street," said Ashermann.

"I think you'd better take me there straightaway."

There was a polite knock at the door to the sheriff's office, followed by its immediate swift opening. Two men strode in. Idaho Jones thought that one had the look of a medical student—a bearded young intellectual. The other had the hard as nails toughness you might expect to see in the leader of a naval press gang. Both were wearing long blue coats, and beneath them what could almost have been a foreign military uniform with rank and insignia removed.

"Sheriff Ashermann?" commenced the young bearded man. "Perhaps you can assist us. My name is Robur."

And with that, Robur removed a hand from inside his coat pocket which held an unusual—at least for this time period—looking revolver, and then struck Ashermann across the face with it. As Ashermann's legs buckled, he hit him again on the back of the head on the way to the floor.

"Restrict your movements, Mr. Jones," ordered Turner. A heavy revolver had appeared in his hand too. "My name is Turner and Captain Robur and I are, or rather were, associates of Deputy Sheriff Frycollin."

Idaho Jones shot a look down at the unconscious form of Ashermann, who was bleeding badly from a gashed scalp, and thought the better of suggesting that first aid be administered.

"You know the sheriff handed Frycollin over to that clan of white-robed murderers who lynched him even though he was under arrest—a good portion of the townspeople saw it happen—in fact, they've scarcely shut up about it," explained Robur.

"I assumed as much," admitted Idaho Jones. "I had the measure of him from the get-go. In fact, the measure of this whole town, and how the rottenness in it links to some new version of the 1752 Conspiracy."

"There you have the advantage over us," said Robur.

"No less, I am sure, than you have over me, Captain. I am puzzled as to which branch of the military you serve... or even which country's..." said Idaho Jones.

"Like a lot of the best titles, it is an honorary one, and it was bestowed upon me by those who sincerely welcome my guidance and leadership," said Robur.

"The solution to all of this lies with questioning Kitty McKenzie, currently at Widow Foy's house on Pine Street. Why did she identify Frycollin as the murderer of her father? I have a terrible feeling that I already know the answer, but we need to get over there to find out," said the detective.

There was the sudden sound of a man clearing his throat, rather over loudly, in order to gain the attention of the room.

"Gentlemen, forgive the interruption. My name is Gideon Spilitt, and I am a reporter for the *Potomac Clarion*. During the war, I was a Union Army correspondent. I can only assure you that my interests are those of Justice and aligned with yours. I would happily throw in my lot with you as an ally and take any reasonable orders. Look into my eyes, my face, if you see any attempt at deception there then leave me right here in this cell. I am held here falsely under a charge of being an agent provocateur carpetbagger."

Robur looked the man up and down.

"I am a fair judge of character and you seem honest enough to me. I hereby accept you into my crew."

The Widow Foy was by now accustomed to admitting the succession of gentlemen callers and well-wishers who pledged themselves to protect the beauteous Kitty McKenzie. She led Spilitt, Robur and Turner into the parlor, with Idaho Jones lagging behind somewhat in the rear.

"Would you gentlemen all like tea?" asked the Widow Foy.

"Only if I may assist you with the preparations in the kitchen," offered Spilitt gallantly.

Idaho Jones nodded knowingly as Spilitt exited with the old woman and Kitty McKenzie looked up from the improving book she was reading. For a split second, Kitty McKenzie reddened with a deep blush and then almost simultaneously all of the color drained out of her face.

"Hello, Trina," said Idaho Jones, his right hand resting on the pistol grip of his six-shooter.

She composed herself, and then seemed to take on an attitude of quiet resignation.

"Idaho Jones, I always thought you'd come walking back into my life... something made it inevitable."

"With the careless clues you left in that hotel in the town of Morgue, California it *was* inevitable. Almost like you wanted to be caught," said the detective.

"I only went to that town because its name amused me... a dead woman hiding in a town called Morgue, and not much of a town at that... I've a feeling it'll be a ghost town before too long; a home from home for those of us involved in the Raiders of Ghost City Affair."

"Where is Alex Morel, alias von Rugen?" asked Idaho Jones quietly.

"Oh, bearing in mind the identity I've assumed, I'm sure a detective with all your cleverness can deduce his fate," she smiled.

"Your so-called 'father.' And you murdered him to free yourself from the 1752 Conspiracy. Playing on the prejudices of this place you would have blamed some imaginary phantom ex-slave assailant—but you couldn't believe your luck when you discovered Deputy Sheriff Frycollin—here on a clandestine mission of his own, which I do not fully understand—hiding out in your barn; a scapegoat as perfect as he was doomed,"

"Of course! I cannot spend decades of my life here sowing discord between black and white, organizing those ridiculous and hateful men in white robes as the puppet masters of this conspiracy intend as part of an attempt to reframe the whole of American politics. And all in the hope that an enlarged Prussian state can seize control of the entire globe during some theoretical war involving practically every country in the world."

"Until today, I had no inkling as to the existence of the conspiracy you both describe," began Robur. "But I had already decided to dedicate my life to pre-empting the possibility of World Wars and the re-emergence of the institution of slavery in the United States by corrupt and foreign-influenced politicians in the aftermath of such wars. I am afraid you will both have to endure a sustained period of debriefing aboard my ship until I have learned all I can from you."

"Well, that is a better offer than I was expecting, and I have always enjoyed a cruise," said Trina Dressard, cheerfully.

At that moment, Spilitt entered the room with a large mahogany tea tray which groaned under the weight of teapot, crockery and multiple home baked cakes. After he had set it down on the table, the Widow Foy clucked around distributing strong sweet Darjeeling and pressing the guests to large slices of cakes whether they wanted them or not.

"I heard from that nice Mr. Widlake—the town photographer—that the Ku Klux riders are going to hold a recruitment picnic outside of town up on Tar Brush Hill tonight. You know, the more members they can drum up and get into the white robes, the safer I'll feel and the more the blacks can be kept in order," said the Widow Foy. "He said they were going to set a huge burning cross, so it can be seen from miles around."

"And perhaps even seen by the Almighty high in the Heavens," smiled Robur, an idea already forming in his mind.

"I don't doubt it, young man," agreed the Widow Foy.

And so, a little later they made their excuses and told the old woman that Kitty McKenzie had a hankering for a horse ride in order to get some fresh air. There were enough horses in the Sheriff's office stable if they doubled up. Robur explained that before departing in his ship—which, of course, he had not revealed to be an airship—they would need to briefly visit his headquarters atop the Great Eyrie.

Idaho Jones rode his own horse, Gambler, with Trina Dressard held tightly in front of him, Spilitt rode with Turner behind, and Robur with the shrouded corpse of Frycollin. Robur led the way, and the miles of pine meadow track were swiftly eaten up.

Finally, they reached the Eyrie's rock-strewn slopes, and Idaho Jones was unhappy at abandoning his horse permanently when Robur broke the news that they would not be returning this way.

"If anything, the approach is too easy," said Robur. "We should blow up this pass to make it more difficult for others to follow and reach our base,"

"Airman Shanks is our best technician with explosives," said Turner. "I'll get him to see what he can do before we leave."

Upon entering the camp at the Great Eyrie, Idaho Jones and Trina Dressard were struck speechless by the sight of the *Venger* and were guided aboard like sleepwalkers.

"Captain Robur, I hope you will grant me the exclusive rights to the story of this unusual vessel," requested Spilitt.

"You have them, sir," granted Robur. "But for the time being you will have to be content writing about them for the ship's own internal bulletin for which you are sole reporter and editor, and founder."

"Orders, Captain?" requested Ellenshaw as Robur boarded.

"Take the lady to the brig and place her under twenty-four hour guard by crewmen least susceptible to feminine wiles. Mr. Spilitt and Mr. Jones may be taken on a short tour to conclude at the Control Deck in about fifteen minutes. More importantly, bring any essential items in from the camp and get the crew to action stations. We will make a bomb-run tonight and I want all tubes loaded with high yield incendiaries."

That night, above Tar Brush Hill, the *Venger* stayed hidden by low cloud and occasionally laid white smoke to camouflage its presence when the cloud became a little thin. Turner was at the helm. Idaho Jones and Spilitt by the map table. Robur busied himself looking through the powerful viewing lenses which had no difficulty piercing the thinner sections of cloud.

"That great burning wooden cross is a gift to our sighting mechanisms. The talkative Mr. Widlake has done us a great favor."

"A flying battleship that even the most feverish writer of penny-dreadfuls would hesitate to submit in a story... how did it ever come to be?" asked Idaho Jones.

"In good time... in good time... for now you must come and look through the sighting lenses at the so-called Ku Klux picnic below."

The image enhancing quality of the lenses produced a pinkish-red scene but they could make out the pale robes, the watching crowd and the rippling heat given off by the immense cross.

"Gentlemen, I am not a madman—though you will shortly think me one—I am not someone who revels in death and the sight of death. What I am about to do is not an act of revenge for my lost friend—the best of men—but an act of justice. I am cauterizing the gangrene which infects this land with the nearest thing to holy fire I have at my disposal," said Robur.

"Inevitably, there will be women and children down there in that crowd too... innocents," said Spilitt.

"Indeed?" queried Robur. "Women to breed more of these Ku Klux riders? Children to grow up and swell their numbers? I find myself filled with very little sympathy."

Robur removed the command speaking tube from its hook on the bulkhead.

"Mr. Ellenshaw, we are above the sighted target. Release all incendiaries from their tubes."

Through the lenses they saw wave after wave of cherry red fire engulf the robed figures and the thronging crowd—concentric droplets of liquid death, blossoming, spreading... joining up... like crimson ink on pink blotting paper. And even at this altitude they could hear the screaming.

With the last incendiary dropped, the *Venger* climbed away.

"What are you thinking, Mr. Jones?" asked Robur.

"I suppose I am thinking about Shiloh, and how the wounded and the dying crawled to a place they now call 'The Bloody Pool' in the middle of that peach orchard to slake their thirst. The pool was made red by the blood of both sides and their act of drinking from it. And it is the origin of the strange and menacing Ku Klux ritual of demanding black folk bring them water. What a pity then that some greater insight was not born in that moment, for it seems to me that all men bleed red and all are brothers."

TO BE CONTINUED

Propeller Island *(in French:* L'Île à hélice*) (1895), also published as* The Floating Island, The Pearl of the Pacific, *and* The Self-Propelled Island, *is one of Jules Verne's lesser-known works, yet one that has attracted the attention of two of our authors, John Peel and now Travis Hiltz, who have chosen to locate their tales on it.* Propeller Island *is a city on a massive ship in the Pacific Ocean, inhabited entirely by millionaires. Anecdotally, the dark social commentary of the original novel did not sit well with its publishers, and numerous alterations and cuts in the text were made. It is only in 2015 that an unabridged, correct English translation (by Marie-Thérèse Noiset) was published...*

Travis Hiltz: *The Floating Island Mystery*

Propeller Island, The South Pacific, 1895

The gentleman's lounge was tastefully ornate, yet comfortably furnished to accommodate its patrons: well-padded wingback chairs and sofas, polished oaken side tables within easy reach, the perfect size to hold a whiskey glass and a pipe. There was a low murmur about the room, as wealthy men of leisure partook in chess, billiards, or merely chatted over the latest financial news.

In a secluded corner, a middle-aged man, trim and well-groomed with an immaculate mustache, looked up from his newspaper, an expression of vague, puzzled annoyance on his face.

Phileas Fogg neatly refolded his paper, and, with a precise gesture, summoned over one of the white-coated waiters.

His top hat retrieved, Fogg exited the lounge and stepped out into the sunny afternoon.

Propeller Island was a large, artificial construct, a masterpiece of electrical systems, steam engineering and ostentatious comfort. It was the creation of some of America's wealthiest Captains of industry, brilliant engineers and machine smiths from all across the globe, brought together by an entrepreneur of Barnum-like skills.

Fogg stood on the edge of the broad main avenue. He peered briefly upwards. Seeing no answers in the clear, blue sky, he then consulted his pocket watch.

As this was happening, a shorter, slightly rumpled man came hurrying down the metallic sidewalk.

Monsieur Fogg!" he stammered, anxiously. "I do apologize for being late!"

"You are not late, Passepartout," Fogg replied absently. "You are quite punctual."

"You left early?" his valet mumbled, his tone implying this was an event as baffling and momentous as if Fogg had said he was going to fly to the Moon. "Are you feeling well?"

"No," Fogg frowned. "Something is wrong...?" He peered upwards, squinting into the sunny sky. "We are off course."

"We are?" Passepartout asked, looking about, anxiously.

He took in their surroundings. The Fogg household was part of the celebrity passenger group partaking on the maiden voyage of Propeller Island Mark 2. Like its predecessor, the enormous man-made island was capable of navigating across the Pacific, like a ship.

It was a quaint resort, an automated utopia, a fashionable modern city that just happened to float. The houses, business and places of leisure that lined both sides of the wide main avenue were all stylish in design, with pristine paint and shining brass trim.

Down the center of the street was a metal strip that allowed an electrically powered streetcar to transverse the island.

At the center of the island, if it weren't for the scent of the ocean on the breeze, one could easily believe one was in some well-to-do neighborhood in a modern city. Besides the streetcar, there were also ornate horseless carriages, both electric and steam powered and the occasional bicycle.

Master and servant stood by a brass streetlamp, as a parade of well-dressed passengers and crew strolled by. Passepartout looked upon his employer with visible concern, while Fogg was as stoic and self-contained as it was humanly possible for an Englishman to be.

He stood, statue-still, oblivious to his valet's nervous fidgeting.

"We need to discover the source of this deviation," Fogg said, calmly scanning the meandering crowd. "Ah, there!"

He inclined his head slightly, before stepping off the curb.

The gentleman he approached was a middle-aged hunchback dressed in grey. He walked along with an uneven gait, barely aware of his surroundings, as he was intently studying a scribble-filled notebook.

"Professor Brainerd," Fogg said, his brisk, precise steps coming into sync with the savants' more uneven motion. "May I have a word?"

The hunchback glanced up from his notes and pushed a stray lock of scraggly black hair out of his face in order to look up at the gentleman.

"I do not wish to appear rude, but I am quite busy," Brainerd replied, brusquely.

"Dealing with the island's unplanned course change?" Fogg asked, with quiet intent.

"What? How could you know that?" Brainerd sputtered, stumbling to a halt.

"I have a very precise mind," Fogg replied, conversationally. "Have you discovered the cause?"

"No," the savant muttered, bitterly. "It has been... This may not be the best place to discuss such matters. Would you care to join me?"

He gestured to the other side of the avenue, towards a most striking conveyance. It had the structure of humble dogcart, but one fashioned from polished metal. Instead of a horse, it was harnessed to a seven-foot-tall metal man who was designed to appear to be wearing a suit, including a top hat. His eyes were polished glass, his nose pointed, like the spout of a funnel, and he even sported a stylish copper mustache.

Brainerd gestured for the two travelers to take a seat. He then pulled a lever on the metal man's right shoulder blade and, standing on the driver's bench, reached up and turned its ear, like a dial.

There was a rumbling from within the metal man and steam began to billow out from the top of its hat.

Brainerd awkwardly lowered himself onto the front bench, next to Fogg, while Passepartout settled in the back.

With a slight lurch, the steam man began to walk down the avenue. Brainerd kept the pace to a stroll, not wishing to startle the pedestrians around them, while he adjusted the pair of control levers.

"If I may," Fogg suggested, consulting his pocket watch. "I am due to meet my wife at the ladies' salon."

"Yes, yes," the hunchback savant nodded, absently, adjusting the steam man's course.

"So, what can you tell me about this odd deviation of the island?" Fogg then asked.

"There have been several occurrences, over the last three days" Brainerd said, not looking up from the oak and brass control panel for his carriage. "At first, they were dismissed. The currents can be tricky and there was that storm... Yet, a vague, but noticeable pattern could be discerned. The Commodore and his crew went to work upon the problem, believing it to be somewhere in the machinery. Your countryman, the noted engineer Banks, myself and another fellow... Elk, I believe his name was, offered our services, but so far have been unsuccessful."

"Do you believe these course deviations are caused by the elements?" Fogg asked, "or by some damage to the island's engines or navigation system?"

Brainerd fidgeted for several moments, adjusting the carriage's controls, obviously pondering how to answer.

"The weather, despite man's efforts, can never be fully controlled," the savant finally replied, his gaze focused on the dials and gauges. "And though I had no hand in its design or construction, I have found no fault in the machinery that propels the island on its way through the Pacific."

"Am I understanding your implication?" Fogg asked, mildly.

"That someone is sabotaging the engine?" Passepartout blurted out from the back seat of the carriage, his tone a mix of anxious excitement.

Fogg cast a disapproving glance back at his valet and then returned his attention to the Professor.

"Not quite how I would have worded it," he said, "but the question must be asked. Do you believe there is someone behind these course deviations?"

"I have no definitive proof," Brainerd muttered, "but the instances are too... not precise per se, but there seems to be a vague pattern to them, and we can find no evidence of damage or mismanagement in either the engines or the navigation... I hate to think it, but there must be some human agent at work here."

Fogg merely nodded, his gaze distant and thoughtful.

"I thank you for allowing us to experience this most unique mode of transportation," he said, "but here is the ladies' salon. We must disembark."

Brainerd seemed taken aback by the abrupt shift in the conversation, as well as his passengers' matter-of-fact tone.

Fogg stepped down, while his valet scrambled to follow him. The Englishman paused and tipped his top hat.

"I look forward to discussing these matters with you further, Professor."

He then turned and walked away, followed by Passepartout, who patted the steam man as he passed. He quickly drew back his hand, as the metal man could grow quite warm when in motion. Blowing on his fingers, the Frenchman caught up to his employer.

Fogg had been joined by a slim woman whose coffee-colored skin, ebony eyes and hair, as well as her style of dress pointed to her origins being somewhere in India.

"My apologies, my husband," she said, demurely. "I did not realize I was running late..."

"No, no, Aouda," Fogg interrupted mildly. "I was a bit early."

She glanced at her husband with the same mix of surprise and concern as Passepartout. She looked past him to the French valet, who nodded in confirmation.

"Come along," Fogg said, offering his arm to his wife. "There have been enough disruptions for one day and I am not willing to suffer lukewarm soup."

After a quiet, orderly dinner had been consumed, the table cleared, and coffee, tea and desert served, Phileas Fogg discussed his afternoon with his wife. She listened intently, aware that any event that could cause her husband to disrupt his scheduled routine must be a serious thing indeed, and worthy of her full attention.

She cupped her hands around her teacup and took a sip. "What do you intend to do?" she then asked.

Fogg merely raised a questioning eyebrow in reply.

"I know you, my husband," she continued. "You will be unable to sit by and let someone else deal with such a distraction. What are your plans?"

Fogg gave her question several moments of thought before answering. "In my discussion with Professor Brainerd," he said, "he outlined three distinct categories: unusual weather, mechanical error, and human action. I wish to investigate each, but I am aware there are... gaps in my knowledge: I have no expertise in meteorology or engineering... Why are you smiling?"

"Because that leaves, investigating the community of Propeller Island, and while you have many fine qualities, navigating social interactions are not one of them," his wife explained, with quiet affection.

Fogg raised a chiding eyebrow at his spouse, but in the end conceded her point and merely nodded.

He stirred his coffee while he further pondered where to take his investigation.

"If I may make a suggestion?" his wife continued, demurely.

"Of course."

"Now, while I'm sure that in the gentlemen's salon, you are dedicated to quiet, intellectual pursuits," Aouda said, "in the ladies' salon, it is a much more frivolous, social environment, and there can be, amongst some of the other wives, a penchant towards gossip..."

"Of which, I am sure my own wife is too refined and modest to take part in," Fogg commented, with a dry amused tone of his own.

"Of course," Aouda said. "But your wife does have ears..."

"Which I have always admired." Fogg said. "One of her finest features."

She gave her husband a brief smile before continuing. "If there are secrets amongst the residents," Aouda continued, "these, most attentive and well informed, ladies will have heard something which could point you in the right direction."

"Would it be inappropriate to ask my wife for an introduction?" Fogg asked. "Or should we arrange an event, and gather the gossip circle to us?"

Aouda stirred in her chair thoughtfully, before looking up at her husband with a small, triumphant smile.

"I believe I know just the person you should talk to," she finally said. "If you would be so kind as to further disrupt your schedule and join me for tea tomorrow...?"

The following day saw no further disruptions to Propeller Island's journey through the Pacific, but there was a low buzz of anxiety amongst its passengers.

Those that had been aboard on the previous island's ill-fated final voyage had no great urge to see its replacement repeat it, and newcomers, who had already been concerned over this unique mode of transportation, stuck close to the areas near the lifeboat stations.

The Island's staff and newspaper did all they could to alleviate such worries, but they themselves were concerned with the mystery and its possible reoccurrence. The country holiday feeling of the Island had faded a touch, and there was now a subdued air of worried expectation.

With the Island back on course, Phileas Fogg's inner equilibrium had returned, and he was, in his own stoic, self-contained way, content to resume his schedule.

Following breakfast, he went, followed by Passepartout, on his morning stroll.

He paused in the park to chat with the noted oceanographer, Professor Aronnax, who confirmed that it was quite unlikely that natural conditions could have been the cause of the mysterious course change.

Upon arriving at the gentlemen's salon, he took a moment to inform his Whist group that he would be unable to attend.

He then settled in his usual corner chair with his preferred brand of cigar, a cup of tea, and a selection of newspapers and books, combining his scheduled reading time with his investigation.

A quiet luncheon was spent with several notable gentlemen with seafaring experience.

Robert Curtis, who had served on the ill-fated voyage of the *Chancellor*, made several observations that were helpful in shaping Fogg's ideas.

He had theories about what might be behind the interference but had little notion of how to conduct such an investigation. His wife was quite correct, in that he had spent most of his life contentedly self-contained and felt a bit at a loss on how to navigate polite society.

Wrapped up in thought, he soon reached the café located by the ladies' salon. He sent Passepartout on some errands, some mundane and a few connected to the mystery, before entering.

The white-jacketed headwaiter led him to a corner table. While it was off to the side, giving it an air of seclusion, it was also by one of the café's large bay windows, allowing the patrons to be in full view of the outside populace.

His wife sat, with her back to the window, while their guest was seated at the perfect angle to both observe and be seen by café patrons and passing pedestrians.

Countess Louise Artoff *née* Charmet was a fashionable matron, presenting a thin veneer of respectability over the rumors of a scandalous past. Her fortune had been accumulated by surviving several rich husbands. People were attracted to her by her air of scandal and the occasional scattered hints of her history. Her *nom de plume* of "Baccarat" was a relic of that past.

She smiled warmly and offered a gloved hand. Fogg diligently bowed over it, gave his wife a brief smile and took a seat.

"Thank you for accepting our invitation, Countess," he said.

"Please, you may call me Baccarat", she lilted in reply. "All my friends do, and I include you and your charming wife in that list."

"Most kind," Fogg nodded.

116

"So, I understand you are investigating our little... detour," Baccarat said, waving over the serving girl to take their order. "Am I on the suspect list? That would be most flattering."

"Nothing so melodramatic," Fogg said, accepting a cup of tea. He added a precise squeeze of lemon, two sugars, and stirred it anti-clockwise sixteen times.

"Pity," the older woman mock pouted.

"Rather, I have been advised that you could be a great help in my inquirers," He continued. "My wife says you are an admirably well-informed woman."

"If by that she meant I am an unrepentant gossip, then your wife is correct—as well as lovely and sweetly diplomatic."

She paused to favor Aouda with a droll smile and take an appreciative sip of her tea.

"How can I be of assistance?" she finally asked.

"As you have stated, I am attempting, for my own reasons, to join in the investigation. My efforts are focused on the theory that some person is behind the disruption, but I find myself at a loss on how to go about this. Propeller Island has a population of several hundred and I am looking to narrow my focus."

In a subtle shift, Baccarat sat back, sipping her tea. Gone was the entertaining, frivolous hostess; a spark of the sharp mind of a fiercely independent woman, who had dabbled in crime and scandal, was now revealed.

"So, you are presupposing someone interfered with the steering of the Island," she mused thoughtfully. "And that person may have some nefarious purpose?"

"Others are investigating mechanical damage," Fogg explained, "but everyone I have spoken to is highly skeptical of such an event being purely the result of some kind of equipment failure. There has to be some human agent behind it. Professor Brainerd and Engineer Banks are looking into whether it was negligence on a crewman's part..."

"...While you are hunting for more sinister motives," Baccarat said, with a brief, sly smile. "Interesting. I can see the difficulty... So many suspects."

"Well, I would imagine that I could eliminate a great many of the families, as they are quite respectable..."

Fogg paused, as the older woman broke out in a sharp laugh and pulled a lace handkerchief out of her sleeve to dab at spilled tea on her sleeve and the linen tablecloth. Even Aouda drew a napkin to her lips to conceal a smile.

"What?" Fogg asked, glancing at the two women over the rim of his teacup.

"You are charming, Mister Fogg," Baccarat smiled, tucking her handkerchief away. "Truly. No family or individual have ever reached the level of wealth as the passengers of Propeller Island without some, er, questionable behavior in their pasts. To reach this stratum of society takes a certain ruthlessness, avarice, guile, and there are some prime examples of it strolling about the promenade at this very moment."

Aouda nodded in quiet agreement, while her husband glanced at them both in thoughtful puzzlement. Fogg was struggling with the concern that his precise, black-and-white view of the world, along with his solitary nature, was perhaps hindering his investigation.

"I see," he nodded, with a slight frown.

Aouda patted her husband's hand.

"I, myself, am too impulsive to be an effective investigator," Baccarat continued, reaching below the table for her handbag. She drew out a small booklet, a slightly tattered, old-fashioned dance card. There were names scribbled on it.

"Your charming wife informed me of the reason for this little gathering," she said, handing the dance card to Fogg. "So, I jotted down this list of suspects. It may give you some help in furthering your investigation."

Fogg put down his teacup and took up the list. His eyebrows rose as he read.

"These are some of the most prominent families on the Island," he muttered, his tone implying a mix of doubt and the dread of having to further mix socially with the rest of the population.

Knowing her husband's moods and thought process, Aouda gave his hand a brief, reassuring squeeze.

"I understand there are some exceptions," Baccarat said, helping herself to a delicate biscuit and dunking it in her tea. "The feud between the Tankerdon and the Coverley families has cooled, following the blessed nuptials of their children, but there are still the Le Brecs, the Belthams, the Waynes and the Wildmans... Or should that be Wildmen?"

"Why have you underlined several names?" Aouda asked, peering over at the list. "The Goldfingers, the Von Wartecks, the Reades and the Favraux?"

"I am no detective," Baccarat said, with a delicate shrug, "but, as the gossip washes about me, like the tide, they are names that have drawn my attention."

"Goldfinger," Fogg murmured. "Yes, he frequents the card room..."

"Disapproving of how he plays Whist is not evidence of a criminal inclination," Aouda said, with a smile.

Her husband's replying glance obviously disagreed.

"I wish to thank you, Countess," Fogg said, tucking away the list and getting to his feet. "I will now excuse myself."

"I will see you at dinner," Aouda said.

Fogg gave both women a polite nod and the merest of smiles, leaving them to continue their leisure time.

He made his way out to the promenade. Passepartout scrambled to fall into step behind his employer.

"What information have you gathered?" Fogg asked, not glancing behind him, as he was sure of his servants' actions.

Passepartout patted his coat pockets, fishing out a paper napkin and several scraps of paper. He consulted his makeshift notes while they strolled.

"I've heard many, amongst the crew and servants, talking about the storm, but there's nothing that implies it affected the ship's engines or navigation."

Fogg merely nodded.

"There has also been a ship spotted that seems to be following the Island," the Frenchman continued. "It's stayed fairly distant, but..."

He looked up, suddenly realized his employer had changed direction and was currently flagging down a passing electric tram. Passepartout hurried to catch up and joined Fogg just as the tram resumed its journey on the track that lined the street.

"Where are we going, sir?" he asked.

"The nearest observation deck," Fogg replied, serenely. "I would like to have a look at this elusive ship."

Passepartout nodded, feeling he was always attempting to catch up to Phileas Fogg, either physically or mentally. He sat, holding his notes, patiently waiting for his master's next instruction.

"What have you heard about the various families?" Fogg asked, quietly.

"Well, there is of course a great deal of gossip," Passepartout said, reluctantly. He shuffled his meager notes, as he attempted to find the best way to voice some of the servants' opinions concerning their masters. "The Tankerdons and the Coverlys are still seen as the... er... 'ruling families' of the Island," he said. "The younger Mr. and Mrs. Coverly are quite beloved, and their fathers' feud seems to have subsided, following their wedding, but there are a few scattered, less... beloved cousins on both sides. At least, three are on this voyage."

Fogg merely nodded, encouraging Passepartout to continue.

"The disreputable Tankerdon cousin has been seen in the company of the Favraux family... who are... well, are... um..."

"Yes, I am aware of the Favraux's reputation as businessmen." Fogg prompted helpfully.

Passepartout nodded, and then became aware the tram had halted and Fogg was exiting the metal vehicle. They then took the bronze cage elevator up to the observation deck.

Soon, master and valet were standing, hands on hats to secure them against the ocean breeze, observing the mysterious, distant, black ship.

"How long has it been following the Island?" Fogg asked.

"As far as I can find," Passepartout replied, "at least for the past week."

"I'll have to speak to the Commodore," Fogg said, thoughtfully. "If he'll allow me to consult the duty logs. But how could it influence the Island, from such a distance...?"

He frowned, pondering silently, then turned to leave.

"It is not that this puzzle is missing pieces," he muttered, as they returned to the street, "it is that there are a multitude of pieces."

Passepartout nodded in agreement.

"Should I make enquiries for appointments so that you may speak with the families on Countess Artoff's list?"

Fogg made the merest shake of his head to indicate 'no', and then perched upon the nearest metal bench.

"Monsieur Fogg, shall I hail a transport? You are due at the card room...?"

"No," was the reply. It was stated quietly and matter-of-factly, but had all the import of a pronouncement that the sky was falling. It was only the direst of situations that kept Phileas Fogg from a game of Whist, and now, he had done so voluntarily!

Passepartout sat next to his employer, unsure of what to do next. He felt as if the ground had been pulled out from under him, and his life was now in free-fall.

"Perhaps I could...?" he began, then halted. "If you would prefer..."

Fogg glanced up, favored his devoted servant with the briefest hint of a smile and stood up.

"I think I will stroll for a bit before dinner," he said. "Go and speak to the officer of the watch. See if you could have a look at the observation deck duty logs. Perhaps get a more precise idea how long that black ship has been with us."

"Yes, of course," Passepartout nodded, before heading back up to the observation deck.

Fogg walked along; hands clasped behind his back. He would occasionally give a passing acquaintance a brief nod.

"Pardon me?" a voice suddenly said. "Mister Phileas Fogg, isn't it?"

A man, dressed in tasteful black, his hat brim pulled low and sporting smoke-lensed glasses, joined Fogg, matching his stride.

"Yes?" Fogg said, with absent, stiff politeness.

"I do hate to intrude," the newcomer said, with a quick smile. "I understand you are involved in a project, and I am sure there have been numerous interruptions from curious and well-meaning members of the community..."

"I do not mean to seem brusque, Mister... Mister...?"

"Yes, of course, I'm being rude."

Without breaking stride, the man in black fished into his breast pocket and brought out a calling card.

"Mister Roberts," Fogg continued, glancing from the card to his new acquaintance. "Please excuse me, but I am not inclined towards social conversation, at the moment."

"I well understand and sympathize," Roberts replied, with a thoughtful nod. "You must be swarmed with the curious and the bored. I am, I hope, neither. I was hoping I could be of assistance."

"I was not aware there were any detectives amongst the other passengers," Fogg said, with forced patience. "Perhaps we could speak another time...?"

"No, no, you misunderstand," Roberts chuckled. "I do not picture myself as a Dupin. As my card says, I deal in nautical trade and salvage, but I feel I can be of some small assistance. I noticed you on the observation deck. You and your valet were expressing an interest in the ship that has been following Propeller Island."

"Yes," said Fogg, casting a more serious glance at Roberts.

"Well, this a bit of a delicate matter," Roberts said, adjusting his dark glasses and then thoughtfully stroking his thin mustache, "but that ship belongs to me."

"Does it now?" Fogg said, keeping his tone casual, while he studied his walking partner.

"Yes," Roberts nodded. "You see, I have lived and worked most of my life at sea. I come from a long line of sea-faring men, but it is time to see about closing that chapter of my life. I have aspirations to settle here, on Propeller Island."

"Do you?" Fogg asked, with a more inquiring eye to his new acquaintance. Roberts' clothes were well-tailored, but sedate. Seen with actual scrutiny, the man gave every impression of wealth, while at the same time appearing discreet to the point that Fogg wondered what the other man was concealing.

"Yes, yes, I do," Roberts replied with a nod and a smile. "A man needs at some point to step away from his... chosen advocation, let younger men blaze their path. I know little of your profession, Mister Fogg, but there comes a time where a man feels he's worked enough, earned enough, and just wishes to experience the years he has left. I no longer have any need for the sea to be my mistress, but I will never wish to be away from her. This island presents the perfect combination of my interests, but it is not without its little... controversies, shall we say?"

"Mister Roberts, I have no wish to appear rude, but you seem intent on dancing around some issue, and I do have a schedule to keep," Fogg said, an undercurrent of annoyance mixing with his curiosity. "Might I hope that we are within viewing distance of whatever point you are endeavoring to make?"

"Yes, of course, your pardon," Roberts said, with a faint chuckle. "In my business, discretion is prized, and a lifetime of habit has caused me to rarely approach things head on. I have high hopes for Propeller Island as my retirement sanctuary, but I do not have a trusting nature."

"So, are you telling me, you had one of your ships follow the Island... and that Propeller Island is the suspicious party in this story?" Fogg asked, as diplomatically as he could muster, given the information that had just been presented to him.

"I'm not the only one who has come here seeking a sanctuary, whilst also carrying a secret," Roberts shrugged. "I'm just a bit more honest about it."

"Honest about being up to something?" Fogg said, eyebrows raised.

He paused, and then waited, hands in pockets, while Roberts took a few more steps, came to a halt, and then turned to face Fogg.

"In fact, I am undecided, as to whether you are mentally addled, a complete charlatan, or sincere in your supposed efforts to be of assistance." Fogg added, thoughtfully.

"Couldn't I be all three?" Roberts replied, airily. "I am a deft hand at organization."

The two men stood, to all appearances casually appraising each other, Phileas Fogg stoic and calm, Roberts slightly bemused.

"I know you have no reason to accept my word," Roberts said, finally breaking the silence, "but my efforts are sincere. I do hope to make Propeller Island my home and am willing to devote my skills to keeping the peace, whether the threats are from within or without. My ship is not a clue, it is merely a distraction."

Fogg nodded briefly to himself, and continued his stroll, indicating that the mysterious nautical adventurer should join him.

"So, tell me, what or who do you think is behind these odd course deviations?" Fogg asked.

"I wish I could be more helpful, past telling you what it is not," Roberts conceded, "but I will say, my own discreet inquiries have focused on if there is a 'who' involved, how are they financing this odd endeavor."

"How so?" Fogg asked.

"How did your culprit acquire a ticket?" Roberts mused, as they continued their stroll. "They are as pricey and difficult to come by, more than if they were printed on gold leaves. It has long been my experience that most, in the well-moneyed class, are not makers or doers, but rather financers of projects, while most skilled artisans toil in obscure and less lavish surroundings."

Fogg nodded, as Roberts theory was a variation of that shared by Baccarat.

"I appreciate your candor," he said. "You have given me much to ponder. If you will excuse me now?"

"But of course," Roberts said, with a brief smile and tip of his hat.

He gave Fogg a finale questioning glance, then the man in black turned and strolled off, leaving the Englishman in a swirl of theories and clues.

"Ah, Monsieur Fogg!" Passepartout breathed, catching up with his employer. "There you are. If we are to meet Madame Fogg for dinner..."

"Passepartout," Fogg quietly interrupted, still looking at the retreating Roberts. "You are well informed, concerning the gossip about the population of the Island: what have heard about a man named Roberts?" He held out the business card to his curious valet.

Passepartout glanced over it intently. "D. P. Roberts, Nautical import, export and salvage... curious," He muttered, thoughtfully. "I am sorry to say, the name stirs nothing... There was once a pirate named Roberts...?"

Fogg contemplated that new tidbit, before shaking his head. His new acquaintance seemed to have some secret, but he hardly seemed the type to be a pirate. Too polite and he dressed like a solicitor.

"Come along," he said. "I have had enough deduction for one day."

Dinner was a quiet, subdued affair. Aouda, sensing her husband's malaise over his new career as a detective, kept the conversation to quiet, mundane matters, such as her own leisurely spent afternoon, the delicious, freshly caught seafood they were enjoying, her interest in attending a musical performance the following night, and various other bits of domestic trivia.

She took no offense concerning her husband's distracted mood and continued to both try to pleasantly distract him from his brooding, while allowing him quiet moments to think.

Fogg would nod along or contribute the occasional brief comment, equally aware of the motivation behind his wife's mood and attempting to show his appreciation for her efforts by occasionally participating in the chat.

In an uncharacteristic display of emotion, he reached across the table and gave her hand a brief squeeze.

"I appreciate your patience while I have discovered that I am ill-equipped for detection," he said. "I am, it seems, better suited to Whist and travel planning."

"My only judgement concerning your recent vocation," she replied tenderly, "is over how you would chastise yourself, if you felt you had failed. You have made a noble effort, Phileas, and a rare instance of participating in a community, and offering to help them, but your sharp, logical mind will sometimes be blunted against a wall of human emotion. Not all problems can be dealt with using logic. The scientific method cannot always succeed when applied to people."

Fogg nodded; his gaze slightly distant. Then his broad forehead furrowed.

"Will you be taking coffee here or on the patio?" Passepartout asked, before being shushed by a discreet gesture from the Princess.

Phileas Fogg eyes refocused, after several seconds, and his first act was to smile at his wife.

"My love, you never cease to amaze me!" he murmured.

"Why, thank you," she replied, with an uncertain smile. "Perhaps if I knew what I had done...?"

"Passepartout," Fogg then said, once again a being dedicated to logic, planning and solutions. "I shall take my coffee in my study. I will then need you to deliver several notes and I will require you to wait for their replies. If you will pardon me, my dear"

There was a quick dab with a cloth napkin, and then Fogg was on his feet. He absently gave Aouda a quick kiss on the forehead and strode away.

"I hope you will forgive me, but I fear, I will be occupied for the remainder of the evening and may be absent from breakfast."

"I will be taking my coffee in the salon, Passepartout," Aouda said, in a bemused tone, giving a faint wave to her husbands' retreating back.

The following morning found Fogg, Professor Brainerd and the English engineer Banks, gathered around a table at one of the fashionable cafés.

The engineer was enjoying a hearty breakfast, while the other two men were satisfied with tea and coffee.

"Thank you for joining me," Fogg began. "I have the beginning of a theory, but it requires some of your expertise."

"Of course," the hunchbacked savant nodded. "Whatever we can do to solve this bothersome conundrum."

Banks nodded in agreement, as he had a mouthful of toast.

"I am working on the supposition, that these course divergences are not, in fact, the final conclusion of some plan or process, but rather the middle. We are experiencing the trial and era period of some nebulous experimentation."

Both of his breakfast companions paused in mid-sip, pondering Fogg's pronouncement.

"Yes," Brainerd said. "That would explain the seeming randomness of the course divergences... trial and error..."

He put down his teacup and steepled his fingers, while he thought.

"It also accounts for why we could find no damaged or sabotaged equipment," Banks nodded. "The Island's mechanics may not be the target!"

He fished in his coat pockets, taking out the stub of a pencil. Unable to find any paper, Banks merely pushed aside his plate and began scribbling on the white tablecloth, much to their waiter's consternation.

He soon had a crude diagram of the Island, with scribbled notes concerning when the incidents had occurred.

Fogg, equally put out by this behavior, pulled out his own pristine-looking notebook and several folded maps.

He spread out one of his maps, then consulted his notebook.

"Proceeding with my theory that we are in the midst of some clandestine experimentation," Fogg explained, using the salt and pepper shakers as markers on the map. He then borrowed Professor Brainerd's spoon as a pointer. "I consulted several charts and the Island's logs to build a list of what I felt was pertinent information."

He touched the spoon to the shakers and then two additional spots.

"These mark where the course deviations occurred," he explained to his rapt audience. He then laid down his open notebook. "I've jotted down the approximate date and times, as well."

"This... this is interesting..." Banks muttered, glancing from his own scribblings to Fogg's. "Those yellow areas are stretches of water with heavy mineral content. It's speculated there are deposits of valuable ores on the ocean floor."

"There is nothing on the Island capable of reaching that deep, is there?" Fogg asked, peering at his breakfast companions.

Banks looked up from studying the map and merely shook his head, before returning to peering in peevish puzzlement at the map.

"No, it can't be," Banks grumbled. "It has stymied many engineers..."

"Magnetism!" Brainard muttered, in sudden surprise.

"What?' Fogg asked.

"Magnetism," the hunchback repeated, glancing up at the other two, the thoughts coming together in his brain obvious on his face. "I and several others interested in automatons did some work together, sharing designs, experimenting with improvements... Anyway, one young fellow... Might have been one of the Reade or Swift boys... played around with using magnetism... both as a way to attach components on our various metal men, or aligned in such a way as to act as a method of propulsion.'

"Yes, but it was fairly impractical," Banks countered. "There was a fellow from the Baltimore Gun Club who suggested a similar method, but nothing really came of it."

"Yes, but I'm reminded of a theory that magnetism could be used to discover and possibly extract large mineral deposits from the ground," Brainerd countered. "And if someone on the Island is attempting a similar experiment, but focused 'on the ocean floor, it would fit the pattern we've experienced."

"I'm sorry," Fogg interrupted, perplexed. "You are suggesting that someone is using a magnet to drag iron ore up from the ocean floor? That sounds... Well, dubious, at best."

"Yes, well, that is to say..." Brainerd muttered.

"It has never worked," Banks added. "And the few instances I have heard of, or read about, ended disastrously."

"Are we in danger?" Fogg asked, concerned.

"No, I don't believe so... no," Brainerd said, shaking his head, while scribbling in his own notebook. "No, whatever they are using is obviously portable, so it couldn't possibly be strong enough."

"Isn't there a danger of large rocks being drawn up and striking the underside of the Island?" Fogg asked, anxiety and puzzlement warring in his expression.

"No," Brainerd continued, adapting a university instructor posture. "What I believe is happening is that... Whoever is behind this is testing their device, but it is not perfected, so rather than drawing ore samples to the surface, it would seem to be latching onto ore deposits and instead pulling the Island towards them."

"So, our mysterious savant is basically endangering Propeller Island with a highly inventive anchor?" Fogg asked, eyebrows raised.

"Succinctly put, but accurate," Brainerd nodded, resuming to his breakfast. He frowned, discovering his coffee was cold.

Fogg sat, back straight as a yardstick, slowly stirred his own tea, while he pondered. "Is there any way to predict or track these events, now that we, presumably, understand what's happening?"

Both of his companions frowned thoughtfully. Banks toyed with his breakfast utensils, buttering a triangle of toast, before absently setting it down.

"Possibly," he eventually shrugged. "It'll take time and I am now concerned we may not have it"

"Yes, "Brainerd nodded. "The cumulative effect on the machinery of the Island is worrisome. We've been looking for large disruptions or damage, but small, cumulative stresses could prove just as disastrous."

He took a final sip of coffee, brushed the toast crumbs off his hands and got to his feet.

"Let's see what we can do," he said, gesturing for Banks to join him. "If we can explain this to the Commodore, he can set out patrols on the Island, while we work with the scientific community for both assistance... and eliminating suspects."

Making plans as they walked, the duo left the café, without a backwards glance at Fogg.

The Englishman sighed and finished his tea. He'd been in the middle of this mystery and now seemed relegated to the audience, once a solution seemed close at hand.

While he appeared, passive and his expression listless and bland, Fogg's eminently logical and well-organized mind was racing. To an outside observer, he was leisurely finishing his morning repast, but internally, he was shifting through clues, theories, and whatever scraps of information had accumulated over the course of his investigation.

Passepartout came and hovered nearby, aware of his master's moods and methods, and waiting patiently, until he was informed if the daily schedule would resume or if there were to be any further disruptions.

Years spent in the service of the methodical Englishman had left Passepartout almost as ridged in his temperament as his employer.

Fogg signed his bill and, after Passepartout had fetched his top hat, gloves and walking stick, went out strolling the picturesque avenue, his valet a respectful couple paces behind.

He appeared to just be aimlessly strolling, his expression neutral, but his eyes were sharp, and he soon found what he was looking for.

After Passepartout caught up to Fogg, the Englishman perched upon a shining brass bench, eyes peering into the distance, back straight and hands clasped over the knob of his walking stick.

"Ah, Monsieur Fogg," the valet said, adjusting his cuffs and his hat. "This close to the edge the sea, breezes are quite strong. Nearly lost my hat, and then I had to assist a young mademoiselle who had stumbled... uh... Monsieur Fogg...?"

"Yes, yes, Passepartout," Fogg said, with a vague gesture. "If you have errands or chores to attend to, feel free to depart. I will be here until..." He paused to consult his pocket watch and do a bit of mental calculation. "Three hours should be sufficient...Let us say, 1:45."

He returned his watch to his waistcoat and resumed his statue-still posture.

"Ah, yes, well," Passepartout muttered, glancing around, unsure of what was occurring. He then looked in the same direction as his employer, hoping to spot what had caught the Englishman's keen attention.

All he saw were passing trams, numerous prosperous pedestrians, several patrolling members of the Island Guard, and a fair amount of fashionable young ladies.

The French valet tipped his hat to a pair of young ladies and took his place, standing dutifully behind the bench, prepared to wait patiently until he was needed.

Luckily, forty-five minutes later, just as Passepartout was shifting from foot to foot, Phileas Fogg cocked his head slightly to one side. He got smoothly to his feet and took several steps, until he was at the edge of the sidewalk.

He looked up at the sun and then glanced intently around at his quaint, stylish surroundings. He could once again feel it: the vague, nagging sense that something was off. The world was slightly out of position.

Fogg then looked down, at the tips of his shined to a mirror finish shoes. He tapped one foot on the packed earth and then, after a moment of thought, stepped off onto the metallic roadway.

Fogg taped his foot again, looking about, yet oblivious to the glances of the occupants of various carriages, rickshaws, bicycles and trolleys passing worryingly close to him.

"Um... Monsieur Fogg...?" a concerned Passepartout asked, gently hooking his arm through Fogg's and steering him back onto the footpath. "Are you feeling well? You shouldn't stare at the sun. You nearly stumbled into traffic!"

Fogg turned and peered intently at his servant.

"Yes, I think that may be it." Fogg nodded, then turned to face his valet, looking as though he'd just noticed his arrival. "Ah, Passepartout! Could you show me where you assisted the young lady who stumbled?"

"Uh, yes, I suppose so," the valet mumbled. "Do you wish to speak with her?"

"What? No," Fogg replied.

The walkway was hard packed earth. It ran alongside the metal plating that marked the edge of the Floating Island. The metal was slightly wider than the path, and it was up against the wall of the bowl-shaped, artificial island.

"It was about... um... let me see... here!"

"Yes, just as I'd hoped," Fogg said, kneeling down.

Set into the copper plate was a smaller, square hatch. It was not set snug: one corner was slightly askew—just enough to catch the dainty toe of a passing lady's shoe.

Fogg handed his cane and gloves to Passepartout and pried up the hatch.

Once it was opened, it revealed a narrow, iron, spiral staircase, leading down into the machinery and maintenance tunnels beneath the Island.

"Excuse me, sir," a young guardsman in an immaculate uniform said. He smartly touched the brim of his helmet. "Passengers are not permitted below."

"Yes, perfectly sound policy," Fogg replied, straightening up, "but I'm afraid a passenger has already broken that rule. If you would be so helpful as to alert the Commodore and Professor Brainard, my manservant and I will attempt to locate him before we go too far off course."

"How did you know we were off course? I only received the alert a moment ago!" the guard asked, losing some of his stoicism.

He jogged away, allowing Fogg and Passepartout to descend into the interior of the Island.

At the bottom of the staircase was a low-ceilinged metal tunnel. Fogg was forced to remove his top hat and leave it on the stairs.

The tunnel was lit by electric lights in wall sconces. The air was full of the hum of machinery. The duo strolled cautiously along.

"What are we looking for, Monsieur Fogg?"

"Someone, like us, who looks out of place, down here, in the workings of the Island," Fogg explained, looking around. "Or perhaps some piece of equipment...?"

"How are we going to find someone down here?" Passepartout asked, nervously. "It's a labyrinth of pipes and tunnels!"

"We are in the right area to search," Fogg said, as they made way their way through the tunnels. "That loose hatch is a good indicator that our quarry came this way. I assumed that, if he is using magnetism to attract ore, he'd want to be at a lower place in the structure. We should also be looking for any stairs or ladders leading further down."

Passepartout nodded, while still not fully understanding what was going on. He merely followed his employer.

They encountered several workers, rough characters in coveralls. They seemed confused to see members of the gentry wandering around amongst the machinery, but questioning well-dressed men of means was not amongst their job description. They merely nodded, tipped their caps and went about their tasks.

Fogg stopped, feet planted firmly, forehead furrowed in thought. His internal compass could feel the island drifting off course, but it was no help in locating a nefarious scientist.

Passepartout, having had time, while they wandered, to sort out what was occurring, pondered how he could help.

The next worker that crossed their path, gave him a bit of inspiration.

"Excuse me," he asked, approaching the grease-smeared young man. "My employer was supposed to meet a gentlemen and... well, it all looks alike, down here..."

"Ah, I wondered what that toff was doing down here," the worker muttered. "Yeah, take the next ladder down, then go left. Can't miss 'em."

"Thank you," Fogg moved to tip his hat and then remembered he'd had to remove it. He instead gave both the worker and Passepartout a nod of approval, before heading off.

The ladder was encased in a narrow tube of metal, and they found themselves in a relatively open area.

"Must be the ballast tanks," Fogg mused, taking in their surroundings.

Passepartout tapped one of the tanks. It made an echoing, sloshing sound, that startled him.

Fogg gave him a quick, disapproving glance, then resumed his search. He reached out to take hold of a pipe in the ceiling, as the Island rocked, and the lights flickered.

They turned a corner, went down another short tunnel, Fogg having to stoop, to keep his head from brushing the ceiling.

Another short tunnel and then another open area, except this one was already occupied.

His back was to Fogg, and his suit was dark, nondescript, and slightly threadbare, easy to mistake him for just another 'below decks' worker. He was intently fiddling with some boxy device, set on a tripod, resembling a camera, except the lens was a glass cone, veined with copper wires.

"There he is!" Passepartout breathed, excitedly.

"Yes," Fogg nodded. "Now, we need to proceed with..."

He paused, realizing his valet had only heard the "yes," as Passepartout rushed past him and tackled the mystery man.

The two tumbled to the floor, a mass of flailing limbs, one of which kicked out, striking one of the tripods' legs. The whole contraption wobbled, like a drunkard, and Propeller Island rocked violently.

Up above, chandeliers swayed, servants rushed to keep lavish knickknacks from tumbling off mantels and passengers who had voyaged on the original Floating Island felt a spike of icy dread.

Below decks, pipes and bulkheads creaked and groaned, lights flickered, and crewmen anxiously adjust the numerous levers and controls that kept the island buoyant and chugging steadily on its way.

Phileas Fogg rushed forward, dodging the two combatants, to steady the tripod. A wire had come loose and main box felt warm to the touch.

With a concerned frown, Fogg inched the tripod out of reach of the struggling duo. He then nudged them with the toe of his shoe.

"Gentlemen," he said. "Might we settle this in a slightly more dignified manner?"

Passepartout got to his feet, dragging his opponent up with him. He was an older man, his trimmed beard streaked with grey. He flailed about, but that was only to retrieve the prince-nez that dangled from a ribbon, attached to his lapel, and secured it to the bridge of his thin nose.

"I think you owe us an explanation, Professor...?" Fogg began.

"Doctor!" The other man said, peevishly, while he dusted off his suit, and eyed his battered device. "Studied hard to earn the title!"

"Where do I know you from?" Fogg asked.

"I know!" Passepartout exclaimed, releasing his grip on the rumpled scientist. "He was at the lecture I escorted Madame Fogg to. He was also amongst the workers when we toured the engine room. His name was... um... Doctor Musk!"

"Doctor Ox!"

"Apologies," Fogg said. "But I am afraid, your activities are disrupting the running of this vessel as well its passengers."

"Good!" Ox huffed. "The purpose of science is to push mankind further! To break boundaries... the limits we put upon ourselves and society. I will not apologize for the discomfort of some pampered tourists while I am attempting to expand the collective knowledge of mankind."

"I am sure the fact that there is money to be made by your device enters into it not at all," Fogg muttered. "I have not come to debate with you, Doctor. However pure and rational you believe your motivations to be, your little experiment is, at best, disruptive—and it must stop."

He patted the top of the wooden, contraption.

"Do not touch it!" Ox exclaimed, lunging forward. "It is a very delicate, precise!"

Passepartout, anxious and protective of his employer, overreacted to Ox's sudden movement and clouted the belligerent scientist on the side of the head.

Ox stumbled forward, and bumped against the tripod, before tumbling to the metal floor, dazed.

Fogg steadied the tripod, raising a concerned eyebrow when a glass tube lit up and there was a low whirring emanating from the box. The glass focusing cone grew warm.

The Island seemed to tilt and all around them, the pipes shook and groaned.

"Oh dear!" Passepartout muttered, stepping over the unconscious Ox to join Fogg in peering worryingly at the contraption.

"Um... Monsieur Fogg...?" he said, quietly. "What should we do?"

Fogg glanced up at the rattling pipes, then back down at the boxy device.

"No need to be panicking, Passepartout," Fogg chided gently. "Doctor Ox is not some conquering madman, but rather a practical, if single-minded, scientist. Let's see..."

He was studying the various dials, lights and switches, his fingers hovering over them.

Passepartout pushed back his hat, and patted at his anxious brow with a handkerchief, while he watched.

As this was going on, Professor Brainerd and several members of the Island guard and the work crew arrived.

"Fogg!" the hunchback scientist shouted. "Be careful!"

"Always," Fogg said, flicking a toggle switch.

The Island shook and Brainerd grabbed a wall pipe to keep his feet. A few of the guards stumbled and Passepartout clamped a hand onto his hat and put his other hand out to steady himself.

There was a faint grinding noise and a wisp of escaping smoke, then the Doctor's magnetic device went quiet, and their surroundings ceased trembling.

"I am no scientist," Fogg said, straightening up and adjusting his cuffs. "But I am technically minded enough to recognize an off switch."

They collected Doctor Ox and his device, placing both in separate, secure rooms. Most were unsure what consequences the scientist would be subjected to, as his experiments were not technically illegal. There was talk of just putting him ashore at the Island's next stop.

The extent of the damage was some broken crockery, frayed nerves, an escaped canary, and the postponement of the afternoon's musical recital due to the piano player stumbling and spraining his wrist.

Once the Island authorities had taken matters in hand, Fogg and Passepartout excused themselves.

As the guard escorted Doctor Ox and his device away, quite a crowd of curious onlookers had gathered. Gossip travels quickly amongst the leisure class.

Amongst the topics of discrete conversation was the presence of A.U. Goldfinger and his interest in Doctor Ox, who he was known to have shared several meetings with.

Of less interest, but of greater significance, was Goldfinger's' brief conversation with a man dressed all in black, who prefaced their chat, by offering his business card.

Even fewer people thought there was any connection between this chat and the Goldfinger family disembarking, deciding to cease sea voyaging and instead finance an expedition to South America, seeking out the lost city of El Dorado.

Later, the next afternoon, Fogg and Aouda were joined at afternoon tea by Professor Brainerd and Countess Artoff.

131

"It is a bit disappointing, to be honest," Brainerd mused, absently stirring his tea. "The principles of Ox's' device have great potential."

"Someone must have thought so," Baccarat added, tipping the contents of a dainty silver flask into her cup.

"What will happen to it?" Aouda asked.

"A great deal of study, most likely," Brainerd replied, glumly. "It overheated something fierce. The internal works are a mess and Ox carried no notes or written instructions in his luggage. Claims he's got it all memorized and won't speak a word about it."

"Well, at least things have settled down," Aouda said.

"Just when things were getting interesting." Baccarat frowned.

Fogg had a satisfied smile as he consulted his pocket watch.

"While this has been most diverting," he said, getting to his feet. "I am afraid I have a schedule to keep and lost time to make up for. Several days of newspapers to catch up on and my Whist partners must think I've fallen overboard. I will see you at dinner, my dear."

"Promptly." Aouda smiled back at him.

"Passepartout, my hat."

132

Rick Lai's jigsaw puzzle of a saga acquires a new piece that has a few recurring elements in common with past stories, such as the ever-malicious Josephine Balsamo and the Black Coats, but takes us across the ocean to Mexico, where we meet a new cast of characters borrowed from spaghetti westerns...

Rick Lai: *The Gunfighter in the Iron Mask*

Mexico, 1869

Alberto Ramirez was often characterized as an ugly man. Most people assumed that his depiction as an ugly man stemmed from the vivid scar on his forehead, but it really had been sparked by the ugliness of his soul. Following a bloodthirsty career as a bandit in the southwestern United States, Alberto had arrived in Mexico in 1862. Using two sacks of stolen Confederate gold, he had financed the creation of a small private army. Now known as General Ramirez, he had allied himself with Benito Juarez in opposing the French occupation of Mexico. The former bank robber had particularly distinguished himself during the liberation of Vera Cruz. When the French were finally expelled in 1867, Alberto was lauded as a heroic patriot.

Many falsely believed that he had purged the ugliness from his soul by supporting Juarez. In reality, he continued to behave like a bandit and ruthlessly confiscated the property of Mexicans accused of collaborating with the French. One of his acquisitions was a gold mine in the Mexican state of Sonora.

A Mexican geologist had once visited the mine. He had been startled to see the shackles on the arms and wrists of the laborers digging for gold. The geologist had protested to Alberto that slavery had been outlawed in Mexico since 1821, but the general had replied that these men were convicts sentenced to work in the mine by the local magistrate. When the geologist had demanded to see the magistrate, Alberto had revealed that he also held that office. The geologist had then accused him of abusing his powers. But charged with the crime of slander, the geologist was given a life sentence of hard labor in Alberto's mine.

One evening in 1869, two brown-haired Americans arrived in a covered wagon at the mine. Both were muscular men of similar height and build. Both wore belts with holstered six-shooters. The driver's hat and clothes were brown. The passenger seated was clothed entirely in black. In addition to his hat, shirt, pants and boots, his ensemble included a black vest and bandana. The most striking thing about him was the superbly carved wax mask that covered the entire lower portion of his face, from his nose to his chin. The mask was gray with the lips being painted dark red. It was attached to cords strung around the wearer's ears. A long slit in its mouth permitted the intake of food and drink.

The masked man's name was Barton Gordon, but he was known by a more infamous alias. Many American gunslingers would later take the name of Black Bart, but Gordon was the first to assume that *nom de guerre.*

Flanked by two armed bodyguards, Alberto approached the pair.

"It is a pleasure to see you again, Blackie," he said.

"This is my partner, Joe Sorenson," Barton replied.

"May I call you Brownie, Joe?" asked Alberto.

"Considering what you are paying us, you can call me anything you want."

"Before I pay anything, I must see the merchandise first."

The inside of the wagon was stacked with crates. Pulling out one of them with his masked partner's assistance, Sorenson opened it with a crowbar. A dozen rifles were revealed.

A deep grin spread over Alberto's face. "A hundred rifles in total. You must be hungry after your long trip. My men can unpack the rifles and load your gold. While that is being done, you shall be dining with me at the main office building. Follow me."

"When I came here last week to negotiate the price, you saw my real face as a precaution against someone impersonating me," mentioned Black Bart. "Do you want me to unmask again?"

"No, your knowledge of that meeting verifies your identity," answered Alberto.

As the general and the two Americans approached the entrance to the main building, two women on horseback arrived. After the duo had dismounted, Alberto's servants led the animals to the stables. Both women were in their mid-twenties. One was a blonde while the other was a redhead. The blonde was attired in a lavender frilled shirt, dark purple pants and black boots. The redhead wore a white blouse and a black necktie, together with a maroon vest, cummerbund and pants. Covered by black gauntlets, her hands griped a black riding crop. A black Cordobes hat as well as boots of the same hue completed her ensemble.

"Josephine!" exclaimed Black Bart. "This is quite a surprise!"

"A lucrative business opportunity compels my absence from my usual European haunts," stated the blonde.

"Is Jenny with you?" asked Barton

"No, Jenny had commitments which require her continued presence in France."

"Hey! I recognize you," said Sorenson. "You're Josephine Balsamo, also known as Countess Cagliostro. Two years ago, you met Arthur and Barton Gordon at Jenny Fancy's casino in Paris. There's a large photograph of you on Arthur's desk in El Paso. It shows you holding a baby."

"My daughter—born last year." The blonde placed her arm around the redhead's shoulders. "This is my friend, Lola Buckhurst."

"Any relation to Jack Buckhurst, the anarchist?" asked Sorenson.

"His wife," said the redhead.

"I've admired your husband ever since he opposed Lincoln's draft laws. I've read his books. They list a person called *La Zorra Roja* as co-author—the Red Fox."

"I am the woman behind that pseudonym. My brother gave me that nickname. While he was born with the dark hair of our father, I inherited my mother's fiery locks. My alias is almost a feminine version of *El Rojo*—the Red One—the sobriquet of Donald Joseph Sorenson, an outlaw far more handsome than his *Wanted* posters.'"

"Thank you, Lola," replied Sorenson.

"Surprisingly, a book review in a New Mexican newspaper criticized us both."

"I've read it. The article compared your incendiary writings to my guns. They both leave a string of bleeding corpses in their wake."

Alberto led his four guests into the dining room where his servants had already placed a hearty meal on the table. Throughout the meal, three servants with holstered revolvers acted as waiters. Their names were Escudo, Septiembre and Gitano. The trio had all fought alongside the general in the war against the French occupation.

Alberto sat at the head of table. Seated on the left side were Josephine and Lola, while Black Bart and Sonderson sat on the right. As the general and his guests dined, Josephine monopolized the conversation by bizarre tales about her great-grandfather, the legendary sorcerer known as Count Cagliostro.

What do you do for a living, Josephine?" asked Sorenson. "Surely you're not a sorceress?"

"I'm a Coalition Maker. I forge coalitions between widely disparate parties with a common political or financial interest.".

"Your great-grand-father was also a Coalition Maker as well," mentioned Sorenson. "He fashioned a coalition between Freemasons and Jacobins that spawned the Reign of Terror."

"I've talked far too long. '" decided Josephine. "We should discuss something else."

"Perhaps *La Zorra Roja* will tell us about her past?" suggested Alberto.

The redhead smiled. "I shall do so, but only if my male counterpart, *El Rojo*, first tells us about his own life."

"I'll accept your terms," replied Sorenson. "My brother Bill decided to move from Utah to New Mexico where he owned valuable gold deposits. In order to steal that land, four men murdered him, and his family, along with our father. A year ago, I tracked down those men and killed them all. It was clearly a justifiable homicide, but the unenlightened Federal Territory of New Mexico viewed me as a vicious murderer. So I appealed to my boyhood friend, Barton Gordon, for help."

"Joe and I had served together in the Confederate army," related Black Bart. "In fact, he saved my life. When the Yankees blew up a bridge, a piece of shrapnel slammed into my head. Examining my unconscious body, Joe realized that I would die without immediate medical attention. Since we were much closer to the Union lines, he decided to surrender. Carrying me on his shoulders and waving a flag of truce, he gave himself up to the Yanks. Alas, no good deed goes unpunished. Joe was confined in the POW camp at Batterville."

Alberto's eyes briefly flashed with rage. "Batterville! I remember that hellhole all too well. My experiences there are a tale for another day. Blackie, were you also interred at Batterville?"

"No. A Yankee doctor, Vincent Gallico, was able to save my life, but not my face. He devised the mask to hide my disfigurement. Members of my family fought on opposite sides of the War Between the States. My uncle was a colonel in the Union army. During my recovery, Gallico was able to contact him. Together, they appealed to Abraham Lincoln and convinced him that my disfigurement was punishment enough for supporting the South. A Presidential pardon allowed me to spend the remainder of the war at my uncle's estate in Nantucket.

"After the war, Joe and I worked together as guards at a casino in Redstone, New Mexico. When Joe became a fugitive, I was working as a bodyguard for a local banker. I quit that job when my father offered me a position at his munitions firm. One of my first acts there was to hire Joe to secretly work for Gordon Munitions."

"Due to the outstanding murder charges in Mexico, I am forced to work in the shadows," admitted Sorenson.

"Brownie has fulfilled his side of the bargain," announced Alberto. "It's your turn, Lola."

The redhead held her riding crop as she proceeded to relate her story.

"I was born in New Mexico in 1843. I was then a subject of the Republic of Mexico. Five years later, I came under the jurisdiction of the United States as a result of President Polk's war of conquest. My parents and nearly all my siblings died during that conflict. Of a family of eight children, only my eldest brother and I survived. I would have starved if not for him. He was 15 years older than I. In order to feed us, he had no choice but to become a bandit. However, as the General here has demonstrated, even a bandit can become respectable. At the start of the Civil War, my brother was universally revered as the founding father of a respectable mining town.

"Recognizing that the Confederacy would soon attack New Mexico, my brother hoped to keep me safe by sending me to a boarding school in New York. At a political rally advocating women's suffrage, I met Jack Buckhurst, the radical orator. We became passionate lovers, and our love eventually resulted in matrimony. In 1863, his public speeches sparked the New York anti-draft riots that left more than a thousand people dead. Incarcerated in the Tombs, my lover made a spectacular escape. Fleeing the United State, we took advantage of the lenient British asylum laws to settle in London. In 1864, we took part in the creation of the International Workingmen Association, an alliance of trade unionists from around the world. Unfortunately, an obscure German professor, Karl Marx, took over the organization. After publicly denouncing Jack as a common criminal, Marx had him expelled from the Association. Jack and I found refuge in Mexico with the hope that the recent defeat of the French colonizers would create an opportunity for a socialist paradise to flourish.

"We soon realized, however, that that paradise was devolving into a blazing inferno. Juarez has used his victory over Maximillian as an excuse to become a tyrant. The Mexican constitution is already being changed to allow him to run for re-election. Only an insurrection led by General Porfirio Diaz will prevent a corrupt dictatorship from controlling this country for decades to come."

"And our host, General Alberto Ramirez has abandoned Juarez to support Diaz," added Sorenson. "Hence his need to purchase rifles from Gordon Munitions."

"Bravo!" shouted Alberto. "Brownie, you have figured out the main reason for our gathering here tonight."

"But there is another reason," asserted Sorenson. "I read about Buckhurst's expulsion from the Association in the newspapers. Marx has accused him of being a secret operative for a notorious crime syndicate, the Black Coats. Buckhurst's goal was allegedly to gain control of the European labor union movement."

Josephine laughed. "The Black Coats don't exist. They are merely a modern fairy tale used to frighten children."

"Spoken like a true agent of the Black Coats," said Sorenson. "The time for pretense is over. For whatever reasons, the Black Coats support Diaz and supply him with guns, while demagogues like Buckhurst seek to smear Juarez's reputation. However, I sense a hidden agenda lurking behind this grand scheme. If at least half the stories that I heard about the Black Coats are true, then there is usually an extra ingredient to their plots—*Revenge.*"

Lola lovingly stroked her riding crop. "Quite true. We enjoy combining business with pleasure."

"Listen very carefully, Lola," advised Sorenson. "My right hand is holding a gun under the table—one pointed at you. If I fire, I'm unsure what part of your body will receive my bullet. Perhaps your stomach? Anatomical details aren't really necessary. Wherever it lands, your death will be extremely painful. I recognized your riding crop as a weapon created by Von Herder & Son, a German competitor of Gordon Munitions. It is a disguised air-gun that fires a single bullet. Unload it!"

Lola unscrewed the small metal handle on the top of the wooden riding crop, then turned it upside down. A bullet dropped on the table.

"Now that you've been disarmed, *La Zorra Roja*, let's clarify something," continued Sorenson. "The mining town which considers your brother as one of its founding father must be Goldhill, New Mexico. Four men were deemed to be its founders, but only two had black hair: Navarro and Ortega. Which one was your brother?"

"Ortega. I was born Lola Ortega."

"There's something you need to know, Joe," interrupted Black Bart. "I removed all the bullets from your gun before we arrived here."

Drawing his own gun, Black Bart pointed it at Sorenson. Alberto and his three servants had also drawn his own weapon.

"Brownie, there are five guns aimed at you," added Barton. "Don't do anything foolish."

"Black Bart only pretended to be surprised to see me here," revealed Josephine. "We planned this little ambush weeks ago. I requested that he trick you into coming here, and he was happy to oblige."

"Bart, is this how you repay me for saving your life?" asked Sorenson.

"That debt was repaid in 1866 when I saved you from being lynched by the L'Ollonais brothers of Redstone," replied Black Bart.

"Revenge is the glue that holds the Black Coat together," explained Josephine. "In exchange for absolute loyalty, our members are granted the power to settle old scores. Take the case of Jack Buckhurst, an effective rabble-rouser fluent in five languages—surely an asset highly valued by the High Council. His lover, another prized member of our society, seeks vengeance on her brother's killer. By punishing that individual, the Black Coats will satisfy the grievances of two of their most valuable agents."

"Yet, only one of the happy couple is here," stressed Sorenson. "Where's Jack?"

"My husband is leading an anti-Juarez rally near the border town of San Miguel. It couldn't be rescheduled because it had to coincide with the famous San Miguel Burning of Lucifer Festival."

"I imagine that the cute woman with the glasses will be attending the Festival with Jack?"

"Jacqueline, my personal secretary... How did you learn of her?"

"For years, she has appeared standing next to Jack in newspaper photos. By contrast, you always are absent. Jack clearly prefers her company to yours."

"A ridiculous conclusion. I could demolish your theory with a single sentence, but I won't waste my breath." Picking up the loose bullet from the table, she reloaded her air-gun.

"If you intend to shoot me, pull the trigger," calmly suggested Sorenson. "I'll be looking forward to our inevitable reunion in Hell."

"There is no Hell other the one we make on Earth," insisted Lola. "Why quickly terminate your existence with bullets when we could transform it into a living hell. You killed my brother in a gold mine. Therefore, Alberto has agreed with my suggestion that you shall become his slave and toil in his gold mine for the rest of your life. Our wise host has added one small provision to the terms of your imprisonment. It is an exercise in sublime cruelty. Louis XIV punished his twin brother by forcing him to wear an iron mask. The same fate awaits you."

Alberto signaled one of the three servants. "Escudo, get the mask!"

Holstering his revolver, the stocky man with the beard left the room.

"Brownie, understand that my usage of the mask is not meant to be an act of cruelty, but a necessary precaution," the general remarked. "Wanted posters bearing your likeness have been circulating widely throughout the United States. The bounty offered for you is very high. Unscrupulous bounty hunters have been known to help criminals escape imprisonment in order to turn them in again elsewhere for the bounty. I was even once victimized by such a bounty hunter. The mask prevents any bounty hunter from learning of your servitude in my gold mine."

"Does Arthur Gordon know about all this?" asked Sorenson.

Black Bart shook his head. "Pa doesn't even know that Josephine works for the Black Coats. Pa may have a ruthless streak, but he lacks my sense of pragmatism. Gordon Munitions was on the verge of bankruptcy. We desperately need the profits from smuggling weapons to the pro-Diaz forces. Pa has an old-fashioned sense of honor. He would never have saved his business by sacrificing the man who rescued his son from certain death."

"I see. And what do you intend to tell him when you return home without me?" questioned Sorenson,

"A lie that will partially resembles the truth," answered Black Bart. "You unexpectedly ran into Ortega's sister and she killed you."

"Your father won't believe it. When we were kids, he could always tell when you're lying."

"Pa never showed me any affection during my youth. I couldn't lie effectively because I always felt nervous around him. Everything changed after my disfigurement. He now views me as the war hero of the family. I am easily Pa's favorite of his five sons."

"But you're still a bad liar. Remember that little fairy tale Bart related about being bodyguard to an unnamed banker? That banker was Ortega! Here's the true story of Bart's role in Ortega's demise. Aware of my plans, Ortega had sought refuge in his gold mine. A dozen men guarded the entrance. Bart was the only person allowed to enter or leave the mine. Lending me his clothes and mask, he allowed me to impersonate him. Disguised as Bart, I walked past the guards into the mine, shot Ortega, and then left. Bart was my willing accomplice in Ortega's death."

"Liar!" shouted Black Bart.

"Don't move, Blackie!" commanded Alberto pointing his revolver at Black Bart. "Put your arms in the air. Stand up. Move away from the table."

Escudo, Alberto's servant then returned. He was carrying an iron mask shaped like a helmet in order to cover the wearer's entire head.

"Your arrival is fortuitous, Escudo," noted Alberto. "Place the helmet in front of me."

The servant deposited the iron mask on the dining room table.

"Now unbuckle Blackie's gun belt and bring it to me."

Taking the holstered gun from Escudo, Alberto placed it next to the iron mask.

"Ladies, we have a problem," said Alberto. "Either Blackie or Brownie is lying about the details of Ortega's death. If Blackie is lying, then he merits punishment. Does he not?"

"Yes," replied Lola. "Both you and the Black Coats promised me vengeance, and I expect that promise to be fulfilled."

"Both of you are being distracted from our primary objective," argued Josephine. "Revenge is a secondary goal. Our main objective is the establishment of a regular supply of arms to Diaz. Barton Gordon is an indispensable ally to maintain that supply line. Furthermore, there is no evidence to support Sorenson's account."

"Not true," countered Lola. "Gordon acted smug and arrogant when describing his resignation as a bodyguard. I had the distinct impression that he was secretly mocking at least one of his listeners."

"He was mocking Sorenson," asserted Josephine.

"No!" objected Lola. "He was mocking me! Why do we need Barton anyway? The High Council ordered you to seduce Arthur Gordon, the real power in the munitions firm. As the existence of your daughter proves, you were extremely successful. Since you control Arthur by sharing his bed, we don't need Barton."

Becoming increasingly frustrated, Josephine spoke in a slow and deliberate manner. "Arthur is a genius at manufacturing weapons, but totally incapable of creating a delivery system that will allow his products to be sold in large quantities. By contrast, his son is a master of logistics. That is why we need Barton. Regarding my daughter, she has no role to play in our deliberations. Never mention her again."

"You two lovely ladies appear to be at loggerheads. Therefore, I, Alberto Benedicto Pacifico Juan Maria Ramirez, must render judgment. Escudo, open the door to the Red Room."

The stocky servant had a large batch of keys attached to his belt. Using one of them, he opened a door to a room totally devoid of furniture Its walls, floor and ceiling were painted a lurid shade of red.

Alberto loudly unleashed a flood of commands. "Although the bullets were removed from your revolver, Brownie, you could still use it as a bludgeon. Unbuckle your gun belt slowly and toss it gently on the table. Good. Septiembre, escort Brownie into the Red Room. Gitano, do likewise with Blackie... *Bueno!*

Now that our two guests are in their proper positions, join me and Escudo outside. I choose the iron mask as the Instrument of Retribution."

Alberto tossed the mask into the room. It rested on the floor in front of the two men.

"Both of you must be confused by my actions," said Alberto. "Stand still. Don't speak. If you speak or move before the door is closed, my men shall shoot you. This is to be a duel. Once the door is closed and locked, you will fight to the death for fifteen minutes. When that time has expired, the door will be opened. If you are both alive, you will both be shot. If Blackie wins, he can leave with the gold. Remember: your opponent must be dead. Not unconscious, not dying, not incapacitated, but fully dead!"

With those final words, Alberto closed and locked the door

"This is madness!" protested Josephine.

"Is it?" challenged Lola. "Maybe you have a secret reason for protecting Barton. During dinner, I noticed him pulling out a chained locket that he wears under his shirt. He looked at it briefly. I could only get a quick glimpse of the photograph inside, however, there is no doubt in my mind that it was of you. It must nave ben fun seducing the son and the father. Perhaps Barton is the true father of your daughter."

Josephine brutally slapped Lola's face.

An enraged Lola attempted to aim the muzzle of her riding crop at Josephine, but the blonde seized the redhead's right wrist with both hands. Pushing Lola's arm downward, Josephine caused the air-gun's trigger to be pulled. The weapon's single bullet was discharged harmlessly into the floor. Maintaining her grip on her opponent's arm, Josephine whirled Lola around into one of the dining room's walls.

"Josephine!" shouted Alberto. "What are you doing?"

Josephine turned her head in order to stare grimly at Alberto. "This is a personal duel between two Black Coat members. Lola Buckhurst has become a liability. It's time *to cut the branch*."

"No!" snarled Lola. "Only the High Council can authorize my demise. The Black Coats need me to control Jack."

"Fool! Even before you met Jack, the Black Coats were already controlling him through his mistress—Jacqueline.

"Jacqueline is not his mistress! She is his sister!"

"She's both his mistress and his sister!"

"Only a filthy pig would peddle such falsehoods!" yelled Lola pulling a thin three-inch blade out of her cummerbund. Fitting neatly into the barrel of her air-gun, the blade had transformed her riding crop into a small sword. "If you're the pig, then I'm the butcher!"

Barely avoiding Lola's first thrust, Josephine felt a sharp pain in her left arm as the blade sliced open the skin of her left arm. A subsequent thrust by Lola created a corresponding cut on Josephine's right arm. Shifting her tactics, Lola pulled her right arm back and slashed diagonally forward with her blade. Josephine stepped back quickly in the hope of fully avoiding Lola's slashing assault, but the tip of the blade scrapped against the blonde's left shoulder. Josephine was now bleeding from three wounds. Delighted by this turn of events, Lola's lips formed a triumphant grin.

"My blade hungers for your blood, Josephine!" she shouted.

Lola launched a powerful thrust directly at her foe. Josephine nimbly avoided injury by moving sideways. However, the force of the thrust propelled Lola past her foe and exposed the redhead's back to an attack. Josephine swung her right fist brutally into Lola's spine.

Losing her balance, Lola fell backwards into Josephine's waiting arms. Standing behind her, Josephine grabbed each end of the riding crop. Yanking the crop out of Lola's right hand, she then harshly pressed the stick-like air-gun against the redhead's throat.

"You have a lovely neck, my dear," whispered Josephine into Lola's ear, "but the world has two types of people: those with pretty necks and those who break them."

Josephine made a slight giggle as she snapped Lola's neck. Releasing her hold, she allowed the body of her vanquished enemy to topple into the floor.

"*Madre de Dios!*" yelled Alberto. "How could you kill her?"

"We'll discuss Lola later!" shouted Josephine. "The Red Room? The time limit must have expired!"

"Escudo! Open the Red Room!"

The burly servant quickly followed Alberto's command. Standing inside the Red Room with folded arms was the unquestionable figure of Black Bart. still wearing his black hat.

"Gentlemen, I believe in being punctual. I don't have a pocket watch on me, but I judge you to be five minutes late. I am entitled to an explanation for your tardiness."

"You shall have one after I determine you are the winner," promised Alberto. "Escudo, keep your gun on Blackie while I examine the other man."

On the floor was the body of a man lying on his belly. The iron mask had been placed over his head, and then smashed constantly until the head itself had been crushed like a grape.

"Brownie is definitely dead!" announced Alberto. "Blackie is the winner! The iron mask is ruined, but luckily, we have spares!"

"You owe me an explanation for your tardiness, General."

"Blackie, my servants and I were distracted."

"Distracted? What is capable of distracting four men from listening to two men fight to the death?"

"Watching two women fight to the death."

The masked gunfighter rushed out of the Red Room.

"Josephine!" he exclaimed.

"Barton, I'm fine." Josephine was kneeling next to Lola's corpse. "Did you know that fox hunters in England cut off the tails of their dead prey and preserve them as trophies. Since I am now the slayer of a Red Fox, this is my trophy." She held up a mass of red hair cut from Lola's head with the air-gun's blade.

"Josephine, you're bleeding. You have to see a doctor!"

Alberto whispered an order to Escudo, who discreetly left the room.

"Blackie is correct," declared Alberto. "Let Gitano take you to your room while Septiembre summons a doctor."

"I will only leave after three matters have been settled," stated Josephine. "First, someone must *pay the law* for Lola's murder. In other words, we need a scapegoat for her death. *"*

"That will be easy," claimed Alberto. "Her body will be found with a noose around its neck hanging from a tree. Since she was a well-known critic of Benito Juarez, most will believe that he ordered her execution."

"Second," resumed Josephine, "a vile accusation was made about the parentage of my daughter. Barton, pull out the locket that you keep on a chain around your neck and show and show Alberto the picture inside."

"Blackie, I must commend you for your taste in women. Who is she?"

"Jenny Fancy. She runs the gambling establishment where Pa and Josephine first met."

"Another beautiful agent of the Black Coats, I presume?"

"No, Alberto," corrected Josephine. "Jenny is not a member of the Black Coats. She's a freelance courtesan."

"That's a polite way of saying she's a highly priced prostitute," added Black Bart. "While she only really cares for my money, she treats me like a human being rather than a freak. She'd probably the only woman who's seen my face since the war ended."

"Which brings us to one final issue," said Alberto pointing his gun directly at Black Bart. "As you can see, Escudo has returned with another iron mask. Brownie told us how he successfully impersonated Blackie in order to kill Ortega in the gold mine. Now a thought occurs to me. How do I know that the winner of the Red Room is really Blackie? Brownie could have killed Blackie and swapped clothes with him. As for the locket, the real Blackie could have showed it to Brownie. Certainly, Brownie knows who Jenny Fancy is because he mentioned her casino when he met Josephine. After swapping clothes, Brownie could have put the iron mask on the real Blackie and crush his head.

"So, the final act in our drama of revenge nears its conclusion. Who is the real winner of the Red Room duel? Blackie or Brownie? Does he get the gold or the iron mask? Of all the people here, only I have seen Blackie's true face, and it was not a pleasant sight. Thus, I demand that the winner of the Red Room remove his mask!"

The man professing to be Black Bart lowered his mask like it was a bandana. His nose and jaw were now fully exposed to everyone. After thirty seconds had passed, Alberto's voice broke the silence.

"Blackie, forgive me for doubting you. Your wagon has been fully loaded with the gold."

Full disclosure: an earlier and slightly different version of this story was originally published in my Prisoner *zine,* Rover *No. 5, in 1980—forty-two years ago—under the title "Encounter at night"...*

Jean-Marc Lofficier: *Foiled Again*

The Village, 1966

No. 6 was walking on the beach. Far behind him, the Village slept. Even those-who-never-slept, the Supervisors, did not care about his lone escapade into the night. Where could he go?

As he walked on the beach, his face was creased with deep thought-lines, thoughts of escape, of freedom...

Suddenly, he heard a clanking, groaning sound, one that broke through the slow whisper of the waves.

A shell-shaped silhouette cut against the dark horizon. There, in front of him, stood an anachronism, a thing that belonged to a world he had never known. It looked like a huge cannon shell, one that could have been fired by the legendary German *Big Bertha* of World War I; but that "shell" had portholes in it, and a door.

The door opened and an old man got out. He was dressed in old-fashioned, turn of the century clothes and wore shoulder-length white hair with a rebellious lock jutting out of his forehead.

"This is not Normandy," he said, looking around him with displeasure.

"Who are you?" asked No. 6.

"Me? I am usually known as Doctor Omega. May I enquire as to your own identity, sir?"

A few thoughts crossed in No. 6's paranoid mind: Who was this stranger? Could he trust him? Was he with *them*?

But somehow, something in the Doctor's sparkling eyes must have reached the Prisoner's soul, for the man known only as Number 6 smiled back, and not one of his canary-swallowing smiles that he kept for his captors.

He offered his hand in trust and began:

"I used to be called..."

"Wait!" the Doctor interrupted. "There is a. high energy concentration nearby. It is coming closer..."

Rover suddenly burst out of the sea and rolled towards them at great speed, roaring.

"Fascinating," whispered the Doctor, not in the least afraid of the Village's guardian.

"You know what that thing is?" No. 6 asked.

145

"Oh, yes. But I never met one before on this planet. I never dreamed that you Earthmen were so advanced..."

"Did you say 'planet?' 'Earthmen?'"

"This is all very interesting, my dear fellow, but your watery friend will do us a lot of harm if we don't go back to my ship at once. Come, follow me!"

No. 6 looked at Rover which was almost on them. He had seen what the thing could do before. But... to get into a cannon shell?

He stepped in, just as the Doctor was going to get out again to get him.

Inside the shell, much to his surprise, he found several small rooms and, up a metal ladder, a brightly lit control room with a console, two rows of two chairs, one large round porthole and two smaller ones on each side.

"Where am I?"

"In the *Cosmos*," the Doctor answered matter-of-factly, as if it explained everything. "And just in time, I see."

On the screen, No. 6 could see Rover trying to push against the metal ship—without any success.

"Fascinating," muttered the Doctor again. "Well, enough time lost as it is. Off we go!"

He pulled a lever, pushed a couple of buttons, and several lights started flashing on and off. The beach started fading from the portholes.

"Where do you want to go, my boy?" Doctor Omega asked the Prisoner.

"You mean, we have left the Village?"

"The Village? Oh, that place. Yes, of course. We are now, er, let me see, hmm, slightly off course again, but nothing too serious. You see, I have to go back to 1906 Normandy. It is a fairly urgent matter. I left my friend Monsieur Borel in charge of my house in my absence, and as is his wont, he touched something she shouldn't have and released a Horla..." Then, as an afterthought, he added: "The damn thing has been tormenting a poor man named Simon Cordier. I must do something for him before it's too late..."

No. 6 stopped the man who called himself "Doctor" (but was he really a man?) before he got totally lost in his train of thoughts.

"So you are a time traveler?"

"Well, yes, my boy, wasn't it obvious?"

"And we are going to, er, Normandy in 1906 in that machine of yours?" the Prisoner said, persistent.

"Yes, this 'machine,' as you put it, is extremely reliable."

Suddenly, the lights on the console started blinking. A blue streak appeared on the front porthole.

"What is this, hmm?... A time-leash! Incredible!"

The *Cosmos* slowed to a standstill, then started to shudder. Like a broken stretch band, a quick backward motion snowballed into a frenzied acceleration.

"What's happening, Doctor?" asked No. 6. "Is there something wrong?"

"It is a time-leash! Babelian technology! We're being dragged back through the aether to your Village."

"Can we do anything about it?"

The Doctor started punching out buttons. "Yes, yes, we can escape—but only by disrupting totally our space-time-coordinates," he replied in an irritated tone. "We shall plunge into another galaxy, another universe perhaps. It'll be quite a strain on the *Cosmos*, but I will not submit..."

A firm hand gripped the Doctor's arm as he was inputing the course changes.

"No, it's me they want. Not you. The Village wants its Prisoner back."

"But you *can* escape! Just let me fix the coordinates..."

"Could you return us to Earth? To London in 1966? Or Normandy in 1906?"

"In time, yes. I would have to fix the *Cosmos*, of course, but..."

"Then return me to the Village and go. You have better things to do."

"But you want to be free. I can give you the freedom of the stars. You can roam with me; we will see the wonders of the Universe..."

"No, Doctor, I want freedom, it is true, but I want it to be able to return and destroy the Village and all that it represents. Erase it from the face of the Earth. This is my duty, my sole responsibility, and I cannot be free from i—ever. No, Doctor, I cannot take your freedom."

The Doctor looked deep into the eyes of the Prisoner.

"I understand. So be it."

Then he turned towards the console again.

"Come on, Old Thing, quick!" he said flippantly.

But the look in his eyes was anything but flippant.

Randy Lofficier carries on with the new adventures of the Phantom Angel, a.k.a. the Sleeping Beauty of legend, who was awakened in modern times by Doc Ardan, and has since set up her own detective agency in Paris. In this latest tale, a prologue for more stories to come, our fearless heroine acquires a new partner, one which fans of 1960s & 70s British TV will remember fondly...

Randy Lofficier: *The Phantom Angel and The Wrong Wolf*

Paris, Today

My new, relatively unwanted, partner Marty Hopkirk and I had set out to solve our first case. Most of you know my story; I had been "asleep" for several hundred years after voluntarily undergoing a magical spell performed by my fairy godmother. I was awakened in the 1920s by the famous adventurer, Francis Ardan, a.k.a. Doc Ardan, and had been living in the modern world ever since, helping others who had moved on from the world of what you call "Fairy Tales," and whom were now coping with a society that was as foreign to many of them as life on Mars! I ran a detective agency of sorts, and now I seemed to be saddled with a ghost partner who lived in my antique lava lamp. This was strange, even for me!

While I had been digesting the arrival of Marty into my life, I'd gotten a call from my old friend, Red Riding Hood, telling me that she needed my help at her grandmother's penthouse on the Île Saint Louis in Paris's 4th arrondissement, a very expensive, exclusive neighborhood. I didn't live far away, not that anything in Paris is really far away from anything else. First time visitors are often surprised by how easy it is to walk from one place to another. So, I walked. Marty did whatever it is Marty does, even though it did look like walking to me. But maybe it was floating. I'm not really sure.

When we got to Red's gran's apartment, Red buzzed us in. There was a tiny elevator that two humans could take if they squeezed. I didn't want Marty to squeeze in with me, because touching him gave me a horrible feeling and I really wanted to avoid it if I could. So I made him go upstairs on his own.

Inside the apartment, Red was shaking like a leaf. We stood by the door to talk before I went inside myself.

"I got here maybe fifteen minutes ago," Red told me. "I rang the intercom downstairs, but Gran didn't answer. I rang a few of the neighbors until I found someone who let me into the building. I don't have my own key, because Gran doesn't really trust anyone to have one, even me. She's pretty old-fashioned that way. The door was cracked open, which was odd because of her paranoia. But I guess she was right, because when I came inside to look around, I found her in her bed, covered in blood!"

Red broke down in hysterical tears at that. I tried to comfort her, but that's not really what I do best. I decided that the best thing to do was to leave her and go look at Gran's body. I walked to the bedroom, being careful not to touch anything on the way. Marty was already there. It wasn't a pretty sight. Gran had been savaged by someone or something. I knew I was going to have to call in the cops, and soon. But I wanted to gather as much information as possible before I did that.

I didn't want Red to know about Marty. I figured she'd had enough of a shock for one day, and finding out I had a ghost helping me out was probably not going to improve her emotions. So I closed the door and tried to speak as quietly as possible.

"Is Gran here, too, Marty?" I asked.

The ghost thing was pretty new to me and I still didn't understand how it worked. I had no idea if everyone became a ghost or not.

Marty looked around a bit then said, "Nope. No other ghosts here but me."

"Why isn't she hanging around?"

"I guess she doesn't feel like she wants to. Maybe she doesn't want to talk to us. It could be that she's got something to hide, or maybe she hasn't realized she's a ghost yet, if she is one. We all adjust to it differently, and sometimes we just move on right away. No way to know for sure."

"I'm going to have to call the *flics* pretty soon if I don't want them to get suspicious when they do come. So let's take a look around and get what clues we can before I do that," I told him.

I looked around the bed and told Marty to look in the closet, in case there was anything weird in there. I noticed a surprising number of grey-brown hairs on the bed near Gran's body. I carefully took a couple of them and put them in a small plastic bag, making sure I didn't disturb anything and leaving a few more in place for the cops to find. Then I carefully got down on the floor and looked under the bed.

A pair of frightened, shiny, bright black eyes and a cute black button nose looked back out at me! I jumped! Then a surprisingly loud growl came out of the little creature attached to the eyes and nose.

"I won't hurt you, buddy," I said, as a small fuzzy dog crawled out from under the bed, continuing its growling. He sat down and stared behind me. Clearly, he wasn't convinced that I was telling the truth. Then I realized he was looking straight at Marty. I guess it's true what they say about animals having senses that humans don't, because it was obvious he had no trouble seeing my ghostly friend.

"Ah," I said. "That's just Marty. He's here to help and he won't hurt you either."

"He's pretty cute for a rat," my partner said with a lot of snark in his voice.

"No need to be insulting, Marty! He's had a shock. He's probably never met a ghost before either."

I heard a faint tapping on the door and went to open it. Red was on the other side.

"I see you've met the monster," said Red when she looked in the room. "His name's Thor, Dog of Thunder. Gran doted on him, although I don't know why. I hate the thing. I guess I'll have to take him to the shelter or something now."

Thor looked at her, narrowed his eyes and growled. Then he clearly decided I was a safer bet and came to stand by my side. He stood up on his back legs and waved his front paws in the air at me, clearly wanting me to pick him up. Which I did. I've always been a sucker for dogs.

"Don't do anything rash," I told Red. "He was under the bed, so maybe he saw what happened. He could be our only witness."

Red scoffed. "Fat lot of good that'll do you. It's not like he talks!"

Thor buried his little head in my shoulder, all the while glaring at Red from his safe perch in my arms. I wasn't completely convinced he couldn't talk if he really wanted to!

It was clear that our time was running out, I needed to make a decision fast.

"OK, Red," I said, "here's what we're going to do. I'm going to call a friend of mine in the police department. She's tough but fair. We've worked together before and she understands about our kind. I think if we get her assigned to the case she'll let me stay involved and she won't freak out about anything unusual that she comes across."

"I don't know, Rose," Red said with a bit of a tremble in her voice. "Can't we keep the police out of it? I mean, this is Enchanted business, after all."

There was something about her reaction that didn't sit right with me. If it had been my gran lying there, savaged, I'd want all the help I could get to bring her killer to justice. I decided I'd see what Marty thought when we were on our own. After all, he had years of detective experience behind him, too.

"You know I can't do that, Red. They're bound to find out and then we'll all be in trouble. I could lose my license and you could wind up in prison. No, we're going to do this the right way."

I realized I was still holding Thor. I put him down on the floor and noticed that when I did, he turned his head away from me so I couldn't see his face clearly. That was suspicious, too. Absentmindedly I patted the breast pocket of my leather jacket. I discovered the ID I always kept there was gone. Before the scoundrel could scamper away I grabbed him and saw that, yep, it was in his mouth. He looked really annoyed when I took it away.

"What a little thief this one is," I said to Red.

"Yeah. He's a real pest that way. One of the reasons I'm going to take him to the SPA as soon as I can. Unless you want him?"

I did *not* want a dog! I loved dogs, but my life was complicated enough. I already had a ghost; I didn't need a dog, too. Then, I looked at Thor's bright eyes. No way was I letting Red get rid of him, even if he couldn't help me solve Gran's murder.

"Yeah. OK, I'll take him," I sighed. I swear that dog smirked at me!

I sent Red into the front room while I made my phone call. Given her odd behavior, I didn't want to have her listen to my conversation, just in case. I called my friend, Captain Laure Berthaud at the Police Judiciaire. As I'd told Red, we had worked a case together before and I knew I could trust her with something as sensitive as this. The phone rang twice before Berthaud picked up.

"Berthaud," she said. Laure was never one to waste words.

"Captain, it's Madame L'Ange," Berthaud preferred to call me that rather than using the name that I was known by to the Enchanted.

"Oh, crap! What is it now? I know you're not calling about going out for a drink!"

"Good catch, Berthaud," I shot back. Our relationship was always a bit snarky. "I'm at a friend's on the Île St. Louis. She found her grandmother dead, and it's bad. And, Laure, there's something weird about the whole thing."

"Weird? With you, is there anything else? Text me the address and I'll get there as soon as I can. You know the drill; keep everything the way you found it." She cut the connection.

I looked at Marty. "Listen," I said, "the Captain is probably going to try to get me out of here for the first part of her investigation, so I'd like you to hang around and find out what's going on. The fact that no one else can see you is going to be a real benefit for me!"

"Hah! You see? I told you you'd find out it was great having a ghost hanging around!" he laughed

"I'm going to go downstairs to meet Berthaud so I can talk to her without Red hearing. Can you keep an eye on her and let me know if she does anything suspicious while I'm gone?"

"Sure thing, Partner," he answered. He looked pretty damned pleased with himself, now that I was letting him officially work the case with me. I rolled my eyes and walked out of the bedroom. While I was telling Red that Berthaud and her team were on their way, I noticed that Thor had gone over to where Red had thrown her signature hooded cloak and was sniffing around in his sneaky way. I couldn't believe she still wore that thing, to be honest. We didn't *have* to bring all our baggage with us into this modern world, after all! Still, it made her easy to spot in a crowd; not a bad thing for a detective on the job!

I took Thor with me when I went downstairs. When we got onto the street, he gave me a knowing look and spit out set of keys onto the sidewalk.

"You're definitely a little sneak," I told the dog, exasperated. But, to be fair, I wasn't really all that annoyed. I had a feeling those keys were going to be important to the investigation, so I picked them up. Thor wiggled his compact little body in happiness when I did. I guess he really had taken them for me.

151

Just then, Berthaud roared up in her little black car. It's a good thing she was a cop, because her driving would have gotten her arrested for sure otherwise!

She parked on the sidewalk (totally illegal!) and got out of the driver's side while her partner, Gilou, got out of the passenger side. I had the feeling they were more than work friends, if you get my drift, but that was none of my business.

"What's going on, Angel," Berthaud asked.

"Red Riding Hood's gran was attacked in her apartment. She's dead and she's a real mess. It looks like she was savaged by an animal. Red's the one who called me, but I don't like it. I've known her forever, and you know what I mean by that."

Berthaud made a face at that but kept her mouth shut.

"Anyway, she acted like she was cut up by it, but somehow, it doesn't ring true. For starters, she didn't want me to call you in, which is, as they say in America, *What we in the FBI call a clue*!

"Then, she talked a lot about how her gran didn't trust her enough to give her a key to the place, but I don't think that's true. Or at least, even if she wasn't given a key, I think she had one. I found these."

I handed her the keys, which were still slightly slimy. I didn't admit that Thor had been the one to find them. I figured it was better to keep his skill set to myself for the time being. Berthaud seemed a bit taken aback by the fact that they were wet though.

"And there's another thing, Laure," I continued. "There were a lot of animal hairs around the body and on the bed. But they didn't look like they were there because of her attacker, more like they'd been carefully put in place. I don't know. You'll have to see for yourself."

Berthaud pushed a bit of hair out of her eyes, something she tended to do when she was annoyed.

"OK, Angel," she said. "I know you want to get involved, and I can't let you in on this officially. But I can't stop you from looking around if you want to, as long as you don't mess up my investigation. And if there's anything *enchanty* going on, I'll probably come to you off the record, like last time.

"By the way," she continued, "what do you think those animal hairs are from?"

"Well, at a quick guess, I'd say wolf."

"Goddammit!" she yelled. "A wolf, on the Île St. Louis? That's all I need!"

She turned, nodded to Gilou to follow her and stomped off into the building.

I hung around outside, waiting for my ghost to show up. Which he did, about twenty minutes later.

"Your friend isn't easy," he said when he blinked into view. "I don't think she really wanted to be there, if you want my honest opinion. And that guy with her? He seemed to find the whole thing a bit upsetting."

"What was Red doing while she was there?"

"Definitely up to no good. First, she looks really guilty if you ask me. Second, she was clearly hunting around, looking for something. I don't know if she found it or not, because she got interrupted by the cops showing up. They took the rest of those hairs from the bed, but they were clearly interested in your friend, too. I think they're going to have her go in for questioning, but I don't think they're going to arrest her yet."

Just then, Red came out the front door. I was hidden in a corner where she couldn't see me. I decided to follow her.

She walked down the street to a café that looked like it was in serious need of gentrification and sat down at a table. A few minutes later, a tall person in a long coat and an old-fashioned hat sat down next to her. To a regular human, he probably looked like a kind of scruffy, middle-aged man who hadn't shaved in a long time. But that was because he was clearly under an enchanted "glamor," something that those of us who don't physically quite fit into modern society use to disguise our true selves. This guy was clearly a wolf in human clothing.

The two of them huddled together. I realized I knew the wolf. He went by the name of Monsieur Legrand-Méchant (or *Mr. Big Bad* in English), kind of stupid if you ask me, but then he wasn't the smartest pup in the litter. I wanted to hear what they were saying to each other, but I couldn't get so close that they'd see me, which meant I couldn't get close enough to hear their conversation. I looked around for Marty, but didn't see him. What good was having a ghost for a partner if he wasn't there when I needed him?

Finally, he showed up.

"Where the hell have you been?" I yelled.

"Sorry, partner," he said a bit sheepishly. "I thought I saw someone I knew from back in the day and went to check them out. But it turned out it was just some jerk who'd bought a 60s outfit from a charity shop. What do you need?"

"Go over to Red and the Wolf and find out what they're talking about," I told him.

He did as I asked, but clearly they were just about finished, because they got up from the table a few minutes later and went their separate ways. Red waited till he was out of sight, then made a call on her phone before heading back to Gran's.

Marty popped back over to me.

"So, what's going on between them?" I asked.

"I only heard the end, but the Wolf is really pissed at Red. He thinks she's set him up to take the fall for Gran. He reminded her they were supposed to split anything she found 50/50, but I don't know if she did find anything or what it is she's looking for."

"Damn. I'm going to have to keep following her until I know what's happening"

"We do know one thing," Marty said. "She made an appointment to meet someone tonight at 11 p.m., and she told him to keep it quiet. She also said something really odd; that she'd gotten rid of the dog and they didn't have to worry about him anymore Oh, and I've got the address!"

"OK, then. I know where we're going to be at 11 o'clock. And I think we'd better get some back up from Berthaud and company. I have the feeling we'll find out what's behind all this then."

I called Laure and set up the details. Then I took my ghost and my new dog back to my apartment, where the dog and I ate while the ghost watched. He looked kind of jealous about it, too. I suppose that was a downside of being non-corporeal, the real pleasures of life were denied you forever more.

After dinner, I dressed all in black, not that I wasn't usually in black anyway. It was a bit more of my rebellion after having been a princess. Modern women didn't realize how lucky they were to be able to dress any way they wanted to. Every time I heard some woman wax rhapsodic about long dresses and crinolines I cringed. They had no idea how inconvenient it was to dress that way. Nothing worse when you were in a hurry to get to the bathroom! Not that we'd had bathrooms back in the day. But you get the idea.

We set off for the 11th arrondissement, which was where Red was meeting her contact. There was a bus stop conveniently located across the street, and I sat on the bench to watch. I'd brought Thor along, figuring he could possibly be useful at some point and Marty couldn't have been kept away from the goings on even if I'd wanted him to. He was, of course, dressed in his signature white suit, which would have been a problem if anyone could have seen him, which they couldn't, luckily.

I didn't see Laure or her team anywhere, but I suspected they were close by, nonetheless. After I'd waited for about fidteen minutes, Red showed up; impossible to miss her in that red cape she was wearing.

She walked up to the door of a sinister little shop called *Au Chasseur Sachant Chasser*, a well-known tongue twister expression which you could translate as "The Knowledgeable Hunter." When the door opened, I saw that it was a pun that only the Enchanted would understand. The owner was a character who had once been known as The Huntsman, and who had done a lot of dirty jobs for Evil Queens, etc. I suppose he figured that being a hitman wasn't something that would ever fall out of fashion, but alternating between from hunting victims to hunting bargains and fencing stolen goods would provide additional financial security. Diversification is key, as they say.

Red followed the Huntsman inside and I decided I needed to get closer to the action. I sent Marty in after them and he told me he'd signal when it was time for me to enter. I rather envied him his invisibility at the moment. Standing outside and waiting was boring as fork!

After what seemed like hours, but was, in reality only about fifteen minutes, Marty stuck his head through the door.

"Come in quick!" he called. "I think you're going to get your answer!"

I tried the door and it was locked!

"Marty! I can't get in! Can you unlock it?"

"Give me a sec," he said.

I watched as he furrowed his brow and pointed at the lock. The door popped open. That boy had some skills for sure!

I pushed the door open and walked in, to the great surprise of Red and the Huntsman. Red was holding a three-pronged garden weeder in her hand and there was a selection of small, but valuable items laid out on a red-velvet cloth on the display counter in front of her.

"What are you doing here, Rose?" she asked in angry surprise.

"I guess I should be asking you the same thing," I said. "This isn't looking good, Red. I don't like what my instincts are telling me about all this."

"It's complicated, Rose. Just walk away, for old-times' sake. Like I said before, this is Enchanted business and the Norms won't understand."

"*I* don't understand, Red. You loved your gran, why would you do something like this?"

"She wasn't who you thought she was. She'd started gambling, because she was bored. And then, she got involved with some bad people, the Dragons, the Beast, you know the type. She was in deep and was going to lose the apartment! Then she got that damned dog!"

Thor, who had been sitting in my backpack this whole time, poked his head out at that and growled!

"Oh, yeah. Everyone thinks he's so cute! But you saw for yourself what he's capable of doing! Gran loved that! She figured she could use him to steal, then fence what he brought back. She used the money to pay her debts. But it wasn't enough; it was never enough.

"That apartment was going to be mine, but not if she lost it! Big Bad Wolf and I were going to use it for collateral to set up a catering business. He's really a terrific vegan chef! We thought we could make a success of it, but not without that apartment.

"So I managed to get a few of his hairs to take the heat off of me, knowing that his alibi would turn out to be fool-proof, and I used this garden weeder on Gran. How did you know it was me?"

"The keys, Red. You said you didn't have your own key, but Thor found the key to the apartment in your red cloak. Once I knew you were lying about that, it was easy enough to see that you didn't want anyone to really investigate what was going on. You thought you could use our friendship to keep me sweet. But you should know by now that justice is something I believe in above all else.

"Your gran may have been wrong to do what she was doing, but what you did was worse. And then you tried to blame an innocent wolf for your actions. I can't stand by and let that happen."

Just then, I heard the door open up. Berthaud and Gilou walked in.

"I've got her confession, Laure," I said. "You're going to have to decide how to handle it from here, though."

The Captain glared at me. "I'm getting really tired of your weird little community, Madame L'Ange," she said. Then, she pulled out her handcuffs and put them on Red, before leading her out.

After she left, the Huntsman spoke for the first time. "I wouldn't have let her get away with it, you know. You may not have liked what I did in the past, but it left me with a certain sense of justice, too. I liked her gran. Red was lucky that you got to her first."

I felt a chill go up my spine as I left the shop. I had a feeling that I was going to be seeing him again one day, and I wasn't looking forward to it.

I walked out into the Parisian night, my new dog by my side and my ghost following behind.

Our Canadian contributor, Rod McFadyen, offers here his own take on the "Haunting" of the Louvre, not only by Arthur Bernède's notorious Belphegor (the novel is available from Black Coat Press, ISBN 978-1-61227-110-1), but by at least three other "phantomatic" characters...

Rod McFadyen: *The Haunting of the Louvre*

Paris, 1925

The sky was clear as the plane descended into Paris-Le Bourget Airport. Richard Curtis Van Loan looked out the window and, even though the airport was six miles northeast of Paris, he was still able to see bits of the city in the distance, including the famous Eiffel Tower. He should have been tired, enduring a seven-day transatlantic sail from New York to Southampton, a train into London, and a flight from Croydon into Paris. However, he felt energized, excited to see his old friend, Chantecoq.

They had met during the Great War, after Van Loan had arrived in France in 1917 as a pilot for the American forces. Chantecoq was already an officer in the French army and served bravely, being awarded the Legion d'Honneur and the Croix de Guerre. Van Loan's accomplishments were more modest, basically reconnaissance flights over enemy territory, yet with their own degree of danger. They had first met briefly at French HQ, along with dozens of other captains, majors, commanders, generals, discussing the information gathered from one of Van Loan's flights. They both happened to slip outside at the same time for a cigarette that evening and had struck up an easy conversation, especially after sharing a flask of brandy. Despite being from vastly different backgrounds, they had forged a connection which had only grown stronger throughout the conflict and kept corresponding after Van Loan's return to America.

After the war, Chantecoq had become a private detective, gaining a prestigious reputation for professionalism and intelligence. He was even dubbed the "King of Detectives" by the French press. Van Loan had followed his career, devouring every French article on his friend that he could find.

Van Loan, once a rich playboy before the war, had drifted aimlessly after it, unable to find meaning in his old life. A challenge by a New York publisher friend of his to solve a crime the police had not, revealed a talent and a passion for detection he didn't know he had. He was seriously thinking about becoming a private detective, too, but before taking the first step down that path, he felt he should seek advice from his friend and real detective, Chantecoq.

When he emerged from the airport terminal with his suitcase, he was surprised to find a lovely, blonde woman standing by a red convertible car, holding a sign with his name on it. He sauntered up to her.

"Chantecoq, you've changed substantially since the last time I saw you," he said with a warm smile.

She smiled back. "My father said you could be a bit of a tease. I am Colette, his daughter and business partner. He sent me to pick you up as he was attending to some important details of a case at the moment."

Van Loan managed to stuff his suitcase into the rear of the car and they drove off. He found she was an intelligent and delightful conversationalist but (unfortunately) immune to his charms.

At the same time, another visitor was arriving in Paris from the south. His journey had begun in the East African country of Bangalla. Traveling by bush trail, river boat and railway, his first destination had been Cairo. From there, he had gone to Alexandria where he had boarded a ship to Marseilles and then had traveled by rail to Paris.

His passport said *Christopher Standish*, but that was not his real name. He was better known in Africa as the "Ghost Who Walks"—the Phantom.

He was the 19th of a line that had started with the original Phantom, Kit Walker, in the 16th century. His ship sunk, his father killed by pirates, Kit had washed up on the shores of Bangalla and had been rescued by the Bandar pygmies. He had sworn a sacred oath that he and his descendants would fight pirates and evil men wherever they were. Ever since, his sons and daughters had carried on that fight, donning the black domino mask and purple costume of the vengeful protector of Africa. That costume was presently hidden in a secret compartment at the bottom of his luggage, along with two M1911 .45 caliber pistols.

The purpose of his journey was the recovery of an ornate ebony spearhead, a remnant of the weapon once owned by a legendary tribal chief revered by the Bandars. It had been stolen months ago by unscrupulous treasure hunters. The Phantom happened upon a scrap of information from a smuggler's files that led him to believe the spearhead had been sold to an even more unscrupulous dealer in Cairo. By the time he had reached the Egyptian city, it had been sold again to a museum curator, and now apparently resided in the Louvre.

This was not the Phantom's first time in France, although he had hoped never to visit that country again. He had fought in the front lines against Germany in the Great War. He was appalled at the carnage that modern weaponry could inflict on a human body. After the war, he had returned to untamed Bangalla, where life was not so cheaply extinguished, intending to limit his contacts with the "civilized" world. This was one of those times, however, when such course of action could not be avoided.

As his train arrived in Paris, the Phantom came to a decision on how he would proceed. Based on what he knew, he felt he had little chance of getting the spearhead back through legitimate means. A theft had taken the spearhead away from Bandar; a theft would return it.

Van Loan and Colette arrived at a mansion block on the Avenue de Verzy in the 17th arrondissement. Chantecoq and his daughter lived on the upper floors while their office was on the ground floor. After depositing his suitcase in a guest room upstairs, the American went down to the office. It was open and decorated tastefully with a large bookcase as the center piece.

"My American friend!" said Chantecoq leaping up from his desk and greeting him with a monstrous hug, kissing him enthusiastically on both cheeks, causing Van Loan to blush slightly.

They sat down with brandies and chatted idly until dinner, Van Loan peppering his host with questions about his cases, investigative methods and the science of detection.

They were joined at dinner by Colette and Jacques Bellegarde, a reporter at *Le Petit Parisien*. Van Loan found the young man reserved, intelligent, and the obvious object of Colette's attention throughout the meal. He sighed internally. Nonetheless, conversation was warm and comfortable over the course of the meal.

"Your daughter says you are involved in an important case right now," Van Loan said after the last dishes had been taken away.

"That is correct," Chantecoq replied. "It is a most unusual case, which, unfortunately, has now taken a tragic twist. Two nights ago, a guard at the Louvre claimed he saw a ghost in a black shroud wandering near the *Département des Antiquités*. It disappeared when he tried to confront it. The man does not have a reputation for drinking. Then, last night, the body of another guard was found, murdered, presumably by this same ghost.

"The Chief of Security at the Louvre is a friend of mine and, because of that, I have inserted myself into the investigation, without a paying client and without the wholehearted permission of the police. They believe it is a simple matter of attempted theft, but I suspect that is entirely the wrong direction.

"The newspapers are now referring to the ghost as Belphegor, the Phantom of the Louvre."

Another individual was reading those same newspapers very closely.

Fantômas was involved in most of the criminal activities in Paris and was keenly interested in anything in which he did not have a hand in, especially if it garnered headlines and a potential profit. A ruthless murderer and a master of disguise, he was the most elusive criminal in France. No one knew what he looked like and, even around members of his own organization, he wore a mask.

It was obvious to Fantômas that this "Belphegor" was looking for something in the Louvre. The fact that he had risked skulking around the museum on consecutive nights, with additional security and the risk of capture greater each night, led him to believe that it must be something extremely valuable.

Whatever it was, Fantômas wanted it. And he had an idea on how to get it.

Chantecoq had arranged with Police Inspector Menardier and the Louvre's Head Curator, M. Lavergne, to stake out the museum that evening. Bellegarde and Van Loan had insisted on accompanying him and the detective had failed to dissuade them. There would also be police and extra museum guards as well, staked out at various places around the museum, but the Louvre was so vast, it was impractical to watch all of the numerous galleries.

After the museum closed for the evening, Chantecoq and his little group headed to the central gallery in the *Département des Antiquités*. The statue of the Winged Victory od Samothrace was clearly visible at one end. Moonlight shone through the high windows of the gallery, bathing it in dim light but also leaving deep shadows in the corners and by some exhibits. The gallery displayed mainly huge statues of ancient deities in stone or bronze, along with a giant porphyry bowl on a central pedestal and a number of relics in glass cases scattered among them all.

"The police are concentrating their presence at valuable artifacts and exhibits elsewhere. However, I believe that whatever Belphegor is looking for centers around here. Let's see if he is brave enough to show tonight," Chantecoq said before they strategically scattered to different hiding places in the gallery and lapsed into silence.

It was well after midnight. To someone used to climbing jungle vines and cliffs, it was child's play for the Phantom to reach the rooftop of the Louvre. Having spent almost the entire day roaming the museum, he'd found the spearhead and scoped out where the nearest potential point of entry might be. A skylight in the ceiling of a neighboring gallery looked to be the most promising. He was clad in his purple costume and mask. They weren't necessary for his task, but it felt right when he was in action.

It was easy to remove a pane from the skylight. He secured one end of a rope to a convenient rooftop pipe and dropped the rest of it through the empty pane, after determining there was no activity below. He then quietly and quickly climbed down.

He immediately crouched when his feet landed on the floor, listening for any sounds. Satisfied that all was quiet, he secured the end of the rope out of sight best he could and made his way to the Egyptian section of the *Département des Antiquités*, a couple of galleries over.

There, he stood before the glass display case that held the spearhead along with a few other items. As he did earlier that day, he snorted that it was classified as an "Egyptian Artifact, Date and Origin Unknown" on the display card.

He opened the case and removed the spearhead and the card, placing them in a small bag he attached to his belt. He rearranged the other items in the case so that it was not apparent that anything was missing.

Suddenly, his keen ears picked up footsteps coming from the direction of the skylight entrance. The bouncing illuminations of flashlights were getting closer. Obviously security guards were making their rounds at the worst possible time.

The Phantom looked around and, in the dim light, realized that this gallery contained nothing but glass cases. Poor hiding places indeed! He had no option but to continue further into the museum and wait for the opportunity to dodge the guards and double back to his exit.

An eerie silence surrounded Chantecoq and his team. Van Loan was aware of the irony of the situation. Here he was, in one of the greatest museums in the world, stuck in a single, dimly-lit gallery with a view of perhaps a dozen statues, displays of relics and a big stone bowl.

He shifted slightly in his spot to accommodate a cramp in his leg. For a man of action, it was difficult to wait and do nothing. Based on discussions with Chantecoq, however, he knew that sometimes patience and a willingness to sit silently for hours was a necessary aspect of being a successful detective.

He held his breath suddenly. He thought he'd heard a faint sound, and he strained his ears for confirmation. Out of the corner of his eye, he saw Belle-garde risk a peek around a column. So he'd heard it too.

At the end of the gallery, a figure suddenly appeared by the statue of the Winged Victory at the main staircase. Van Loan could only make out the silhouette of a figure wrapped in flowing robes. Belphegor, he assumed. The figure stood there, in the dim light, for long seconds.

Van Loan felt as though the pounding of his heart was loud enough to alert Belphegor that he was not alone.

The figure then started moving slowly in their direction. It seemed to float rather than walk. Van Loan could make out a hood and cape atop the robes. When Belphegor reached the middle of the gallery, the silence was suddenly shattered by the sound of a police whistle as Chantecoq sprang from his corner. Bellegarde and Van Loan emerged from their hiding places as well, each brandishing Browning revolvers.

Belphegor pulled out a pistol and ducked behind a stone sarcophagus, keeping it between himself and the three men as they closed in on him. He swung the pistol back and forth from one man to another.

At a standoff, no one made any further moves.

No one had noticed the figure of the Phantom slip into the gallery at the far end and immediately crouch in the shadows during the commotion, caught between security guards behind him and the tableau in front.

The sound of running feet grew closer. Two security guards ran into the gallery, revolvers out. They joined the standoff, one behind Chantecoq and the other beside Bellegarde, both pointing their guns at Belphegor.

"You are trapped, Belphegor!" Chantecoq exclaimed. "Additional police will be here within minutes. Surrender peacefully!"

Belphegor remained silent.

Suddenly, a shot rang out. The guard beside Bellegarde dropped to the floor, dead, shot by the other guard.

Chantecoq then felt the warm barrel of a revolved pressing against the back of his head.

Van Loan kept his pistol pointed at Belphegor, who trained his on Van Loan, while Bellegarde pointed his towards the new threat. Because of the guard's position behind Chantecoq, Bellegarde had no good line of fire.

"What is the meaning of this?" Chantecoq growled, indignant despite the gun against his head.

"Allow me to introduce myself," the fake guard said. "I am Fantômas. You may have heard of me. I need to have a word with this so-called Phantom of Louvre. Assuming the disguise of a security guard and letting you flush him out seemed to be the most expeditious way of arranging that."

"You are insane, Monsieur, if you expect to get away with this!" Chantecoq said calmly. "Others will be here shortly and you will be surrounded."

"I have men strategically placed among the police in the museum tonight. They will be causing some delays, so we have time to conclude our business quickly." He pushed the barrel of his revolver tighter against Chantecoq's head. "Tell your friends to drop their guns. Now."

Van Loan watched the scene with Chantecoq and Fantômas out of the corner of his eye, his pistol never wavering from Belphegor's direction. His friend stood firm, displaying the same cool and courage he had during the war.

Suddenly, four shots thundered through the gallery and a glass case near Chantecoq shattered loudly.

Pandemonium ensued as everyone scattered and ran for cover. Fantômas ducked and rolled behind the porphyry bowl in the center of the gallery, wildly firing towards the end of the gallery where the shots had seemed to originate.

Bellegarde rushed towards Chantecoq and pulled him behind a large statue. Van Loan dove behind a display table as Belphegor let off a wild shot and ran back the way he came, towards the main staircase.

Fantômas disappeared down a shadowed corridor branching from the gallery.

The smell of cordite filled the gallery as the echoes of the shooting died away, leaving only the odd tinkle of glass shards hitting the floor.

Van Loan peeked over the edge of the table towards the end of the gallery where those unexpected shots came from, his gun ready. An amazing figure, clad in purple and wearing a mask, strode towards the center of the gallery, guns in each hand.

Chantecoq fearlessly stood and stepped from behind the statue.

The masked man stood before the detective and put his guns back in their holsters. Van Loan and Bellegarde stood as well, lowering their own guns but remaining ready to raise them again if necessary.

"I presume I have you to thank for the distraction that may have saved my life?" Chantecoq asked. "That was intended to be a distraction, wasn't it?" he added.

The figure nodded. "Based on what I witnessed, you were on the side of the law in all this. That fake guard was standing too close to you to risk shooting him without potentially hitting you in this dim light, but I gambled that something loud and chaotic might resolve the situation without bloodshed. I'm sorry that your quarry escaped. Both of them."

"I'm sure we will have another chance to apprehend them again," Chantecoq said. "We escaped with our lives, *mon ami*. That is enough for now. But, who are you? And why are you here?"

"I have many names," the purple-clad man said. "The Ghost Who Walks. The Guardian of the Eastern Dark. You may call me the Phantom. I am here to right an old wrong," he said vaguely.

Chantecoq glanced at the small bag at the Phantom's belt. "And has that wrong been righted?" he asked.

"Yes," the mysterious man responded, not offering any further explanation.

Voices were echoing throughout the museum, getting louder.

"We have many questions, but I expect you will want to be on your way, before the authorities arrive," Chantecoq said. "We owe it to you not to delay you. Merci, once more."

The Phantom nodded once more and disappeared into the dark, just as running footsteps and bobbing flashlights appeared at the main staircase.

Van Loan and Bellegarde had stood mute during this exchange. They both were still trying to wrap their heads around the unexpected turn of events as police and security guards flooded the gallery.

Van Loan finally found his voice. "So... the Phantom of the Louvre... Fantômas... the Phantom... and wasn't there a story about an opera house a few years ago? What is it with Paris and ghosts?"

Chantecoq was thoughtful for a moment and then gave a very Gallic shrug of his shoulders.

Van Loan boarded the ocean liner to New York a few days later. His mind drifted over the events of the past few days. He decided that his destiny was to be a detective and he couldn't wait to get started when he reached home. He would have to train himself in a variety of skills—criminal psychology, disguise, hand-to-hand combat. He would need the latest in crime fighting equipment. He had some ideas on trustworthy people that could assist him as well, given his recent experience on the value of teamwork.

His thoughts continually drifted to the figures he had encountered in the Louvre. The idea of a disguise appealed to him. A costume, or a mask at least, was intimidating and he could keep his identity and his friends safe.

He chuckled to himself as a random thought leapt into mind. Perhaps he could be a... *phantom detective*?

Arnould Galopin's Doctor Omega is well-known to our regular readers, but it is very unusual to see characters created by Arthur C. Clarke show up in Tales of the Shadowmen. *In fact, the only time one such character, or rather a place, appeared in one of our books, it was the city of Diaspar in our* Shadow of Judex *collection in a tale written by the undersigned. Nigel Malcom easily tops that one with...*

Nigel Malcolm: *When the Children Leave Home*

The *Cosmos* shook as Doctor Omega frantically worked the controls. They rode the space storm together. He had suddenly come across some invisible force—something new and unwieldy.

"This storm is too powerful!" said Omega. "I can't get anywhere near Earth-119901125664 before its destruction! Any suggestions?"

He was speaking to Thea, a robotic head mounted on a special resting hook on the console, who was plugged directly into the ship's instruments.

"Gravitational forces are random and currently seven hundred times more powerful that the *Cosmos*' ability to withstand them," the robotic head replied.

Omega finally pulled one last lever and the ship came to a rest.

"That's the best I can do," he said, grumbling. "Aethereal ambit. At least, it'll give us time to get our bearings."

He sat there looking at the controls for a moment, before the penny dropped and he looked at Thea suspiciously.

"What did you mean, gravitational forces are random?"

"Analysis shows that the gravitational forces are fluctuating without consistency," replied Thea.

"But surely, there must be some pattern to it," muttered the Doctor. "We may as well all pack up and go home if we can't rely on the Laws of Physics anymore!"

"There is simply not enough data to discern logical patterns," said Thea.

Doctor Omega paused for a moment and sighed.

"I see," he said more calmly. "I'm sorry, Thea, I shouldn't have snapped at you. Please forgive an old duffer." He then changed the subject. "Let's focus our attention on the planet's surface. Is there anything noteworthy about the destruction of this particular Earth?"

As he asked, he flicked a few switches on the control console. New readings and images flickered in front of them.

"There appears to be a high level of energy, manifesting itself in an aurora of light. Much of it is in a condensed upward motion."

"Hmm... A column of energy," murmured the Doctor, summarizing the robot's description.

He typed a command into the console computer with his bony fingers. Ticker tape rattled out. He tore a strip off, read it, and gasped in horror.

"That energy is… people!"

He checked the readings further, and asked the robot to analyze the energy patterns again. More ticker tape came out. He read the latest printout, and compared it to the first.

"This is extraordinary. It looks like a tree made of human energy. So that's what has become of the human race here, hmm?"

The Doctor considered the instruments in front of him and wondered if he ought to look at a visual image of the phenomenon, or not. He'd seen plenty of horrific sights in his long life, and it probably wouldn't be very long before he saw more. He didn't have to go looking for them.

He turned to Thea.

"Are there any…" he searched for the right word, "…corporeal human beings left?"

"Scans indicate that there is one person. A human being is sending a transmission to an alien spaceship," said Thea.

There was a split second, and then Doctor Omega sprang into action, activating the *Cosmos'* communications unit and tuning it in on the source of the transmission.

"Let's try to eavesdrop," he said.

"Doctor, did you not once tell me that eavesdroppers never hear any good of themselves?" asked Thea.

"Well, yes, yes, but never mind that now," replied the Doctor, irritably.

They picked up, through the crackle and with a bit of fine-tuning, a monologue from the last man on Earth. As he described what was happening around him, Omega and Thea watched as the outer surface of the planet began to fade and dissolve.

With a jolt, the Doctor stood up. Then, he sat down again, looking intently at the controls. Thea could tell that he was working out how to get down to the surface and rescue the last man—whose name they now knew was Jan Rodricks. She had to intervene:

"Please do not disable the hostile action protocols, Doctor. Without them, these forces will rip the *Cosmos* apart, killing you and destroying me. You cannot save Jan Rodricks."

The Doctor clenched his fists in frustration. That frustration turned to horror as he saw on the screen in front of them the Earth's outer layers fade into transparency and vanish, unleashing the inner core. This lit up very brightly before burning out. It, too, disappeared. And then, there was nothing left.

Omega sat back, looking at the emptiness thoughtfully. He put his finger on his upper lip. He became aware that it was rough. He then felt his chin and realized that it had been a long time since he had last shaved. Piloting a space/time vehicle made it easy to lose track of time, ironically enough. It was probably very late at night for his own biological clock.

He suddenly felt a little hungry and thirsty. He got up and walked over to a little side table where there was a decanter with some water and a glass tumbler upside down over the rim. Omega picked up the tumbler and poured out a near glass full of water. The decanter was now empty.

As he drank the lukewarm water, he looked at the blackboard next to it. It had two tallies chalked up on it. One marked *Earths Saved*, and the other *People Rescued*. It reflected a long day of hopping across diverging timelines and dimensions, preventing the end of different Earths and different people— sometimes rescuing alternate versions of the same individuals.

"Well, I suppose I've mostly succeeded," he said. "Eight Earths and seventy-eight people relocated to new homes. That isn't a bad day's work. What a pity to end the day on a disappointing note."

Omega finished his water and put the tumbler down.

"Thea, check our systems while I trace the destination of that signal," he commanded. He swiftly tapped a few keys, and laid in some co-ordinates.

"Valve eight has reached 98% of its lifecycle," said Thea.

"Has it indeed? Hmm. Well, let's give it an excuse to go out in a blaze of glory, shall we?"

He suddenly pulled a lever, and the *Cosmos* spun round and shot off through the juddering remains of the solar system.

"Possibly even back to our own Normandy afterwards for some beef bourguignon and a glass of wine." he added.

Somewhere near Pluto the spaceship was stationary, pointing towards the third planet and observing its disappearance. Moments afterwards, the ship turned around in the direction of the Overlords' home world and engaged its stardrive.

On its bridge, chief supervisor Karellen looked thoughtfully at the big screen, watching the Sun disappear into the distance. As he looked, he mentally saluted those people of Earth. The rest of the ship's crew knew not to disturb him in these moments. Leaving a race that had successfully ascended to the Overmind was always a time of mixed emotions.

Nothing disturbed Karellen's reverie until he heard the invasive wheezing, groaning sound.

He looked around. The other Overlords on the bridge were glancing anxiously at each other. In one corner of the bridge, its metal grey clashing with the metal green walls, was a spaceship. A bizarre looking thing, like a primitive rocket built by a child.

An old man with a lock of unruly white hair marched out and stood looking at them. He drew himself up to his full height and put his hands on his lapels.

"You're a dashed difficult fellow to keep up with." he said.

Karellen looked at this intruder. He had studied humanoids for long enough to realize that while his bluster was clearly a front; this crazy man was not fazed by the Overlords' devilish appearance. He seemed to take no notice of their horns, tails, red skin, or the fact that they were all much taller than him.

Also, despite his appearance, the intruder was not from Earth. The ship, and the man's demeanor, suggested another race. Maybe one he was familiar with.

"It's all right," said Karellen to the rest of the crew. "Stand down. This person is harmless. Resume your duties."

The bridge crew went back to their assigned tasks. Some immediately. Some hesitantly, as though expecting this intruder might suddenly turn violent.

"My men are harmless and unarmed. Who are you?" Karellen asked.

"I, sir, am Doctor Omega. And who might you be?"

"My name is Karellen."

"And are you responsible for the destruction of this Earth?"

Doctor Omega's question was loaded with anger. Karellen chose his words carefully:

"I am the supervisor of the project to help the human race evolve to the point where it could ascend to join the Overmind."

Omega took a couple of steps forward.

"So that's what you call it, hmm?"

"Did you watch the people of Earth as they ascended?" asked Karellen.

"Yes, I did. That's millions of years of development and growth now up in smoke." That hard edge returned to Omega's voice.

Karellen responded calmly.

"On the contrary, it is the conclusion of millions of years of development and growth. It is the next stage in their evolution."

"That is death! Genocide!"

"They are beyond death," said Karellen, before his tone changed to curiosity. "I think I know your race. They made incredible advances in their technology and civilization. They can traverse all of space and time. And yet, like my own race, they cannot evolve any further than they have. Both your people and mine have become stuck at an impasse."

At this, the old man seemed to almost jump in revolt. He took a step back. His body language adopted a more defensive tone.

"Impossible. My people have evolved over billions of years!"

Karellen knew this, of course, but decided to politely ignore it. He continued:

"As a matter of fact, I seem to remember that the Overlords considered coming to your homeworld. They even sent out ships. But the Overmind instructed us to go away and leave you untouched. We assumed it was because either your people didn't need our help, or because you were in no position to even be helped."

Omega drew himself up to his full height again.

"My people do not need your help sir. And to meddle with their affairs would cause some very dire consequences. Not just for us, but for every other planet in the universe. Tell me; what are your plans now? Hmm?"

"We will return to my home planet. From there, I will no doubt get instructions to go to another planet and help their species' progress," said Karellen.

"And how would you like it if your own civilization was 'helped' to join this 'Overmind'?" asked Omega, who was clearly hoping this was a master card to play in the argument.

Karellen sighed.

"I would like that very much," he said sadly. "Doctor, you seem to be afraid of what you see as death. I think that is because you see it as the end. You are a man of science, and I suspect you are also a widely traveled man. Does it not occur to you that something as complex and diverse as the universe—with its measures and counterbalances—could lead to something more than the end? We only see what we can see from our limited perspective. Even you, from your point of view, can only perceive a limited amount." He looked directly at Omega. "The Overmind is not the end. It is the beginning of something else."

The Doctor just stood there. For once, he was lost for words.

"Go home, Doctor Omega," continued Karellen. "Or resume your travels. There is nothing you can do for us. Nor your own people. My race means other races no harm. We are merely helping them."

"Very well," said Omega at last. Then in one last impotent gesture he raised his index finger and added: "But I will be watching you so-called 'Overlords', and if you meddle in the affairs of other planets, then I will step in and meddle with yours! Good day to you, sir!"

He turned round and quickly stepped back into the *Cosmos* before Karellen could respond. Even though the Overlord did not intend to.

A moment later, the *Cosmos* vanished.

Back at his controls, Doctor Omega flew his craft away from the Overlords' spaceship, and steered it back to early 20th century Normandy. His Normandy.

He didn't speak a word to Thea, who just remained perched on the console, looking at him in silence.

With the co-ordinates set, Omega then slumped back in the chair, and rubbed his eyes wearily. He remained slumped as he weakly pulled out a handkerchief and fumbled with his pince-nez, cleaning them.

He looked over at the blackboard, with its *Earths Saved* tally and its *Last People Rescued* tally.

He was so young. He still had so much to learn.

After reintroducing us to Tod Browning's "Unholy Three" in our previous volume, Christofer Nigro returns to the story that was the basis for Browning's 1932 classic, Freaks. *That story, "Spurs," by Tod Robbin, was originally published in February 1923 in* Munsey's Magazine *and becomes here the basis for a new "Unholy Three" gang invented by Christofer. Before we go on, a historical note: French politician Pierre Laval who is featured here served as Prime Minister (in French: Président du Conseil) of France from 27 January 1931 to 20 February 1932 and then again from 7 June 1935 to 24 January 1936 (when the story takes place). Laval sought to contain Germany, and pursued foreign policies favorable to Italy and the Soviet Union, but his handling of the Abyssinia Crisis, which was widely denounced as appeasement of Benito Mussolini, prompted his resignation in early 1936, leading to the accession to power of Léon Blum's Popular Front. Laval returned to the post during the German occupation, from 18 April 1942 to 20 August 1944. After the War, Laval was tried and found guilty of plotting against the security of the state and of collaboration with the enemy. After a thwarted suicide attempt, he was executed by firing squad in October 1945.*

Christofer Nigro: *The New Unholy Three*

Deep beneath the Opéra Garnier. Paris, December 1935

Erik, better known and feared as the Phantom of the Opera, was having a rather heated discussion with his close friend and frequent partner-in-murder, the present-day incarnation of the freakish bell-ringer named Quasimodo. The master assassin sat on his comfortably plush orange Streamline Moderne lounger, one of the most prized articles of furniture in his opulent subterranean quarters. The contemporary Hunchback of Notre-Dame was seated on an equally comfortable navy blue sofa directly across from Erik. The subject of the conversation was not one that the former resident of the world-famous cathedral wanted to hear.

"You must go easier on those working ladies I hire to service you, *mon ami,*" Erik said in a frustrated tone that conflicted with his soft, mellifluous voice. "They do not easily endure such rough treatment from one with your level of strength, especially not when that is coupled with the incendiary temper you display if you do not receive precisely what you want."

"What I want and what I need, *mon bon ami et cher bienfaiteur,* is to be *loved,* not merely 'serviced,' as you put it," the Hunchback retorted with massive irritation evident in his deep, scratchy voice. "I need to feel like a man! Like one of the many Parisian gentlemen walking the streets with Clark Gable looks garbed in waistcoats and tuxedos of luxurious sharkskin! The ones proudly striding about the 9th arrondissement with a beautiful woman in the latest Schiaparelli dress and boasting a Greta Garbo figure!"

"Come now, Quasimodo..." The Hunchback's distorted visage frowned as Erik's tone took the familiar shift of tenor that indicated he was about to initiate some verbal tough love. "Let me be frank with you, as I learned to be with myself on this matter. We are not ordinary men. We do not have the same entitlements that the handsome members of the rabble take for granted. Instead, we were fated for other sorts of privileges, such as power and wealth. Our lot in life is never to be loved; but in its place we get to be feared like few others outside that accursed Colonel Bozzo-Corona, leader of the fearsome Black Coats.

"So, you should celebrate all that you have acquired when you joined up with me. This includes the women of the night which I hire to provide for your physical needs, even if those of your heart must remain unfulfilled. That is considerably more productive than griping and complaining over what the Fates have denied you."

"I cannot be so grateful!" Quasimodo pounded the mahogany wood arm of the sofa closest to him with his huge, spade-like fist. The hard natural substance splintered under an exhibition of strength comparable to that possessed by the likes of Charles Atlas. "I need more than just the physical, Erik. I am dying inside without the requirements of the heart that you mentioned."

The yellow eyes deeply sunken in the Phantom's skull-like face glared at the broken section of expensive furniture wrought by his friend's display of angst. Erik rose to his feet, his cape flowing about him like a dark-hued sheet fluttering in the wind.

"What did I just tell you about curbing your temper? The décor in this chamber is the finest one can purchase anywhere in the world, and one of the privileges I have provided for you, the value of which you now overlook."

Quasimodo never tolerated that tone from anyone, regardless of how often it was justified. Erik, however, was an exception, in part because he was the only friend and kindred spirit the Hunchback had ever known. This was more than he ever expected to have, one who had helped him live in a type of splendor unimagined by his more famous predecessor whose story had been recorded by the scribe Victor Hugo. It was a bridge he was loathe to burn, no matter the agony inflicted by the void in his heart.

"*S'il vous plaît, pardonnez-moi,* Erik," Quasimodo said as his homely visage looked downwards in shame. "I did not mean to jeopardize my friendship with you. For you have given me so much, and I should not be so bitter about the things which no one can provide, no matter what resources are at their disposal. But... sometimes, it really hurts, right here." Quasimodo pointed to that which was beating within the left side of his massive chest.

The Phantom was rarely forgiving of any sort of affront to himself... but again, in this case, he made an exception. Quasimodo was also practically the only friend he had ever known, a rare kindred spirit. And truth to tell, Erik fully understood his malformed comrade's sense of emptiness and longing. Thus, he could not help but sympathize with the Hunchback's plight.

"All is forgiven. I sometimes forget that one of our entitlements is to anger over the simple but important pleasures of life, the ones that those of our ilk are denied. But be aware that one of the privileges I have provided for you is a way to channel that inner fury in a manner that is simultaneously cathartic and financially lucrative. Tonight, we shall be presented with another such opportunity."

"Oh?" Quasimodo slumped forward and cocked his misshapen head with an expression of interest.

"*Oui, mon ami.* A mysterious millionaire said to have powerful political connections has a dangerous but very profitable assignment requiring the services of those who make murder their profession. I, of course, was pre-selected for the job above all others, and you will come along for it."

"What is the nature of this 'job?'"

"The man said it could only be mentioned in person, never written down on paper or entrusted to any messenger. We will meet him tonight at the Underground for full details."

"Is there a chance this could be some type of trap?"

"Every chance, but that is one of the hazards of our vocation. It is the reason why we are paid so handsomely, and also why we always go to these meetings prepared for anything."

Within the hour Erik and Quasimodo strode through some of the back alleys of the notorious Porte de Clignancourt district. Also known as the Zone, it was a shantytown slum located near the northern gates of Paris. Though street crime was pervasive in such a place, no miscreants who lurked in the dark dared approach the likes of the Phantom when he had cause to walk through these thoroughfares of poverty. His reputation as one of Europe's deadliest assassins more than preceded him, and he was easily recognizable with his operatic mask, dark billowing cloak, and distinctive fedora hat. Thus, Erik was practically the only personage who could wander about this area, particularly after dark, with no fear of being accosted, despite having pockets filled with lucre.

"This place is truly squalid," Quasimodo remarked as he looked around. "My flimsy quarters at the top of Notre-Dame was a palace by comparison. Must we trek through here to reach the Underground?"

"It is necessary," Erik replied. "The Underground must be well hidden, and in a location where even the Parisian constabulary would prefer not to enter. But you need fear no molestation while in my company."

"It is not fear of attempted robbery that concerns me. I would simply rather not look at this place. And with the way it smells, one would think the residents use these streets as a communal outhouse."

"That is actually quite accurate, so I would be mindful of where you step in this darkness. Use your nose to alert you to the presence of human refuse in your path if your eyesight is not as keen as my own in the absence of light."

"Mon Dieu," the Hunchback whispered to himself, as he began closely monitoring the path in front of him.

That was when, near the edge of the Zone, the death-dealing duo witnessed a most unusual sight. The silhouette of a very tall woman with what looked like a doll perched on her right shoulder was walking just a few yards in front of them. At her feet was what looked like a massive wolf or an unusually large dog with wolf-like features. The woman staggered a bit, as if afflicted with great fatigue or painful bunions on her soles.

Erik and Quasimodo could hear a shrill, high-pitched voice saying, "Move along now, *mon chéri.* You have covered only slightly more than half the total length of France at this point."

Curious about these individuals, Erik produced his Deluxe Lux flashlight manufactured by Duebe Industries and illumined the figures before him. It revealed the following details:

The woman was a buxom blonde dressed in tatters. Her attractive facial features and flaxen hair were covered in grime and bore the look of one who had endured suffering for a long time.

The "doll" perched on her shoulder was actually a man barely over two feet in stature. He was dressed in an expensive courtier outfit with a miniature scabbard affixed to a leather belt that held a gold-hilted little sword. His tailor-made boots, small enough to fit a toddler, were adorned with shiny gold cowboy spurs that he was using to cruelly prod the woman forward as if she were some beast of burden.

The mite's appearance, demeanor, and vocal intonations reminded Erik of the unique voice possessed by a tiny criminal named Tweedledee, with whom he had once recruited for a mission many years earlier. That homicidal dwarf was the leader of a trio of dangerous American criminals that had spent a year wreaking havoc in the City of Love while on the lam from the authorities from their native country.

As for the wolf-like dog, it possessed a bushy gray coat and a fearsome muzzle clearly capable of easily rending a person limb-from-limb. The animal glanced in the direction of the sudden influx of light and bared his sharpened teeth at the two interlopers. The canine's vicious growl indicated that he meant business, and Erik knew a killer when he saw one, whether it was human or otherwise.

Before the Phantom could react, he and his misshapen friend noticed some movement several feet to their right. Three figures dressed in dingy Cossack jackets and beret caps emerged from the shadows between a nearby shanty to bar the path of the strange party.

Each one of this new threesome swiftly brandished stiletto blades. Erik's keen eyes immediately recognized them as members of a gang of violent youths who would demand tribute from any outsider who passed through the Zone (save for him, of course). Their sudden appearance quickly diverted the canine's attention from the Phantom and Quasimodo to the triad of ruffians that posed a more obvious threat.

"Good evening, Mademoiselle," the lead thug addressed the woman. "Hand over whatever valuables you may have, including the gold-handled sword on the doll you're carrying on your shoulder. Do it, or we will take more than just your money and jewelry."

"No one touches her but me!" the voice of the "doll" forcefully squeaked. The huge canine began growling in tandem with the small man's angry words. "Go back to the filthy alley you crawled out of, or my dog and I will make you wish that the wenches who spawned you had miscarried."

The mite of a figure then drew the sword with the gold-plated hilt, revealing a blade tailored to his size but no less sharp than a full-sized version.

"*Mon Dieu,*" the youth to the left of his leader said. "Géraud, that doll is… alive. It's a man!"

"And is that… a knife that he holds?" the thug to the right queried aloud.

"It doesn't matter!" Géraud decreed. "Hand over all your valuables, including that little knife. You will also give us the woman as a penalty for mouthing off at the rulers of the Zone. Give it, or we will cut you and that mongrel of yours to pieces, little man."

"In a pig's eye you will!" the defiant mite exclaimed. "We shall see who will cut whom to pieces this night."

The smallish figure leapt off the woman's shoulder to land on the canine's back. The sword-wielding imp had now mounted the animal as a normal-sized man would a stallion.

"St. Eustache, attack!" the miniature figure commanded.

Before the leader of the gang could react, the canine had dashed forward and leapt upon Géraud. The leader of the gang was taken down to the concrete by the animal's over 100 pounds of weight. The small man thrust the blade of his mini-sword directly into his victim's left eye, penetrating the brain and killing the young man immediately.

The canine then swiftly rushed at the startled youth to the left, jumping at him and slamming its skull into the thug's stomach. The young malcontent was likewise knocked to the ground with the wind knocked out of him. The small man jumped off the animal's back and onto the torso of the fallen gang member. Like a savage toy out of Hell, he preceded to repeatedly stab the youth in the face and neck until a fatal skewer was delivered directly to the jugular vein. A thick scarlet spurt that formed a pool around the severely lacerated gang member's head indicated that he was mere seconds from bleeding out.

St. Eustache immediately changed trajectory after knocking the second youth down and leapt on the final thug standing to the right. The powerful beast ripped out the would-be robber's throat as effortlessly as a man might take a bite out of a bologna sandwich, only with a far bloodier result. The grisly deed was done before the would-be mugger could attempt to bring his stiletto to bear in his defense.

The woman merely stood still while watching the homicidal spectacle with a tired and haggard expression that displayed no emotion. With the triple murder quickly accomplished, the small man re-mounted the canine, which carried him back to the lady in their company. He ordered the woman to lift his tiny body off the animal's furry back and return him to her shoulder. She quickly and easily complied with this demand.

"*Très impressionnant,*" the observing Erik said quietly to himself as he moved the illumination of his flashlight from the three mutilated corpses and back onto the trio that were still standing. "How useful one such as that would be to us—much like a similar man I was once acquainted with."

The homicidal mite then turned his beady little black eyes directly at the two individuals who were shining a high lux light on his party.

"Who goes there now?" the diminutive but deadly man queried in his squeaky but firm voice. "State your business or St. Eustache and I will make mincemeat of you, much as we did those fools now coloring the street red."

"At ease, *mon bonhomme,*" the Phantom said, tipping his fedora in a friendly manner. "My friend and I present no threat to you, but we understand your concern after the encounter you just had with those miscreants. We are merely curious of the unusual sight that you and your companions present."

The dog continued to growl, causing Erik to stealthily move his hand to the blade he carried at his belt in preparation for the worst.

"Heel, St. Eustache!" the small man cried. *"Heel,* I say! This one says he and his friend pose no menace, and they have already seen what we can do to those who threaten us."

The animal instantly obeyed, his raised ears going down along with his defensive snarls. Quasimodo seemed to be oblivious to the strange little man and the ferocious canine, however. His gaze was instead fixated solely on the blonde amazon of a woman standing dejectedly before him.

The Hunchback could not help but notice that her facial features would match Marlene Dietrich herself in beauty if the film of grime were to be removed from it. Further, her tattered dress did nothing to hide the shape of the ample breasts covered but emphasized by the thin veneer of cloth she wore. And this amazing lady appeared to be tamed by this small sliver of a man, one who could no more call himself a true man than the Hunchback.

"My name is Erik," the Phantom said while removing his hat and bowing respectfully. "My friend here is Quasimodo. Who might you be?"

"My name is Jacques Courbé," the doll-like man replied. "This... charming lady is my wife, Jeanne Marie. My faithful companion and guardian at our feet is St. Eustache. Do you and your friend have surnames to go with your first?"

"We do not," Erik answered. "So, am I to understand that you are completely in control of this magnificent animal? One who will effectively tear apart any who might present an obstacle to your well-being?"

"He will do so at a simple command from me, regardless of their behavior," Jacques replied.

"If I may ask, is your St. Eustache a wolf?" the Phantom queried.

"He is actually the result of a mating between a dog and a wolf," Jacques explained, "and has been in my care since he was a pup. St. Eustache is also the only friend I have ever possessed. He has shown more loyalty to me than any person ever has or would, including this treacherous wife of mine."

"Your woman, whom you speak so poorly of, appears to be under your command much as your dog," Quasimodo noted after finally recovering from being mesmerized at the initial sight of Jeanne Marie. "Only not as well treated."

"How I treat my wife is my business," Jacques fired back. "Rest assured she did much to earn my ire when I offered her both my love and a life of wealth. In return for my heartfelt generosity, Jeanne Marie and a man whose bed she shared decided that she could make a laughingstock of me by forcefully carrying my person across the entire length of France on her shoulder. I merely turned the tables and have spent the last few months compelling her to do precisely that, only under *my* control instead of hers. That is some poetic justice, *non?*"

"It's a travesty to treat such a magnificent woman that way, is what it is," the smitten Quasimodo opined.

"Do not be so quick to judge, *mon ami,*" Erik reminded his friend. "The treatment meted out by Jacques to his wife is actually more benign than that which you inflicted upon the last woman you had."

"That is not the same thing," the Hunchback insisted. "Jeanne Marie is his wife, not some lady he picked off a street corner. This is a lady he should love as he professed."

"What *she* loved was the money I inherited," Jacques rejoined. "And by the looks of you, I cannot imagine that the fair sex has treated you any better than they have me, Quasimodo. Frankly, you could have been part of the circus sideshow I performed in before I became independently wealthy."

"You were part of a circus?" Erik asked, now more intrigued than ever.

Jacques did not understand why he was opening up to these strangers. Quasimodo was a misshapen hunchback, but his deformed features were not shocking to one who since his earliest days had performed alongside the likes of Grippo the Giraffe Boy and Lupa the Wolf Lady.

176

The tall, slim one named Erik wore a mask similar to those who performed in an opera, and the mite of a man could well imagine that the countenance it concealed was no easier for the lay person to look upon than the visage of the Hunchback. Both men looked as if they could accept him as a friend, something he had never received, even from his fellow sideshow performers. This is what caused him to lower his guard.

"I was once part of Copo's Circus, as was Jeanne Marie," Jacques explained. "She titillated the crowds as a performing equestrian of great skill. As for me... I provided them amusement as part of the sideshow merely by looking as I do. Her feelings for me were unrequited in favor of one of the handsome acrobats she shared the stage with.

"That is, until a year and a half ago when my uncle, a wealthy farmer I barely knew, died and left me his entire estate because I was his sole living relative. My mother died soon after birthing me, so my uncle left me in the care of the circus. He certainly wanted no part of raising me; and unlike an orphanage, they would pay him for leaving me with them.

"Papa Copo was good to his sideshow performers, but I grew up employed as an object that the crowds paid to laugh at rather than admire like they did my wife and those cursed acrobats. I loved Jeanne Marie, but she was among those who laughed at me, agreeing to be my bride only after she learned of my inheritance. It was her intention, at the suggestion of her dear departed lover, to poison me so she could acquire what was mine and provide him with the prosperous life I gave to her. She deserves no less than this for such crimes against my person and my heart!"

Quasimodo continued going back and forth between looking yearningly at Jeanne Marie and derisively at her miniature husband. St. Eustache seemed to pick up on this and periodically released a low growl at the Hunchback while baring his blood-caked teeth in warning.

"I must ask you, Jacques," Erik continued. "You resemble a man of similar... stature, general appearance, and even demeanor that I once worked with. He had also been previously employed at a circus, but this one in America, before he fled to Paris to seek his own fortune, so to speak. He called himself Tweedledee. Is this resemblance a mere coincidence?"

Jacques's button-like eyes gaped wide with astonishment. *"Mon Dieu!"* the dwarf exclaimed. "The man of which you speak... he was my father! He paid for the services of a working lady during his own circus's tour of Paris a few years prior to his year-long stay here while fleeing the American authorities. The woman whose 'services' he paid for was my mother. She was impregnated by him, and I was the sad result."

"How interesting," Erik proclaimed. "Much like the lineages of Quasimodo and I, it would seem that your own tends to grow apples that do not fall far from the proverbial tree."

"I always hated apples," the Hunchback grumbled.

"Please stifle yourself, Quasimodo," the Phantom requested as he turned back to the shoulder-mounted mite. "It would seem, Jacques, that you are every bit as proficient at the art of homicide as your sire was."

Jacques had by now figured out the identity of this intimidating figure, as few in France were unaware of his fearsome legend.

The miniature killer's reply to the Phantom's inquiry was colder than an Arctic breeze. "I most certainly am. You should see what became of Jeanne Marie's lover courtesy of the sharpened combination of St. Eustache's jaws and my blade." The dwarf unsheathed his small but razor-sharp sword in a blinding blur of motion to demonstrate his point in quite a literal fashion.

"Splendid," Erik responded with a clap of his gloved hands. "I think it would be most fortuitous for one to have you and your canine friend at their side on a mission to deliver death to some unfortunate fool. That being the case, I would like to present you with an offer."

The mysterious millionaire who was providing a most profitable proposition to Erik sat staring at the motely troop before him in the darkened room of the hidden chamber known simply as the "Underground." It was situated at a locale just outside the Zone that only a carefully chosen handful of people were privy to.

This enigmatic figure was well aware that the Phantom of the Opera had partnered up with the present-day version of the Hunchback of Notre-Dame. He was not, however, expecting to see a dwarf carried on the shoulder of a disheveled woman, let alone what appeared to be a fearsome wolf keeping a close eye on the safety of the tiny man.

The mystery millionaire sat across from the others behind an oaken desk wearing a tuxedo. His facial features were effectively concealed by a wide-brimmed hat, but a bushy walrus mustache was evident.

"How many of you will be going on this mission?" the mysterious man asked Erik in a gruff voice that may or may not have been his real one.

"That would be me, Quasimodo, Jacques—he's the, er, little one on the lady's shoulder—and the wolf-dog," the Phantom answered.

"Is this woman one of your famed Angels of Music?" the mystery man queried.

"She is not," the Phantom replied. "No such femme fatales are in my employ at this time. The lady is Jacques's wife."

"His... wife? I see," the mystery man said. "If she is not an official member of your crew, then she must be removed from this room before I can give you the particulars of the assignment. I did not exaggerate when I said the fate of the very world may well hinge on its success. We cannot take even the most remote chance of the target being somehow tipped off."

"My wife goes where I go and stays where I stay," Jacques contended.

178

St. Eustache began growling at the man in the shadows upon seeing this person rile his master. "Heel, St. Eustache," the dwarf commanded softly but firmly.

"Keep that animal under control," the mystery man snarled, "and I will not have to shoot it."

"The wolf-dog is under control," Erik noted, "and Jacques will mind his manners in your... home. His wife will leave the room and wait outside."

"Very well," Jacques agreed with a huffy sigh.

The dwarf motioned for Jeanne Marie to put him down on the back of his dog and then drew his sword. With that small but deadly blade in hand and St. Eustache at his side, the diminutive man feared little.

He then spoke to his wife just before she turned and stumbled towards the door. "If you try to run off, St. Eustache and I shall hunt you down and have a lot of fun both before and after your capture. So, do not be a fool."

The broken woman nodded weakly in compliance as she left the room and waited outside. Quasimodo then turned and began following her out.

"Where do you think *you're* going?" Jacques queried brusquely.

"I will keep her company out there," the Hunchback replied. "It can be dangerous in this part of the city. Erik can give me the details of the mission afterwards."

"You will not be alone with her!" Jacques warned his new ally. "And if you dare touch her...!"

"Jacques, please calm down," Erik requested.

"Now, the assignment!" the mystery man loudly stated to get the order of business on the table. "As you all know, there has been much chaos throughout France since Serge Stavinsky's credit bonds were discovered to be worthless and the man subsequently turned up dead."

"But of course," Erik responded. "Was it not I who was hired to kill him?"

"*You* did that?" Jacques asked with an astonished expression on his little round face.

"None other," the Phantom affirmed before turning his attention back to the topic at hand. "Is this current assignment likewise of a political matter?"

"*Oui,* Monsieur Erik," the man in the shadows replied. "You are also aware of the Nazi Party that has come to power under Chancellor Hitler, who now calls himself the *Führer* of Germany. In the short span of time since he took power, his regime has initiated a series of atrocities. Particularly placing people of Jewish and Gypsy heritage into concentration camps, with horrific treatments that include monstrous medical experiments similar to those being conducted on people of Chinese heritage in Imperial Japan's Unit 751. There are incessant rumors that Hitler plans to conquer all of Europe, including the invasion of France in the not-too-distant future."

"I am aware of that much," Erik confirmed.

"But there is more, which connects these two things," the mystery man continued. "The Popular Front has emerged as a confluence of socialists and radicals to oppose the government, as it is now moving toward the Right. Hearing of this, Hitler has contacted Prime Minister Laval and set up a clandestine meeting with him here in Paris. My spies have informed me that this will take place in an expensive suite at the top floor of the Ritz hotel, Place Vendôme.

"This presents the perfect opportunity to have Hitler killed before he can convince Laval to align himself with the Nazis, and thus end his reign of terror. Your assignment would be to surreptitiously enter the hotel and kill the *Führer*."

"Are your sources absolutely certain of this meeting?" the Phantom enquired. "If they are wrong or have been fed misinformation…"

"My spies are correct," the strange millionaire interjected forcefully. "Their credentials are impeccable. You will note how well guarded the Place Vendôme is when—if—you accept the assignment. But you must achieve this without killing Laval, for that is not necessary. I can assure you that the Popular Front, which I am helping to fund, will see to it that his time will be done within a month or so through conventional political means.

"However, because of the importance of this assignment, you must provide me with proof that the assassination is successful. Do this, and fifty thousand francs shall be yours."

"Such money!" Jacques said ecstatically. "I have not seen its like even with my inheritance! Say we will accept, Erik!"

"That is for *me* to decide, *mon ami,*" the Phantom curtly informed his newest ally. "And I have decided that we shall take the assignment."

"Merveilleux!" the mystery man exclaimed. "You have only tonight to prepare, however. The meeting will occur tomorrow at 7 p.m. But it should take a professional of your caliber no longer than that to formulate a plan. I could not give you more time because this meeting was kept so secret that my spies only uncovered it six hours ago."

"You hired the right assassin, Monsieur," Erik confidently reassured the enigmatic millionaire. "A plan will be enacted by tomorrow evening to ensure that the man with the toothbrush mustache does not leave the hotel alive tomorrow. You have my word."

Just outside the door, Quasimodo gently put his enormous hand on Jeanne Marie's shoulder. "Do not worry, Madame. I shall protect you from harm, including further cruelty from that pint of a man you foolishly married."

She pulled herself away from the Hunchback, obviously reviling him. Unlike Jacques, whom she had initially found amusing, she could see nothing funny about the massive monster of a man now determined to get uncomfortably close to her. Jeanne Marie was a circus performer who had grown used to the freakish abnormalities occasionally spawned by humanity due to living and working around the sideshow freaks… but she had never cared for any of them actually touching her, certainly not when attractive acrobats were at her beck and call. It was bad enough having to give certain liberties to Jacques after marrying him, but this Quasimodo presented an even worse nightmare.

"Please... do not touch me," Jeanne Marie said in a bedraggled voice.

"I was offering you sympathy and succor," Quasimodo said in an irritated tone. "I believe a beautiful woman such as yourself deserves better than what Jacques has done to you. I am offering a protective hand."

"But at what price?" Jeanne Marie asked as she began to break down in tears. "What madness has that cursed pygmy gotten me into now? I don't want to be in the hands of freaks anymore. Lord, I am sorry for what I tried to do to Jacques. Please don't punish me any longer, I have already paid enough for that. I... I can take no more of this."

"I am only trying to help you, damn it!" Quasimodo hollered in frustration while grabbing both arms of the statuesque woman and shaking her like a leaf in the wind. "And this is how you treat me?"

"I told you not to touch her!"

The Hunchback turned to see Jacques standing just outside the door on the back of the snarling St. Eustache while pointing his small but sharpened sword directly at the malformed man-monster.

"I was only offering her comfort!" Quasimodo exclaimed.

"And she no doubt spurned you for your trouble!" the angered mite correctly surmised. "Now, remove your hands from her body before I order St. Eustache to bite one of them off while I detach the other with my sword."

Quasimodo released the trembling Jeanne Marie to turn his full attention to the threat he now faced. "Try it, and I shall choke your dog to death by shoving your stunted little body down its gullet."

St. Eustache seemed to sense the challenge, for he began growling in preparation to meet it. This caused the Hunchback to move into a defensive stance in preparation for the coming attack. The battle was ended before it began, however, when Erik leapt between the two conflicting parties in a quick and graceful whirl of motion.

"That is quite enough, you two!" the Phantom demanded. "Jacques, kindly sheathe that sword and make your wolf-dog heel. Quasimodo, do not touch that man's wife again, for she does not belong to you. We have just been offered fifty thousand francs to complete a most dangerous assignment and we must work out a viable plan before tomorrow night. I will need both of you for this, and the two of you must focus your respective rage on killing Hitler rather than each other."

Qusimodo quietly strode through the lower levels of the Ritz with Jacques riding atop St. Eustache at his side. It came as no surprise to them that the Phantom knew a hidden ingress into the building that bypassed having to enter through the heavily guarded front entrance.

"That Arab whom Erik left my wife in the care of had better not touch her," the murderous mite decreed.

"That man is a Persian, not an Arab," Quasimodo corrected his diminutive ally, "and he can be trusted to cross no lines."

"Unlike you, *non?*"

"We shall discuss that matter later. For now, we are under strict orders to provide a required diversion down here while Erik takes care of business above. His orders forbid us to kill each other, so save our wrath for any guards that come our way."

The armed security forces of the French government assigned to Laval and his special guest did not leave them waiting long. St. Eustache snarled and perked up his ears to alert his master to sounds emanating from the stairway leading up to the ground floor.

"Be silent, Quasimodo," Jacques whispered. "St. Eustache hears something. Being practically deaf, you would obviously not have noticed until it was too late."

"I thank you—and the dog—for that."

A few seconds later, two security guards stepped out of a doorway and entered the hallways as part of their patrol of the hotel's lower levels. Neither were prepared for the sight of a tiny man dressed in courtier clothing, wielding a sword scaled down to his size and sitting on the back of what looked like a large growling wolf.

"Que diable?" one of the men exclaimed as both drew their firearms.

The two guards, unfortunately, failed to see Quasimodo perched above them on a metal beam. He promptly dropped down on top of the guard standing a few feet behind the other. A sick crunching sound was heard as the Hunchback's almost 400-pound frame broke the man's spinal cord and splintered several of his ribs. The sentry's attempted scream of agony and surprise came out sounding more like a raspy cough.

The other officer was startled and turned to point his weapon at the misshapen man that stood over the broken and bleeding body of his colleague.

"St. Eustache, sic him!" Jacques commanded.

The security man's aim was spoiled as the mighty canine bit into his extended gun arm and crushed the bones of his wrist. The wolf-dog effortlessly pulled the watchman to the floor while Jacques jumped off his pet and onto the torso of the man. The hapless guard was barely able to let out a cry of agony before being muted by the dwarf's mini-sword puncturing his larynx. The man was soon bereft of all movement and much of his body's blood supply after being stabbed repeatedly in the neck and chest with maniacal intensity.

"I must say I was surprised to see an individual of your bulk manage to climb onto that beam so quickly," Jacques conceded to his ally while using the dead guard's collar to wipe the blood off his blade.

"Many years of climbing the balconies and statues of Notre-Dame have helped one to develop such skills," the Hunchback replied. "I again thank you for saving my life."

"I must thank you for doing the same. We would be much better to each other as friends and colleagues than enemies and rivals, Quasimodo. You need only stay clear of my wife and that is how it can be."

"She does not want to be with you, Jacques."

"Nor with you, I would confidently wager."

"We must again put this matter aside and make our way to the top floors. Erik may need our assistance."

After making short work of each patrol guard they encountered, Quasimodo and the team of Jacques & St. Eustache had arrived at the top floor. The meeting room reserved by Laval was located at the opposite end of a long corridor. As the deadly duo cautiously made their way there, they stumbled upon the corpse of a guard. The sight of the cadaver's eyes bulging from their sockets and its mouth wide open with a swollen tongue, along with an ugly dark bruise across the length of his throat, instantly revealed the cause of death.

"Erik is quite proficient with that Punjab lasso," the Hunchback muttered.

Several feet down the corridor they found another body, this one laying in a pool of his own blood. His throat had been slashed and one of his eyes was missing.

"It would seem Erik does not require our assistance after all," Jacques noted.

Prime Minister Pierre Laval sat comfortably on a Marisol sofa inside the posh room reserved by the French government as he discussed important political matters with his very important guest from Germany. The *Führer* was seated directly across from him on an equally lavish lounger. Situated between the two was a long rectangular wooden table bearing cups and a pitcher of tea. One security guard stood alert several feet in front of the door.

Their discussion was interrupted by what sounded like a brief cry of agony from the guard posted just outside. The door was suddenly kicked open and in stepped a cloaked figure with a mask and fedora hat. The interior security officer drew his pistol, but his shot went awry as a result of a dagger skillfully hurled into his trachea. The sentry fell to the floor with a dull thud, never to rise again.

"Gott im Himmel!" Hitler shouted as he jumped to his feet.

"What is the meaning of this?" Laval demanded to know as he likewise stood up.

"Salutations, gentlemen," the Phantom said cordially. "And to answer your question, Monsieur Laval, I have come here to kill your guest."

"Kill me?" Hitler responded incredulously. *"Me?* Do you realize who I am, you *schweinehund?"*

"Of course, I do, you madman," Erik replied. "And I am here to hasten your inevitable journey to Hell. I will be sure to say hello when I eventually see you there."

"You shall not take me so easily!" the *Führer* shouted as he moved to draw a pistol he had holstered on his belt.

The chancellor had one of the Phantom's daggers in his left eye before he could brandish the weapon. Within a second he was lying on the throw rug in a bleeding heap.

"It would appear you were wrong," the masked man remarked.

Laval cautiously backed up while attempting to hold his composure. "I suppose… you are going to kill me next?"

"*Mais non, Monsieur le Ministre*," the assassin replied. "Your execution was not included in my assignment. You are to be dealt with in another way, one that is out of my hands."

"What do you mean by that?"

"I am not at liberty to answer. Now, kindly stay where you are while I take a minute to procure an item from this room to prove the worth of my services."

The mystery man looked up as he saw Erik enter his hidden chamber on the outskirts of the Zone. He noticed that the Phantom was carrying a laundry bag with a large dark stain on the bottom.

"The assignment was completed," Erik casually stated.

"I take it you have photographic evidence to prove it?" the mysterious millionaire queried.

"I do not carry a camera on missions, as such a device would be cumbersome. So, I brought you much better evidence of my success."

Erik opened the laundry bag and dumped the severed head of Hitler onto the desk. To his credit, the mystery man barely cringed at the gruesome sight despite not being prepared for it.

"You will take note of something unfortunate when you examine this," the masked murderer said. "Those barely visible scars on the face indicate a series of surgical alterations. And when I confronted this man in the room, I observed that he seemed somewhat taller than the *Führer* was supposed to be. My theory is that Monsieur Laval's guest was a fake, likely something that even our esteemed Minister was not aware of."

The millionaire put his face close to that of the wide-eyed, mustachioed head slowly rotting on his desk and likewise noticed the deception.

"So, Hitler is not dead," the man solemnly muttered.

"He is not," Erik said, "but I was hired to kill the German with the toothbrush mustache who was Laval's guest at the Ritz. I did that, after my team and I risked our lives to fight our way through the government security officers hired to protect Laval and this imposter. So, I am requesting payment for professional services rendered."

"Here," the enigmatic man said with a sigh as he reached under his desk and handed a briefcase filled with a fortune in francs to the Phantom. "Now, be gone from my sight."

"It was a pleasure doing business with you, *cher ami,*" the masked killer commented as he departed the chamber with his bounty in tow.

After Erik had long departed, the exasperated mystery man removed his wide-brimmed hat to expose a full head of brown hair and handsome facial features beneath. He then peeled off the bogus moustache stuck over his lips with spirit gum. Thus was revealed none other than Jacques de Trémeuse, a very wealthy man who secretly dealt harsh justice to criminals as the darkly attired vigilante known and feared throughout Paris as Judex.

I was loathe to hire the likes of that assassin—a man I have tried to kill in the past—but the dispensation of justice sometimes forces one to resort to such measures, and if the Phantom of the Opera is to be at large, I may as well make use of his skills against others like him when required. Despite how much I would have enjoyed eliminating Hitler personally, Judex cannot involve himself directly in the murder of a head of state, no matter how vile that man may be.

Despite today's failure, I have at least gleaned some very important intel: Hitler is employing doubles and may have a large number of them at his behest. I now must prepare for the repercussions of what I set in motion today. I need to contact the Nyctalope and let him know that his help is greatly needed.

A hidden location in Berlin, the next day

An irate Adolf Hitler was fuming with rage as he addressed Hermann Göring, one of the top leaders in the Nazi Party.

"Someone hired that son of a *schwein* to kill me!" the *Führer* bellowed like the madman he was. "This Phantom of the Opera will pay dearly for this, as will the one who hired him once I discover his identity. Get some of our top men in the Gestapo on this!"

"Right away, *Mein Führer,*" Göring replied respectfully. "You shall also be pleased to know that more of your doubles have been produced based on the surgical procedures developed by Herr Doktor Cornelius Kramm. It has been reported that the latest altered subjects are even more convincing, as there is now negligible facial scarring with the addition of bone reduction in the legs so that your *doppelgangers* can match your, er, distinctive height. In addition, the early tests in cloning techniques also seem to be promising."

"*Wunderbar!* We shall be needing more of those doubles in the days to come. Plenty of potential subjects can be acquired from the camps, so let our doctors know that the brainwashing process must also be improved."

"*Ja,* Herr Hitler. It shall be done as you wish."

What are the odds? After Travis Hiltz's tale, another story of dastardly intrigue taking place on another one of Jules Verne's sea-faring novels this time, A Floating City *(French:* Une ville flottante) *(1871) which tells of a woman who, on board the ship* Great Eastern *with her abusive husband, finds that the man she loves is also on board. But here, the concept is a grand heist to be perpetrated by one of popular fiction's greatest criminal minds...*

John Peel: *A Thief in the Floating City*

March/April 1867—the Atlantic Ocean

When I booked passage of the steamship *Great Eastern*, I had been certain that I was in for an unusual experience; I did not expect it to include being hauled before Captain Sir James Anderson and being accused of being an international thief.

Naturally, my companion, Dr. Dean Pitferge, found this a source of great amusement. "What?" he cried? "If M. Verne is to be a great and successful thief, then surely I must be a renowned international anarchist!" He chuckled. "I assure you, I can think of any number of political personages whose views might be distinctly improved by the judicious application of a bomb or two."

"You are not aiding the situation, my friend," I informed him, knowing that he could no more rein in his attack of humor than he could cease breathing. "I am sure the good Captain has his reasons for suspicion."

"I am embarrassed to bring the matter up," the Englishman said, with his stiff formality. "In normal circumstances I should never have dreamed of asking a guest to prove their credentials. But—" He sighed, loudly. "You have been asking very suspicious questions of various crew-members about my ship."

"Because I am a writer of adventurous travel stories," I explained. "And, faced with such a wonderful vessel as this, is it not natural that I should be curious about its statistics and operations?"

The captain looked uncomfortable. "If you are who you claim to be," he said, "then I would understand perfectly. My only question is: Can you prove your identity?"

I was somewhat taken aback. I had never before been required to prove that I was, in fact, myself. I considered the point. "I have in my wallet several papers to that effect," I said slowly. "But, of course, if I *were* indeed some clever rogue, then I would certainly have several papers to the effect that I was actually Jules Verne, would I not?"

"You understand my problem, sir," the captain admitted.

Dr. Pitferge chuckled. "Why not quote him some passages from a few of your works?" he suggested.

"There are two problems with that idea," I replied. "The first being that unless the good captain has copies of my works scattered about his ship, then he would have no way of knowing whether the quotations are accurate or simply invented on the spur of the moment."

"Ah. And the second problem?"

"That once I finish a work, I banish it from my mind so that I can concentrate on the work I have currently on hand." I sighed. "Which, of course, I am still hatching, like a chicken brooding."

The captain's first officer had been standing in the background and, until this point, unspeaking, cleared his throat. "If I may, sir," he said, politely, to his captain, "I may be of assistance here."

"By all means," Anderson agreed. "Any assistance to resolve this matter is welcome."

"I—ah—have been enjoying M. Verne's stories myself," the man admitted. "In fact, I have a copy of the final magazine installment of his latest work in my cabin. I was quite interested to see how the tale would turn out." He smiled diffidently at me. "I would not require you to quote from it, but I should imagine that you are familiar with it."

"*The Children of Captain Grant?*[5]" I nodded. "But of course." He then asked me several questions pertaining to the tale, which I shall not bother detailing, but which I answered to his full satisfaction.

"I am certain, sir, that this man is indeed the celebrated author," he informed his superior.

"Then, M. Verne," Anderson said heartily, "I must apologize to you for my suspicions and offer my sincere apologies. And if you would be willing to be my guest at dinner, I have a wine that you might find interesting and appealing."

"Aha!" Dr. Pitferge cried. "Oh no, my dear captain, you do not dismiss us so easily. Though, I confess, I will certainly look forward to your amiable vintage."

"What do you mean?" the captain asked, bemused.

"I mean that your questions have exposed *you*, my dear sir," the doctor exclaimed. "You informed us that you would not have asked such potentially embarrassing questions of my friend *in normal circumstances*. You therefore imply that we are *not* in normal circumstances. And the fact that you accused my companion of being a possible thief implies that you expect to discover an actual thief aboard this vessel."

These points had, of course, already occurred to me, but I would not have mentioned them. Pitferge—being an impulsive wretch at times with a rather high opinion of himself—simply could not forbear mentioning them. And it was quite evident from the expressions on their faces that both Anderson and his first mate had hoped that we would not.

---

[5] More usually known as *In Search of the Castaways*.

"There is a... certain amount of truth in what you conjecture," the captain finally admitted.

My friend smiled complacently, quite happy to have forced the issue. "Perhaps you would be so kind as to share the relevant facts with us?"

"We are sworn to secrecy," the first mate said.

That was a mistake, because I knew the character of the doctor. Once he was onto a scent, like a bloodhound he could not be sidetracked. "You have already admitted to much," he pointed out. "And since you even considered the possibility of M. Verne being an imposter and a thief, it is clear that you are floundering about somewhat. Perhaps it is not too much to suggest that you might benefit from having two extra minds to consider your problem—a remarkable author and a no less remarkable man of science, namely myself."

In truth, I felt a little sympathetic towards Anderson. Unlike me, he was unused to the forcefulness of Dr. Pitferge's mental abilities. I was not, therefore, overly surprised when the captain gave way and acquiesced to my companion's suggestion.

"You are both aware, I am sure, that the recent Civil War in the United States has come to a close," he said. Both of us nodded. "And, as I am also certain you are aware, there has been a great deal of political wrangling as a result of this. Whilst there is still a good deal of animosity between representatives of both factions, there is also a strong desire to repair the rifts the war created and to move onwards in amity."

"An admirable aim," I agreed.

"And we have yet to see how this works out in practice," Pitferge remarked. "Lofty ideals often run aground in the waters of practicality."

"And you may or may not know," Anderson continued, "that while the official stance of Her Majesty's Government was neutrality to both sides in the conflict, there were... ah... influences on that policy."

"You mean," I offered, "that the many textile mills in your industrialized north required a substantial influx of cotton from the Southern states."

"Yes, quite," the captain agreed. "As a result of which the Southern states were strongly inclined to send ships carrying cotton to England."

"And the Northern states responded by blockading ports in the Confederacy," I added.

"Resulting in substantial attempts—many successful—to run these blockades," Anderson finished. "The cargoes were the lifeblood of our industrial mills, and payments for these shipments would have been a great assistance to the war efforts of the Southern states—if they were able to get through. Some payments made the journey; many did not. Instead, they accumulated back in England."

"Understandable," I said. "And fortunate, as it turns out. I am very interested in the issue of the emancipation of the slaves in the South, feeling that the institution of slavery besmirches the entire human race—and not simply those

188

who insisted on its survival. Whilst I admire the bravery of many in the Confederacy, I was strongly opposed to their policy."

"As all men of humanity must be," the doctor murmured.

"Quite, quite," Anderson agreed. "Be that as it may, what the ending of the war meant in practical terms to our English authorities is that a substantial sum of money had accumulated in London that was technical due to the Southern states. The *defeated* states."

"I begin to see the problem," Pitferge said, chuckling. "The English government could hardly pay these states the accumulated monies as this would have vastly annoyed the peoples of the states who had won the war. But neither could they, in good faith, keep it."

"Precisely," the captain admitted. "And so there have been negotiations under way between the English government and the one in Washington as to the fate of the funds. He spread his hands helplessly. "Needless to say, it has taken a degree of wrangling and the passage of two years to come to an agreement. Finally, a deal has been struck."

I smiled. "Now I see the issue," I said slowly. "You have been entrusted to resolve the issue, in utmost secrecy."

"Well, hardly myself," Anderson said. "But we do carry in our ship's vault, gold bullion with which to make the payment to the American authorities. I am informed that they monies are to be used to assist in rebuilding the Southern states, so that everyone is in essential agreement on the disposal of the sums."

My companion chuckled. "And you are in a highly nervous state as to the safety of this bullion," he deduced. "Which is why you suspected my friend's innocent questions of having an ulterior motive."

"Yes indeed," the captain agreed. "We had been warned that, despite the veil of secrecy cast over this transaction, it is possible that certain interested parties may have learned of the existence of the money. There are plenty of people who might be tempted to steal the gold."

"Supporters of the defeated Confederacy, no doubt," I realized. "Let alone common thieves and robbers."

"Exactly. So you perhaps understand the source of my worries."

"You have a responsibility I do not envy," I admitted.

"And are we allowed to enquire the amount of bullion you carry?" Pitferge asked.

The captain and his first officer exchanged glances, and then Anderson replied: "Close to three million pounds."

"In gold?"

"In its entirety," the captain agreed.

Pitferge gave a chuckle and sat back in his seat. "Then you have very little to worry about," he said.

Anderson stared at him curiously. "I'm afraid I do not follow you," he admitted.

"By my estimation, three million pounds of gold would weigh approximately 670 kilograms—or about two thirds of a ton. It is, shall we say, far from a negligible weight. It could not be carried off in a thief's pocket—nor even in his hand luggage. And—look about you!—we are in the middle of the Atlantic Ocean. If a thief did indeed somehow manage to steal your bullion, where would he go?" He shook his head firmly. "No, the very fact that it is such a large amount mitigates against its being stolen. I should say that you are substantially more likely to be robbed of a hundred pounds than of three million."

The captain and his first officer exchanges glances again, and a look of relief passed over their previously-worried features. "Indeed," Anderson exclaimed. "You make a very good point!" And he shook hands with my friend, thanked him heartily and again iterated his request that we join him for dinner.

After we left the captain's cabin, I smiled at my friend. "Well, you seem to have settled that issue rather well."

Pitferge looked at me speculatively. "You think so?" he asked me. He shrugged. "I said what I did merely to relieve their minds. Their worried expressions would have given the game away to any genuine robbers."

I studied him with astonishment. "You do not accept your own arguments?" I asked him.

"Pish." He waved his hand dismissively. "There are two very substantial arguments *against* my points," he stated.

I was somewhat amused. "And what are they?"

"The first is that the *Great Eastern* is a cursed ship, and, as you know, I fully expect this trip to end in a disaster."

I raised an eyebrow. "Really, doctor? You—a man of science—calling this a cursed ship?"

He snorted. "How else do you explain that this vessel—a true marvel of our age!—has never managed to succeed at anything? On her very first voyage, she crashed into a New York dock. She then set out for Virginia, and a burst pipe ruined much of her food supplies. The voyage was a financial disaster and alienated most of her passengers. In 1861, caught in a storm at sea, both of her paddlewheels were destroyed. In 1862, she struck an uncharted rock off Montauk Point on Long Island that cost $350,000 and months to repair. By 1864, the ship had lost so much money it was auctioned off and converted into a cable layer. Its first attempt to lay a cable resulted in a breakage of the cable in the mid-Atlantic." He shook his head. "No, my friend, this is a ship with a curse."

"It appears to me to be more a victim of bad luck and poor decisions," I replied.

"And can there be worse curses than those?" he countered. "However you label it, the fact remains that the *Great Eastern* is a failure of gigantic proportions."

I saw that logic wouldn't help convince him, so changed tactics. "And your second argument against yourself?"

190

"Why, precisely the same one that was *for* myself—that we are alone in the Atlantic." We were walking the deck, and he gestured at the sea about us. "There is no other vessel that could come to our aid. If a thief, or gang of thieves, strikes in a city, policemen could be summoned instantly. But—here?"

I smiled. "Come now, doctor," I said. "Surely it has not escaped your notice that there are a decent number of military officers aboard, and that they each of them carry a sword and probably a revolver? What need have we for police when we have gallant soldiers?"

"And what better way for a gang of thieves to disguise themselves than as military officers?" he countered. "Can you say with any certainty that the ones we observe are actually what they appear to be?"

"We know of many that are," I argued. "My friends Captains MacElwin and Corsican spring to mind."

"And their foe, Harry Drake?" Pitferge enquired. "We know for a certainty that he is a scoundrel and a blackguard. Do you assume that he is the sole villain aboard?"

He did have a point there. Drake was ostensibly a gambler, spending much of his time in the smoking salon where the passengers engaged in games of chance. And we had seen him on more than one occasion already speaking intimately with others who had decidedly unprepossessing appearances. That they *might* be crooked could not be denied. But we had no other reason to suspect them than their acquaintance with a known villain. "You think that we should keep an eye on him?" I asked.

"We are already observing him so that he might not accidentally meet Captain MacElwin," the doctor reminded me. This was indeed so, for the two men were ferocious enemies, but—as yet—the captain was unaware of the presence of his foe on the ship, as Drake hung about the gaming room, and the good captain had, like me, no interest in gambling. "And then," added Pitferge, "there is the ghost to account for."

"The ghost?" I echoed, unable to restrain a smile.

"You are aware that several people have seen this dark-clad figure at night in the corridors of this vessel," he said.

"Given the amount of intoxicants consumed aboard, I am very much surprised that there haven't also been reports of pixies or leprechauns," I commented. "And surely, as a man of science, you do not believe in ghosts?"

"As a man of science," he responded, "I cannot afford to *disbelieve* in them."

One of the reasons I was friends with the doctor was because I enjoyed our conversations, which engaged in many strange turns and his odd application of facts. "How can you say that?"

"With the greatest of ease," he replied airily. "The scientific community did not believe in the existence of meteorites until a few decades ago. Their reasoning was that stones could not fall from the sky as there were no stones *in* the sky to fall. The entire scientific community was proven wrong by their disbelief. I do not aim to be caught out in the same error. So, though I do not necessarily *believe* in ghosts, I cannot *disbelieve* in them, either. And neither should you, my friend, if you consider yourself a good Catholic. The existence of the soul is bound up in your religious faith. So why should you not also be able to accept the persistence of the soul in this world?"

"Because in the course of history, vast millions of people have died, and yet only a handful of them have been claimed to return as wandering spirits. Why are there not millions of ghosts, if ghosts exist?"

"Because, I imagine, the vast majority of departed souls must have far better things to do than to stalk the corridors of this ship," he replied. "Which does not mean that *some* may not. As Samuel Johnson observed about the existence of ghosts: *All argument is against it, but all belief is for it.*"

"Well, I cannot imagine that any ghost—if such even exists—would have any interest in gold bullion," I remarked. "Of what use would it be to them?"

"What use is it to most men, except to serve as an object of envy?"

"Speaking for myself, I am always glad when I have a handful of gold in my pockets," I replied. "It enables me to live my life as I wish."

"But would you desire hundreds of kilograms of the stuff?"

"I would have little use for it, and it would take up room in my home that could be put to better use," I admitted.

"Precisely."

I considered his points. "Let us, for the moment, accept that there may be some person or persons who wish to rob this store of bullion," I said. "How do you propose that they would undertake the task?"

He shrugged. "That's hardly my area of expertise," he replied. "I am but a simply doctor. You are the teller of imaginative tales—how would *you* have characters of yours proceed?"

That was worth considering. "Well," I said slowly, "it seems to me that the first thing that any would-be robber would need is a method of escaping capture. As you said, the weight of the bullion precludes it simply being walked away with—nd there is nowhere on this ship to hide such an amount."

"Well, then?" he prompted.

"They would require another ship to transfer it to."

"And how would you provide that?"

I smiled. "These waters may be lonely at the moment, but our general course is known and fairly predictable. It is unlikely that a second ship could keep up with us, as the *Great Eastern* is the fastest ship afloat. Such a ship could not be behind us then, but must approach us from the United States."

"Capital!" he applauded. "So if there is to be a robbery of the gold, it will most certainly be when another ship approaches us closely from ahead. A gang of thieves isn't likely to want to wait any length of time after the robbery for their escape, so they are unlikely to strike until they see their salvation approaching." He chuckled. "Which means we need not fear any action until we sight another vessel."

"And the chances are that any such vessel will be an innocent traveler," I added. "While we have only seen one other ship so far, as we draw closer to the United States, such traffic will increase."

"Which means we should be free to accept the captain's gracious dinner invitation." He considered. "Is there any other information that we currently require?"

"Two things," I replied. "Both of which we might discover over our evening meal. Firstly, the location of the vault aboard this ship and, secondly, how it may be opened."

The doctor chuckled again. "If you ask the captain about either, my friend, I fear you will rekindle his suspicions. Can we not perhaps deduce the information for ourselves?"

He had a good point there, so I thought for a moment. "Well, I, for one, have not seen a vault in my peregrinations about our ship; have you?"

"Not I."

"And we have been everywhere that the passengers are allowed to access—as well as some that they are not, thanks to the kindness of the crew. I therefore conclude that the vault must be located in an area that is accessible only to the crew."

"Capital reasoning," he replied. "Anything further?"

"Well, as you said, the bullion weighs a good deal. Even assuming it is broken down somehow—either as coin or as gold bars—it would probably not be carried about by hand. The easiest method of transport would be by crane. So the vault is likely located within reach of one of the ship's decks for simpler access."

"Splendid," Pitferge agreed. "And, further?"

"If it was loaded aboard by itself, it would surely have drawn attention. So the most obvious way of disguising it would be if it came along with necessary supplies. That would suggest that the vault is located close to the food or luggage areas." I thought for a moment. "Not the luggage areas, as many passengers need to access their bags while traveling, so close to the kitchen storage is more likely."

"I agree. And when we were shown around the kitchens, there was a corridor we were not given access to, and I saw a sailor loitering at the entrance."

I smiled. "So that is likely where the vault is situated," I concluded. "And for our hypothetical robbers to strike, they would need to remove that obvious guard. No," I corrected myself, "to *replace* him with one of their own number."

"Unless the guard himself is one of the gang," the doctor suggested.

I considered the point. "That is unlikely—any man in such a post must clearly be one that both the captain and the ship's owners would trust implicitly, given the nature of the cargo."

"I concede the point. Now—the vault itself. Do you have any thoughts?"

"Well, this ship was not *designed* as a transport for bullion—in fact, this is clearly a rare occurrence, as our captain is unusually worried. But it *does* carry many wealthy passengers, and they are likely to require storage for their jewelry and such items. People of that ilk do like to make ostentatious displays of their finery at dinner and of an evening. Therefore the vault would have to be accessible at short notice. An inventor, Yale, has developed a combination lock for doors, but only as recently as 1861. As the *Great Eastern* was built in 1858, its vault would therefore not possess a combination lock. It is most likely, therefore, to be accessible by means of two keys."

"We are doing splendidly," the doctor said approvingly. "And those keys would be held by...?"

"Clearly, one would be in the possession of the captain at all times," I said. "The other would most likely be held by the chief steward, as he would be the one approached by the passengers who required their precious items."

"And that means," he concluded, "that any would-be robbers would have to obtain the keys from both men." He shook his head. "Is it possible, do you think, that our robbers might attempt to blow open the door using explosives?"

I laughed. "It is unlikely," I replied.

"I read of banks being so robbed constantly, it seems."

"But always at night, once the staff have gone home," I pointed out. "In our case, the ship *is* home, and the kitchens are working all day and night. An explosion would attract far too much attention. Stealing either the keys or else kidnapping the persons holding the keys is far more likely."

"True." He considered a moment. "So, then, the best course of action would be for us to constantly follow the captain about?"

I chuckled. "I hardly think that he would approve. Besides, he's the *captain*—he's in the public eye all of the time."

"Except while he sleeps."

I raised an eyebrow. "Do you propose to establish a cot for yourself in his cabin?"

"It would be... problematical," he agreed. "Still, if *we* cannot think of a way to get both keys at the same time, surely any would-be robber would have the same problem?"

"But our hypothetical thief has a criminal nature." I pointed out. "And we—I trust!—do not."

"Then you propose we do nothing?" the doctor asked.

"Properly speaking, it is neither our right nor duty," I replied. "I am sure that Captain Anderson has his own measures in place, and anything we might do could interfere with his own arrangements." I softened slightly. "But we *might* keep our eyes open as we negotiate about the ship and look for any potential thieves."

Pitferge grinned. "So, we do what we have been doing all along, only with a more wary eye? I am all for that."

And, thus emboldened by our resolution, we took a turn about the deck, and then went below to examine our fellow passengers in the various salons. The problem, of course, is the eternal one of being able to differentiate between good and evil souls. It would be of a distinct advantage to us all if the theories of the physiognomists were to be proven accurate, and one could simply glance at an individual and say: "By the slant of his brow and the spacing of his eyes, I can tell that this fellow is a crook". Sadly, of course, there is very little evidence of the efficacy of the method and the most we can manage is to decide that we do—or do not—like the look of a man's face. The most evil man's face I have ever seen—according to these theories—belonged to the personage of a judge of the court of appeals, and I have to hope that he features belied his attitudes.

We did come across Harry Drake—whom we knew to be a villain—in his usual place in the smoking saloon, intent on some game of chance, but he appeared to be alone, so we could not even judge his companions by association. He was clearly planning nothing worse for the present than fleecing one or more of the other players. I could not bring myself to have any compassion for his potential victims as I feel that anyone who indulges in gambling—beyond those mild lotteries played on the ship to guess miles sailed—deserves to lose everything that they hazard in games of chance.

It did, at least, aid us in passing the day in a fairly amusing fashion, as Pitferge felt compelled, as always, to comment on the personages and histories of everyone he was acquainted with; and he somehow knew or knew of a great number of the passengers and one or two of the crew. He kept me entertained by his wide-ranging comments and frequently scurrilous tales of everyone from minor nobles to major rogues—at least, where their villainy ranged from flirting to over-indulgence in alcoholic beverages.

In the late afternoon we were strolling around the deck and observing our fellow travelers when we heard the cry of: "Sail ho!" We immediately proceeded to the bow of the ship and scanned the horizon.

"Ah—there!" the doctor exclaimed, pointing almost due west. His eyesight was clearly better than mine, for it took me a few moments to spot the vague whiteness on the waves indicating a companion vessel. It was impossible to make out anything further at this distance, other than it was definitely proceeding from New York in our general direction.

"You think it might be allies of our robbers?" I asked.

Pitferge shrugged. "The odds are against it, my friend. It is most likely simply a passing vessel heading for Europe." Then his eyes sparkled. "Ah—but suppose it is not?" He sighed. "It is a fair distance from us, and it will be a matter of more than an hour before we shall be able to tell whether it aims to pass or to intercept us. And it is quite close to dinner time. Once our meal is over, we shall be able to tell, eh?"

By the time that the bugle sounded to announce that seating for dinner was to commence we had promenaded about the ship three and one half times and were not an inch closer to discovering any possible robbers. I imagine, though, that it had at least improved our health a good deal, and most certainly our appetites.

Captain Anderson greeted us warmly as we approached his table, and welcomed us to the impending feast. "And how are your investigations progressing?" he enquired, with a twinkle in his eye.

"Investigations?" I echoed, innocently.

"Oh, come now, gentlemen," he said, chuckling. "You are a writer, M. Verne, and you—if you will pardon my saying so, doctor—an irredeemable busybody. Given the information that I handed you earlier, I fully expected the pair of you to decide to play detectives." And he smiled warmly. "And I saw you walking the deck fully three times in the course of the afternoon, both deep in conversation. What else could you have been so intent upon?"

"It sounds to me, captain," cried Pitferge gaily (and not at all insulted by the captain's description of him), "that we have not been the only ones engaged in detection."

Anderson chuckled. "I must confess, you did live up to my expectations. But have you learned nothing, my friends?"

"Oh, yes," I replied. "I have learned that I should stick to writing about detectives instead of attempting to emulate one."

"Ah." The captain sighed. "Well, it is always possible that I am simply being an alarmist. But let us not allow the day's events to detract from the enjoyment of our meal, gentlemen. I can assure you that I shall not."

And so we indulged ourselves to the fullest in a fine dinner. The captain was proven correct in his estimation of the wine—a remarkably opulent Bordeaux—and both of us enjoyed a second glass with our desserts. We finished off with cups of strong—if somewhat bitter—coffee, and the captain's steward offered us both cigars, which we happily accepted.

Then the captain noticed a slip of paper peeking out from under the edge of his saucer. He frowned, and removed it, unfolding the small note. And then his face paled.

"Is something wrong, captain?" I enquired. Wordlessly, he passed me the note. In block capitals were the words:

YOU HAVE JUST BEEN POISONED.

We three looked at one another in concern. "Could this be some kind of an attempt at humor?" I asked. "No matter how misplaced?"

"I can assure you gentlemen that it is not," the steward answered in a confidential voice. "Please—let us keep this conversation to ourselves; we should not wish to alarm the general public."

Anderson scowled at the man. "What the devil do you mean?" he demanded—but he kept his voice low, as requested.

The steward smiled slightly. "Why don't you gentlemen enjoy those fine cigars on the deck?" he suggested. "We can converse more freely there."

It was clear that the captain's first inclination was to tell the impudent scoundrel to go to the blazes, but then he reconsidered and gave an abrupt nod. "Gentlemen," he said to Pitferge and I, "let us promenade."

We walked as casually as we could through the dining room and onto the almost-empty deck, trailed by the steward. My emotions were in a turmoil—we had been vaguely anticipating trouble, but it had seemed more like a sport than reality. And this—well, *this* was certainly nothing that we had anticipated. Poisoning the captain! What could it mean?

Once we were upon the deck, I noticed that the breeze had stiffened somewhat. Pitferge nudged me and indicated the seascape. The vessel we had seen earlier was now closer, and quite clearly heading to intercept our course.

Anderson, however, had eyes only for the steward. His scowl had intensified. "What does this mean?" he asked the man. "You are not the regular steward.

"No, indeed," he agreed. "He is… indisposed. I took it upon myself to substitute for him for one meal."

"You have a name?" the captain enquired. Had the sea been as cold as his voice, I should have looked for icebergs in it.

"Of course, though it will be meaningless to you." He smiled slightly. "You may call me Moriarty."

"Well, Moriarty—would you care to illuminate me as to the meaning of that note?"

The man pretended to be puzzled. "I should have thought that it was obvious," he replied. Then he glanced at the doctor and myself. "Ah, of course! You gentlemen are French, and my note was in English. And there is no discernable difference in English between the second person singular and the second person plural, unlike in your more descriptive tongue. I meant the second person plural, of course. You have *all* been poisoned. My apologies for not having made myself clearer."

I had been poisoned also? I confess, I felt more than a momentary shock at the news. "The poison was in the wine?"

"My dear sir!" Moriarty exclaimed. "In that delightful vintage? What kind of a monster do you take me for? No indeed—it was in the coffee. Which means, of course, that anyone who drank the tea is perfectly safe. Anyone who is willing to drink that wretched coffee *deserves* to be poisoned."

What an audacious madman! Though I was far from calm with the news, I almost had to admire his skill and humor. "And the purpose of poisoning half of the passengers?" I enquired.

"Come now, M. Verne—my men have been observing you and your amusing companion. I think you must have a good idea by now what the purpose of my plans is."

"The gold," Captain Anderson said coldly.

"Precisely."

"And how will killing my passengers and myself get you an inch closer to the gold?"

"My dear sir," Moriarty answered. "It is not my desire to kill *anyone*. The poison I introduced into the coffee is quite harmless for several hours. No one else will even suspect that they are in any danger—provided you see reason."

"And that reason is…?" the captain asked.

"I will provide you with the antidote for the poison—in exchange for the two keys to the vault and time enough to transfer the gold to my approaching vessel. How you chose to get the passengers to imbibe the cure is up to you—I would suggest placing it into the beverages at breakfast. That way there will be no panic and no need to inform anyone that they were ever in any sort of danger."

Anderson thought for a moment. "You appear to have thought this out quite thoroughly."

Moriarty bowed slightly. "I certainly hope I have," he agreed. "It is my aim to build up an organization to conduct crimes on a scientific basis." He smiled at me. "A concept worthy of one of your tales, M. Verne. A criminal enterprise—with the emphasis on the latter word. Most crimes are matters of opportunity and yield slight rewards. I aim to build up, if you will, a criminal business, organized like any regular company, which will take the uncertainty out of crime and make it serve as a regular, salaried occupation. And your three million dollars, captain, with provide me with an admirable initial investment."

Dr. Pitferge snorted. "You appear to have gotten off to a fine start," he commented. "However, if I may question you? Do you have any proof at all that you have poisoned *anyone*?"

"I beg your pardon?" Moriarty asked.

"We have only your word thus far that you have actually poisoned anyone. Conveniently, you tell us that the effects won't be observable until *after* you have left us. Given that you admit to being a criminal, I find it rather difficult to accept the fact of the mass poisoning based solely upon your unsupported word." He scowled. "It would be rather… embarrassing, shall we say… if you were allowed to pillage the vault only for us to later find out that there was, in fact, no poison."

I had expected Moriarty to be annoyed at this assault on his word, but, to my surprise, he laughed heartily. "My dear doctor, I do declare that you have a wonderfully criminal mind. I am sorely tempted to offer you a position in my enterprise. You are quite correct in suggesting that I might well be—as our American cousins would have it—running a bluff. To be truthful, the idea did appeal to me initially. But then I realized that someone might have similar suspicions." He reached inside his jacket pocket and removed a small vial, which he offered to Pitferge. "You are a doctor, sir—feel free to examine my sample."

The doctor accepted the vial and unstoppered it. He tasted a few grains and then resealed it. "A derivative of thallium?" he asked.

"My own formula," Moriarty replied with a slight smile, taking the sample back. "I assure you, it works as I described."

"Yes, I imagine it would." He turned to Captain Anderson. "He is correct in saying that it is very dangerous and inevitable fatal if untreated. However, there *is* an antidote."

"But not one you are likely to carry aboard in any quantity," Moriarty added.

"No, quite," Pitferge agreed.

"I have more than enough stored aboard," the criminal mastermind said. "And I will be more than happy to provide you with the location—*after* you accede to my demands."

Captain Anderson tried to maintain his usually impassive English expression, but I could see that his nerves were badly affected by this threat. "My duty to the lives of my passengers must come first," he said slowly. "It would appear that I have no other option but to agree to your demands." He seemed to shrink in size as the burden of this decision weighed upon his mind and body. "I shall send for my first officer—and the other key."

"Perhaps we should limit the number of people aware of this... problem to as few as possible," Pitferge suggested. "I volunteer to fetch the gentleman and key in question."

"Acceptable," Moriarty agreed. "There is no need to alarm the passengers or crew. I can trust you to be discrete, I believe."

"I will speak only with the first officer," the doctor promised. "Believe me, I fully understand the importance of silence." He hurried away, leaving the three of us to await his return.

I faced Moriarty. "The ship that we observed earlier," I murmured. "It is, of course, your vessel?"

"Indeed," he agreed. "My men will board this ship and unload the gold on my instructions. I assure you, the passengers will in no way be molested or severely inconvenienced." His chuckled. "Though if you have entered the shipboard sweepstakes over how far the vessel will travel in 24 hours, I hope you have a low number, as you will, of course, have to remain at rest while the transfer is effected. Captain, you may need to prepare a story of some minor repairs to the paddles—this has happened before, so it will not alarm anyone."

It was a scheme so well-planned and intriguing that I could almost forget that we—the captain and I—had both ingested poison and were actually in peril of dying if anything went wrong with Moriarty's scheme. This knowledge, however, was clearly preying upon Anderson. Like any good captain, his main concern was with the safety of his passengers and crew. He was a conscientious man, though, and surrendering cargo given into his safe-keeping did not sit well with his spirit. I had no doubt that he was wracking his tortured brains to try and circumvent the theft without endangering anyone further. I cannot fault him for being unable to do so.

Pitferge returned in surprisingly short time, accompanied by the worried-looking first officer. "I have advised him of the predicament we are in," the doctor informed us all. "Naturally, he has kept silent."

"It is appreciated," Moriarty said solemnly. "Now, gentlemen, shall we proceed? He turned to Pitferge and myself. "I apologize for inconveniencing you both, but I should prefer it if you accompanied us."

"Speaking for myself," I informed him, "I am quite intrigued by the thought of seeing three million dollars in gold—no matter how fleetingly."

Moriarty chuckled. "An understandable attitude," he said cheerfully. "Well, then, I shall endeavor not to disappoint you. Captain?" he inclined his head. Anderson growled, but led the way below decks.

We did pass other passengers and crew, but none of them suspected our purpose, of course, and did no more than nod greetings to the officers. Captain Anderson, for the most part, ignored them all, concentrating on his task at hand. He was clearly suffering internal stress, and I felt sorry for the unfortunate man. I was also trying hard not to allow my imagination to concentrate on the idea that poison was even now ravaging my insides.

It was not the easiest of tasks.

My companion didn't appear to be suffering from my dark thoughts. As we approached the food storage area, he chuckled to himself. "Aha! See, my friend, our surmises were quite accurate—the vault is located in this part of the ship."

"Forgive me if I don't share your enthusiasm," I muttered. "I cannot help being concerned that we are, even now, facing the possibility of death."

He waved his hand airily. "It is a factor that we face every single day of our lives," he said. "We can never be certain that we shall survive the day."

"Well, I am a little more certain that we shall not survive *this* day," I pointed out.

"Ah, well, sometimes certainty is overrated. We have, let us not forget, no tangible proof that a poison has in fact been administered to us."

"You yourself held and examined the poison," I pointed out.

"Oh, I grant you—the poison Moriarty mentioned certainly exists. But that it was actually placed in the coffee?" He shrugged. "It could be merely a bluff."

"Can we take that chance?" I inquired.

"Ah, no," he admitted. "If I were hazarding only my own life, perhaps I would risk it. But the lives of so many of our innocent fellow passengers?" He shook his head. "I would require something more certain than suspicion."

Moriarty had clearly been listening to our conversation, even though we had carried it out in subdued tones. His sense of hearing must have been exceptional. "Bravo, doctor," he approved. "Excellent reasoning." Then he turned to the captain. "I see that we have arrived."

I could see this also. There was a single member of the crew standing watch by a large steel door. The locks for the two keys were visible, as also was a wheel to be turned to open the door. The sailor stiffened at our approach.

"It's... all right, Sanders," the captain informed him. "We need to enter the vault."

"Sir." The man stood aside. His face showed no suspicion that anything was wrong. And why should he even think that there might be? The captain and first officer were here with a couple of passengers to access the vault, and there were no signs of duress being employed.

Scowling, Anderson and his first officer removed their keys and unlocked the door. The captain glanced at Moriarty, who merely inclined his head towards the door. The first officer gripped the wheel and turned it, and the door sighed open. There were lanterns by the door, and the two men lit one each and led the way into the vault.

It was not large—possibly ten feet on a side—and one wall was lined with boxes such as you would find in a bank. These were clearly where the valuables deposited by the passengers resided. Oppose them was a stack of heavy-duty shelving, and on that shelving sat numerous heavy-looking sacks.

Three million dollars in gold...

Moriarty rubbed his hands together in anticipation. "Splendid, captain. Now we shall have to..." He had started to turn and his voice trailed off as he saw the revolver in Doctor Pitferge's fist. "You surprise me, doctor," he said gently.

"I meant to," my companion replied. He chuckled. "I suppose I might have done this at any time, but, like M. Verne here, I found myself with a desire to gaze upon such a large sum of money."

"And what is your intention with that weapon?" Moriarty enquired.

"To put a stop to your little scheme, sir."

Moriarty frowned slightly. "And condemn yourself and your fellow passengers to an unpleasant death?"

"Certainly not." Piferge smiled and turned to the first officer. "If you please...?"

The man reached into his pocket and withdrew what was clearly a flask of the type gentlemen use to carry alcoholic drinks. He opened it and held it towards Moriarty. "Drink," he ordered.

"That's very civil of you," the villain replied. "But I make it a strict rule never to take intoxicating drinks. It interferes with the smooth operations of the mind, you understand."

"This isn't whiskey," the officer growled. "It's coffee."

"Ah." Moriarty turned to Dr. Pitferge. "You plan to utilize my own poison on me?"

"Quite." The doctor grinned cheerily again. "If you *did* poison the coffee, then you will have to tell us where the antidote is to save your own life. And if you *didn't*, then we can be certain that we have no need to fear."

Whatever was passing through Moriarty's mind at this point, nothing of it showed on his face. "And if I refuse to drink, then you propose to shoot me?" He shook his head. "If you kill me, then you condemn everyone to death."

"I do not prose to kill you," Pitferge replied. "I am, after all, a doctor, and I am sworn not to take life but to save it. But, as a doctor, I know *precisely* where to shoot you so that you will merely be in such pain that you will *wish* to die. At which point, we shall simply pour the coffee down your throat anyway." He shrugged. "In any event, drink the coffee you will. You may decide how much pain you wish to take with it."

Moriarty considered the matter thoughtfully, but made no move to accept the proffered flask. "Ah. Well thought-out, doctor," he said. "I admit that I did not take this possibility into consideration." He appeared to be thinking rapidly. "Very well, I accept that I have been beaten. I shall reveal the location of the antidote to you—without requiring the payment of three million dollars." He sighed softly. "Such a shame."

"No, sir," Pitferge replied.

The would-be robber looked startled. "No?"

"Drink the coffee, and *then* we shall discuss the antidote."

Surprisingly, Moriarty laughed. "You think I would offer you a fake cure otherwise?"

"Would you not?"

Moriarty nodded. "I should have indeed. Very well." He accepted the flask and drank the coffee very visibly. He appeared to be taking the failure of his plans with equanimity. I admit that I found this rather disturbing. He did not strike me as the type of person to accept defeat quite so easily.

Something occurred to me, and I turned to the captain. "He has his accomplices on that ship we saw earlier," I said. "Perhaps it would be as well to avoid contact with it."

"Indeed," Anderson agreed. He nodded to the first officer, who hurried away. Then he turned to Moriarty. "And now—the antidote," he prompted.

Moriarty complied, and Anderson arranged with his staff to serve it in the morning with breakfast. He then had Moriarty locked in the brig. I was rather surprised to discover that the vessel even had one, but apparently most larger sea-going vessels possessed one, though they were rarely utilized.

"Drunken sailors and all that," Pitferge commented.

"Quite," the captain agreed. "And now, gentlemen—a further favor from you both would be greatly appreciated. I would ask that this incident remain between the few of us concerned. It would hardly do my company a great deal of good if it should become known that we almost suffered a mass poisoning."

"And the *Great Eastern* has a—shall we say—*delicate* history as it is," Pitferge said, unable to resist himself.

"We do not have the greatest reputation," Anderson was forced to admit. "I would appreciate it if further scandal were not attached to my ship's name."

"Perfectly understandable," I replied. I sighed. "A pity, as it would make for a good story. But I shall promise not to reveal anything of it during my lifetime."

The doctor scowled. "I confess it would make for a fine after-dinner story," he said. There was a glint in his eye. "Particularly after coffee. But I shall respect your wishes also. Though I confess that you may have a problem prosecuting Moriarty without the full story coming out."

"I am sure that he would not wish it to be known that he had been involved in a mass poisoning attempt," Anderson said. "He is likely to get a lengthy sentence as it is for attempted robbery on the high seas."

As it turned out, he didn't. When the ship docked in New York, the brig was discovered to be empty.

"I suppose he had assistance from some confederate on the ship to escape," I suggested to the doctor when we found out.

Pitferge grunted. "You have always had such a generous and innocent nature, my friend," he observed.

I frowned. "What do you mean?"

"I mean," he said as we disembarked from our eventful journey, "that it would not have been in the best interest of the company if Moriarty's tale were to be told in court. They might be faced with problems booking passengers, and they desperately need to make money."

"You think, then...?"

He stared off into the distance. "I think that life is full of possibilities—don't you?"

The hero of this tale, Maciste, who previously appeared in this volume in Matthew Baugh's story, and, prior to that, in Matthew's "The Heart of the Moon" in our third volume, is an Italian silent film character, played by the herculean, Bartolomeo Pagano, who first appeared as a slave in the 1914 film Cabiria. *The character then returned in several more films, in the silent era and beyond, popping up in different settings and eras, righting wrongs, always fighting for the common person and overthrowing all kinds of villains. Anthony Perconti heartily recommends Jacqueline Reich's 2015 book,* The Maciste Films of Italian Silent Cinema, *a wonderful examination of this character in the greater context of Italian society during the early 20th Century…*

Anthony Perconti: *Maciste Contro il Negromante Cremisi*

> *In sunset cycles of the sombering years,*
> *He sips an amaranth wine.*
> Clark Ashton Smith

Zothique, The Far Future

The lone figure walked up the dirt road, the red sun having breached the horizon at his back. As he approached the small farmstead, Fulo could make out his features. A towering, broad-shouldered, barrel-chested man with dark brown skin. He was bald and he wore a salt and pepper spade beard. The stranger cut a figure of heroic proportions. His dress was that of a farmer or laborer, a simple woolen tunic, with a blue sash about his waist and sandaled feet. The young man waved.

"Good morning, young lord," the stranger said.

"Good morning, sir. How can I be of service to you?"

"I was hoping to quench my thirst and perhaps obtain a morsel to eat. I'm passing through." The man turned his head towards the orchards of olive trees. "I'd be more than happy to help with any chores that need tending. Are your parents about?"

The young man said, "My name's Fulo. My mother will be back later in the day. We could use some help with the harvest." Fulo's eyes had a haunted cast to them. He was courteous, but on his guard.

The giant nodded and said, "I'm called Maciste. I'm obliged to you."

After a simple morning meal of flat bread, dried olives, hard cheese and watered wine, Maciste was put to work in the orchards. He and three other farm hands, both bronze-skinned men past their middle years, worked the rows of olive trees. They used long green sticks to bring the fruit down, collected them into wicker baskets and hauled these to a small stone barn. Fulo and three younger children, a boy and two girls, worked the rows alongside the laborers. The stranger judged them to be his host's siblings by their features.

Sometime during the mid-afternoon, a mule drawn cart made its way up the road and towards the farmhouse. A woman walked down the path that bisected the orchards. She was over medium height, lean and bronze-skinned, with black hair, shot with a few strands of gray. Her left eye was covered with a plain leather patch. Like the other farmers, she wore a simple woolen tunic, a cord sash and sandals. She gave the group an expansive wave and walked back to the homestead.

Once the harvesting and other chores were completed, the laborers went to the well to wash off the dust and sweat of the day. Once dry, they made their way to the farmhouse, wood smoke rising into the red tinged sky from the hearth.

The farmhands, the children, Maciste and Nisa, the lady of the house, all ate at the same table. There was no time to put on airs on a working farm—the three farm cats being the exception. These people worked together, cheek by jowl, day in, day out. They ate together as well. The evening meal was a simple, yet hearty affair, a soup of lentils and carrots, flat bread and cheese. A young red wine helped wash it all down. After the meal, all hands pitched in to clean up.

Once the cooking area was tidy, the farm hands, Fulo, Maciste and Nisa, sat around the table, imbibing a bit more of the wine, conversing. The three younger children played with the cats, by the hearth.

"My man and I were in King Gandash's service, part of his Majesty's Royal Archers," said Nisa. She brushed the leather eyepatch with a finger, smoothing a stray black lock behind her ear. "That's how I lost this. Lamiae are formidable and wily brutes."

"Ah," Maciste said, taking a sip from his bowl.

"After our term was up, we pooled together our few specie and brought this place." She stared off in the middle distance for a moment and said, "It was a good run. Nearly made it a score of years."

"What happened?" Maciste asked.

"One day, our eldest went missing. Delva just passed her nineteenth summer." Nisa took a sip of her watered wine. "Arwia, the local temple priestess, informed us that Grenier might be the author of our troubles."

"Grenier?" Maciste repeated the name.

"Yes. Known about these parts as the Crimson Necromancer, or Grenier the Red. It is rumored that he hails from the far western isles. He arrived here about two years or so ago, bringing along a retinue of revenants with him. Word is, he is obsessed with the bloody color. He even had his manse built up in red marble. He's a strutting, black hearted little peacock." She shook her head. "And a collector of people, too. They say he can revivify them and make them his playthings."

Maciste examined the contents of his wine bowl and muttered, "So that's why I'm here." He quaffed the dregs.

Nisa glanced at Maciste, questioningly and said, "What do you mean?"

He asked, "Did this necromancer take your Delva from you?"

"Aye," she said. "And Adiur, her sweetheart, too. A nice, hardworking boy. He made the journey to Grenier's manse, looking for answers, but never returned."

The sun was making its slow descent behind the hills. Rosh, one of the old hands, snatched a twig from the hearth and began lighting a few clay oil lamps scattered about the room and on the dinner table.

Nisa sighed and continued, "What could I do? I have my other daughters and sons to look after. Not to mention my hands. Who'll look after these rickety old scoundrels, eh?" she grinned at the men, playfully. "We all have to eat. The land needs tending."

Maciste rose from the table. "I thank you again for your hospitality, Lady. At dawn, I'll be off to pay this Crimson Necromancer a visit. How long a journey did you say it was?"

Nisa, the three farmhands and Fulo stared up at Maciste, looks of bewilderment apparent on their faces.

"We could use your strong back here on the farm," said Fulo. "Not much glory to be had. The pay isn't exactly the King's coin, but it's good, honest work. No lamias around these parts, either. We don't go to bed hungry. The wine and food are plentiful and the sunsets are something to behold."

"Just the same, I'll be leaving tomorrow," replied Maciste. "But I appreciate the offer."

Fulo gave a little sigh and nodded. "Half a day's walk. Follow the main road, back that way," he pointed out the window, "due north. Impossible to miss it."

Maciste nodded.

"And, Maciste," Nisa added, smiling up at him, grasping his hand, "you have my thanks."

The man seated at the table, taking his mid-day meal, was garbed foot to crown in deep crimson robes. A freshly reanimated serving girl was seated on his lap, hand feeding him. His aquiline face, sculpted mustache and beard were also of a matching scarlet hue. He sipped wine from a ruby encrusted goblet, while his other hand absentmindedly twirled a lock of the girl's brittle brown hair. An armor-clad revenant, the plume of his helm bobbing in time with each clanking step, approached the feasting necromancer. The soldier put his right palm over his still heart, took a knee and croaked, "Your pardon, my Lord."

The necromancer turned to the man at arms, a look of disdain on his red face and said, "Why do you disturb my repast, Shahin?"

"A man at the main entrance, Lord. He requested an audience with you. When the guards told him to be off, he became... agitated."

"Agitated?" Grenier asked. "How so?"

"He has destroyed six of the men thus far. I am reinforcing the gateway as we speak," the officer said.

The necromancer's eyebrows raised in something like surprise. "Six, you say? Single handedly?"

"Aye, my Lord."

Grenier rose to his feet, pushing the naked girl to the floor. He crossed the sumptuously furnished room, to a small worktable beneath a window. Amidst other sorcerous tools sat a silver bowl, with runes etched onto the sides. The bowl was filled with a milky, viscous liquid. Grenier traced a series of geometric patterns over the fluid, uttering a few guttural syllables. A scene slowly materialized on the liquid's surface.

A span before the colossal bronze doors stood a dark-skinned giant, with several cuts about his arms, shoulders and torso. He was crouched in a wrestler's stance. At his feet were strewn half a dozen of the manse's guards, helmet's stoved into skulls, arms and legs broken at odd angles.

"By the Lord of the Seven Hells!" the necromancer said. "He is a spirited one to be sure... Shahin, he is to be taken alive. Is that clear?"

"Aye, my Lord," said the officer.

Maciste kept low, while three more armed revenants came at him, stepping over their broken comrades, short swords at the ready. Maciste went for the one to the right, rushing into his guard, wrapping his right arm about his waist. With his left hand, he gripped the guard's right arm, where the wrist joined the hand. He then twisted until a snap of bone and a clang of bronze on stone could be heard.

Maciste picked up the guard and threw him at his two approaching companions. The three fell into a huddle on the paving stones. The giant ran over to the group, bringing down sandaled feet, crushing skulls and bones.

"Grenier! Come out and face me!" the giant yelled, his voice ringing off the red marble edifice.

A rhythmic *clump clump clump* sound grew louder. Six pikemen in serried ranks methodically marched towards the giant, pike-points glinting in the sun. Maciste stepped back, away from the small phalanx, turning his head left and right. Clusters of guards surrounded him on all sides, cautiously making their way closer and closer.

He rushed the group coming in from his left. Tucking his chin and coming in low with his shoulder, he bowled over the first three guards, but hands gripped his ankles and calves, dragging him down. He felt a kick at the small of his back, sending him to his knees. His left arm covered his face, while he lashed out in a devastating hammer fist with his right.

The revenants were now closing ranks on him, striking with sword pommels and kicking him down to the paving stones. Maciste rolled onto his back and lashed out with both legs, snapping the femurs of two of his foes. A weighted net was thrown on him, while hands gripped his calves and arms. Several of the guards straddled his legs and torso, pinning him down. A few more weighed down his biceps and wrists.

Maciste bent at the waist, slowly, slowly, making his way up to a sitting position. He felt a sharp sting on the right side of his neck. Reeling, the back of his head hit the paving stones.

In his field of vision was a cadaverous hand holding a long bronze needle, its length coated with a sticky amber substance. A drop of blood fell from the point.

His vision dimmed and the world went black.

Maciste floated in velvety darkness, comforted in its warm embrace. Images slowly coalesced. Visions of cities, nations and entire planets materialized before him. With names such as Carthage, Rome, Lemuria, Turin, Selene, Vienna, Tikal, Gotham, Leptis Magna, Mu, Karanog, New York, Aztlan, Yasodharpura, Edo, Meroe, Hy-Brasil, Los Angeles, Itchyma, Castle Rock, Dis, Varanasi, Atlanta, Brunse, Byzantium, Ys, Saint-Domingue, New London, Ilium, Cerebos, Neo-Tokyo, Venusburg and Paris, among others. All places that he recognized, all places that he had frequented at some point in his existence. These images were followed by a torrent of faces: male, female, androgyne, even non-human visages: metallic, crystalline, reptilian, all bearing the same name—*Maciste*. Recognition passed between that long procession of countenances and the man floating in darkness. They were aspects of the same being. All aspects of himself. A sibilant speech filled his ears.

"Who will lift the Heel from the Neck of The People?"

"Maciste."

"Who will repel the Wolf at the Gate?"

"Maciste."

"Who will strike a Blow for Justice?"

"Maciste."

The speech was repeated again and again, myriad voices joining in, a gigantic chorus, rising in intensity and volume.

"I hear you," Maciste said.

The chorus grew louder.

"I hear you!" he repeated. "I hear *all* of you!"

The chorus grew louder, still.

The giant put his hands to his ears and screamed.

Maciste woke up screaming. A stabbing pain radiated from his wrists, down to his shoulders. He could not feel his hands. He hung from manacles fastened around his wrists, the connecting chain draped over a stout oak beam. His toes scraped the damp stone floor.

He swiveled his head, left and right. He assumed he was in a small stone cell, somewhere beneath the necromancer's manse. Light filtered in through the barred door. A hulking, freshly reanimated revenant came into his line of sight. Maciste felt woozy, like he was standing on the deck of a pitching ship. Whatever substance he had been injected with, its effects had not worn off yet. He tried pulling his hands down, straining against the bronze links, to no avail.

"That *aqrabuamelu* venom's keeping you weak as a lamb, meat. Don't bother," the hulking figure said.

The revenant unleashed a flurry of punches to Maciste's midsection, finishing up with a right hook to his ribs.

"Boss wants me to tenderize you a bit," he rasped.

There was another series of blows to his midsection. Maciste gritted his teeth through the beating. When the revenant had finished delivering the second volley, Maciste spit a wad bloody phlegm at his face. It dripped down his forehead, into his unblinking eyes.

The hulking figure shook his head, *tssking*. "Not very nice, meat. Not very nice at all."

A ham-sized fist caught Maciste on the left side of the face. Once again, the world went black.

Maciste awoke on a filthy straw pallet. The metallic tang of blood filled his mouth and his tongue found split lips and several empty spaces where his teeth should have been. He couldn't see out of his left eye, swollen shut courtesy of his tenderizing session. Everything hurt. He had no way of knowing how long he had been unconscious and the effects of the *aqrabuamelu* venom still lingered.

The room pitched. Maciste vomited up bile onto the straw, causing a coughing spasm that racked his entire body. Pain shot through his chest with each cough. He lay back down and closed his eyes, drifting in and out of consciousness.

The sound of his cell door creaking open and closing awakened him. The revenant that stood before him must have been an elder figure at the time of her death. She bore the telltale signs of advanced age, stooped back and white wisps of hair on her head. The mummified flesh covering her bones was parchment-thin and just as delicate. Within her hollow eye sockets, twin amber flames burned with an unearthly glow. She wore a tattered saffron robe, with the remnants of a red silk sash wrapped around her skeletal waist. Her voice was a susurrus-dead leaves blown by the winter wind.

"Be still, warrior. I mean you no harm."

"No harm, eh? A friend come to pay a visit?" Maciste let out a weak chuckle.

"In a manner of speaking, yes. My name is Ilalotha. In life, all those count-less years gone by, I held the rank of Queen and Sorceress. My compatriots and I were well versed in the dark arts. The enemies of our kingdom trembled when they spied us upon the field of battle."

"Good for you," Maciste said.

"But also, good for you," Ilalotha said.

"How so?" Maciste asked.

"By comparison, Grenier's skills are blundering at best, albeit formidable. He is like a perverse child with a dagger. The way he has enslaved all of us," she waved a skeletal hand above her head, as if taking in the entirety of the manse, "for example. But thanks to the knowledge I gained in life, I have a degree more autonomy than my fellow reanimates. A slave still, but one with a longer chain. That fool," she pointed up, "is all but blind to this fact."

"Why are you telling me this?" Maciste asked.

"At midday tomorrow, once he has slept off the debauches of the night, Grenier will grace you with his august presence," she said with a dry chuckle. "You will be brought to him, and he will regale you with all the tortures that he has in store for you, prior to murdering you—and bringing you back, of course."

"A pleasant fellow," Maciste said.

"Indeed. This meeting will present an opportunity," Ilalotha said.

"An opportunity? How so?" Maciste asked.

"An opportunity for us to be rid of this wretched creature. When you are ushered to his throne tomorrow, it will be the only time that you will see him while still living. Once he brings you back from death..." the woman shook her head.

"A comforting thought," Maciste said. "What of this opportunity?"

"As I said, Grenier does have a bit of talent. A protective enchantment shields him from bodily attack. If someone were able to puncture it," she nodded at Maciste, "he would be as helpless as a newborn fawn."

"Even at the best of times, my strength is no match for raw thaumaturgy," Maciste said. "And, as you can plainly see, my condition is far from optimal, Lady."

"True enough. However, I may be able to help in this regard," the revenant said.

She bent down onto one knee and held up her index finger. It began to glow with the same amber flame that was present in the orbits of her skull. It grew brighter and brighter still, reaching incandescence. Ilalotha traced a com-plicated series of runes in the air, a light trail following her finger as she weaved.

When she finished, she said, "This will hurt, I'm afraid."

She pressed the flaming digit against Maciste's chest. The skin sizzled and hissed. The giant gave a groan of pain.

"There. All done. You are now able to pass through his protective shield. It will be painful, but it will not kill you."

She reached into one of the robe's sleeves and retrieved a small stoppered phial, containing a red liquid.

"Drink this." She poured the contents into his mouth. "It will ease the pain of your injuries and help you regain some of your strength."

"My thanks, Lady."

"You pummeling him into a red ruin is all the thanks that I require. Remember warrior, you have one chance only. Strike swiftly. Without pity or mercy."

"I shall."

"Good, good," she placed a skeletal hand on forehead. "Now rest. And may Mordiggian guide your hand."

Maciste was awakened by a sharp kick to the leg. Three armored revenants stood before him. Two were armed with tridents, pointed in his direction, while a third held a pair of chained manacles.

"No sudden movements," the guard holding the fetters said.

The two trident wielders moved in close, one on each side of him. The third affixed the shackles to his ankles and wrists. The chain between his ankles was just long enough for Maciste to take short, mincing steps, while the chain between his wrists was a handspan in length.

"Get up," the third guard said to him.

Maciste rose to his feet. The pain from the punishment that he endured was still with him, yet subdued. He felt rested. He gave the chains between his wrists a discrete tug, testing their boundaries.

"Where are you taking me?" he asked.

"To see the Master," a trident wielder said. "You try anything and we'll skewer you like a carp. Understood?"

"Understood," Maciste replied.

He was led out of his cell and down a long stone corridor. At the terminus point, the unarmed guard took a key from his belt and unlocked a heavy wooden door, reinforced with strips of bronze. They marched him up two flights of stairs, the trident bearers to either side of him, into a palatial chamber, all in red marble. The unarmed guard peeled away from the trio, while they made their way to a dais at the far end of the room. When they reached the edge of the platform, one of his warden's pushed Maciste to his knees.

Gilles Grenier the Red sat upon a throne carved from a single gigantic carnelian. It was flanked by two monstrous red marble mandrakes. He took a sip of wine and smiled down at the giant.

"Well! What a fine specimen we have here. Tell me your name, warrior."

"I am known as Maciste."

"Maciste, eh?" The necromancer sipped at his wine. "I trust you found my accommodation most welcoming? My servants attentive to your every need, yes?"

Maciste kept silent.

"Well, Maciste, you now have my undivided attention," the man in red said, grinning. "How may I assist you?"

"A girl was taken from her parent's holding, half a day's journey from here. When her betrothed came to inquire after her, he never made it back home. This is your doing."

Grenier burst into a fit of laughter. "So?" the necromancer said, wiping tears from his eyes. "What care I about these insignificant peasants? Of course, I had them killed. They are my servants now. As you soon shall be. That is, once you've had the opportunity to sample *all* the pleasures afforded to an honored guest of the Crimson Necromancer."

The dream-state chorus began its familiar refrain in Maciste's mind.

"Who will lift the Heel from the Neck of The People?"

"Who will repel the Wolf at the Gate?"

"Who will strike a Blow for Justice?"

"I will. As I always do," the giant whispered.

With clenched teeth, Maciste pulled his arms apart, straining, straining against the constricting bronze chain. A link snapped and *clinked* to the marble floor.

The dark-skinned man acted with a speed that belied his size. He delivered a combination of left, right punches, putting his hips into it, to the revenant's legs, standing at his right shoulder. The guard's shattered knees gave out from under him and fell to the floor.

Maciste picked up the fallen trident and pivoted left and up, catching the second trident guard in the neck with the triple tines. He gave a sharp wrench to the weapon in hand, partly separating the revenant's helmeted head from his torso, collapsing him in a clanging heap. The giant bound to his feet and stomped shattered knee's head.

Grenier's eyes opened in surprise. He clapped his hands enthusiastically. "Bravo, warrior! Bravo! Your strength is truly remarkable! You will be a prized addition to my collection."

Maciste gripped the trident in both hands, shifted his stance, squatted down and launched himself onto the dais.

The necromancer rose from his throne and said, "Oh, well done, Maciste, well done! So courageous! So heroic!"

Maciste shifted the trident in an overhand grip and replied, "Your time is finished, Grenier!"

The Crimson Necromancer laughed. "Yes, hero, yes! Come, strike your avenging blow!"

The giant lunge-hopped against the constraints of his ankle fetters, aiming the trident at Grenier's midsection.

A blue nimbus materialized around the Crimson Necromancer, enveloping him. When the triple tines struck the sorcerous enchantment, sparks flew at the impact. A sensation of cold burning ran up Maciste's arms, snaking into his chest and down into his belly. The smell of ozone permeated the air.

Maciste anchored himself, pushing off the ground, channeling all of his strength into and through the translucent barrier. Incrementally, the trident passed into the membrane. The giant strained all of his muscles against the protective ward.

A commingled expression of bewilderment and panic formed on the necromancer's face. He stumbled back onto his carnelian throne. "No, it can't be!" he said.

The skin on Maciste's hands, forearms and biceps hissed and blistered. His beard smoldered. The stink of burning hair clogged his nostrils.

The triple tines inched inexorably closer towards Grenier's heart.

Realizing his barrier would not save him, the necromancer frenetically sketched a sequence of runes in the air, uttering guttural syllables.

Suddenly, a deafening *pop* echoed throughout the great chamber, followed by a gurgling cry.

The Crimson Necromancer was sprawled on his carnelian seat, his left hand gripped the haft of the trident, feebly trying to pry it from his chest. Blood poured from wounds, soaking through his robes. It flowed down the throne in an expanding pool on the dais.

A bubbling utterance came from the lips of the dying sorcerer. His eyes gradually growing dull. "This cannot be. No man can resist my will."

"I am no man," the giant said. "I am Maciste."

The blistered giant tamped down the embers in his smoking beard and wiped the sweat from his brow and pate. His breaths came in exhausted gasps. He turned his back to the throne and the dead necromancer and stepped off the platform.

Ilalotha and Shahin came to him. Shahin put a hand to Maciste's heart and bowed his head.

"We are forever in your debt, mighty ursang," said Shahin. "Now, we can finally rest as the true dead."

The throne room was thronged with the reanimated dead men, women and children, all victims of Grenier's art. Unblinking eyes and hollow orbits all on the giant, their hands placed over their lifeless hearts. Shahin called out a name to the crowd. A mummified man, with remnants of a long wispy beard, in tattered indigo robes stepped forward.

"This is Orang. He was court physician to King Euvoran in ancient days. He will see to your wounds. Even in death, his skills in the healing arts are unequaled."

The physician dipped his head. He placed a desiccated hand on Maciste's arm and croaked, "Rest, now champion. The scales have been balanced."

The damage to Maciste's body was tended to with a combination of Orang's healing arts and Ilalotha's elixir. He recuperated in Grenier's manse for two days more.

On the dawn of the third day, Maciste began the journey south, back to Fulo and Nisa's olive farm. He carried with him three objects, bound in red silk. A bronze arrowhead affixed to a leather thong, a copper bangle and a lock of long black hair. He could feel the heat from the devouring flames at his back. Thick gouts of black smoke poured from the crimson manse, extending to the dawn sky. Grenier's victims were at peace at last.

Once Maciste delivered these familial keepsakes to the farmers, he would make his way eastward, to the coastline of that boundless and turbulent sea. There he would await the arrival of *The Dark Ship That Sails Across the Seas of Fate*, with its mysterious blind Captain, mute Helmsman, and contingent of nomadic warriors. To what marvelous itinerary he was bound for next, he could not say.

"Who will lift the Heel from the Neck of The People?"

This he knew with every fiber of his being. He had always known it. In all of those places and in all of those times. Throughout those countless lives.

"Maciste."

Jean-Paul Raymond is the author of a Madame Atomos *novel published by our French sister imprint,* Rivière Blanche. *He also contributed a* Harry Dickson *caper to* Harry Dickson vs The Spider. *This latest story of his breaks one of our cardinal rules, in that it doesn't feature a crossover with a French character; but then, its protagonist, Jules de Grandin, is French! So read on as Seabury Quinn's indomitable little French sleuth faces…*

Jean-Paul Raymond: *The Specter of the Valkyrie*

Harrisonville, New Jersey, 1925

It had been an abominable night. Gusts of wind and vicious downpours, one after another, without relief. Plus, an unexpected phone call had got me out of bed at two in the morning. Who would call me on such a night? A Puerto Rican worker, one of those working in the cannery run by Mr. Bentley, was complaining of almost unbearable pains. I went to his bedside and quickly diagnosed appendicitis.

I brought my patient—a strapping young man—to the Saint Philip's Hospital. Once there, my night was over for good. I felt vaguely annoyed and, I must admit, it put me in a sour mood.

"So, my dear Trowbridge, don't forget that today's the big day and it would be impolite to keep the charming Virginia waiting."

Even though it was morning, Jules de Grandin was already in his evening clothes, a gardenia in his buttonhole, the Legion of Honor conspicuously pinned to the lapel. With his thin fingers he was delicately twirling the tapered tips of his precious moustache.

"Of course, I haven't forgotten," I shot back. "I'd even say I'm impatient. Anyway, what's going to happen will bring the greatest happiness to my ward…"

"Hey, hey!" De Grandin exclaimed. "What ideas you have, my friend, so poetic and a little old-fashioned. When you say happiness, are you thinking of marriage? What a risky prospect! Even more so since some insidious imp so often slips into the life of young couples that can break what looks like the strongest bonds. We've seen it happen in the most stable couples."

This time I felt downright aggravated.

"You're not very optimistic. The union of two young lovers… but there's no reason for the marriage of my dear Virginia to turn into a disaster. Benjamin and she are charming together and truly smitten with each other. That's all that needs be say."

I went on my way with a quick nod. I had no need this morning to discuss the matter with De Grandin. Why would he mock such a lovely, delightful institution that pleases everyone?

For the rest of the morning, I dealt with my patients with my mind elsewhere, namely on Virginia. I'd known her forever. Her father had been one of my classmates at Saint James College. Then there was the War and Lieutenant Bushrod had fallen, mowed down by a machine gun near Seicheprey.

His young widow, Alexia, brought up their only child, little Virginia. I became her guardian and was full of affection for the charming girl. Oh, how captivating she is! And when she came to announce that she had met the most marvelous young man and they were going to be married, I was overjoyed.

Saint Patrick's Church was beautifully decorated for the ceremony. Gorgeous flower bouquets adorned all the pews. My role as guardian was to lead the young bride to the altar. Her betrothed awaited there. The guests were all smiles, brimming with emotion.

Finally, after fulfilling my obligations, I went to my pew and stood next to De Grandin. He was already a little tipsy thanks to the cognac he had drunk after breakfast and he talked too loudly.

"Very pretty ceremony, isn't it, Trowbridge? My eyes are stinging and I fear it won't be long before I give in. I already feel the sniffles coming on."

The voice of Jules de Grandin was the farthest thing from low-key. Faces turned to him. To quiet him down and make him find a little dignity. I squeezed his arm, but it did no good. The little Frenchman, as usual, was uncontrollable while the vows were being exchanged at the foot of the altar before us.

"I, Benjamin, take you, Virginia, to be my lawfully wedded wife, for better and for worse."

"I, Virginia…"

A shout accompanied the end of Virginia's promise.

"And till death do them part!"

The conclusion had been yelled spontaneously and was obviously not planned for. It had been let loose (must it be said?) by De Grandin who always found a way to cause trouble with his unexpected and unwelcome outbursts. At the moment he shouted this, he turned to me and smiled. But among the guests, brows furrowed and some ladies sneered. The old gentlemen who were sticklers for tradition raised a disapproving eyebrow.

By chance, cutting short the embarrassment that was spreading through the gathering, Mendelssohn's Wedding March prompted the newlyweds to leave the church. A mountain of flowers covered the courtyard, ready to soak up the tears; a colorful ornament to the warm and enthusiastic cheers.

Nobody was thinking of the awkward outburst that De Grandin's rudeness was guilty of.

When everyone had gathered in the understated luxury of a reception hall, I finally had the boundless pleasure of congratulating my ward, Virginia. But before I managed to utter a single word, Jules de Grandin slipped in before me and bowed elegantly to perform that outdated custom that the French love so much: he kissed her hand exquisitely, carried it out like a master.

"Madame Chetwynde," he said to the young lady, "allow me to wish you all the happiness in the world. Marriage is a delight that has been denied me. If you only knew how sorry I am for that."

When the reception was over, as we were heading back home, Jules de Grandin remained strangely silent. You might even say gloomy. The reminder of a marriage that had been refused him probably brought back smoldering, sorrowful, painful memories. His old, secret life...

I was fated not to spend a peaceful night in bed, to sleep like a log. Was this going to become a habit? The telephone rang. Again! I picked up: on the line was a female voice on the verge of panic.

"Doctor... Trowbridge..."

I recognized her right away, "My dear Alexia... at this hour, what's wrong?"

It was Alexia, the attentive mother of lovely Virginia who had only that day been wedded to the charming Benjamin Chetwynde. Good God, had some disaster struck? The explanation came pouring out.

"It's Virginia... Oh, I don't understand... she's just left her husband! Right now she's with me. Come quickly, doctor. I'm totally lost. Please, come as soon as you can!"

Miraculously, my ideas organized themselves without the least effort on my part. They suddenly became clear and lucid. Awoken by the phone call, De Grandin was up and dressed, from head to toe, ready to play his part in the battle against adversity.

"Was that sweet Mrs. Bushrod?" he asked. "Does she have any idea? Waking up the good doctors like this in the middle of the night." Then a little slyly said, "Is our young bride, Mrs. Chetwynde... having a little trouble? And on her wedding night?"

This was proof to me, as if I needed any, that he would listen in on my conversations, even the most intimate.

I forced myself to answer, "Exactly, old friend. But I know nothing more. Only that she's gone back to her mother's house."

"Hey, hey, isn't this some kind of record? A marriage that doesn't last even one day!"

A bittersweet comment! I looked at him without hiding my surprise. My French friend was not usually so sarcastic and glib. But I was soon reassured: he went away and rushed back, hat on head and medical bag in hand, ready for any emergency. He pressed me to hurry up.

"Let's go see what's happening, come on! If your Mrs. Bushrod needs our help, we shouldn't keep her waiting. Especially since it's young Virginia who appears to be in trouble. It really looks like your mind is somewhere else!"

A little taken aback by such a sanctimonious attitude, I wasted no time getting into my suit. Meanwhile, De Grandin was already in the street waiting for me.

"Well, well," he bellowed when he saw me, "you took your sweet time! You didn't need to get all dolled up!"

There was no need to rush me. I jumped into the car and did not go easy on the driver to get to my old friend as quickly as possible. In less than 15 minutes we were in front of the big, colonial style house. A prim and proper butler was pacing the sidewalk, waiting for us to arrive.

He whispered to me, "The ladies are waiting in the bedroom. It's upstairs."

Jules de Grandin was already gone. He had bolted through the open door. I followed him but less athletically. He was far ahead of me. It was like he was flying.

Upstairs, a door was open. It was the bedroom where Virginia was staying. The new Mrs. Chetwynde was lying on the bed. She was as pale as a sheet. Her eyes were half-closed and her lips were mumbling incomprehensible words. From time to time she let out a groan.

Her mother knelt at her side, full of dignity. The noble widow's face was addled. You did not have to be a saint to know why when you saw the condition of her dear child. I wanted to know more but Jules de Grandin was ahead of me and started asking questions.

"Tell us what happened! What's wrong?"

Mrs. Bushrod answered. It was obvious that she was on the verge of panic.

"I... I don't know," she stammered. "It was two in the morning and I was still in my evening dress. I was getting a little fresh air at the window and..."

"Go on, madame, continue," Grandin encouraged while tapping her gently on the hand.

"That's when I saw a figure appear at the corner. It was dark and I didn't recognize it right away. But when it got closer, I saw that it was my daughter..."

"Your daughter! Oh, madame..."

"Exactly. My daughter, the one who had just left in the afternoon in the arms of a man who had always seemed very honorable and whom I took for a real gentleman, that Benjamin Chetwynde!"

"Now, now," Grandin interjected.

"If only you'd seen the state she was in! She had no coat on, not even her dress. The hem of her silk nightgown was torn and there was blood on her feet!"

Mrs. Bushrod straightened up, her face in anguish. She was reliving the scene and tears rolled down her cheeks.

"I didn't waste a second," she resumed. "I rushed down into the street and I grabbed my daughter who collapsed in my arms, completely exhausted."

A question was torturing me… I could not help asking, "And her husband? Where was he?"

"I don't know, but he wasn't there."

"So, then, your daughter was alone in the street on her wedding night and in a frightful state. This is all so unbelievable."

"And yet," Mrs. Bushrod sighed, "it's true."

A wave of anger washed over me and I felt like I was about to choke. I reacted verbally. "What a creep! Benjamin! We had no idea! Leaving his young wife like this in the cold, dark night!" I took a breath and let out, "A monster of perversity unworthy of the air he breathes!"

"Calm down now, Trowbridge,' De Grandin tried to soothe me. "You're talking without knowing. Remember that it might be possible that Benjamin isn't responsible for what happened."

He turned to Mrs. Bushrod who was still in tears.

"I give you my most solemn promise that we'll do everything we can to find out the truth of this astonishing story. When Jules de Grandin tackles a problem, he puts his whole heart and mind into it, which I assure is nothing to sneeze at."

A quick examination of Virginia's neck and throat showed that she had not been injured in her ramble through the city. On the other hand, De Grandin and I agreed that the bride was a victim of a nervous shock that had hit her hard and numbed her senses. In short, she was no longer herself and seemed possessed by an unnamable terror!

One question was critical: what or who had caused this shock?

More questions crowded my mind. From my medical bag I took out a hypodermic needle and filled it with digitalis. I chose where to inject her and I stuck in the needle.

She reacted quickly. Her eyes started blinking, her breath slowed and her heart started beating normally. And right away she fell asleep.

Jules de Grandin and I were back in my office when the sun rose. The telephone rang. De Grandin jumped on it before me and answered. I tried to listen in.

"Dr. De Grandin? I'm happy to get in touch with you. Can you imagine, I have a strange person in my office who claims to know you. Last night a policeman picked him up in the street. Oh, he was half-dazed, the artist! We got him a drink and between two slugs he told us the most unbelievable story. He said he'd just been married and…"

"His name?" De Grandin cut in. "Tell me his name!"

"His name? I think it's Chetwynde. Benjamin Chetwynde."

De Grandin did not act surprised. He put a hand over the mouthpiece and whispered to me, "Did you hear that? This is Lieutenant Costello. Last night in the street his men picked up Virginia's delinquent husband... If I understand correctly, he's a little deranged." He started to laugh, but there was no joy in it. "Oh, these two kids make a funny couple!"

On the other end of the line Costello was getting impatient, "It'd be nice if you could come get him, though," he said. "On the quiet, of course. If you wait too long, he could end up with the crazies, counting sheep in a padded cell."

"Okay, we're on our way. Keep him warm!"

I was not so sure. Grandin turned to me, "Come on, get a hold of yourself! The best thing we can do is to go and get him as soon as possible."

We found Benjamin Chetwynde sharing a cell at the station with a shaggy drunk and a scruffy whore whose face was buried under a thick layer of powder. The poor kid greeted us with a blank stare. He had clearly suffered a terrible ordeal. He was mumbling off and on, something incomprehensible, but I could make out a few words and almost put together a coherent thought: it was about a kind of warrior come from the northern mists, one of the Valkyries who, around the year 1,000 had sailed in a big ship shaped like a bright and colorful dragon.

"Drakars," I muttered. "But I don't see what drakars have to do with anything... to be blunt, I think the boy has become completely mad." And I added, "Poor Virginia, I'm thinking of her and I truly feel sorry for her."

On hearing me pronounce the name of his beloved wife, Benjamin changed his attitude. He seemed to wake up.

"Virginia! No, really... And that awful old woman come from the depths of time! Oh, please, I don't understand anything."

My face froze. But my friend was looking unresponsive. So, I reacted.

"What's wrong with you, De Grandin? Aren't you shocked by what he's saying?"

"I'm thinking he should try to find out what's hiding behind this Valkyrie... a strangely powerful woman, as it so happens, I have to admit... a woman coming out of her cocoon or rather out of the past, from a thousand years ago. See, in this curious case I really doubt we're going to find even a trace of logic. The mystery, my friend, the mystery. It's fast approaching!"

In the meantime, at the Bushrods, our lovely new bride was getting over the shock she had suffered on her wedding night. Jules de Grandin and I had the pleasure of paying her a visit and spending time in her charming company for an hour or two.

That night...

Virginia was cozy in her pillows. It was late, nearing dusk. The young lady had slept and was just waking up. Slowly, free of trauma, her memories were coming back and settling into her mind. But she had still not said anything to us about what really happened on that night.

Was it the still of the night or maybe the soft light coming from the candles on the night table? Whatever the case, my French friend was able to find the right words.

"Dear girl, we're here now to listen to you. Of course, Trowbridge and I are friends of your mother, but more than that we're ready to help you overcome any obstacle that lies in your way."

"Oh, doctors, my dear friends, if only you knew… if you knew…"

"Poor Virginia, that's all we're asking of you is to know."

The young lady looked more assured, "What happened that night defies all common sense. I risk sounding foolish if I talk about what very well might be a ghost story."

"Well now, that's interesting. Might there be an old woman mixed up in this, all get up for war and getting off a boat that looks like a dragon?"

"Exactly, exactly! But how did you know? And what do you really know?"

She looked astonished. I cut in to explain a little more, but not too much.

"Just a few details, not many."

Jules de Grandin smiled. Like a greedy tomcat about to lap up a bowl of milk, he twirled the ends of his blonde moustache—he smoothed them out, then rolled them until he got them as he wanted.

Virginia started coughing. She forced herself to speak firmly.

"We'd just left the guests. We were eager to be alone together. Benjamin had booked the luxurious bridal suite at the Excelsior Hotel, which is probably the swankiest in Harrisonville County."

"We know, yes. You're right, it's a very elegant hotel. And then…"

"While my husband was parking the car in the hotel lot and smoking one last cigarette in the garden, I was getting all gussied up and putting on my frilliest nightgown… which I had bought with my mother, quite an emotional experience…"

"A completely normal feeling," Grandin interjected, "a feeling that all brides feel on the brink of their first night."

Virginia went on, "I was waiting for Benjamin. I imagined him excited and impatient, climbing the last steps up to our room."

She paused, frowned, tried to hide the faint blush coloring her cheeks.

"All of a sudden there was a lot of noise in the hallway. I heard bumps and then footsteps… I was waiting for the big moment, my husband was there, he was coming in… and then…"

She let out a sigh, a little sensual, provocative, innocently naughty.

"I slipped off the thin straps of my nightgown, almost baring my chest. I blew out the candles and let night slide into the room. Oh, not a dark night but a kind of darkness where things fade away but don't disappear."

"And while waiting for the big moment, what was happening in the hallway? Those footsteps came closer?" De Grandin asked.

"Oh yes, the footsteps. I could've forgotten them. But they stopped right in front of the door. Before going away, then coming back and scratching at the door like some clown was trying to pick the lock."

"Maybe it was Benjamin?"

"Oh no, not Benjamin! My husband is good with his hands and is very dexterous under any circumstances. Anyway, he had keys, so why play a joke and pretend to be breaking in? To surprise me?"

"You're right," Grandin muttered. "Doesn't make sense."

"In fact, none of this seemed normal to me. So much so that I started getting nervous. My heart was racing. I told myself it was Benjamin, all the while knowing that it wasn't him."

"Of course. Because otherwise…"

"At that very moment, the lock turned and the door opened. At first I didn't see much… only an outline, a short one… but stocky. A shadow that looked like nothing."

"And so… an image, a ghostly apparition, maybe," Grandin suggested.

"Yes, a little like you say. Either way, I was alone in that room with some vile thing, something terribly strange. A weird shadow, in fact."

This time De Grandin looked like he was struggling to contain his joy and excitement. He loved the occult, the eerie, those strange accounts of mysterious auras that defy all logic. So, he looked pleased. He straightened his collar and in a curiously gentle voice said, "My dear young lady, be aware that Trowbridge and I are here to ease these painful memories that are burdening your mind. But I've interrupted you…"

Virginia took her handkerchief and wiped the tears that were welling up in her eyes.

"Finally, the thing approached me and I could see it better. It could have been a woman, an older woman. I didn't know her. She had long hair that reached all the way down her back. Otherwise, she was nude, or almost. She wore a belt, a piece of fabric in which she carried an axe and a short sword.

"I can't say why but this apparition seemed to come out of a different age, magically transported into our time and I felt like it had just broken through the invincible barrier of centuries.

"I started shaking and pulled the covers up to my eyes. But I was plagued by curiosity and kept my eyes open.

"The figure came closer and so I could finally see it. The unknown woman was gnashing her teeth horribly. Her skin looked tanned, she was covered in scars that carved deep grooves from her cheeks down to her chest. Her breasts were small but a little puffy. All around her throat were swollen pustules, horrific growths and the rancid spirits that engorged her body oozed out of the corners of her mouth.

"I was in no condition to think straight. But I did ask myself one question: where did this monstrosity come from? Was there a theater putting on a performance with monsters and ghosts? A play with satanic, demonic rituals of some voodoo cult maybe?

"The creature kept coming closer. She ended up putting her hand on my wrist. It was like a streak of fire, a kind of radiation, a burning... Look, you can see..."

Virginia pushed her frilly sleeve up to her elbow. The burn in the shape of a hand had scarred her flesh.

Jules de Grandin bent over to get a closer look. He concluded, "It looks to me like there's no way this burn is self-inflicted. On the other hand, Mr. Chetwynde..."

Virginia reacted violently, "You mean that Benjamin attacked me! But you can't think such a thing! He couldn't hurt a fly. He's the gentlest of men."

"Okay, okay, I get it. But go on. Your nocturnal ghost, apparently fallen from the moon, is all she did was grab your arm?"

"Of course not. The old woman started caressing my face and I smelled her breath, which reminded me of the repulsive stench of rotting meat. She ended up saying something to me in weird words I hardly understood."

"She said something... but what? What did she tell you?" De Grandin urged.

"Well, dear doctors... excuse me but in my memories of the awful night nothing is very clear to me. I was so terrified... But the gist of it was something like this: Don't try to run or even leave this room. You chose to unite with the worst procreator of a cursed line, to mate with a traitor who, on the battlefields like on our nights of love, had sworn to be faithful to me... and who ended up betraying me. He fell for a girl he met in some tavern or on the docks or who knows where. He had two kids with her and never looked at me again—he forgot about me.

"'But that's impossible'—I answered back, sitting up in bed. 'My Benjamin would never do such a thing! If he were already a father, I'd know about it!'

"The apparition answered me: Who's talking about your husband? He's just the descendent of my former lover. But you can be sure that he, too, your wonderful Benjamin, won't act like a swine. And it's on him that my vengeance and ancestral hatred will fall.

"Then she added: So, you can be sure, my pretty, that you won't be spared. The fact that you became the wife of a renegade puts you in the front line. You're going to suffer, just as much as the traitor, the punishment that my vengeance demands."

"Well, just listen to that!" De Grandin exclaimed.

Like him, no doubt, I was only half-convinced of Virginia's story. Logically, it could all have been made up. Nobody passes through time like crossing the street. But at the same time, I knew Virginia and tended to believe her. Not completely, though, I still had my doubts, just like De Grandin again.

Trying to clarify the situation he asked, "So, if you can continue... what happened next?"

Virginia looked to me like she was about to gasp for air, but she kept calm and went on, "The apparition told me that she was called Inghen Ruaidh, that she was a foreigner coming from Northern Europe, that she was born in the mists that cover the North and Baltic Seas, and what else..."

Her voice faltered. She closed her eyes and fell back. I thought she had fainted, but that it was not so. I brought out the smelling salts and they had an immediate effect.

Jules de Grandin swore under his breath, "By the Great God of the Little Green Pigs!"

Virginia was rattled, "I don't know what could've happened next. When I woke up, I was here in this bedroom." She stopped, but not for long. Her delicate face looked pained again and she continued, "There's something bothering me—what's become of Benjamin? Why isn't he with me? He hasn't come to see me even once. Is he hurt? The creature who came into my room... did she get to him? Kill him?!"

De Grandin smiled at her, "No, no, rest assured, nothing like that. Your husband suffered the same shock as you, a trauma like the one that's laid you up. But don't worry, Trowbridge and I are doing our best to pull him through. We have high hopes."

Pretty Virginia almost jumped with joy. Her face lit up, which made her look like a little girl seeing presents on Christmas morning.

"Oh, thank you! Thank you for taking care of Benjamin and trying to make me feel better. You can't know how good it makes me feel."

But De Grandin pinched his lips and confessed, "The fact remains that the improbable existence of this hideous stranger from another time is still a mystery. Hard to understand and therefore to accept, you'll agree. And yet, in this troubling enigma you were very lucky. Let me explain.

"You have before you an intelligent, I'd even say a kind person. By the Beard of the Blue Fish, you'll find no one, in any place or time, who will tell you that the eminent Jules de Grandin has ever been intimidated or refused to face a thorny problem. They will certainly tell you the opposite. So, young lady, I'm asking you to remain confident, keep the faith... for I am on your case!"

And he added with dramatic flair:

"From now on I will dedicate my life to restoring your happiness. By gum and to hell with the dead cats!"

Three long days went by. Jules de Grandin and I pooled out medical acquaintances to find the best facility for Benjamin Chetwynde. As a result, over time, with rest, he quickly regained his love of life. It was even so sudden, so spectacular that we arranged a little freedom for him. We were getting him out one morning and were sitting, all three of us, in the room.

"De Grandin and I think that this afternoon, at teatime, we might bring you to see your dear Virginia," I told him.

His reaction was violent. He shot up, full of anger, which left us dumbfounded. We would never have imagined such an objection.

"Out of the question!" he shouted. "I never want to see her again for the rest of my life. Not once, get it!"

I did not understand anything and sat there astounded. That this loving marriage, on the eve of the honeymoon, could be shattered to pieces, made no sense at all.

I shouted back at him, "What did you say? I'm having a little trouble following you. You have a young wife, pretty and gentle and in love with you, who's waiting for you. And you, in this selfish fit, state outright that you reject her, that your only desire—an unbelievable horror!—is that she never again be a part of your life! Is that it? So, what happened?"

I came down from my self-righteousness, I was in no condition to react too violently to the man scorning my ward. I was growing weak, no doubt; I suddenly felt sorry for myself. But Benjamin started to explain, without being too clear, apparently hesitant to give us certain details. He addressed himself to me.

"Excuse me, Sir, if I shock you, but don't be so quick to judge. Let's just say I'm cursed. The word is not inappropriate. It's an old story that's been haunting my family for a long time. I should've known! But, in fact, I didn't want to believe it. If I decided to see Virginia again, today for example, or any other time, it would be reckless of me, could even cause a terrible disaster. Know this... and believe me, I don't want to see her facing a bleak and dismal future with death as the only prospect."

During this conversation between Benjamin and me, Jules de Grandin listened very carefully off to the side. From time to time he rubbed his slender hands, then twirled the ends of his little moustache. He looked like a sated cat licking his chops after a savory meal.

He seemed interested in what Benjamin was saying. I'd even say intrigued. This story of the old woman who was claiming to have parachuted into our time out of the gulf of ages was far from ordinary. When mystery reared its head, the spirited De Grandin right away started quivering like an eel.

He spoke up, "Even if Jules de Grandin is sure that there is, from the day of our birth, a place reserved for well-born souls in Paradise, so it is that that's not enough for some people who will try to find out what's hidden behind all that. Hell's bells and Holy of all Holies!" he raised his voice. "We have here a charming young lady who surrendered her little girl dreams to put herself, in all innocence, under the natural protection of an admirable and beloved spouse. But then, right quickly, this young man, traitorously, broke the supposedly inalterable vow that he and his wife took at the altar.

"Bravo! Bravissimo! And after a night that looks nothing like any other wedding night, here's the unworthy husband shamelessly rejecting his charming wife while the poor child keeps on living in the fever of love because she can't imagine her future, at this moment, without her despicable husband at her side. But don't you see, sir, that there's something wrong, something crazy in this determination you're showing and in the choices you're making?"

When his speech was over, De Grandin made a majestic, theatrical wave of his hand and bid farewell to Benjamin ceremoniously. I, who knew him well, knew that he took great pleasure in these grandiose actions.

Benjamin reacted, "I'm fully aware that the decision I made, which I've told you, doesn't speak in my favor and if I were in your place, I'd probably react in the same way. Nevertheless, I guarantee you, most assuredly, that I love Virginia, more than my life, and I'd risk this life to confront him—or her—who want to do her harm."

With his vow Benjamin seemed to get a grip on himself. But right after, he sank and darkened again.

"But there's a curse between us, a curse of the blood I inherited, the blood of my ancestors. This curse will be the cause, the seed of future tragedy. In a way, I'm responsible for whatever happens to Virginia, even if nothing, absolutely nothing, is really my fault."

Well now, I said to myself, and glanced back over my shoulder.

Jules de Grandin raised his chin and said, "Excuse me, dear boy, for pushing you to the limit. To tell you the truth, it's what I was hoping for, that you'd react. And believe me, you haven't disappointed.

"You're an honest man, worthy of confidence and, above all, you're brave. But here you are in the throes of some nameless agony that we have no idea how to get you out of. But hope is not lost! I can see marvelous days of happiness ahead for you!

"For, in your misfortune, you have an admirable person to help you. his name is Jules de Grandin and he's not just anyone. He's smart and he's going to solve this mystery he's faced with. That's how I see the story ending. But I'll still need information, extra information, basic information. It's indispensable for success. Sir, I'm all ears."

The morning was not over, so a little early for cocktails, but I still went to the bar to serve us some aged brandy that lit up the eyes of Jules de Grandin, who was a serious drinker.

We both sat down in the comfortable, buffalo-skinned, chesterfield armchairs. Benjamin preferred to remain standing. He lit a cigarette with a hand I saw was trembling. Finally, getting his momentum, he bravely jumped right in.

"You might not know it, but all the men in my family died young. More precisely, they left the world a few weeks after their wives gave them their first child."

"Your father…" I started.

I'd just remembered the event, hazily at first, then more details came back. I was a young doctor then. During a heatwave—so hot that the tarmac on the road melted—they came looking for me to treat a patient. He was pretty much the same age as me but unfortunately, at first glance, I saw that he was dead and there was nothing I could do. He had no wounds. There was just a look of hideous fear frozen on his face! Nobody knew what happened.

Nobody except a 10 year-old kid, a distant cousin, who confessed, "I saw an old woman like in storybooks. She had red hair and there was a knife in her belt."

Nothing more. They shut the kid up with a hard slap. The dead man… it was coming back to me now… it was Benjamin's father.

"Yes, my father," Benjamin went on. "Died of fear. He wasn't even 30. And his father before him suffered the same fate."

"Like a macabre chain of…" I muttered.

"Exactly. In my family, nobody talks about it, but everyone knows. In fact, fear runs rampant."

"I suspect—I doubt it, true, but…," De Grandin spoke up, "that it's an ancestral fear passed down through the ages. The question I have is: how did you know?"

"One day I was with one of my great uncles, Gideon. He was about to calmly celebrate his 100th birthday and his mind sometimes let down its barriers, especially after a drink or two."

"I understand completely," De Grandin smiled. "But go on, please."

"It was a kind of incantation, anyway nothing rational, no logic to it at all…"

"Rationality and logic," I said slowly, "I feel are in short supply in this story."

Benjamin turned to me, "Dr. Trowbridge, you only know about the death of my father, if I leave out my complicated wedding night. But there's something else."

"Well, don't hold back. Tell us, please."

"After my father's sudden death—could we call it murder?—the health of my mother declined. Her nerves were shot. She dragged on for years in psychiatric hospitals and nursing homes and finally died of lethargy."

"What a tragedy. I had no idea…"

"Yes, a tragedy, but whose origins lie elsewhere. I have to get back to my great uncle, old Gideon. The day he talked to me, he told me that my direct ancestors all died suddenly and afterwards their wives, sometimes within weeks, sometimes years later, they all became mad. The archives confirm the fact, gentlemen. If you look into my family tree, you'll get lost in all the disasters of this kind. It goes back along an endless chain, a dizzying succession of tragedies. On the other hand, and this is the only luck that couples in my family seem to have..."

"What is it?" I urged.

"They have time to give birth to a child. Thus, the lineage perpetuates and the chain remains unbroken. The curse, therefore, can continue to flourish, always with a new generation to target."

"And in this case here, it's got you in its sights... and Virginia," De Grandin commented.

"Right. But at first I didn't want to believe it. I was sure that they were just old wives' tales. And then on that night in the hotel when I was going back to be with Virginia in our room, when I saw that long-haired, old woman slipping down the hallway, get up like she was going off to war, and enter our room... I knew. For my part..."

"Yes, exactly, for your part..."

"I had some kind of fit. An attack that left me dizzy and petrified. The one glance that the apparition cast at me was enough! It burned into me, pierced me like an ice pick. It was hair-raising. And yet, I assure you, it's the truth!"

Jules de Grandin put down his glass. His wide eyes were bright enough to melt steel.

"We believe you, young man, we believe you. We know the devastating effects that a stroke can have on sensitive people. But still, be aware, I think it's very improbable that the mere appearance of a strange woman could cause such a state. So, my friend, I believe there must be something else. That this startling ghost was not a stranger to you. It matters right now... but go on, please."

"My great uncle, the almost 100 years-old man, certainly did all he could to tell me all he knew, but me, being young and carefree, I scoffed. I laughed at his hesitations and insinuations. To be frank, I didn't even remember most of what he said.

"I do remember snatches of it: a thousand years ago there was a Viking warrior named Inghen Ruaidh, a rather pretty woman, but terribly cruel. Simply put, she was probably possessed by a real frenzy for murder, pillage and conquest. They called her the Red Maiden because of the color of her hair. What's more, she was the partner of a man just like her, another grisly ravager named Egil Borbrander."

He paused briefly.

"That's all I know. At any rate, to get back to my wedding night, just when I was blacking out, this woman came back to me and whispered out of her toothless mouth, 'Enjoy your young wife, but don't forget that you belong to me. Yes, both of you belong to me. You've belonged to me since the first minute of your union, the same union as the one forged centuries ago by your piddling, traitorous ancestor. In a word, you're mine. And I won't let you go. My vengeance will soon be fulfilled like it was on all those couples, your ancestral couples in bygone years.'"

"Astounding!"

"Isn't it? Out of the depths of my stupor I thought right away of my dear Virginia. There was no way I could let this happen to her, that I could accept the dreadful fate of seeing her poor mind wander lost in limbo. Especially since she wasn't responsible for what was happening. In this case, I was the only one, me with my cursed blood…"

"If we accept that this woman is real, that she has the ability to travel through time, then we're dealing with a warrior named Inghen Ruaidh and her lover named Egil whom we can imagine was your ancestor. And that's all we have to go on."

In any case, young Benjamin brooded over the story, wringing his hands in despair. "This time, my friends, you know the real reason that compelled me to leave my wife. By separating from her, separating her from my life, I might manage, in time, to break this curse. If I am no longer here, there's no reason for Virginia to become a victim of this ancient vengeance. On the other hand, by making this painful decision to leave, everyone'll think I'm crazy. Especially if there's no way to justify myself, at least no credible way."

Benjamin was absolutely right. But for my part, to be honest, I did not know what to think. I told myself, "What if he's pulling our leg, what if the whole thing's made up, a ridiculous pack of lies?"

Maybe we were being naïve.

Jules de Grandin looked up, straightened up his short frame in front of Benjamin and declared, "But no, dear boy, I don't think you're crazy, I'd even say the opposite. And the Good God, rest assured, has the same opinion. Still, by the Great Horns of Satan, you've got me troubled. And I must press on. Even if Judas Iscariot and whoever invented Prohibition used all their influence to stop me, I know it's my duty to confront the repulsive thing trying to trouble the intimacy of your honeymoon.

"And once I get my hands on her, I'll just have to turn her into a scaly bat with parrot wings! Bloody hell, you'll see if I'll deal with her, that crazy old woman! Oh yes, I promise you!"

Jules de Grandin and I were once again alone in my consulting room after making sure to bring the rest of my stock of alcohol, which had just suffered a considerable drain. I felt a little groggy, my mouth a little furry, my mind woozy, ready to lose it. Which almost happened.

De Grandin asked me, "What should we think about all this?"

I raised my arms and my voice, "Not much, I'm afraid."

It was a truly weird scene.

De Grandin laughed, "I should've known. It's hard to trust you and hard to put any confidence in your reasoning skills. That's why I have to have a word with a specialist, a scholar who knows every last detail about the 10th century Vikings."

"Are you kidding?"

"Not at all or at least not completely. Because if we want to have any chance at retracing the dubious travels of our Valkyrie, there's only one person to consult: Professor Hajlmar Hjerson from the University of Michigan."

"Hjerson? Who's that? With a name like that…"

"The Professor is Swedish. He's considered the best specialist in everything to do with Vikings. He's spent his life digging up tombs where the bones of the ancient conquering sailors are buried. And I assure you, he has enough knowledge to enlighten us."

"If you say so."

A lead was finally opening. The spirited Jules de Grandin seemed very self-confident. He was brimming with enthusiasm.

The petite secretary was like a little mouse—a sweetly sour face, thin lips, a tiny body but a little wide in the hips and a professional smile. She spoke in a confidential voice.

"The professor is waiting for you. If you'd follow me…"

Jules de Grandin and I entered the office that was as big as an exhibition hall. Behind glass on long shelves were countless objects sparkling lightly. They reflect the electric fixtures in the corners of the huge room.

In the middle of all the odds and ends stood Professor Hjerson, leaning back against a big bookshelf like a spider in its web. The man was smiling and made an excellent first impression in me. He offered us a firm, dry handshake.

"Ah, Dr. De Grandin, what a pleasure to see you again after all these years! And you brought one of your good friends. Dr. Trowbridge, I presume? Welcome. Please, sit down."

"We came…" De Grandin started.

But he cut him off, "I believe you've forgotten the good old habits. Don't you think the powers of the mind are stronger if they're stimulated by a fine, delectable beverage?"

This was really not the thing to say. De Grandin's eyes looked ecstatic, even more so when the professor opened a side table and brought out a cut crystal bottle along with three glasses. He poured us a generous dose of his Swedish Elixir, a bitter drink created in the 16th century by the famous Paracelsus. He dropped in ice and a lemon twist to each glass.

We all drank and clicked our tongues to express our appreciation. But De Grandin was impatient to state his business. He was fidgeting in his chair, having a hard time staying calm.

Finally, he went straight to the point, "What brought us here is the controversial existence of a Viking warrior named Inghen Ruaidh. She just showed up in one of our cases. But the whole matter is rife with mystery. That's why I'd like to ask you very directly: in the course of your research have you ever come across a woman by this name?"

We were expecting a puzzled response from the professor, so were quite surprised. Because he laughed and shook his head.

"That worthy dame!" he boomed. "She's certainly not unknown. You might even say that in certain ways she's famous."

"Is that right?" De Grandin exclaimed. "What do you mean?"

"At the start of my career I was part of the team of Professor Anna Stolpe. Together we did some excavating around Birka in the southeast of Sweden and we unearthed a magnificent burial site dating back to the 10th century. There were many tombs, among which was a huge sepulcher of a local nobleman entombed with his weapons and with his hair hastily sacrificed to be buried with him."

"Very interesting," De Grandin said. "But commonplace, too common and nothing to do with this woman, our Inghen."

"Not quite," the professor continued. "Over the following years we identified other sources that gave more information. The first thing we learned was that this warrior... was a woman!"

"Is that right? How..."

"Put yourself back in that time if you can. Since researchers started digging up those conquerors who roamed the cold seas, it was always believed that they were all men and that the presence of a woman on board a ship was rare. Well now, they were wrong! There were many fighting women and they went to war equal with men."

"Ha, ha!" De Grandin let out. "If these facts get known, if they grow and spread, the feminist leagues are going to hit the streets and start stepping on our coattails!"

That damned De Grandin never missed a chance! Misogynist that he was! Was it the memory, the regret from a pretty girl he watched walking away on the quays of the Seine around Melun?

"That's one way to put it," the professor muttered. "Anyway, the tomb, in reality, was the final resting place of a warrior woman whose name was Inghen Ruaidh."

"What?"

Our surprise was incalculable. It took me a long moment and half my glass to gather my thoughts. One question nagged me:

"How did you find out?"

The professor answered, "You know, it was some epic research, a complicated matter that lasted... in my case... almost a lifetime. First, I had to convince my colleagues—most of them of a ripe old age—that in the time of the Vikings a woman counted for as much as a man and that she could fight and lead like a man. Secondly, we thought it necessary to put a name on our discovery. Okay, to be honest, we were lucky. On the armor we found on the skeleton's chest were runes. We translated them. They were an archaic version of an old Irish text of an epic about a fleet that once conquered Ireland under that command of Inghen Ruaidh."

"Well, then," De Grandin was on pins and needles, chewing at the bit. "This warrior whose name we know is not a just a legend! We can stop talking about a dream or raving madness. Isn't that right, Trowbridge?"

Jules de Grandin was bubbling over with excitement and wanted to know everything down to the minutest details. He continued without waiting for an answer.

"Dear professor, here's another name while you at it: Egil Bordrander."

"Oh, De Grandin, I didn't know you'd become an expert in the history of ancient melodramas."

"So, there's something there to lights your fire?"

"Maybe. You be the judge. If you dig through the old archives about Ireland in the year 1,000, we'll find really splendid tales of love, burning and passionate love."

"There you go," De Grandin pressed on, "So, Egil Borbrander?"

Professor Hjerson was all smiles. Nothing could disturb the domineering calm on his face. With a sweeping gesture he served us another drink, which made the good mood even better in the inveterate drinker, Jules de Grandin.

"This time," the professor said, "with what we found in the piously preserved old manuscripts of the archives at the National University of Maynooth, we'll meet again your friend Inghen Ruaidh. But in a different sense. This is about, let's say more intimate conquests."

"Like in what we're dealing with—matters of the heart?"

"Exactly. It would seem that this ancient warrior was buried while crazy in love with a certain Egil Borbrander, another bloodthirsty, pillaging conqueror. But in this case it was not so simple. See, this handsome, young man had the bright idea—which turned out to be pretty foolish—to dump his lover and in one of his ports of call to marry a fair maid named Dagmar.

"No need to tell you what happened next. Inghen was furious. That's all she needed to murder her young beau and his sweety, but another circumstance, most regrettable to be sure, came to prevent her would-be vengeance. In fact, our Inghen had really bad luck and was mortally wounded in a bloody raid that history remembered as the Battle of Assandun. It took her three days to die, three days of agonizing suffering. But this didn't keep her from cursing poor Egil and his wife Dagmar along with their descendants."

"That's it, the whole story of our curse!" De Grandin shouted with glee. "I understand everything now. Great God of Artichokes, our Benjamin is obviously a direct descendant, a real Swede and way back when had some shady ancestors who were not very Catholic, some sea-faring, battle-loving looters who died as they lived."

"Maybe so, after all," I concluded.

All Americans, especially the whites, have European origins even though they've forgotten about it, especially the younger ones.

A long pause during which De Grandin twirled his thin moustache. Then he addressed the professor again.

"So, tell me, what happened to the skeleton?"

Hjerson looked surprised. "But how could you know? No one ever talked about it. Not a word was published."

De Grandin replied, "You know, there are other sources besides the traditional media, interesting channels other than the *New York Times*. If you want to satisfy your curiosity, you can discover wondrous things. So, your skeleton..."

I really had no idea where the little Frenchman with his waxed moustache was trying to lead the Swedish professor, but one thing was certain: we were heading deeper into the mystery.

The professor explained, "Once the last bones of old Inghen Ruaidh were unearthed, our lab took over to identify and catalogue them. That's how we archeologists, on further examination, can claim to extract from the past a bunch of information that otherwise would slip through the cracks and remain unknown. And in the case of our warrior woman, we had plenty of surprises in store."

"Aha!" De Grandin interjected.

"See, in less than a week, just a few days later, all the bones had disappeared! Not a single one to be found."

"Stolen?" De Grandin inquired.

"I hardly think so. Who would be interested in remains like that? They were all pretty well deteriorated. No market value for anyone. Plus, at the same time some other objects showed up, ancient artefacts that made us think of Fenrir, the Great Wolf."

"Another detour into Scandinavian mythology. Fenrir? Isn't that the monster that the gods of Valhalla tried to chain up but never could? Isn't he the one who feasted on proud Odin, the majestic father of all creation?"

"Exactly. In short, a rather undesirable, wild beast who has sown panic among men for ages."

"So, your bones?"

"Vanished. In three days and without a trace. And yet, in their place we found these medallions I mentioned, crudely forged in old bronze. All of them, on both sides, bore the outline of Fenrir the wolf, which made us think that the red-headed warrior might have taken refuge under the protective paws of the mythic canine."

We got back to out Harrisonville neighborhood. Jules de Grandin seemed to me to be in excellent spirits. I teased him, a little ironically:

"I wholly share your opinion about Professor Hjerson. He is remarkably knowledgeable, a great scientist and a talented storyteller to boot. But now, after all this, maybe it's time to tell me what you're going to do. Can you put a little order into this chaotic situation?"

"That's your question?" my friend Grandin answered back in the same tone. "By the Parrot's Bellyache, I'll tell you that Jules de Grandin can do it all and there's no misty, old, asthmatic wolf hooked up with a thousand year-old fury who's going to stop him. No, certainly not, pal."

I raised an eyebrow. "What do you have in mind?"

I was aware of the risk, but the little Frenchman, after taking a moment to reflect, surprised me again.

"I would like to ask you to honor me with your presence, knowing full well that you will be witness to a rather unordinary scene that will undoubtedly delight your nice lovebirds."

The gardens of the Excelsior Hotel were radiant in the moonlight. There were flowerbeds studded with forget-me-nots and those varieties of roses so precious to poets that are called Ann Boleyn and Sharifa Asma.

Jules de Grandin and I were once again with the young Mrs. Chetwynde who was looking a little peaked. I had no idea what we were going to do. Night had not yet fallen but there was nobody around. It was like we were the last survivors on earth. For the moment, at least, we heard no noise, not a trace of life. And I knew this devil De Grandin was fully capable of reserving the entire hotel for his own, personal use.

There was not a single employee in sight, no guests wandering the hallways. Of course, you could imagine that De Grandin had taken all precautions: he wanted to have no unfortunate interruptions or unexpected incidents foiling his well-planned scheme.

He went over to Virginia and took her arm, murmuring to her confidentially, "I admire your courage, my dear girl. And I can assure you that during this coming night we are going to pull off a brilliant victory. At least if you accept to put a little trust in the marvelous intelligence of Jules de Grandin and his exceptional tenacity and remarkable character. For, this is quite an extraordinary man you have with you tonight."

Virginia Chetwynde looked at him with her eyes full of tears. She did not look convinced and seemed to hesitate. She could only answer timidly, "If you really say so…"

"Very good, very good," De Grandin jumped in. "Let's go up together. We have to get there first."

The three of us went upstairs, still without meeting a living soul. When we were on the landing Virginia stiffened up. We could see the "honeymoon suite" where what should have been a wonderful wedding night had turned into a dark tragedy.

"Don't be scared, child," De Grandin tried to sound reassuring. "We're here with you. No one's going to touch you. No one's going to attack you. Jules de Grandin knows how to defend himself and his friends. And those are not empty words. By the Great God of Rats!"

He opened the door and entered the silk-upholstered room.

"Now's when you can settle in."

More determined than ever, De Grandin had put a luxurious vanity case on a small table.

He explained, "I brought you everything you need to get yourself ready: a nightgown, makeup... Don't forget, dear girl, it's important that everything be perfect."

Virginia obeyed him and went into the bathroom. She came out soon after, wearing a nightgown with flounces that flowed all the way to her ankles. She had on light makeup and had highlighted her eyebrows.

De Grandin continued his suggestions, "It's important that you remember, once and for all, that I am Jules de Grandin. This simple fact and my presence should be enough to keep you calm."

And he added, "It's necessary, no, indispensable I'd say, that you fall asleep. If you can't, we have the means to help. Either way, to make sure we get off to a good start, let's have some of this excellent potion."

He held out a tiny, finely chiseled vial. And explained further:

"The hours to come will no doubt be very trying. That's why I'm asking you or rather ordering you to sleep... come now, sleep, don't fight it..."

"Doctor... yes, I think..."

Her voice was sorrowful, stammering, then fading away. Pretty Virginia lay down on the bed. Her head rested on the embroidered pillow, but her eyes were not closed—they were white, turned up and staring into an invisible void.

A long moment passed, silent, endless. Jules De Grandin suddenly jumped up, went to her and tapped her.

"Mrs. Chetwynde, are you awake?"

The only answer he got was a slow blink.

"I think my concoction, an Indian recipe directly out of the old provinces of what we call New France, has done its duty. She's asleep, Trowbridge. But at the same time she's conscious of everything happening and she will remember what is soon going to break into our festivities. Original, don't you think?"

I said nothing because I was still waiting to see what would happen.

De Grandin went on, "You're going to see arrive on the scene a fabulous, extremely cruel fury. I have named Inghen Ruaidh, cast forth to us out of the depths of the ages by the magic of a little trick—very cunning nonetheless— orchestrated by a legendary wolf. No, no, don't be scared. Remember that Jules de Grandin is on the job and won't let down his guard for a second. Do you believe me? And you, madame, do you believe me?"

"Yes, with all my heart," Virginia whispered, still lying there with her empty stare. But she clenched her fists reflexively.

235

De Grandin went on. His voice resonated in the silence. He kept talking to the young lady. "This savage warrior will remain unknown to you. At least in the beginning. It will only be at the end, when you open your eyes... and then..."

"And then?" I was getting fed up with all these assurances. "Really, my friend, you don't know what you're doing!"

He answered, "Old chap, please, don't worry. I'm in control of the situation. Convince yourself that Virginia is in no danger. Truly, she's in no danger at all. She won't be aware. What she'll say and do will not be her. I'll stay behind her and it will be me acting in her place!

"A kind of hypnotism, if you want, like taking control of a defenseless mind. You know, as we've talked about and I won't insult you by suggesting that you've forgotten, I have mastered the inductive methods demonstrated by Dr. Sigmund Freud. As well as those of Carl Gustav Jung. And many others. Because my mind is strong. Yes, don't forget, I've got a strong mind!"

I frowned, all the while feeling very anxious. I didn't much like the turn that our nocturnal adventure was taking.

De Grandin came close to me and tugged my sleeve, "Come, it's about time we saw our brave Benjamin."

"Yes, I almost forgot about him."

In the small living room adjoining the bedroom, which together formed the "suite" of the Excelsior Hotel, Benjamin was waiting. He was obviously very fidgety. When he saw us he jumped up.

"I was worried sick," he blurted out. "I've been waiting for hours. Can you assure me that it hasn't started yet? And that the Creature—Good God, I can say our enemy—hasn't shown up yet?"

De Grandin's big smile reassured him. "Stay calm, young friend, it does no good to be impatient. The night is still young. In fact, the evil being we're tracking feels uncomfortable in the daylight, even in the dying rays of twilight."

Personally, contrary to what De Grandin was saying, I was sure that we would not be waiting long. We went back into the bedroom where Virginia was sunk in a strange lethargy inflicted on her by Jules de Grandin and went into the little closet to wait for the darkness to deepen. My breathing was fast, just like Benjamin's. Only De Grandin kept his unshakeable calm.

The sounds of the city, very muffled, barely reached us. It really felt like we were out in the country, far from the city's hue and cry. The moment we had been waiting for came... It was the slow advance of a crowd.

At first faint, far-off, then closer and clearer it came. Not wanting to believe it, we felt bewildered. Was this De Grandin's expected arrival of the old ghost from bygones times. Were there other ghosts? Souls wandering in perdition?

I turned to De Grandin. He looked almost ecstatic. I left him alone for the moment and looked out the little window in my door. And then... I saw...

It looked like an ancient boat, a drakar with its bulging hull, its oars lined up on the sides and its big sail. What astonished me the most was seeing the sculptures erected on the stern and bow—the dragon heads and tails.

More striking still were all the sailors, hairy and dressed in leather, armed for war and standing on the deck, totally silent. Their faces like wild beasts did not look human.

How did this drakar get here? A ship of this size? Was this some new devilry cunningly cooked up by the old Valkyrie? The impossible, the inconceivable was before our eyes, at our very feet! We were going to be attacked by a Viking army! What's more, it must be said, by an army of ghosts against which De Grandin's ever-present Browning would obviously be as useless as a child's peashooter.

Presently I heard clicking, like the nails on the soles of leather boots stomping the ground. The floor groaned. The man—or woman—approaching was not trying to be subtle.

We heard scraping on the door and then it flew open. The darkness in the room barely allowed us to make out a silhouette, a faint, stocky shadow. The slope of its shoulders, the soft curves of its chest and thighs, gave us the impression of warped, pustular flesh.

The woman—for, it was a woman—stood completely still for a moment before throwing her head back. She cackled, full of hatred and evil intent. I was startled and shivered. I closed my eyes for a few seconds and when I opened them again...

The ghost was walking to the middle of the room. It was an appalling, truly obscene spectacle. Was it a slimy, fleshy, old woman or a toad like out of some child's nightmare? She held a hatchet with a sharp, glistening blade and was pointing it towards Virginia's throat.

Jules de Grandin was shaking. I felt like he was about to pounce. Yes, but for the moment I realized that he was going to do nothing. He just breathed deeply and went over to Benjamin who had turned pale.

"I'm asking you not to move," he whispered. "If you move, all will be lost."

Meanwhile, the creature had moved and was going around the bed to caress one of the sleeping girl's wrists. With a hand whose touch must have been foul and intolerable, she pushed up the sleeve to the shoulder. The hideous face looked like a toad snout or, from a different angle, a monstrous lizard. An infestation of boils covered her skin. There were so many that they were like scales. The horrid phantom let out a frightful, disgustingly carnal laugh.

Next to us, Benjamin was losing control, struggling to contain himself. "I'm going out there... I'm going..." he muttered in total confusion.

"Absolutely not," De Grandin said with his moustache a mess. "If we want your wife to survive the coming ordeals as best as possible, I order you not to move."

And this order was definitive. Benjamin moaned a little, but once again he obeyed. Big beads of sweat were rolling down his forehead.

The foul and savage Valkyrie was now getting down to business. She reached out for the sleeper. I noticed her long, deformed fingers ended in sharp nails like a carnivore's claws.

"I came for you and I suggest you believe me. Your love, which you think is eternal, is going to be annihilated. For, you're like all women when they're in love: you believe your love will last forever and can't imagine for an instant that your lover will betray you. He's innocent, isn't he? Well, no! You're wrong! In a month or a year he'll make you cry tears of blood. It's obvious, inevitable. So much so that I'm offering you... come with me. Together we will enjoy the taste of vengeance."

The creature swung around suddenly and strode away from Virginia. Her flaming eyes were glued to the closet in which we were observing the scene. The demonic entity let out a whistle that sounded like the wheezy death throes of the dying.

Jules de Grandin tensed up. Again he calmed Benjamin who seemed completely discombobulated. But Benjamin did not obey and slipped free, stumbling into the room like a clumsy bird tripping out of a muddy pool.

"There you are at last!" the Valkyrie growled.

Straightaway her hand went to the dirty rag she used as a belt and grabbed a thin blade that looked as sharp as a razor.

"You'll see, sweet boy, how nicely I can cut off heads!"

The tragedy was off and running and if I followed the logic of my thinking, it was going to turn into a massacre worthy of the Dark Ages. Luckily, my pessimism was resisted. For, De Grandin was not taken by surprise. His eagle eyes were staring at the petite silhouette lying on the bed, looking so far away, completely ignorant of the horrible scene unfolding around her. But all of a sudden, enveloped by his gaze, Virginia sat up and to my astonishment let out a frightful, beastly howl. The wail was so unexpected, so strange, that the creature from the past was jolted violently. I could see a veil of bewilderment floating in her eyes. The Valkyrie did not understand what was happening. Even less when Virginia leaped out of bed and snatched the lethal weapon out of her firm hand.

"That's good, yes, very good, my girl," De Grandin murmured.

He seemed thrilled, like he was slowly sucking on sweet candy. He was panting, not missing one detail of the scene in the middle of the room.

I stood there confused and in awe. For, Virginia was docilely executing the orders of De Grandin. My ward was acting with a prowess that no one—me first of all—would have believed her capable of. Above all, to carry off such a work of death.

With her white eyes gazing into some void she raised her arm, brandishing the weapon she had taken off her enemy—and a flash of light.

Virginia in a state close to rapture did her work to perfection. The blade of iron, which must have taken the lives of many a man during the past thousand years, sliced through the Valkyrie's neck like butter.

At first, nothing happened, she did not even flinch. Then, blood came gushing out of the wound. The old warrior tried to lunge at her attacker, spouting incomprehensible words from her severed throat. But the attack wilted into a vomiting of blood and she dropped to the ground.

But Virginia, still obeying De Grandin's orders, did not leave her there. She raised the weapon again and cut the head of the hideous Valkyrie clean off.

Then everything froze. The monstrous creature had lived. Now she was just a heap of slime slowly spreading over the floorboards. We finally breathed. Virginia gradually woke up, but she did not seem to remember anything, especially not the murder she had committed. She merely threw the mucky, putrid blade to the other side of the room.

"What happened here?" she asked.

Her voice was hoarse and muffled. She was still listless and Benjamin was holding her in his arms. She put her head on his shoulder and cried softly, sobbing a little, while her husband stroked her hair.

"The beast is dead," Jules de Grandin assured them as his eyes sparkled. "Your courage and your composure, dear lady, have made sure that this monstrosity from the past has gone back into the cesspool she should never have crawled out of."

I chanced to cut in, "And yet, this horror was really here and she was truly menacing. And let's not forget about the men on that ship that was in the garden. They got off! Maybe we should remember that they might still be there!"

I was sure I was being the voice of reason. I did not feel like it was over and we were wrong to be rejoicing. It was too soon. But Jules de Grandin, with a firm grip, grabbed my arm and led me to the window. The sight of the garden stunned me completely. I let out a long sigh.

The Viking drakar was disintegrating. The proud sculptures ornamenting the prow were rotting at breakneck speed and crumbling to dust. They split and cracked, then splintered again into shards.

And the men, if you could call the resurrected ghosts on board as such, were falling to pieces. Their skin dried up so that the brittle bones were breaking through the leathery envelope. Their already hideous faces hollowed out to look like demons. Their eyes started bursting. Then putrid puss dripped down their withered cheeks. One after another the corpses fell to the ground in a pool of oily goo that was absorbed by the earth.

I looked on, astonished by the spectacle just like the one I had witnessed minutes before. It was just like the demise of the Valkyrie but on a grand scale.

"Now it's over," De Grandin said.

His tiny eyes glimmered. The ends of his moustache were even thinner than when he spruced them up. He raised his hand and started twirling them. Then he summed everything up in a few words.

"In the beginning, when Virginia was found driven to despair because of her lost love, we could've told her that it was over, that there was nothing to do, that the female monster called Inghen Ruaidh would conquer all. Yes, we could've done that…"

"Of course," I agreed.

But the little Frenchman started growling. I thought he was losing control. But it was only for a moment before he resumed his calm demeanor.

"I have to admit, we were lucky to have with us such an admirable person. I'm talking about Jules de Grandin who, from the start, took charge and forced the hand of fate, bravely, without ever backing down."

"That's a fact, without a doubt!" I exclaimed laughing. "But now tell me, during this fateful night, taking control of Virginia was kind of an abominable crime, wasn't it? Think about it. Cutting the throat and then beheading an old lady! There are people who would end up in the electric chair for less!"

"Please, Your Honor," the ineffable De Grandin as suddenly agitated and barked out, "that a crime was committed, yes, I am fully aware, but any jury in the world would acquit me. It was legitimate defense! Think about it, as you say—a weak young lady, your ward, attacked by a monster! Guided under my care, she was only protecting her life. And in fact, tell me, the victim's corpse, where it is? In this case we're lacking evidence, aren't we?"

A little annoyed, I had to admit he was right. "Indeed, the corpse has completely disintegrated."

"You see, the, my dear Trowbridge, there's nothing substantial left in this case. And for no one! Who would believe in a warrior from the time of Vikings travelling into this world today? And a weird Valkyrie who lived around 1,000 years ago?"

Here I could argue. "Don't forget those wacky ideas of your Swedish friend, Professor Hajlmar Hjerson. You believed them and used them yourself to describe the ploys of a wolf coming out of the frozen lands whose name was given by legend as Fenrir."

"Right, right," De Grandin replied. "But all that nonsense is just folklore. Who today would be crazy enough to think all that claptrap was real? Except for you, my dear Trowbridge?"

"Okay, okay," I muttered, a little irritated that my arguments were so easily refuted. I scowled in disillusioned silence. Then I looked up and saw my ward and her Benjamin hugging and kissing each other.

"Isn't that a beautiful thing?" Jules de Grandin concluded as we left the loving couple.

I agreed wholeheartedly, even more touched by the sweet little tear, prickly as hell, well up in the eye of the Frenchman as well as my own. Would we, too, someday, have a promise of love, a fiancée? I thought of lost opportunities, the ones crushed by the Great War.

De Grandin, I knew, even though he never spoke of it, treasured in his heart the memory of a little French girl, pretty and elegant, who ended up in a convent, surrounded by wimpled nuns and dressed in a religious habit herself. It was like a thorn in the flesh of my dear friend.

But he was strong and straightened up, twirled his moustache again and got back to his jolly self.

He asked, "Gadzooks, in the back of your cellar, under a pile of dust, don't you have a secret cache of old brandy? Or maybe Armagnac? Even some Sherry?"

A brief pause and then, "After a trying night like we've just had and as an eminent doctor of the University, in order to recover from our efforts, I recommend that we take out some glasses and fill them up. For me, the bigger the better."

Frank Schildiner is currently at work on a novel that will feature the green-masked Fantômas, who was the star of a trilogy of French films in the 1960s starring Jean Marais and Louis de Funès. Recognizing that this version of the character owed more to James Bond than the original dark-clad psychopath created by Allain & Souvestre, Frank has been practicing by penning a series of humorous homages, of which this is the latest...

Frank Schildiner: *The Emperor of Crime*

The French Alps, The 1960s

Sir Gerald Tarrant woke in darkness. A soft, yet gauzy cloth covered his head and face and he wondered if he'd been in an accident.

No, the British spymaster thought, *I am sitting upright, and my arms and legs are pinned. I have been waylaid.*

Then Sir Gerald remembered his last moments before the darkness had enveloped his body and mind. He had exited Blades after a fine dinner with Miles Messervy, entered his car and found the backseat flooded with green gas. Other than a momentary feeling of euphoria, nothing else occurred as far as he recalled.

"Ah," a French-accented voice purred, "you are awake. Excellent. It was so very boring waiting for the return of your intelligence."

Not Colonel Straik or Mister Sexton, Sir Gerald thought, remembering his last kidnapping and the supposedly dead members of that gang.

"You are each my guests, so I do believe introductions are in order," the French voice said as the cloth fell away from the elderly spymaster's head. "I gathered each of you here for reasons of my own."

The room was as dark as the lowest layer of a coal mine, a stygian gloom suddenly broken by a yellow light above the head of a man opposite Sir Gerald's seat. He was of medium height with a slim, slightly blocky build, a strong jaw, a somewhat prominent nose, and salt and pepper hair. His eyes narrowed and he looked left and right, searching for something in the surrounding murk.

"Monsieur Macdonald of the American division known as ICE. I believe that name is an acronym for Intelligence and Counter Espionage; however, it is quite silly. Must you Americans behave like schoolboys when naming your various spy organizations? UNCLE, SHIELD, OSS, ZOWIE, HEAT... Such nonsense!" the French voice said from the darkness.

"You'll get nothing from me!" Macdonald said, growling his words.

"Oh, do by quiet, Monsieur Macdonald, or these introductions will take an eternity," the voice said while chuckling softly. "Next, we have Sir Gerald Tarrant of the Britishh SIS. A valuable gentleman with a willingness to utilize any resource in the battle for his country's security."

Sir Gerald blinked as the light appeared above his head, but simply nodded once at the shadowy presence in the darkness.

"Now we come to a most impressive person from our neighbors behind the Iron Curtain. Welcome, General Nicholai Sergenovitch Grubozaboyschikov, formerly of SMERSH, now second in command of Department V of the KGB. Your supervisor, the one some Englishmen refer to as Karla, found your vanishing most upsetting. How very concerning... for you," the other continued.

The Soviet general proved to be a bald man with a bullet shaped head, dark brown eyebrows, and the tough, burly body of a brawler. He stared at the others with dark eyes that were hard, unyielding, and to Tarrant, resembling gun barrels.

A final light illuminated a fourth man, a short, podgy figure with a harsh, Puritanic face, thin brown hair, and a narrow, downturned mouth.

"Please allow me to introduce the legendary Chief Inspector Charles La-Rousse Dreyfus of the French Sûreté. A pleasure, Monsieur, a true pleasure," the French-accented voice said.

"And who are you, Monsieur L'Ombre?" Dreyfus asked, his face twitching slightly.

"Thank you, monsieur, but I am not L'Ombre. However, you do know me... All know me... I am the Prince of Terror, the Master of Strange Deaths, the Lord of Darkness... I am Fantômas!"

A light appeared above a wide wooden desk littered with silvery devices and switches. Seated in a highbacked leather chair sat the infamous international criminal himself.

A tall, broad-shouldered figure dressed in a black suit and black gloves with a head hidden beneath a green mask, the image of this man was known throughout the world. He was the number one most wanted criminal on every country's list. Rumor had it that, when any other person rose above his position in this hierarchy, Fantômas hunted the individual down and sent the dead person to the authorities.

"You monster!" Macdonald said, "How dare you kidnap us!"

The Lord of Terror laughed as he shook his head.

"Do you believe there is anything that Fantômas would not attempt, messieurs? Your respective organizations have scrambled every available agent in the world in hopes of recovering you immediately. A team is preparing an assault upon this position in a matter of minutes. Shall we view their progress?"

The lights dimmed and a table rose between the four captives. It was made from the finest dark wood. Then, a series of screens rose before them. The images flared to life, revealing a group of men crouched near the mouth of a dim cave.

"Mon Dieu!" Dreyfus said, his eye twitching.

"Oh, my," Sir Gerald said, feeling sweat trickle from his brow.

"Bohze Moi!" General Grubozaboyschikov said. "Not him."

"Oh crap, I'm dead," Macdonald said, shaking his head.

"Task for Jaguar, are you prepared?" Commissioner Juve asked, pulling his pale raincoat across his chest despite the lack of rain and high heat.

Juve was a tiny man with a bubble shaped bald head, a long, pointed nose, tiny eyes, and protruding ears. He appeared perpetually in motion, with tiny fussy gestures making him a quite distracting figure.

"Jaguar?" a languid English voice asked. "I thought we'd agreed upon Turtledove?"

This was the semi-famous spy, Charlie Bind. He was about as tall as Juve with a narrow face dominated by an enormous, misshapen nose, and bony, spidery limbs that resembled pipe cleaners.

"No, no, no, no, no!" Juve said, pressing his face close to that of Charlie Bind. "A jaguar is a symbol of power, a dove is that of peace. We have declared war on that beast, Fantômas, Agent Triple Zero!"

Producing a bone China teacup and saucer from nowhere, Bind lifted the vessel to his lips. "I prefer to be referred to as Agent Double Oh, Oh!"

"Why do we discuss silly creatures like kittens?" a short, wide, man with a pencil mustache asked, his vaguely Eastern accent almost a cliché.

Dressed in black from head to toe and possessing a wide, oversized smile and tiny, beady eyes, this Soviet secret agent was the Hollywood image of a Communist spy.

"That's enough, Badenov!" Agent 86 said, straightening and throwing back his shoulders. He was a few inches taller than the others, though still resembled a hotel detective rather than a secret agent.

"Go ahead, Juve," he said, shooting his cuffs and somehow stumbling in place.

"We shall now enter the lair of the evillest man in history, Fantômas. Our every second will be a life-or-death struggle to survive. We will be in terrible danger every minute…"

"And loving it," 86, Bind and Badenov said together.

The screens turned black and, a moment later, receded into the table. The floor then opened and the table slowly lowered out of sight.

"Juve," Dreyfuss said, his mouth twitching as a high-pitched giggle emerged from his lips. "He is the second biggest booby in all of France! The theories of that man were so demented he nearly brought about a world war."

"Why did you not fire him?" Fantômas asked.

Dreyfus cackled with crazed laughter. "What if he was right? Only Clouseau is worse than him, and he will die soon enough!"

Just then the far door burst open, and Task Force Jaguar/Turtledove burst inside. The walls slid back revealing a series of men in white plastic helmets bearing old fashion Sten guns.

"Fantômas!" Juve said, raising a revolver. "Now I have you!"

"Um, Mister Juve," Charlie Bind said, lowering a tiny silver gun that lay between his overlong fingers, "I believe we are surrounded."

Badenov slid back out of the doorway, closing the door behind him, "I will stand guard out here."

"It doesn't matter, Fantômas," Agent 86 said, stepping forward, his hands raised. "As we speak, this evil lair being surrounded by the entire Sixth Fleet of the United States Navy!"

"I find that hard to believe," Fantômas said.

Agent 86 frowned, leaned forward and asked, "Would you believe... the Fifth Fleet?"

"I don't think so," the Prince of Terror said.

"Three sailors in a rowboat?" he asked.

Juve stepped forward, his hands raised, his odd face grinning broadly, "No, now, let's talk, Fantômas."

A pair of hands then burst from his trench coat, each clutching a revolver. He fired wildly and was soon joined by 86, Bind, and Badenov who had snuck into the room when the shooting commenced. The men in the walls did not move and Fantômas slumped over.

"The old fake arms in the raincoat trick," Agent 86 said. "Well done, Juve!"

"It is one of my cleverer ideas," the French detective said, rushing forward towards the fallen Fantômas. "Mon Dieu! What is this?"

"Oh, dear," Bind said, sipping his tea. "That is a bit of a disappointment. I hoped to meet the man."

"Free me, you imbecile," Chief Inspector Dreyfus said, only later discovering their captor was a robotic Fantômas... one that lacked legs or arms...

Fantômas—the real one—flipped a switch on his desk and four faces appeared upon his viewscreen. The first was an angular, hard-faced Asian woman with dark eyes that appeared bottomless. The second proved to be a tall, scrawny man with thick silver hair, no earlobes and a syphilitic infection of his nose. The third man was a sad-faced man with a downturned face, bags under his watery eyes, a scar on his right cheek and a massive forehead. The final face was that of a beautiful woman with ebony hair and green eyes that reminded one of a cat and lovely bronze skin.

"As you see, my friends," Fantômas said, "Not only did I divert the attention of the United States, the Soviet Union, Great Britain, and France, I embarrassed their top agents. One week you were promised, and one week Fantômas delivered!"

"A bold plan, Monsieur," Gabriel said. "I have paid the full amount agreed upon as well as the bonus."

"Your services are priced quite high," Madame Atmos said, pressing a button that paid the full amount, "however, I see the results are worth it."

"Agreed," Sumuru said. "I dislike relying on your assistance. However, I could not commence work upon my secret base with the Soviet Union observing the location."

"I have paid as well," Ernst Stavro Blofeld said, "though I have a question. Why do you perform these missions, Fantômas? You do not lack resources. My analysts believe you are the wealthiest man in the world."

Fantômas leaned closer to the camera, his green masked face suddenly dominating their viewers.

"Because it amuses me to do so, Monsieur Blofeld... or should I call you Comte Balthazar de Bleuville? Shatterhand?"

"Um..." Blofeld said, raising his skeletal hands as he leaned back with obvious terror in his eyes. "I meant no offense."

"None taken," Fantômas replied. "Simply remember this, each of you. You are great kings and queens in your own worlds. But only Fantômas is the true Emperor of Crime!"

David Vineyard's latest clever caper is a perfect little thriller that fits neatly in both John Buchan's adventures of Richard Hannay and Arsène Lupin's later years, left relatively unreported by his creator, Maurice Leblanc...

David L. Vineyard: *Army of Shadows*

London, 1939

"It was mules that won the last war," Richard Hannay said.

Lord Charles Lamancha, who had been discussing the logistics of the new war with Palliser-Yeates, who was something in the War Cabinet in charge of providing troops with their needs from food to ammunition, spoke up:

"Oh, I don't know Dick, I wouldn't argue that mules, and horses for that matter, weren't important in the War, transporting and the like, and I can see an old infantry man like yourself holding that, but I can't really say I agree."

Palliser-Yeates spoke up as he swirled his brandy in its snifter. "I have to agree with Charles. I mean, mules were vital to that war, but winning..."

Major General Richard Hannay chuckled. "Gentlemen, I am not discussing moving goods or artillery to the front. I am merely saying that mules won that war, or at least, played a significant role in winning it."

It was the early days of the "Phony War," in the Fall of 1939, and things looked increasingly dark. The three men were gathered in the Rungates Club for dinner and brandy, something rare these days. The War had drawn them all out of retirement, with Hannay training young men in wilderness survival, going back to his youth in South Africa, and all the others recalled to various positions.

Neddy Leithen had died in Canada, more the pity, and Sandy Arbuthnot, as usual, was in the back of the beyond somewhere doing God knows what. Archie Roylance was an Air Marshall, and Peter John, his and Mary's son, was in the States, training with the RAF somewhere in Texas. The three friends had seldom the chance to gather and simply talk. Still, Hannay's broad statement had both Lamancha and Palliser-Yeates ready to argue, especially considering the conspiratorial smile on Hannay's face.

But before either man could protest further, Hannay held up his hand.

"No, hear me out and I think you'll agree with my point. Mules most certainly won that war—mules and a Spaniard. Sit back and I'll explain."

Lamancha and Palliser-Yeates recalled earlier days when, in a much more crowded room, each member of the Rungates Club had recalled some past encounter with adventure, whether uncanny or ordinary, and knowing Hannay's history, they were happy to follow his lead.

"It was just after that business in Turkey," Hannay began, "Blenkiron and I had gotten out by the skin of our teeth and Sandy was still leading the Turkish troops as their prophesied Greenmantle while I had returned to England, hoping for a regiment, but instead, I found myself called in by Sir Walter again and on my way to Spain..."

The Basque Country, 1916

If you have never seen the Basque country of Northern Spain, it is one of the glories of the world, but I wouldn't recommend it in winter. Especially not in winter in wartime, when skullduggery is afoot. It's a harsh country populated by tough people, and to make things worse, I was there under false papers, none too sure who, if anyone, I could trust, equally apprehensive of a German knife in my ribs, or the hand of a Spanish policeman on my arm with me interned for the rest of the war in a Spanish jail.

According to my papers, I was one Captain Hans Vanneker, an old *Voortrekker* from South Africa buying breeding stock, sheep, and primarily mules. I had been a few weeks in Spain gathering information on various aspects of the trade when I received information that I was to head to the Basque country.

As I had yet to get any information that I could see might be of any use to anyone, I was relieved to think something might finally be happening.

It wasn't the first time I was in rough country, nor the first time I had no idea why I was there, or what I was doing. I was getting orders out of Switzerland through Dick Ashenden, the novelist, who was operating there with a Mexican national under old R. Anyway, he got word to me that I had a rendezvous in the Basque country and would receive further orders there.

Nothing unusual about that. One of the more annoying parts of the whole intelligence business is how much of it is about sitting around and waiting with no idea what is actually going on, or what your role might be. I thought of Adam Melfort, who was somewhere behind German lines patiently playing at being a simple farmer and sending vital intelligence daily. At least, my job wasn't that nerve-wracking.

They also serve and all that, but I had been about two weeks in a small village at the base of the Pyrenees, and I was running out of sheep-men and muleteers to visit and discuss purchases with, especially as there didn't seem to be a mule within two hundred miles of the place for sale.

I knew the value of livestock in wartime, but it seemed there was a run on mules in Spain that seemed quite out of proportion to the need. Nor would anyone tell me who had purchased the animals, if it was an individual like me, a representative of some government, or a syndicate of some sort. I could understand there being some interest in buying up livestock and cornering the market, considering Spain was almost a direct conduit to France or Germany.

Someone willing to profit from the war—and there were always men willing to profit from the war—could make a tidy sum.

I assumed it was because of the war, and in a way, I was right, but not in any way I could have imagined. Meanwhile, I entertained a few theories, including that the Germans were buying up stock to prevent the French from importing it, but that presupposed there was a shortage in France, which I had no reason to suspect was true.

The inn I was staying at was run by a jovial Spaniard of the old Catalan blood and his dark, small, Basque wife. I had spent the day walking around talking mules until I hoped I never heard the subject again, and was having a drink after an early dinner, when the owner called me over.

"You are interested in buying mules, señor?" He asked the question in a low tone, his stale wine breath and face like the rough side of a boxing glove leaning in towards me.

I nodded. "I am. Not having much luck, but if you know of someone..."

"There is a man, señor, He came to me today and asked if you were still interested in mules. I said I thought so, and suggested he speak with you this evening, but he seemed concerned and asked it you could come to him. He said he would be waiting in the storage house behind the inn this evening. and asked if you might meet him after dark, and as it turns dark early here..." He nodded toward the shuttered windows where it was clear the last light of day had already gone out.

I thanked him and said I would certainly meet with the man. But first, I went to my room and dug my Webley out of its concealed place in my trunk and stuck it in the heavy shearling coat I was wearing against the cold.

There was likely no reason for this kind of concern, but there was a familiar tickling at the back of my neck that had played true for much of my life. I was sure I had spotted more than one German agent since arriving in Spain, some taking an interest in what I was doing, and though I had spotted no one particularly suspicious since I had arrived, we were close to the French border and I couldn't be certain I was the only spy in the place.

The prospect of a knife in my back in a storage house behind a small Spanish inn was not worse than catching a bullet in the trenches or a broken leg in the ever-present mud, or gas, or any of the myriad humiliating ways to die in a war, but just then, it was more likely than I cared for.

I stood in the shadow of the inn for a good long while watching the storage building. It was a moderate sized building that looked as if it might once have been a small stable, probably used now to store a few barrels of wine and ale, some smoked meats, and various fresh foods as well as gardening tools. There was a little lot by the inn that was no doubt the owner's wife's small allotment.

The only light came from the back of the inn, a pale buttery light coming from the kitchen that illuminated the sparse snow about halfway between the two buildings. Still, it was bright enough that, despite the low clouds, I had a good view of three sides of the storage building while the fourth side was hard up against a fair-sized tree.

I saw a few footprints outside, no doubt made by the innkeeper and his wife immediately behind the inn and adjacent to a few refuse bins. Beyond that, there was enough snow on the ground that I would have seen any others approaching the building, and while there should have been at least one set, there were none. It had snowed a little before dark, just enough to cover prints, and that meant the individual I was meeting with had been there for some time already.

He was anxious to see me, it seemed. At least, I assumed it was a man. I still had nightmares of that Greenmantle business with Hilda Von Einem. Tragic as her end had been, the thought of encountering another agent of the fair sex as dangerous as her still gave me a chill.

It was only a short way to the storage building. Not more than twenty-five feet, but there was no cover, and no amount of maneuvering would save me from being exposed when I approached the door. The building had no windows, but it was an old wooden structure and there were almost certainly cracks large enough for someone to watch me.

There was nothing for it, so with a last reassuring brush of my hand across the bulk of the Webley, I stepped out of the shadows, bold as if I were actually Captain Vanneker, a South African stockman looking to enrich his herd. I strode across the distance with purpose, as if I expected to meet nothing more sinister than a wary farmer, and for all I knew, that was all I was going to meet when I got there.

The door was partially open, and still keeping my cover in mind, I opened it casually, as I normally would have, with no more caution than I would show entering any strange dark building.

I pushed the door open and, for one of the longer moments of my life, filled the doorway, knowing the light framed me from behind.

If anyone wanted to put a knife in my ribs or a bullet between my shoulder blades, this was the perfect opportunity.

"Hello," I said. "Is there anyone there?" I spoke in my poor Spanish with as much of an Afrikaner accent as I could muster. I tried to mimic old Peter Pienaar as best I could, knowing I wouldn't fool anyone really familiar with the breed.

I stepped into the darkness, closing the door a bit behind me, putting at least a little more ground between me and whoever was waiting. My eyes adjusted to the darkness quickly enough, but I could make out nothing. My ears were sharp as a deer-hound on the heels of a stag, but I heard nothing and sensed no movement in the darkness.

Maybe my mysterious mule-seller had decided to stand me up?

I was about to strike a match and look for a lamp when a soft voice spoke in Spanish.

"Just place your gun on the floor, Colonel Hannay, and step away from it... No, no quick movements. I should regret wounding you, and even more having to kill you."

Even after he spoke, I still wasn't sure where in the dark the man was. When he had uttered these words, my hand had gone to my pocket, but fortunately, I hadn't tried to draw the Webley.

"Two fingers, Colonel. Only two fingers."

I did as he instructed, lifting the Webley by its butt with only two fingers. The voice commanding me was faintly aristocratic, and the accent just off the tiniest bit, as if he had spent much of his life away from his homeland.

I placed the Webley on the floor and stepped back as he instructed.

"Now push the gun across the floor with your foot. Yes, like that."

I wasn't going to risk a bullet in the gizzard at this point. There might be an opportunity later, but I was too much at a disadvantage at that moment.

"There," the man said.

For the first time, I got the impression of a tall, slender figure in the dark. He bent and retrieved the Webley, but his head stayed level facing me and the barrel of his Luger, which had caught a bit of light from outside, never wavered.

"That is so much better, Colonel Hannay."

"I'm afraid you have me at a slight disadvantage, señor..."

"Don Luis Perena," he said, and I saw a slight incline of his head in a bow. "And may I commend you for your nerve. Another man might well have forced me into an unfortunate action, and that would not have been good."

"Thank you, and I command you, sir, for a steady finger on that weapon, or I might already have my liver ventilated. Now, if you would indulge me, just out of curiosity, mind you, I assume the innkeeper was in on this—one of your men?"

Don Luis chuckled softly.

"Actually, they are all my men. The entire village. Very loyal, the Basque people. Everyone you have spoken to since you arrived in these mountains has been one of my agents."

"Even the mules?" I asked. The fellow's self-assurance was wearing on me a bit.

"Especially the mules. But now, I fear time is growing short, and I have other, less pleasant allies joining us. Listen to me with great care, Colonel. If you do, I can assure you that you will survive this night, and I hope many more to come. Don't make any assumptions and don't act until I tell you. You seem intelligent enough and you do have the nerve. You will certainly need it tonight. Above all, listen and learn. Your life, and perhaps the course of this war, may well be determined here. This night's history will be written in blood."

With that, I heard footsteps and realized we had been joined by two others. I half-turned and saw two heavy-set, square men, and a third taller and painfully slender figure with the bearing of an officer, almost certainly of the Jünker class. They needed no uniforms for me to recognize them as German.

"Well done, Don Luis," the tall man said in German. "Though you might have saved us all a great deal if you had disposed of this meddling Englishman."

"I never waste a perfectly good human being, Herr Baron Von Horsell. Besides, Herr Von Stalhein may want to interrogate him afterward. In any case, we have work to do this night..."

"You need not remind me of my duty, but it is growing late. My men are waiting at the entrance to the pass to accept delivery of the animals from your Basque. I trust they can be expected to arrive on time?"

This Baron struck me as typical of his class, but I couldn't quite fathom why someone like the Spaniard would put up with his arrogance. The fellow didn't strike me as the type to be so greedy he would put up with any fool easily. Still, I kept my council and played the fool. Besides, I was more than a little curious about how the Spaniard had known my name and fairly recent rank. Had I been exposed before I even reached Spain? Betrayed before I left England? I knew Old Bullivant would want answers if I ever got back.

"You need not worry about my men. Le Cagot will be at the cabin to deliver the message that they have made rendezvous with your men when we reach there, but as you say, it is a difficult climb in this weather, and we should start. You brought the extra snowshoes for our guest?"

"We should shoot him now and get it over with," the German said.

"Now, now, that would never do. We are in Spain, and stray bodies might still disturb the civil authority. There is enough risk in your Herr Doktor Krueger's scheme without risking drawing Spain into the war on the wrong side."

The German shrugged as if dismissing Spain as inconsequential, but gave into Don Luis demand. He spit something out at one of his men and the brute threw snowshoes at my feet.

"Put those on, Englishman," his officer commanded.

They kept a close eye on me while I put on the snowshoes though there was no need to. I had no desire to make a break before I knew what was going on. The name Doktor Krueger had triggered memories, and I knew he was a German scientist with an unpleasant reputation.

What he might have to do with mules being delivered to a pass in the mountains, I couldn't guess, but it could not bode well for our side. I would no more have run at that moment than leaped in front of a cannon.

While I was putting on the snowshoes, so did the others, one of the Germans keeping a gun on me while the other booted up.

Once we were all outfitted, we went outside where, in the short time we had been in the storage building, the snow had begun to fall heavily from pregnant gray clouds that seemed to sit on the mountains that hung over us.

"I do not care for this snow," the man Don Luis referred to as "Baron" said.

Now, in the better light, I had a chance to study both men better. The Spaniard was tall and distinguished, almost a caricature of a Spanish grandee, full of pride and dignity. The German was younger, and yet somehow prematurely aged and almost withered in appearance. I immediately thought of him as the Withered Man.

"The snow is in our favor, Baron, I assure you," said Don Luis. "It will be easier to move the livestock through the pass without being seen, especially as we get nearer to the French border. We could not have asked for better conditions."

The Baron dismissed that with a grunt, but ordered us on. The Spaniard took the lead, followed by the Baron, then the smaller of the two Boche, with me carefully watched by the larger of the two coming up last. Frick and Frack, as I had come to think of them, were taking no chance.

We hiked half-a-mile up toward the mountains as the temperature dropped and the snow fell heavier. By the time we reached a well-worn path, I could already feel the weight in my legs and the cold seeping into my bones. The trees were burdened with fresh, wet snow that weighted the limbs and, without the snowshoes, we would have been up to our ankles in fresh snow.

The snowshoes were awkward and difficult to walk in, but at least, I wasn't the only one struggling as the incline became steeper and the snow grew deeper. The Spaniard had been wise enough to carry an alpenstock and leaned into it. I found myself wishing I had one as well, but I couldn't see my guards letting me wield the equivalent of a quarter-staff.

The Baron swore steadily, and Frick and Frack grunted in an ill-tempered growl. Only the Spaniard seemed to move more or less with ease and I found myself admiring the man, despite his being an enemy. He had a cool head, a commanding manner beneath the easy charm, and an air of assurance. I regretted very much that I might have to kill him before the night was out, or him me.

I estimated something like an hour and a half had passed before we stopped to rest. The Withered Man looked as if he was on death's doorstep, but he was made of steel.

The Spaniard walked over to me and offered me a flask and I took it gratefully. It was brandy, and a good one. It burned all the way to my belly warming me, though I knew from experience that alcohol was a good way to freeze to death. I sensed the Spaniard had something to say to me that he didn't want the Withered Man to hear.

"We are almost there, my friend, only a short distance from here." In a softer voice he added, "When we reach the cabin, follow my lead if you want to live."

"What was that?" the Withered Man asked.

"Merely a warning, Baron, not to try anything. My Basque are everywhere, and escape is impossible."

The Withered Man made a harrumph noise.

My mind was whirling, though I struggled not to show it on my face. Whatever the Spaniard's game was, it was not simply helping the German's smuggle a few mules through a pass into France.

And there was the rub, because no matter how I played it, I could not see the value of this obviously well-planned operation. Perhaps if they had been smuggling mules into Germany, it could have made some sense, but why they should want to smuggle them into France?

It has something to do with Doktor Krueger, who was known for his outrageous schemes, but mules seemed unlikely saboteurs, and short of sending them across the border packed with explosives, nothing I could think of made sense, and even that was absurd and unlikely to do anything worse than kill the mules themselves.

Mules are fine animals in their place, but I could not see them taking to training in large numbers.

Our short rest was over, and we were up and on our way again. Almost another hour had passed, and we had climbed steadily, if not steeply, when I spied a small cabin, little more than a shack carved out of a small clearing in the woods, for we were still well below the tree line. A pale light was coming through a partially curtained window.

Grey smoke curled out from the chimney, and, at that moment, the idea of a warm fire meant far more than the idea this might be my final destination.

We stopped a dozen yards from the cabin and the Spaniard whistled. The door opened quickly and a small Basque boy of around ten appeared in the doorway.

"Le Cagot," the Spaniard said. "My runner. I told him to prepare for us."

Outside the cabin, we took off the snowshoes. My feet ached in my boots and I wanted nothing more than the be out of them, but it occurred to me that there was little dignity in dying in my stocking feet. Not that there was that much dignity in dying anyway.

Frick and Frack hustled me through the door the Basque boy Don Luis had called Le Cagot had opened. I was pushed toward a straight-backed chair and told to sit, and did so with some relief. The Withered Man pushed past and went straight to the fire, drawing off his gloves and holding out his hands to the fire before turning to warm his backside. True to type, he left no room for anyone else before the small hearth.

The Spaniard ignored him and seated himself at the small table in the center of the room. Before him there was a jug of wine, cheese, and bread. He poured wine in a mug and sipped it.

"Perhaps our guest...?" he began.

"I don't think the swine will be needing refreshment," the Withered Man said, pouring a stiff mug for himself. He took a drink from the mug and then turned and violently spit the contents into the fire. "What is this swill?"

"Algerian red," the Spaniard answered. "I acquired a taste for it when I was serving with the Foreign Legion in Morocco. It isn't to everyone's taste though."

"Only fit for..." the Withered Man surely meant to say something rude, but the look in the Spaniard's eye deterred him. "By all means, share it with the

Englishman. He deserves it."

A glass was poured and Frick handed it to me. It wasn't half as bad as the German had made out. I noticed an envious look on Frick and Frack's faces. Their commander had offered them nothing, not so much as a glass of water.

The Spaniard took a knife from his pocket and carved a piece of cheese and a little bread. "Might I share this too, Baron?"

"The condemned man... I don't see that it matters whether our guest dies with a full or empty stomach."

I took the cheese and bread gratefully. In this weather, a full stomach might provide some advantage in whatever play the Spaniard had in mind, because I was almost certain at this point that the game being played was beyond anything I had imagined.

"I must leave for the rendezvous with my men soon," said the Withered Man. "Your Basque will deliver the mules at midnight as arranged?"

"As I have assured you, Herr Baron. Though it took some persuasion to convince them. They fear the disease might be carried back to their own animals."

"We have taken precautions," the Baron said. "We have no wish to carry it back with us to Germany either. When we have delivered the animals into France, we will burn our uniforms and don clean clothes we are carrying with us. Your men will do the same before they return home. The fire will cleanse any germs from their clothing. You only have to make sure they destroy anything that came in contact with the diseased animals...

"Ah, see how our English friend's ears have perked up, Don Luis. He begins to comprehend a little. He overhears Doktor Krueger's name and diseased stock and little wheels begin to turn in that thick English skull. No doubt he is imagining the Black Plague, cholera, or some horrible influenza, but we are much more subtle than that.

"Listen, Colonel Hannay, and appreciate. The disease we are importing among the French tonight will likely not kill a single soldier, but it will destroy the Allied war effort as surely as any plague. A nation and an army cannot function without livestock, food, transportation... There are a hundred ways in which livestock are of value, and when we have finished tonight's work, in six months to a year, all the livestock in France will be decimated—perhaps worse.

"Tell me, Englishman, have you ever heard of hoof and mouth disease, anthrax?"

A cold chill went up my spine. I had seen cattle devastated by the disease in South Africa when I was younger. It spread like wildfire, and the only cure was to isolate healthy stock and slaughter and then burn the diseased animals. Six hundred infected mules could quickly be moved to the front, infect animals, and, despite the Baron's assurances, men, women, and children. The effects could easily turn the tide of war in Germany's favor.

I had thought poison gas an atrocity, thought the bombing of London the low point of this war, but this was inhuman. This was not merely warfare, but a crime against humanity, destroying not only lives but livelihoods, the ability to rebuild after the war.

I looked at the Spaniard but his taciturn features showed nothing.

"Well, Englishman," the Withered Man's smile was almost a rictus, "what do you think of our brilliant coup?"

"I think it's about the foulest Boche trick I can imagine. I can't believe the High Command approved it."

"The High Command? A bunch of old men with old men's dreams of honor. This came from Von Grundt and Krueger. Even Stalhein doesn't know the extent of our operation."

Von Grundt—the one they called Clubfoot. I had heard of Okewood's encounters with him and knew of what he was capable, and Krueger was even more monstrous if that was possible.

"It's a shame you won't live to enjoy the results…"

With that, his hand went inside his tunic and he produced a Luger, smoothly cocking it and lifting the barrel toward me.

I stared down the little black hole as I would the eyes of a cobra poised to strike.

The Spaniard quietly reached up and laid his hand on the weapon. The Withered Man snarled at him.

"Not to deprive you of your pleasure, Baron," said Don Luis, "but I would rather the boy not see this. He will guide you to your destination and after you have gone, I will tend to this fellow. If you will be so kind?"

The Baron looked at the boy whose eyes were quite wide. The red went out of his face and his hand ceased shaking with rage under the Spaniard's touch. He pulled the Luger back sharply and I thought for sure that he would shoot me anyway, but then, he uncocked the weapon and slid the safety on and returned it to his tunic.

"Very well," his voice was strained by suppressed anger. "You may have the honor, señor, but never lay hands on a German officer again."

"I wouldn't think of it, Herr Baron," the Spaniard said unperturbed.

I knew the wings of the angel of death had just cast their shadow over me as surely as they did that day Blenkiron and Sandy had been penned down with me by German shelling on the Turkish border. I have been behind enemy lines and in combat, and often afraid since then, but no closer to death than that moment, and it dawned on me the Spaniard had shared the same close brush.

"You should get going, Herr Baron. It is a difficult trail and neither you nor your men will be able to travel as quickly as Le Cagot."

"We will keep up, I assure you," the Baron snarled, and I couldn't imagine why the Spaniard was risking goading him other than the German was a pompous ass.

But, if his reason was to goad the German into moving, it worked.

Arrogance to one side, even the Junker had to know he was no match for the Basque boy who had grown up on this mountain. He curtly ordered Frick and Frack to get their gear on and snapped at the boy who looked toward the Spaniard, who nodded his ascent, which did not go unseen by my Withered Man.

"See you in Hell, Englishman," the Baron commented, his rictus smile both cruel and mocking. The door shut behind him.

The Spaniard leaped to his feet and went to the door listening. After a moment, he drew his Luger out and cocked it as he had earlier.

And fired twice directly at me.

I leaped back, but both bullets kicked up splinters in the wooden floor at my feet.

"For God's sake, man, lie down and play dead," he snapped.

Still seeing visions of my own mortality, I did as I was told, and only just in time.

I heard rather than saw the door flung open, the cold wind blow in causing me to repress a chill on the cold floor.

"Ah, good," I heard the Withered Man say. "Shall I have my men help you with the body?"

"There is no time, Baron. In any case, my own men will be here soon enough. If tonight's work is to succeed, time is vital."

The Withered Man grunted, and, after an agonizing pause in which I half expected him to draw his own Luger and finish the job, the door closed. This time, the Spaniard bolted it behind him.

'You've rested long enough, Colonel. Quickly now, we haven't much time."

I pulled myself up from the floor. "Just who are you?" I asked.

"A friend, and an ally. Your Webley is there on the table. We may need it. I suggest another glass of wine and some of that bread and cheese to fortify us for the climb ahead. I'm told you are no mountaineer, but a good man in a tight, and our path is hard, but not particularly difficult."

I sat at the table, poured more wine and used the Spaniard's knife to slice a chunk of the cheese and then tore a piece of bread from the loaf.

"I take it this is not a sudden change of heart on your part?"

"If you mean, have I been on your side from the beginning, then yes. While we gird our loins, so to speak, let me fill you in on what has been going on. You know who A.E.W. Mason is, of course?"

"The writer chap?"

"That's the one, though in this case, we are more concerned with Lt. Commander Mason of your Admiralty Intelligence."

"One of 'Needles' Hall's boys."

"I believe so. Lt. Commander Mason has a great love for Spain and many friends here. Even before the War, he established a network, the 'Spanish

Network' as it is called—agents loyal to Spain, but also friendly to Great Britain. Naturally when this war began, the Network was activated with the idea of protecting Spain's neutrality as much as a base from which to monitor German activities in the Mediterranean.

"It was the Network that first uncovered the curious interest in the German's purchasing mules and notified Mason. He followed leads until he uncovered this business of infecting the animals with anthrax and smuggling them into France."

I repressed a shudder thinking of what that hideous plan could mean, but waited for the Spaniard to go on.

"I was brought into this little game fairly late. I had recently returned to Spain from Morocco, having undertaken a small diplomatic mission. Friends of mine in the Network informed me what was going on and I chose to insert myself in this action.

"There was some debate how to best handle this. Reporting it to the Spanish authorities was the first thought, but alas, there is enough corruption at all levels of government and there are German sympathizers as well as those favoring the Allies, so that was quickly abandoned.

"Next, there was some talk of simply keeping the Germans from purchasing enough stock to make their plan effective, but even a relatively few anthrax-infected animals could prove a devastating disaster.

"Finally, since the best route for the Germans to smuggle these animals into Spain was through the passes in these mountains, it was decided, since I have allies among the Basque, for me to volunteer my services as a mercenary in pay of the Germans. This way, we have control of all the animals and which pass the German's intend to use.

"Your own mission was largely to panic German Intelligence so they would be moved to act quickly, but when I saw who had been sent to do the job... You are not a great strategist, Colonel, but you have experience, you are good in rough country, and you can be trusted to keep your head in a crisis. In other words, you are exactly the kind of man I need tonight.

"At midnight, my men will deliver the infected mules to the Germans. We were unable to find a way to fool them, so the animals are actually infected, but they have been carefully guarded so as not to infect any other stock. Doktor Krueger was able to create a slow developing virus that will not be fully infectious until shortly after the animals are dispersed throughout France, so as of now the animals are relatively safe."

"Six hundred time bombs, hardly seem safe," I said, finishing my last bite of bread.

"As safe as such volatile elements can be rendered. Tonight, at 1 a.m., the mules will reach the midway point in the pass, a narrow point chosen because the animals will be bunched together in a tight formation. My Basques have already planted explosives above the pass, and you and I will be waiting there.

258

At the given hour, the boy Le Cagot will go ahead to make sure the pass is clear, and when he is far ahead enough to be safe, he will light a flare—the signal for you and I to set off the explosives and bury the Germans and the mules under tons of snow, rock, and ice."

The enormity of it, the sheer horror of it, must have shown on my face.

"I am not a cold-blooded man, Colonel, but there is no other way we can guarantee this horror dies here. Come spring, when the snow thaws, my men will burn any remnants they find, but until then, there is no other option."

"No, I suppose not. Still..."

"These men did not pause to consider the innocents who would starve and lose their livelihood, the innocents who would suffer, the women, children, infants... They devised this plan with that fully in mind. Our own ruthlessness is at least directed at soldiers, not innocents."

He was right, of course, and there was no other option. As a soldier, and as a man, I am not unfamiliar with death from the veldt in South Africa to the Turkish steppes. Whatever horror I felt about cold bloodedly killing German soldiers and six hundred innocent animals, it was nothing compared to the idea of what would happen if they successfully moved them into France.

We prepared for our ascent up the mountain quickly. It was close on eleven and the snow was falling more heavily than before. The only advantage of that was that if it slowed us, it would slow the Germans as well.

On that journey up the narrow trail into the thinner and bitterly cold air, I will not dwell. The Spaniard, though older than I by some years, was nimble, but even he struggled, and while there was no real rock climbing involved, no precipice and crevasse or ice sheets to traverse, my legs were screaming and my feet numb, while my face was stiff and my hands felt like blocks of ice.

We halted seldom and then, only long enough to catch our breath. We pushed on, and though I did not consult my watch, I knew we were racing the clock, and the Germans below us driving those deadly damned beasts through the pass.

When we finally reached the overhang above the pass, the snow was blowing so hard that pellets now stung our faces. I feared we would never know if the Germans were beneath us or not, but the Spaniard seemed satisfied.

After catching our breath and taking a swig of wine, he showed me where the explosives had been set by his Basques. They were not sappers, and the set up was crude, but effective. Without military supplies to work with, they had set up two sets of explosives at opposite ends of the overhang, and I saw for the first time why the Spaniard had needed me with him.

We would have to trigger the explosions with our pistols, and the thought of that nagged at my gut. Just how good were the Basques with explosives. A brief vision of the two of us riding the rock, ice, and snow down the steep slope teased the back of my mind. The Spaniard had said I had a cool head, but it did not feel that way in that moment.

259

So, we waited.

And waited.

I tried to keep my hands warm, concerned they would be too numb to even fire my Webley when the time came. All the while, I watched for the boy's flare. A million questions danced through my mind. Had the convoy of animals been delayed? Were they still coming? Had the Spaniard been betrayed by his Basques for German gold? Was I going to freeze on this overhang, waiting for a parade of death that never came?

I cursed my self for too much imagination, then had to smile at the thought of Sandy's face if I claimed too much imagination. My great strength in his view was a narrow focus on the matter at hand, entirely unhindered by imagination,

I noticed the Spaniard had raised his hand. He pointed to his ear.

I strained against the wind, and for a time could only hear the whistle of the wind among the rocks. Then, I heard it. It was faint, and if the Spaniard had not held up his hand, I would never have detected it, but now that I was listening, I made out the unmistakable sound of the mules braying and protesting the conditions they were being driven through. Even though they had probably tried to silence them, a few were bound to work their mouths free and protest the cold and hard climb. They were not animals to suffer silently.

If anything, that made it more difficult to do what had to be done.

The sound came closer, and I no longer had to strain to hear the animals. I even imagined an occasional German soldier cursing the poor creatures that could be heard above the icy wind.

Well past the overhang, there was a sudden burst of red light in the sky.

The boy's flare! He was clear of the pass and had given the signal.

The Spaniard had his Luger out and was cocking it. I pulled my Webley flexing my fingers before leveling the barrel at the charge.

The Spaniard had raised his free hand. I could not hear him shouting above the wind, but I understood his directions were to fire as soon as he dropped his hand.

My nerves were gone. The fear was gone. My head was clear. The cold, the wind, the ice and snow, none of that seemed to exist in that moment. My whole focus was on the Spaniard's hand.

And it dropped.

I fired.

For a moment, all that was heard was the almost simultaneous crack of the two weapons.

The world seemed frozen in time, hanging on a thin edge.

I threw myself backwards when the fuse reached the explosives. There was a roar and leaping flame beneath a burst of white, and just as suddenly, an even louder roar as the wall of snow and ice beneath us slid forward and then collapsed in a growing wave of blinding white with a continuous thundering sound that grew louder even as it swept away tons of ice and rock and snow.

How long before the first screams of men and beasts reached us, I couldn't calculate. I tried not to picture men and animal under that fallen mountainside, seeing inescapable death fall upon them. I will never forget the sounds that rose up from that cauldron of death as long as I live.

The silence came suddenly. It was worse than the thundering roar and the screams of man and mule.

I startled when I saw the Spaniard above me.

"We must get back. There is no point freezing on this mountain now."

I nodded and stood up, realizing I still had a death grip on my Webley. I tucked it away.

The rest was anti-climax. The boy Le Cagot joined us halfway back to the cabin. He reported none of the mules had escaped, but that he believed the German I thought of as the Withered Man may have.

That seemed to bring an end to it. No other attempts were made to smuggled diseased animals into France, and the whole business was quietly buried, like the men and animals in that narrow pass known only to a few Basque smugglers and ourselves.

I said goodbye to Don Luis and made my way to the coast where a ship picked me up and, in a short time, I was back in London reporting to Sir Walter. I had done my service for the moment, and took a quiet week in Scotland hiking as a reward. By the end of it, I could even sleep without hearing the dying screams.

But however hard it might be to accept it, the war was won in many ways that night, by six hundred dead mules and that Spaniard whom I never saw again.

London, 1939

Lamancha and Palliser-Yeates were gone, having heard out Hannay's story and now taken their last drinks and said a more sober goodnight than either had intended earlier.

Hannay lingered on for a final brandy, briefly lost in an old man's thoughts of glories and horrors of the past. Just before polishing off the last of his drink, he removed a thin blue envelope from his pocket,

He had received it just after war had been declared in September and carried it with him still

He opened the letter, grateful he could still read without glasses at his age, and read it once again with some of the wonder he had felt when he had read it with the first time.

To Major-General Sir Richard Hannay
My dear Hannay.
It is with some grief I write you as our two nations have again been

plunged into inevitable war with an implacable foe, one I fear even greater than the monster the two of us confronted in that narrow Spanish pass so many years ago,

We are both old men now, and this will be a young man's war to fight, but we may both still contribute in our own way to its successful conclusion and the ultimate defeat of yet one more evil in the world.

In that spirit, I know you will be participating in the events to come, as will I in my own way, but should you at any time require my services you may contact me at the address below and be assured I will reply as quickly as possible.

Yours, in peace and in war,

It was signed *"Don Luis Perena"*, but it was the signature scrawled beneath it that caught Hannay's eye. That signature explained so much and opened so many new avenues of exploration, but somehow it was very reassuring. A sort of continuity in these days of change and doubt of the future.

Like England, like France, some things did not change. Some things were true and steady and held so across the years.

The letter was signed in a bold hand:

Arsène Lupin.

Credits

The Brasher Bat

Starring:	**Created by:**
Harry Dickson	*Anonymous*
Mr. Quelch	Charles Hamilton
Billy Bunter	Charles Hamilton
Harry Wharton	Charles Hamilton
Bob Cherry	Charles Hamilton
Johnny Bull	Charles Hamilton
Singh	Charles Hamilton
Inspector Lestrade	Arthur Conan Doyle
Dr. John H. Watson	Arthur Conan Doule
Peter Wimsey	Dorothy Sayers
Bulldog Drummond	H.C. McNeile
Petrie	Sax Rohmer
Raffles	W.W. Hornung
O'Hara	Rudyard Kipling
Moriarty	Arthur Conan Doyle
Ruthven	John William Polidori
Rupert Giles	Jess Whedon
Tootles	Arthur Conan Doyle
Darling	J.M. Barrie
Co-Starring:	
Uncle Huree	Rudyard Kipling
Sherlock Holmes	Arthur Conan Doyle
Mycroft Holmes	Arthur Conan Doyle
The Mandarin (Fu Manchu)	Sac Rohmer
The Seven Golden Vampires	Don Houghton
Dracula	Bram Stoker
The Black Coats	Paul Féval
Also Starring:	
Raymond Chandler	Kim Newman
(The Narrator)	based on the author
Plum (P.G. Wodehouse)	*Historical*
And:	
Dulwich School	P.G. Wodehouse
Watchers' Council	Joss Whedon
Diogenes Club	Arthur Conan Doyle

Tim Newton ANDERSON is a former daily newspaper journalist and PR executive who recently started writing fiction, including a self-challenge to write a story a week during lockdown. His story *The Pataphysical Detectives* was published in *Emanations 9: When a Planet Was a Planet* and another story, *Letters to my Daughter*, will soon appear in *Parsec* magazine. He is a member of the London Institute of Pataphysics and an enthusiastic collector of science fiction and fantasy. He is a regular contributor to *Tales of the Shadowmen*.

Hercules and Samson vs the Russian Vampire and the Zombies of Frankenstein

Starring:	Created by:
Yvgeni	Matthew Baugh
Jean Ténèbre	Paul Féval
Ange Ténèbre	Paul Féval
Casimiro	Juan García & Gilberto Martínez Solares Francisco Cavazos
The Zombies	Francisco Cavazos & Alfredo Salazar
Maciste	Gabriele d'Annunzio & Giovanni Pastrone
Santo	Rodolfo Guzmán Huerta
Blue Demon	Alejandro Moreno
Mil Mascaras	Aaron Rodríguez Arellano
Mujer Murcielago	Alfredo Salazar based on Bob Kane & Bill Finger
Co-Starring:	
Dracula	Bram Stoker
Baron Brakola	José Díaz Morales, Rafael García Travesi & Fernando Osés
Dr. Irving Frankenstein	Fernando de Fuentes, & Alfredo Salazar

Matthew BAUGH is the author of oodles and oodles of short stories and several novels, who aspires to keep writing until there are no more stories left to tell. He is represented by Rebecca Angus of the Golden Wheat agency and lives and writes in Torrance, CA. He is also the author of *The Vampire Count of Monte-Cristo*, and a regular contributor to *Tales of the Shadowmen*.

Orpheus Omega

Starring:	Created by:
Dr. Omega	Arnould Galopin
Orpheus	Jean Cocteau
The Princess (Death)	Jean Cocteau
The Beast	Jean Cocteau
	based on Gabrielle-Suzanne Barbot
	de Villeneuve & Jeanne-Marie
	Leprince de Beaumont
Co-Starring:	
Glenarvon	Lady Caroline Lamb
And:	
The *Cosmos*	Arnould Galopin
Tormance	David Lindsay
The Zone/The Room	Andrei Tarkovsky
	based on Arkady
	& BorisStrugatski

Atom Mudman BEZECNY is the editor-in-chief of the independent pulp press Odd Tales Productions, a position she has occupied for five years. Her previous publications include the novels *The New Adventures of the Flash Avenger, Flint Golden and the Thunderstrike Crisis*, and *So Be It... Desecrator*. She has written two official movie tie-ins: *The Return of the Amazing Bulk*, a sequel to Lewis Schoenbrun's superhero film *The Amazing Bulk*, and *The Bryan Gospels*, an expansion of Seth Landau's horror movie *Bryan Loves You*. She is also the author of many short stories, including a series starring her original heroine Bloody Mary. She is a regular contributor to *Tales of the Shadowmen*.

The Worthiness of the Wielder

Starring:	Created by:
Milady de Winter	Alexandre Dumas
Solomon Kane	Robert E. Howard
Constance Bonacieux	Alexandre Dumas
Charles de Batz de Castelmore,	Alexandre Dumas
a.k.a. D'Artagnan	based on a historical
	character
And:	
Járngreipr, Mjölnir, Megingjörð	*Mythological*

Matthew DENNION lives in South Jersey with his beautiful wife and daughters. He currently works as a teacher of students with autism at a Special Services School. Matthew writes giant monster stories for *G-Fan* magazine and he has recently published three giant monster novels, *Chimera: Scourge of the Gods*, *Operation R.O.C.: A Kaiju Thriller* and *Atomic Rex*. He is a regular contributor to *Tales of the Shadowmen*.

The Projector of Death

Starring:	Created by:
Lance Corporal Frančišek Zupančič	Brian Gallagher
Captain Marić	based on the painting *Death Laying in Wait for a Cavalryman* by Lazić, 1916
Simon Hart	Jules Verne
Professor Marcus	Cesare Zavattini, Federico Pedrocchi & Giovanni Scolari
Warrant Officer Duval	Brian Gallagher
Lord Astor Burydan	Gustave Le Rouge
Lady Ellenor Burydan	Gustave Le Rouge
Dr. Cornelius Kramm	Gustave Le Rouge
Countess Irina Petrovski	Arnaud d'Usseau & Julian Zimet
Josip	Brian Gallagher
Lieutenant Vuljanić	Brian Gallagher
Sergeant Mayr	Brian Gallagher
Darko	Brian Gallagher
Kata	Brian Gallagher
Co-Starring:	
The Saturnians	Federico Pedrocchi & Giovanni Scolari Brian Gallagher
Fritz Kramm	Gustave Le Rouge
The Red Hand	Gustave Le Rouge
Professor Saxton	Arnaud d'Usseau & Julian Zimet
Dr. Wells	Arnaud d'Usseau & Julian Zimet
Also Starring:	
Stjepan Radić	*Historical*
Archduke Karl	*Historical*
Emperor Franz Joseph	*Historical*
Gabrielle D'Annunzio	*Historical*

Brian GALLAGHER has a BA in Politics and Society and lives in London. He works in the media and for many years has written on the politics, economics and many other aspects of Croatia and has been quoted in Croatian and international media. In relation to that he has written extensively on Croatian-related cases at the International Criminal Tribunal for the Former Yugoslavia. He has always been interested in SF, classic horror, comics and is proud to be a lifelong *Doctor Who* fan. His latest BCP collection is *The Return of Captain Vampire.* He is a regular contributor to *Tales of the Shadowmen.*

Young Robur and The Thirst of Shiloh

Starring:	Created by:
Robur	Jules Verne
Thaddeus Frycollin	based on Jules Verne
Tom Turner	Jules Verne
Serafina	Martin Gately
Ellenshaw	Martin Gately
Elsa von Merck/Trina Dressard/Kitty McKenzie	Luci Ward & Morgan Cox
Erich von Rugen/Alex Morel/Lionel McKenzie	Luci Ward & Morgan Cox
Sheriff Ashermann	Martin Gately
Idaho Jones	Luci Ward & Morgan Cox
Gideon Spilitt	Jules Verne
Widow Foy	Martin Gately
Co-Starring:	
Grand Pater Platanus'	Martin Gately
Steve Clarke	Luci Ward & Morgan Cox
The 1752 Conspiracy	Luci Ward & Morgan Cox

Martin GATELY is the author of the official prequel to Philip José Farmer's *The Green Odyssey (Samdroo and the Grassman* in *The Worlds of Philip José Farmer 4—Voyages to Strange Days).* His writing career commenced in 1988 when he wrote for D C Thomson's legendary *Starblazer* comic. He is also a contributor to the UK's journal of strange phenomena *Fortean Times.* For Black Coat Press, he has provided stories for two collections, *Exquisite Pandora* and *The New Exploits of Joseph Rouletabille,* and contributed to the following anthologies: *Night of the Nyctalope, Harry Dickson Vs. The Spider* and *The Vam-*

pire Almanac Vol. 1. His latest work is an adaptation of Edgar Rice Burroughs' *Pirate Blood* into comic strip form, drawn by Anthony Summey and available on the official ERB website. He is a regular contributor to *Tales of the Shadowmen*.

The Floating Island Mystery

Starring:	Created by:
Phileas Fogg	Jules Verne
Passepartout	Jules Verne
Professor Brainerd	Edward S. Ellis
The Steam Man	Edward S. Ellis
Princess Aouda	Jules Verne
Professor Aronnax	Jules Verne
Robert Curtis	Jules Verne
Baccarat (Countess Artoff)	Pierre-Alexis Ponson du Terrail
D.P. Roberts	based on William Goldman
Engineer Banks	Jules Verne
Dr. Ox	Jules Verne
A.U. Goldfinger	based on Ian Fleming
Co-Starring:	
The Gun Club	Jules Verne
Chevalier Dupin	Edgar Allan Poe
Tankerdon	Jules Verne
Coverly	Jules Verne
Le Brec	Paul Féval
Beltham	Pierre Souvestre & Marcel Allain
Wayne	Bob Kane & Bill Finger
Von Warteck	Jean de La Hire
Reade	Harry Enton
Favraux	Arthur Bernède & Louis Feuillade
Wildman	Arthur Conan Doyle
Swift	Edward Stratemeyer
And:	
Propeller Island	Jules Verne

Travis HILTZ started making up stories at a young age. Years later, he began writing them down. In high school, he discovered that some writers actually got paid and decided to give it a try. He has since gathered a modest collection of rejection letters and a shelf full of books with his name on them. Travis lives in the wilds of New Hampshire with his very loving and tolerant wife and a staggering amount of comic books and *Doctor Who* novels. He is a regular contributor to *Tales of the Shadowmen*.

The Gunfighter in the Iron Mask

Starring:	Created by:
General Alberto Tuco Ramirez	Age & Scarpelli, Luciano Vincenzoni, Sergio Leone & Roland Kibbee, James R. Webb, Borden Chase
Black Bart (Barton Gordon)	Mario Casacci, Rate Furlan, & Antonio Giambriccio
Donald Joseph Sorenson (El Rojo)	Mario Casacci, Rate Furlan, & Antonio Giambriccio
Josephine Balsamo	Maurice Leblanc
Lola Buckhurst (La Zorra Roja)	Rick Lai based on Robert W. Chambers
Escudo	Renato Izzo & Gianfranco Parolini
Septiembre	Renato Izzo & Gianfranco Parolini
Gitano	Renato Izzo & Gianfranco Parolini

Co-Starring:	
The Black Coats	Paul Féval
Jenny Fancy	Emile Gaboriau
Arthur Gordon	Emile Gaboriau
Jack Buckhurst	Robert W. Chambers
Bill Sorenson	Mario Casacci, Rate Furlan, & Antonio Giambriccio
Dr. Vincent Gallico	Rick Lai
Von Herder & Son	Arthur Conan Doyle
Ortega	Mario Casacci, Rate Furlan, & Antonio Giambriccio
Navarro	Mario Casacci, Rate Furlan, & Antonio Giambriccio
L'Ollonais Brothers	Rick Lai based on Renato Izzo & Gianfranco Parolini
Jacqueline Buckhurst	Rick Lai based on

	Robert W. Chambers
Also Starring:	
Abraham Lincoln	*Historical*
Karl Marx	*Historical*
Benito Juarez	*Historical*
Porfirio Diaz	*Historical*
And:	
The Iron Mask	Alexandre Dumas
Gold Hill	Mario Casacci, Rate Furlan,
	& Antonio Giambriccio
Burning of Lucifer Festival	Mario Casacci, Rate Furlan,
	& Antonio Giambriccio

Rick LAI is an authority on pulp fiction and the Wold Newton Universe concepts of Philip José Farmer. His speculative articles have been collected in *Rick Lai's Secret Histories: Daring Adventurers, Rick Lai's Secret Histories: Criminal Masterminds, Chronology of Shadows: A Timeline of The Shadow's Exploits* and *The Revised Complete Chronology of Bronze*. Rick's fiction has been collected in *Shadows of the Opera, Shadows of the Opera: Retribution in Blood* and *Sisters of the Shadows: The Cagliostro Curse* (the last two titles are available from Black Coat Press). He has also translated Arthur Bernède's *Judex* and *The Return of Judex* into English for Black Coat Press. Rick resides in Bethpage, New York, with his wife and children. He is a regular contributor to *Tales of the Shadowmen*.

Foiled Again

Starring:	**Created by:**
No. 6 (The Prisoner)	Patrick McGoohan
	& George Markstein
Dr. Omega	Arnould Galopin
Co-Starring:	
Denis Borel	Arnould Galopin
The Horla	Guy de Maupassant
Simon Cordier	Robert E. Kemnty
	based on Guy de Maupassant
And:	
The Village	Patrick McGoohan
	& George Markstein
Rover	Patrick McGoohan
	& George Markstein
The *Cosmos*	Arnould Galopin
Babelian Technology	Kurt Steiner

The Phantom Angel and The Wrong Wolf

Starring:	Created by:
The Phantom Angel (aka Madame L'Ange, Briar Rose, Sleeping Beauty)	Randy Lofficier based on Charles Perrault
Marty Hopkirk	Dennis Spooner
Red Riding Hood	based on Charles Perrault
Gran	based on Charles Perrault
Captain Laure Berthaud	Alexandra Clert & Guy Patrick Sainderichin
Gilou	Alexandra Clert & Guy Patrick Sainderichin
Big Bad Wolf	based on Charles Perrault & James Halliwell
The Huntsman	based on Charles Perrault
Co-Starring:	
Dr. Francis Ardan	Guy d'Armen
Introducing:	
Thor, Dog of Thunder	Himself

Jean-Marc & Randy LOFFICIER have collaborated on five screenplays, a dozen books and numerous translations, including *Arsène Lupin*, *Doc Ardan*, *Doctor Omega*, *The Phantom of the Opera* and *Rouletabille*. Their latest novels include *Edgar Allan Poe on Mars*, *The Katrina Protocol* and *Return of the Nyctalope*. Randy has written a number of animation teleplays, including episodes of *Duck Tales* and *The Real Ghostbusters*, and Jean-Marc comics featuring such popular heroes as *Superman* and *Doctor Strange*, as well as (in collaboration with Randy) original characters such as *Robur* and *Tiger & The Eye*. Jean-Marc is currently publisher and editor-in-chief of Hexagon Comics; Randy is/was a member of the Writers Guild of America West and Mystery Writers of America.

The Haunting of the Louvre

Starring:	Created by:
Richard Curtis Van Loan (The Phantom Detective)	D. L. Champion
Colette Chantecoq	Arthur Bernède
The Phantom	Lee Falk
Chantecoq	Arthur Bernède
Jacques Bellegarde	Arthur Bernède
Belphegor	Arthur Bernède

Fantômas	Pierre Souvestre & Marcel Allain
Co-Starring:	
Inspector Ménardier	Arthur Bernède
Phantom of the Opera	Gaston Leroux

Rod McFADYEN has been dabbling in creative writing for a number of years now, although generally doing more dabbling than writing. While an avid reader of books of history, science fiction and fantasy, he is also a fan of the pulp genre and was delighted to come across the French pulp heroes. He's also a sucker for a good cross-over. He is a regular contributor to *Tales of the Shadowmen.*

When the Children Leave Home

Starring:	**Created by:**
Dr. Omega	Arnould Galopin
Thea	based on Thea Von Harbou
Karellen/The Overlords	Arthur C. Clarke
Co-Starring:	
Jan Rodricks	Arthur C. Clarke
The Overmind	Arthur C. Clarke
And:	
The *Cosmos*	Arnould Galopin

Nigel MALCOLM lives in Kent, England. He works as a Teacher of English as a Foreign Language. He is a long-term *Doctor Who, Star Trek* and *Prisoner* fan, long before all the new-fangled versions came along. As well as being a regular contributor to *Tales of the Shadowmen,* he is working on various novels and audio plays.

The New Unholy Three

Starring:	**Created by:**
Erik (The Phantom of the Opera)	Gaston Leroux
Quasimodo (The Hunchback of Notre-Dame	Sean Todd based on Victor Hugo
Jacques Courbé	Tod Robbins
St. Eustache	Tod Robbins
Jeanne Marie	Tod Robbins
Jacques de Trémeuse (Judex)	Arthur Bernède & Louis Feuillade

Co-Starring:

Colonel Bozzo-Corona	Paul Féval
Tweedledee	Tod Robbins
Grippo the Giraffe Boy	Tod Robbins
Lupa the Wolf Lady	Tod Robbins
The Persian	Gaston Leroux
The Angels of Music	Kim Newman
Leo Saint-Clair (The Nyctalope)	Jean de La Hire
Dr. Cornelius Kramm	Gustave Le Rouge

Also Starring:

Adolf Hitler	*Historical*
Pierre Laval	*Historical*
Hermann Göring	*Historical*

And:

Duebe Industries	Matt Hickman
Copo's Circus	Tod Robbins

Christofer NIGRO is a writer of both fiction and non-fiction with a strong interest in pulps, comic books and fantastic cinema, and a regular contributor to *Tales of the Shadowmen*. He may be known to some by his websites *The Godzilla Saga* and *The Warrenverse*, as he is an authority on the subject of *dai kaiju eiga* (the sub-genre of cinema specializing in giant monsters), and the characters featured in the comic magazines published by Warren. He has recently revived and expanded Chuck Loridans' classic site MONSTAAH, and has since been published in the anthologies *Aliens Among Us* and *Carnage: After the Fall*. He is a regular contributor to *Tales of the Shadowmen*.

A Thief in the Floating City

Starring: **Created by:**

Captain James Anderson	Jules Verne
Dr. Dean Pitferge	Jules Verne
James Moriarty	Arthur Conan Doyle

Co-Starring:

Fabian McElwin	Jules Verne
Harry Drake	Jules Verne
Archibald Corsican	Jules Verne

Also Starring:

Jules Verne	*Historical*

And:

The Great Eastern	Jules Verne

John PEEL was born in Nottingham, England, and moved to the U.S. in 1981 to marry his pen-pal. He and his wife ("Mrs. Peel") and their rescue dog Dickens (named for as favorite author!) live on Long Island, New York. He has written more than a hundred novels, including tie-ins based on shows like *Doctor Who, Star Trek* and *The Avengers* (the one with the *other* Mrs. Peel!). His most popular works are the *Diadem* series (12 volumes so far) and the *Dragonhome* series (a mere 3). Two volumes of his collected short stories are now available from Black Coat Press: *Return to the Center of the Earth* and *Twenty Thousand Years Under the Sea*. He is a regular contributor to *Tales of the Shadowmen*.

Maciste Contro il Negromante Cremisi

Starring:	Created by:
Maciste	Gabriele d'Annunzio
	& Giovanni Pastrone
Gilles Grenier	Clark Ashton Smith
Ilalotha	Clark Ashtn Smith
All other characters	Anthony Perconti
And:	
The Dark Ship	Michael Moorcock

Anthony PERCONTI lives and works in the hinterlands of New Jersey with his wife and kids. He enjoys well-crafted and engaging stories from across a variety of genres and mediums. This is his first contribution to *Tales of the Shadowmen*.

The Specter of the Valkyrie

Starring:	Created by:
Jules de Grandin	Seabury Quinn
Dr. Trowbridge	Seabury Quinn
Professor Hajlmar Hjerson	based on Agatha Christie
	& Patrik Gyllström
All other characters	Jean-Paul Raymond

Jean-Paul RAYMOND has contributed a *Madame Atomos* original novel to Rivière Blanche (Black Coat Press' French sister imprint) and several short stories, including "The Mystery of the Byzantine Mosaic" included in *Harry Dickson vs The Spider*. This is his first contribution to *Tales of the Shadowmen*.

The Emperor of Crime

Starring:	Created by:
Sir Gerald Tarrant	Peter O'Donnell

Macdonald	Donald Hamilton
General Nicholai Sergeno-vitch Grubozaboyschikov	Ian Fleming
Chief Inspector Charles La-Rousse Dreyfus	Blake Edwards & Maurice Richlin
Fantômas	Pierre Souvestre & Marcel Allain / Jean Halain & Pierre Foucaud
Commissioner Juve	Pierre Souvestre & Marcel Allain / Jean Halain & Pierre Foucaud
Charlie Bind	Talbot Rothwell & Sid Colin
Boris Badenov	Jay Ward, Alex Anderson & Bill Scott
Agent 86	Mel Brooks & Buck Henry
Madame Atomos	André Caroff
Ernst Stavro Blofeld (aka Comte Balthazar de Bleuville, Shatterhand)	Ian Fleming
Gabriel	Peter O'Donnell
Sumuru	Sax Rohmer
Co-Starring:	
Sir Miles Messervy	Ian Fleming
Colonel Jim Straik	Peter O'Donnell
Mister Sexton	Peter O'Donnell
Karla	John Le Carré
L'Ombre	Alain Page
Jacques Clouseau	Blake Edwards & Maurice Richlin

Frank SCHILDINER has been a pulp fan since a friend gave him a gift of Philip Jose Farmer's *Tarzan Alive*. Since that time he has written the *Frankenstein* trilogy, the *Napoleon's Vampire Hunters* series (3 vols.), *Irma Vep and the Great Brain of Mars*, and *The Last Days of Atlantis* fantasy series, all for Black Coat Press. Frank has been published in many other anthologies. He works as a martial arts instructor at Amorosi's Mixed Martial Arts and resides in New Jersey with his wife Gail, who is his top supporter. He is a regular contributor to *Tales of the Shadowmen*.

Army of Shadows

Starring:	Created by:
Richard Hannay	John Buchan
Lord Charles Lamancha	John Buchan
Palliser-Yeates	John Buchan
Don Luis Perenna (Arsène Lupin)	Maurice Leblanc
The Withered Man (Baron Von Horsell)	John Creasey
Le Cagot	Trevanian
Co-Starring:	
Edward "Ned" Leithen	John Buchan
Sandy Arbuthnot, Lord Clanroyden	John Buchan
Archie Roylance	John Buchan
Peter John Hannay	John Buchan
Mary Hannay	John Buchan
John S. Blenkiron	John Buchan
Sir Walter Bullivant	John Buchan
Richard Ashenden	W. Somerset Maugham
R	W. Somerset Maugham
Adam Melfort	John Buchan
Peter Pienaar	John Buchan
Hilda von Einem	John Buchan
Von Stalhein	aptain W. E. Johns
Doktor Krueger	Robert J. Hogan
Adolph Von Grundt (Clubfoot)	Valentine Williams
Desmond Okewood	Valentine Williams
Also Starring:	
Admiral "Needles" Hall	*Historical*
A(fred) E(dward) W(ooley) Mason	*Historical*
And:	
The Rungates Club	John Buchan

David L. VINEYARD is a fifth generation Texan (named for his gunfighter/Texas Ranger great-grandfather) currently living in Oklahoma City, OK, where the tornadoes come sweeping down the plains. He has useless degrees in history, politics, and economics, and is the author of several tales about Buenos Aires private eye Johnny Sleep, two novels, several short stories, some journalism, and various non-fiction. He is currently working on several ideas while battling with his cat for household dominance and the keyboard of his PC. He is a regular contributor to *Tales of the Shadowmen*.

WATCH OUT FOR

TALES OF THE
SHADOWMEN

VOLUME 20: FIN DE SIÈCLE
TO BE RELEASED DECEMBER 2023

N° 3. CHAQUE RÉCIT EST COMPLET EN UN VOLUME 25 Cent.

GUSTAVE LE ROUGE

LE MYSTÉRIEUX DOCTEUR CORNÉLIUS

LE
Sculpteur de Chair Humaine

LA MAISON DU LIVRE 28 R. MONSIEUR LE PRINCE PARIS.

www.ingramcontent.com/pod-product-compliance
Lightning Source LLC
Chambersburg PA
CBHW030356020726
47493CB00003B/843